Also by B J Scott:

THE ANGEL TRILOGY

Angel of the Gold Rush

Angel's Daughter

Legacy of Angels

Light on a Distant Hill
(MANAKWA NOOVIGADED PA'A TAVIDUAGA)

A Novel of the Indian West

by

B.J. Scott

Dave —
May You Enjoy !

— BJ Scott

authorHOUSE®

AuthorHouse™
1663 Liberty Drive
Bloomington, IN 47403
www.authorhouse.com
Phone: 1-800-839-8640

First published by AuthorHouse 12/2/2010

ISBN: 978-1-4567-1226-6 (sc)
ISBN: 978-1-4567-1227-3 (e)

Printed in the United States of America

Any people depicted in stock imagery provided by Thinkstock are models, and such images are being used for illustrative purposes only. Certain stock imagery © Thinkstock.

This book is printed on acid-free paper.

FOREWORD

When the true horrors of Nazi atrocities were revealed after the close of World War Two, a burden of guilt settled upon the German people. It is accurate to say that there is no counterpart to this guilt in America regarding the equally murderous tragedy visited on Native Americans during westward expansion.

Americans still react with outrage, more than half a century afterward, at mention of the merciless cruelty of Japanese soldiers during the Bataan Death March in World War Two. Yet two other marches—the relentless extinction of over 5,000 Cherokee during the Trail of Tears in 1838-1839, and the flight of 800 Nez Perce from pursuing U. S. Cavalry during the late 1800s—draw no similar outcry, no feeling of remorse. Manifest Destiny—the notion that it was Divine Will that mandated the sweeping away of Native American cultures—still holds sway in America.

In memory of the original Ellen O'Hara, my great-grandmother,
January 3, 1834—May 3, 1888
and
For the Peoples who were once widespread across this land, mostly
forgotten now, memorialized too often in such things as children's writing
tablets, chewing tobacco, automobile names, and team mascots.

SALINA, KANSAS, 1874: *A young girl stands at her window. She is fourteen, on the edge of womanhood. Looking out across the vast sea of grass that is the Great Plains, she dreams of the day when she might set sail upon it.*

Two years later she does, venturing forth into that vast unknown, from which she will emerge later, older than her years and wiser than her age, having been shaped and burnished in one of the great tragedies of American history. This is her story.

Light on a Distant Hill

1930
ON THE PACIFIC COAST NEAR CAPE MEARES, OREGON

Robbie McIntire wrestled with the steering wheel of the battered Chevrolet panel truck as it bounced over the rutted dirt road through the forest, ever higher into the coastal hills of Oregon. And with every jarring twist in the road, he cursed the day he had accepted his new assignment.

But as a rookie reporter for the Portland *Oregonian*, fresh out of journalism school, he had been in no position to turn it down. Still, he had been taken aback when his boss, crusty city editor Seamus O'Flynn, had dumped it on him.

"You want to write for the *Oregonian*, you take the job, boy," the bushy-browed old inkslinger told him in a gravelly voice. Seeing Robbie's discomfort at the prospect, O'Flynn jabbed a finger in his direction. "When *I* was new on the job, I would have begged for an assignment like this." He stood up and came around his big wooden desk. "Now, I've got a nose for a good story. I was reading about this old woman in a rest home over by Cape Meares. They say she's chock full of tales about the Old West, that she was witness to some amazing things. Our readers could do with something to take their minds off the Depression. Now, it won't be easy. I got the impression she's a bit of a recluse. Guess no reporter's been down there in years." He clapped a big hand on Robbie's shoulder. "Go to it, my boy. Bring back something worth reading."

Robbie knew the moment he was handed the pitiful advance that it would be gone before he could complete the assignment. Nevertheless, he packed a bag and caught a rattletrap old bus to Cape Meares. There, he managed to talk the owner of a local garage into renting him the old panel truck.

Now, as he jounced over the rugged road, grinding gears, posterior aching and kidneys beginning to float, he cursed his lack of intestinal fortitude once again. He should have had the guts to turn the job down. Just when he thought he must have taken a wrong turn and was ready to go back, a dusty wooden sign came into view ahead.

MOUNTAIN MEADOW REST HOME

Set on a rise in a clearing, surrounded on three sides by pine and fir trees, the dusty building was long and relatively narrow, with wood clapboard siding, fading paint, and a porch that ran the length of the front. It was topped by a clay tile roof that looked out of place among the mountain setting.

With a sigh, he turned into the driveway, the old panel whining in protest as it climbed the slope up to the entrance. He hit the brakes and the truck jerked to a halt in a bare area in front of the building. Weary but grateful to be there at last, he turned off the ignition. The panel coughed a few times in protest, then finally fell silent. Robbie opened the door, put his left hand on the top of the door frame, and levered himself out to a standing position. He stretched his aching back, looking back the way he had come. Now he knew why the home was located at this spot. An opening in the trees provided a view into the distance, all the way to the ocean. He could see sunlight playing off the water. A tall promontory stood on the coast, punctuating the otherwise low coastline. It looked like a loaf of french bread stood on end. It must have been hundreds of feet high, and looked to be right on the surf line. The top of the promontory was mostly open ground, with scattered tall trees dotting a lush meadow. A patch of sunlight fell on the meadow and seemed to make it glow a vibrant green.

He was still admiring the view when the sound of a screen door creaking open and then banging against a door frame behind him spurred him to turn around. He found himself facing a stout middle-aged woman in a print dress covered partly by an apron. She had short curly brown hair held in place here and there with bobby pins. She frowned at him.

2

"Reckon you're the reporter fella that big-city paper called about couple of days ago," she said sternly. "You must be him; no one else would bother to come up."

"Yes ma'am," Robbie said. He stepped forward, hat in hand. "I'm Robbie—ah, Robert McIntire from the *Oregonian.*"

The woman snorted. "Hmph. You're a young 'un, aintcha. Fresh out of college, I reckon. Come up here to make a name for yourself, interviewing *her.*" She almost spat out the last word. "Well, no sense in standin' out here jawin'. Come on in." She turned back to the house and went inside, leaving Robbie to catch up to her. "Mind you, she don't cotton to visitors much," she said. "No one ever comes to visit anymore 'cept her daughter." She turned back to look at him. "Maybe you'll get lucky and catch her in a good mood." She turned away again. "Hah!" she snorted, walking away from him into her kitchen.

Robbie trailed hesitantly behind, fearful of committing a breach of etiquette.

"The ladies are having lunch on the back patio," she said. "There'll be no visiting until they're finished." She opened an icebox and withdrew a large pitcher of amber liquid. "Iced tea?" she said, holding it out toward him.

"Yes ma'am, that surely sounds good about now, but—"

"Down the hall, second door on your left," she said, understanding the meaning of his hesitation. She chuckled as he scuttled off. "That road'll do it every time."

Robbie was back from the bathroom in minutes. The woman was standing by the front screen door, holding two glasses of tea. "Come on out," she said. "We'll sit a spell."

They settled into padded chairs on the porch. Only then did the woman finally introduce herself. "Edie Maitland," she said, extending a broad hand and shaking his firmly. "Don't get much traffic up here," she continued, looking out into the distance. "I get a hankerin' to talk to someone else now and then, besides the residents."

Robbie took a sip of his iced tea. It was wonderful, like he had tasted rarely, if ever. He decided to start the conversation with something that had nagged at him all the way up the long dusty road. "Mrs. Maitland," he ventured, "this place is half an hour out of town, up a long bad road. Why are these residents of yours—these women—way up here?"

Edie was silent for long seconds, the quiet punctuated only by the buzz of insects. Finally, she spoke, still looking off into the distance. "Waiting to die, most of 'em," she said softly. "Most got no family left, leastways none that care to visit much. So they come up here to commiserate—and wait. 'Cept the one you came to see, Ellen O'Hara. Her, I don't know *what* she's waitin' for." She turned and looked at him. "Maybe it's *you*." She drained her glass and set it down with a thunk on a small table, then laboriously stood up. "They should be about done now. I'll let her know you're here."

She went back in the house, the screen door slamming shut behind her. She was back in under two minutes. "She says you're to wait for her in her room, and she'll be in shortly. Come on, I'll show you the way."

Edie led him down a dim hallway past the bathroom, all the way to the end. She opened the door of the last room on the left. "Go on in, and wait here," she said. She turned to go, then paused. "Try not to get her wound up with those nosy questions about the Old West. She gets on a roll, we won't hear the end of it for days. None of us believe that fantastical stuff she goes on about anyway. Mostly we just humor her until she winds down." She turned down the hallway. "Good luck," she called out to him as she walked off.

Robbie looked around nervously. He had no idea what to expect. The room was comfortable in a homey way, with country-style furnishings. A patterned quilt was spread over the queen bed. Drapes with a subtle farm-scene design flanked the large window, which afforded the same fine view of the ocean he had seen from the front yard. An oval area rug was spread over the polished wooden floor between the bed and two chairs near the window. There was a dresser to one side. Two items on top of the dresser caught his eye. They looked out of place compared to the rest of the furnishings. Curious, he moved closer. One item was what appeared to be a thick notebook in a leather case. It looked well-traveled and worn, and when he bent over close to it, it smelled faintly of sage and woodsmoke. The other object was a gray rock about the size of his fist. One side was ground flat, and polished to a high shine. He realized it was a thunder egg. Looking closer, he could see something was inscribed into the smooth surface. Unable to make out whether it was a pattern or lettering, he picked it up and held it in the window light for a better look. He was peering at the it closely when a stern voice from behind made him jump.

"Put that down."

Startled, Robbie nearly dropped the rock. He put it back on the dresser top and turned around to see who had spoken. "Ma'am, I'm so terribly sorry—" he began. "My, ah, my manners surely slipped."

A slender woman of medium height stood before him. One wrinkled hand rested on a cane. She had long white hair that flowed past her shoulders. Her features were well defined, almost delicate. Age had left its mark on her tanned and lined face, but it would take little effort to realize that she had once been a beautiful young woman. Her eyes were clear and an arresting golden-brown. She looked at Robbie with a gaze so unflinching it almost made him shiver.

"Ma'am, I'm really sorry to be so thoughtless," Robbie said, desperately trying to make up for his *faux pas*. "I'm afraid I'm not off to a very good start."

"Hmph," she said, walked slowly across the room, and lowered herself into one of the chairs by the window. She looked up at him, frowning, one hand still on her cane as if she had a mind to whack him with it. "Well, sit down, young man, unless you want to do this standing up."

Robbie sat quickly. "No ma'am," he said, setting his shoulder bag on the floor.

"They told me you were coming," she said, fixing him with a penetrating stare. "What do you want?"

Haltingly, nervous to his core, Robbie briefly told her what his boss had told him, and what he hoped to bring back from the assignment. "Ma'am, I read what I could find about you on the way down here," he said. "They say there are few people left who saw the Old West the way you did. They say you were there when the West was alive. Are they right?"

Ellen O'Hara turned her head and looked out the window at the coastline for long seconds. Then she turned back to him. "I was there."

The heaviness, the sadness in her voice as she said the words left Robbie bereft of any response. Desperate for something to break the mood, he reached down into his shoulder bag and pulled out his notebook. "Well, can you tell me something about your time in the Old West?" he ventured tentatively.

She tilted her head and looked at him, as if studying something caught under a microscope, trying to focus on its true nature. "Tell me, young man, are you here for yourself or because your boss sent you?"

Robbie bit his lip. He knew there was no chance of misleading this woman. She would see right through any falsehood he concocted, he was sure. "Well, ma'am," he said, taking a deep breath, "the truth is, at first I didn't want to come. It's a far piece from Portland, and it didn't sound all that interesting."

"You mean visiting some crotchety old woman in a rest home out in the middle of nowhere, who'd spin tales that may or may not be true, and probably fall asleep halfway through?"

Robbie hung his head. This interview might be over before it started. "Yes ma'am," he said softly. "Something like that."

"But you're here anyway," she said.

"Yes, I am. Because the more I read about you, the more I felt there might be a great story here. I'd be pleased to stay as long as you'll let me. I'll write faithfully what you tell me."

Ellen looked down at the thick notebook in his lap. "Is that all you brought?" she said.

"Well, yes," Robbie said, somewhat startled. "Do you think I'll need more?"

Ellen leaned forward slightly and fixed her golden-brown eyes on him. "Young man, if you're serious about your purpose here, you'll need a lot more than that. You can get more in town when that one's full up."

She moved her body around in her chair, achieving a more comfortable position, glancing once more out the window. "You asked me a few minutes ago if I was there when the West was alive. I was." She turned back to look at him. "And I was there when it died." Her expression took on a new intensity, eyes seemingly focused on some faraway place and time. "Open up your notebook, young man."

Robbie did so, pen poised, relieved she was going to talk to him after all.

"We'll start at the beginning," she said.

*"My convictions upon this subject have been confirmed. That those
tribes cannot exist surrounded by our settlements . . . is certain.
They have neither the intelligence, the industry, the moral habits, nor
the desire of improvement which are essential to any change in their
condition. Established in the midst of . . . a superior race . . . they must
necessarily yield to the force of circumstances and ere long disappear."*
—President Andrew Jackson before Congress, 1833

SALINA, KANSAS
1876

April 23, 1876—Salina
*Hello to my beautiful new diary! How exciting it is to fill your pristine
pages with the prospect of our journey. For we are to depart at last this very
day! Nettie, Liza, Clarence and I will travel by buggy and steamboat to
Omaha, where I shall board the train and begin the journey westward to
Sacramento, and thence northward to Washington Territory. What took
months only a few years ago can now be done in just days. And can you
imagine—I am to be a bride! Captain Morrow's reply to my acceptance of
his proposal of marriage arrived just last month. I am sure he is as handsome
as his photograph! He has sent me one hundred dollars toward my passage
on the railroad. As he is a U. S. Cavalry officer, I hope that was not too great
a strain on his account. Nettie nags that it is high time I showed an interest
in marriage, but she is such—*

"ELLIE! ELLEN O'HARA!"**
The young girl's reverie was shattered by the shrill voice of her
aunt calling from outside the house.

"Ellen O'Hara, you put that diary away and get out here this very minute! The buggy is loaded and ready to go."

—an old busybody, Ellen continued. *I try not to take her seriously,* she concluded in deliberate fashion, then quickly closed the cover on her diary, a going-away gift from her Aunt Liza, leaped up from the desk, and bolted out into the packed dirt yard.

A red-wheeled buggy, hitched to two horses, stood at the ready. In the back of the buggy were three leather traveling bags. Ellen's Uncle Clarence was in the driver's seat, holding the slack reins. Ellen's Aunt Liza, Clarence's wife, stood beside the buggy, next to Ellie's other aunt, Nettie.

Nettie was plain, and at thirty-three, resigned to spinsterhood. With the end of the Civil War only a few years distant, there was still a tragic shortage of young men of marrying age in the area. Many of them had gone off to fight—and had not come back. It was all the more reason Nettie was determined that her little niece, Ellen, would not suffer the grueling burden of life on the plains as a spinster herself. Attractive though Ellen was, Nettie fussed that the girl's outspokenness and independent nature would drive off what few would-be suitors might find their way to their neck of the woods—or plains, as it were.

"Well, come on," Nettie said impatiently, waving her over to the buggy. "Have done with that fool diary for a while and hop on in," she said as Ellie did so. "Land O' Goshen, child, if you ain't a bothersome little bug. Every since your mama died o' grief when your papa didn't come back from that accursed war, I've had to take you in tow, and t'aint been easy."

Ellen's father had gone off in 1864 to supply horses to the Union troops. He was not a soldier and did not expect to encounter the dangers of battle. Even so, he was caught in a Confederate ambush at the October 23rd Battle of Westport, Missouri, and killed. His body was brought home to Kansas by family friends. Barely a week after he was laid to rest on the farm, between the house and the barn, Ellen's mother, who had barely spoken since her husband's body came home, wandered off late one night onto the plains. They found her the next day, dead. There were no marks on her body. "It was the plains that killed her in the end," Uncle Clarence had told Ellen. "She'd been on the edge for a long time. Too many tornadoes, too many long winters, too many grasshopper plagues, too little rain, too many failed harvests—your father's death just pushed her over."

"You have the money that Captain sent you tucked away, I hope?" Nettie's sharp voice brought Ellen back to the present.

Ellen rolled her eyes and nodded. She knew her aunt's lament all too well; she'd heard it enough. She also knew there was more to come.

"You're a lucky girl, you know," Nettie went on. If that captain was here to know you better, why, he might not be so eager. This might be the only proposal you'll get. You're just a little tomboy, stubborn in your ways and far too outspoken for your own good. You'll have to put all that away if you intend to be a military wife."

Ellen bit her lip to keep from sassing her aunt, and settled into a gloomy silence as Clarence clucked the horses into motion and the buggy pulled away down the path through the tall prairie grass that stretched away as far as eye could see. She looked back only once, feeling a sharp pang of loss, then steeled herself to look forward, as the only home she had ever know receded into the distance.

It would take longer to reach Omaha—about 10 days—than it would to cross the whole distance west to Sacramento. What had once taken six months could now be accomplished in less than a week. But before Ellen could board the train, the party would have to head east to Kansas City and catch a riverboat north up the Missouri River to Omaha.

The money that Captain Morrow had sent her after she accepted his proposal of marriage would enable her to travel first class on the train. She would have a plush seat that could be converted at night to a snug sleeping berth. She would also have steam heat and fancy furnishings. For meals, though, Ellen would have to eat on the run at whatever stops the train might make along the way. Meals on board would have cost an extra $4 per day.

They reached Kansas City in five days, and there boarded a northbound steamboat. The voyage was uneventful, and Ellen, impatient and nervous, whiled away the time sitting near the bow, watching the steamboat push the placid water away and to the side. The boat was bustling with river men, gamblers, families, and people whose livelihood she couldn't guess. The rear deck of the boat was piled high with cargo— boxes, barrels, bales of hay, implements she couldn't identify, and more.

As the boat pushed northward, stopping all too often for her taste, Ellen would time and again pull from inside her diary a well-worn envelope and open it up in her lap. There was a photograph, a yellowed newspaper clipping, and a packet of letters written in a neat hand. The photograph showed a handsome young cavalry officer in uniform, posed in a studio looking very solemn, captain's insignia on his shoulders. He had dark wavy hair, cut short, and a well-trimmed mustache. Ellen had tried time and again to read gentleness and compassion into his expression, but she was only guessing. When she tired of looking at the photograph, she would carefully hold the newspaper clipping in her hands. It was an advertisement her Aunt Nettie had seen in the Kansas City *Times*, and it had started everything she was now caught up in.

CAVALRY OFFICER SEEKS WOMAN OF MARRYING AGE FOR MATRIMONY. WILL PAY PASSAGE WEST. CAN PROVIDE A STABLE HOUSEHOLD. HAVE A PROMISING CAREER, AND A GOOD INCOME. WILL CONSIDER CHILDREN. REFERENCES CAN BE PROVIDED. REPLY VIA TELEGRAM OR LETTER TO CAPT. E. MORROW AT FORT WALLA WALLA, WASHINGTON TERRITORY

Ellen had shown no interest at first, but Nettie's insistence had gradually won her over to at least writing to the man. She knew that Nettie, overbearing and fussy as she could often be, had her best interests at heart. She also knew she was not looking forward to aging into spinsterhood like Nettie. Not to mention that with her parents both gone, there was no one to run the small farm she grew up on. Her two aunts and Clarence were all she had left, and the loneliness of the long prairie days could be unbearable.

So as a bit of a lark, she had written in reply. To her amazement, she had received a response in just under two weeks. She had opened the letter, heart pounding. More letters between her and the Captain followed over several months, the gentlemanly tone of his writing slowly sparking her interest. She had gone to the lone photography studio in Salina to get her photograph taken to send him. Three weeks after she had sent it, a reply came. It was a proposal of marriage. She was speechless for a while; not having expected it would really come to that, and uncertain how she should reply. She had written more out of boredom than anything, entranced with the notion of communicating with someone out on the frontier.

Nettie had no such ambivalence. "You don't have to love him, child," she had said, sitting with Ellen one evening on the porch of the small farmhouse, watching the light fade over the prairie. "You can't live on just love, after all. He's young, handsome, well-employed. There's nothing for you here. Your Aunt Liza and Clarence and I are leaving too, you know. We can't manage the farm by ourselves. Now with the railroad done, we can endure the trip. We'll sell the farm and use the money to go west. I've got a powerful desire to see Oregon."

Ellen had had a feeling that news was coming. She had risen from the porch swing, gone to her room, and flung herself down onto her bed, tears coming fast. At sixteen, she didn't feel up to such change. But before long, she had written Captain Morrow back and accepted. The money for her trip had come swiftly.

THE RIVERBOAT REACHED OMAHA LATE on the third day. They stepped ashore, Ellen amazed at the bustle of the docks. She had never seen a city so big. Nettie wasted no time in getting her to the train station and seeing to it she purchased the proper ticket. Then they sent a telegram to Captain Morrow announcing that Ellen was to depart the next day.

The Pacific Express departed daily, bound for Sacramento. The day following their arrival in Omaha, Ellen stood on the train station platform in the morning light, trying hard to keep tears from falling.

Nettie put both hands on her shoulders, smiling broadly, her own eyes moist. "Look at you in that new travelin' dress," she said, softening from her usual stern demeanor. She suddenly put her hands to her face, stifling a sob. She saw before her a pretty girl, slender, of medium height, with long wavy light brown hair shot through with golden highlights brought forth by the sunlight. She had a beautifully shaped mouth, and refined features with a smooth pale complexion. Her most arresting feature, though, was the golden-brown color of her eyes.

"Child, you're the spittin' image of your mama, God rest her soul. You'll be a woman soon, sure enough." Nettie put a hand under her chin as she saw Ellen's lower lip trembling. "Now, you be the young lady your mother meant for you to be," she said. "A bright future is waiting out west for you. I think this Captain Morrow will be a fine husband. And if he doesn't treat you right, he'll have *me* to answer to! I'll come all the way to Washington Territory to set him straight, you may be sure of that!"

Ellen managed a small smile and hugged Nettie tightly. Then she did the same with Liza and Clarence.

"We'll be along to Oregon as soon as we can get the farm sold," Liza said. "Then we'll come for a visit. Now, young lady, you write to us regular, you hear? Send a telegram if you can, when the train stops at a station."

"I will, I promise," Ellen said, face contorted with sorrow.

The boarding whistle sounded. Uncle Clarence picked up her bag and carried it for her to the passenger car entry. Ellen took it from him reluctantly and stepped up into the waiting car. She walked down the aisle and took a seat at the window. Within minutes Ellen heard two long blasts on the whistle. The American Standard 4-4-0 locomotive gave a roar, spun its big drive wheels briefly, and began to move out of the station. Ellen waved to her family until they were out of sight. Then she sat back in the seat and broke into heavy sobs. The tears would be denied no longer.

The locomotive sped westward, a smoking arrow shot across the endless sea of grass.

ELLEN CRIED SOFTLY FOR A long time, unable to cope with saying goodbye to all the family she had left, and to all the world she had ever known—the vast plains that had made her what she was, for better or worse. *All to marry a man I've never met*, she thought. *I so hope he is kind. If he is cruel, I shall run away.* She looked out at the featureless plains rolling by the window. *But to where? I am too young for this.*

She was drying the last of her tears on the sleeve of her new dress when a soft voice interrupted her.

"You look like you could use a friend."

Ellen looked up to see a girl about her own age, or perhaps a bit older, standing in the aisle next to her. She had short blond hair that covered her head in a mass of tight curls, and blue eyes. She was smiling broadly.

Ellen put a hand to her face, embarrassed. "Oh! No, I'm—I'm all right, I—"

"Nonsense," the girl said, taking a seat next to her. "You most certainly are not. You've been crying since the train left the station." She extended a hand. "I'm Rachel."

Ellen wiped her cheeks and took the girl's hand briefly. "Ellen. You can call me Ellie."

"Done," Rachel said firmly. "Now, it's not right for girls our age to be alone on this contraption. I must sit with you a while." She looked closely at Ellen. "You must be missing someone terribly."

"It's—it's more than that," Ellen replied. "I'm a bit scared."

Rachel waved a hand in dismissal. "Well, who wouldn't be? The west is still quite wild. I hope we shall not encounter any red Indians on this trip. But they say we should be safe on the train."

"It's not that, so much. You see, I am to be wed. I'm going to meet my husband-to-be."

Rachel looked taken aback. "You're going to marry a man you haven't met?"

Ellen blushed. "Well, the truth is—I'm a mail-order bride. So to speak."

Rachel's eyes flew wide. "How fantastic! I must hear the whole story!"

Still embarrassed, Ellen recounted the story of how her Aunt Nettie had found the advertisement in the Kansas City *Times*, encouraged her to reply, and, more as a lark than anything else, she had.

"You must have been terribly surprised when he actually proposed," Rachel said.

"I was," Ellen admitted. "I didn't know what to do—at first." She smiled ruefully. "My Aunt Nettie can be very persuasive. By the time she was through, I realized that with my mama and papa dead, the only other choice I had was to go westward with my aunts and uncle when the farm was sold." Ellen looked out the window briefly then raised her voice as the train passed between low hills close on either side; the roar of the locomotive ahead increasing. "That wasn't something I wanted to do! Aunt Nettie is very old-fashioned, to put it kindly. She's always tried to stuff me into her notion of what she thinks is proper for a girl—marriage at a young age, and motherhood. Me, I just want to do something more, something exciting. Something *important*."

"But now you've agreed to marry this man you've never met," Rachel said.

"I *have* met him, in a sense, through his letters." She smiled. "My acceptance of his proposal is conditional. I wrote him that if he is the

13

gentleman he seems to be in his letters, I will marry him. If not—" She left the sentence hanging.

"They must be some lovely letters," Rachel mused, sitting back in her seat and looking away.

Ellen got her diary out of her shoulder bag. "Would you like to read one?" She held up a packet of envelopes frayed from travel and handling.

"Could I?" Rachel said eagerly.

"Yes, I see no harm," Ellen replied, having overcome her initial embarrassment about her status. "Here's the one he sent when he proposed to me." She opened her diary folio and retrieved a single envelope from an inner pocket.

Rachel took the envelope gingerly, and eased the letter out. She opened the folded pages, the paper crackling as she did so. She began to read:

My Dear Miss O'Hara,

I received your last letter of February the 27th with great pleasure. I feel that I have gotten to know you quite well as we have exchanged letters over the last few months. Each letter has made me more certain that you would make a fine mate for me. As you have come to know, I am an educated man of means, possessed of a good career, and working my way up in the U. S. Cavalry. I can provide a woman with a good, comfortable home and a solid household in which to raise children. Indeed, such a home is already purchased and awaits only the touch of a woman's hand to bring it to life.

Therefore, I feel confident in asking you at this time for your hand in marriage. Will you accept my proposal? Please respond at your earliest convenience; I am anxiously awaiting your reply.

Faithfully Yours,
Capt. E. Morrow,
U. S. Cavalry

Rachel looked up from the letter. "Goodness!" she said, sighing. "Such gallantry! A girl could do worse."

"This is his photograph," Ellen said, laying the Captain's photo in Rachel's lap.

"Dashingly handsome," Rachel said in admiration. "I would have accepted his proposal as well, I have no doubt."

The two girls talked on for some time as the train rumbled westward. Rachel, as it turned out, was traveling with her parents to establish a new life in Oregon's Willamette Valley. "We shall practically be neighbors!" she gushed when Ellen revealed where Captain Morrow was stationed. "It would be little trouble to visit now and again."

Rachel at last returned to her seat with her family toward the front of the car. Worn out from the strain of parting at Omaha, Ellen was lulled into an exhausted slumber by the rhythmic click-clack of the rail joints. She awoke two hours later when she felt the train slowing. They were rolling into Grand Island. The train stopped there for just ten minutes, then it was speeding away again.

Night fell as they approached North Platte. Drained from the constant travel ever farther from her home, Ellen longed for the train to rest for the night. It was not to be. They were stopped long enough for her to dash off a telegram homeward, but after taking on water and fuel, the locomotive once again chuffed its way out of town into the featureless blackness of night on the plains.

WHEN ELLEN AWOKE THE NEXT morning in her sleeping berth, for a moment she did not know where she was. Then she realized the truth as the noise of the moving train invaded her consciousness. The sun was up, illuminating seemingly endless stretches of grassland, the tall prairie grass rippling in the wind like waves on the ocean. *It is very much like an ocean*, she thought. A porter came and converted her bed back into the seating position.

Hunger pangs were assaulting her when the train came into Cheyenne. The train had no sooner rolled to a stop than a gathering of people waiting on the platform stepped up onto the train and began walking through the cars. They turned out to be local farmers, who began offering a variety of fruits, vegetables, preserves, and baked goods to the hungry passengers. Ellen was delighted with the selection, and quickly purchased items that made a fine breakfast. Down the car, she could see Rachel motioning her to join her, which she did.

Except for such good fortune, the train travelers, excluding the Pullman car occupants, were forced to practically eat on the run when the train stopped for meals, which was usually for only twenty minutes. Whether breakfast, lunch, or dinner, they usually encountered the same fare—beefsteak, fried eggs, and fried potatoes.

After breakfast, Rachel invited Ellen to explore the rest of the train with her, and so they walked from car to car, holding onto seat backs to cope with the periodic swaying and lurching of the train over the uneven, hastily-laid frontier tracks. Ellen was amazed at the appearance of some of the people she saw in the day coaches, and confided this to Rachel.

"My father says that many of them are not going far. There are over two hundred stops on the way west, and many of these people are going only between one stop and another. I would think some of them are cowhands, hunters, or farmers. That's why they are dressed more for work than travel. Good thing, because those who *are* going through have to sleep on these horrid benches, the poor dears. It must be almost impossible." There were even two Indians aboard, much to Ellen's surprise. She had seen very few in her lifetime, and rarely up close. The sight of them made her shudder.

"Not to worry," Rachel assured. "As you may notice, many of these men have guns stuck in their belts." Indeed, the gun-toters were a rough-looking lot who talked loudly and profanely, and blew out clouds of noxious tobacco smoke, which rose to the ceilings of the coaches. Opening the windows to let in fresh air was often not possible, as sparks from the locomotive smoke sometimes entered the cars if given the chance.

As they made their way toward the rear of the train, they came to a car at which Rachel halted. "This is the Pullman car," she said. "We can't go in there. It's for the very rich only. So, our tour is at an end."

THE JOURNEY TO SACRAMENTO WOULD take only an amazing four and one-half days. It was a speed that staggered the imagination of anyone who had experienced the hazardous six-month crossing by wagon train, with its attendant dangers of floods, prairie storms, wildfires, Indian attacks, starvation, snow-bound mountain passes, and a thousand other perils which could scarcely have been imagined to those raised in the east.

As there was little to do when the train was streaking across the featureless landscape, Ellen and Rachel spent considerable time together visiting and comparing notes about their childhood. They quickly became fast friends.

Around noon of the second day, east of Green River, Wyoming, Ellen felt the train slowing to a halt. Puzzled, she lowered a window and stuck her head out for a look. To her delight, she saw that the train had stopped for an enormous herd of buffalo rumbling its way across the tracks. "Why, there must be thousands of them!" she said to Rachel.

"Easily," Rachel answered. The herd stretched from one horizon to another, on its way to a place only the buffalo could know. The ground shook with their passing. Enormous clouds of dust were thrown up, and before long Ellen was forced to raise the window. Even at a steady gallop, it must have taken fifteen minutes for the end of the herd to at last clear the tracks. But the last of the great shaggy beasts finally crossed over, and the great brown mass began to recede toward the far horizon, the thunder of its passage slowly dying away.

"I had expected to see them more often by now," Ellen said.

"Me too," Rachel agreed.[1]

THE PACIFIC EXPRESS ROLLED ON into Day Three across northern Nevada. But when it pulled into Elko, bad news awaited. A conductor came through each car announcing that a bridge had washed out several miles west of town, and the train could not continue. Repairs would take several days at best.

Ellen stepped off the train onto the dusty platform in confusion and disappointment. Not knowing what to do, she went into the station and sent a telegram back east informing her aunts of her progress. Just as she had seen the telegram off, Rachel found her.

"I have heard news," she said. "There is a chance to continue westward now. There will be a small wagon train party departing in

---

1   Even as early as 1870, the buffalo had been severely decimated. Thousands were killed to feed the crews who had built the very railroad Ellen was traveling on. Buffalo Bill Cody alone killed some 4,300 over a period of eight months.

17

the morning. It will head north several miles to where there is a safe crossing to the other side. On the other side, the wagons will come back south to the tracks. A train will be waiting there to continue the trip to Sacramento."

Ellen was taken aback. Such a side trip seemed very risky indeed. "Do you not think it would be better to remain here until repairs are made?" she said.

"Piffle!" Rachel replied. "Look around. There is nothing here. We would be stuck on the train, and the food is sure to be horrid." She looked down at the scuffed wood floor for a moment, her excitement suddenly seeming to deflate. "Truthfully, we can't afford the expense of staying and buying food for several days. Father says we are nearly out of money, and we must move on. The railroad will charge us nothing for the wagon trip. Please, come with us! It would make it so much more bearable."

Ellen was still dubious.

"Oh, I am so weary of train travel!" Rachel said, excited again. "We shall be back on the tracks in no time, I am sure. Then in about a day and a half, we will arrive in Sacramento! Dear friend, please come."

Ellen looked away out the window at the locomotive hissing clouds of steam as it sat on the tracks at the platform's edge. For the first time on the trip, it didn't seem in a hurry to be away. She twisted back and forth in indecision for long moments. Then she finally looked back at Rachel. "All right, I will come. But only because we have become such good friends. I wouldn't want to separate from you now."

Rachel threw her arms around Ellen, pressing her blond curls to Ellen's cheek. "Wonderful; it shall be a great adventure!"

Before retiring on the train that night, Ellen opened her diary and made an entry:

May 5th, 1870—Elko, Nevada

We are stranded here temporarily on our journey west. It is said there is a bridge out some miles west of here, and we must wait for repair. But my new friend Rachel and her family, along with some of the other passengers, are going to take up the railroad on their offer to take us around the bridge by wagon, there to re-board a westbound train on the other side. She has asked me to come. I am reluctant to venture such a distance from the train tracks,

18

but I have decided to go with them tomorrow, as Rachel has become such a dear friend on this short trip.

Ellen awoke with a feeling of unease she could not shake. Something about the proposed detour by wagon train unsettled her. But hunger soon overcame her reservations. With no vendors in sight offering farm produce, she dressed, did her toileting, and stepped down onto the platform and into the station. She was sitting down with her lackluster breakfast when Rachel came sweeping in the door.

"Well, Miss Sleepyhead, about time! Hurry up and eat; the last wagon is waiting for your baggage behind the depot."

"I'll be there." Grimacing, she wolfed down her food, rushed onto the train and retrieved her suitcase, and laboriously lugged it around to the rear of the depot. There she found three covered wagons garishly painted red and blue, as many western-migration wagons were, the white canvas tops offset by the blue bodies and red-spoked wheels. Two sturdy draft horses were hitched to each one. Three men with rifles sat on horseback nearby.

Ellen did a quick count. There looked to be about twenty people who had volunteered for the trip, an even mix of men and women, but no young children. She found Rachel, who helped her hoist her heavy suitcase up into the last wagon in line. Then Ellen climbed up underneath the covering top, and took a seat atop her suitcase, next to Rachel.

Rachel smiled and squeezed her hand, just as the wagons lurched into motion and headed north. Ellen looked ahead, squinting in the bright morning sunlight far out into the distance. She clutched her stomach. The feeling of unease had returned with a vengeance.

They traveled through mostly level country—arid, treeless land dotted with sagebrush and alkali flats. Heading slightly northwest, they were soon rolling alongside a great dry wash, the bottom of which was dotted with willow and other scrub bushes.

"What awful country," Rachel said. "I'll be glad when we get to the tracks again. We can't leave this place soon enough." She looked down at the wash. "This must be the riverbed the tracks cross. I hope we reach our own crossing point soon."

The sun climbed higher in the clear sky as the wagons bounced along over the dusty terrain. After about an hour and a half, they reached the crossing point. The sandy banks of the wash had been broken down and shoveled into slopes which the wagons could negotiate. The bottom of the wash had been made firmer by the laying down of willow saplings to form a crude bridge.

The wagon drivers eased their charges down the slope into the wash, then across. At the beginning of the upslope on the other side, everyone got out of the wagons to lighten the load and help push them up the slope. In just fifteen minutes, all three wagons were across.

"We'll rest here," one of the mounted guards announced. "The horses could use it."

Everyone gathered near their respective wagons as the guards dismounted but continued to scan the area. Rachel's parents were in the second wagon. Rachel and Ellen stood beside the third wagon, taking sips of water from a tin cup.

"We shall be back on board the train very soon," Rachel said reassuringly. She looked at Ellen's diary, which was slung across the girl's shoulder by homemade straps. "Do you ever part from that thing?"

"Not often," Ellen said. "I got tired of fishing it out of my shoulder bag, and fashioned these straps for my shoulder. That way I can open it and write any time the notion strikes me."

"Very efficient, I suppose," Rachel replied.

What happened next would be forever burned in Ellen's memory as if by branding iron. She would remember later that the air around them had grown very quiet. The sound of insects in the bushes had died away to nothing. Only the faint breeze made any noise at all. Ellen reached out with the tin cup for a refill from the canteen, but the cup slipped out of her hand and fell to the ground. She bent over to retrieve it.

She had just grasped the cup handle when there was a loud *thunk* above her and she heard Rachel gasp. She straightened up and saw Rachel's eyes wide in shock, staring at an arrow sunk in her chest. Her hands fluttered in the air around the arrow as bright red heart blood pumped from her chest and down her calico dress. She looked up at Ellen in disbelief. Then the color drained from her face and she collapsed on the ground.

Ellen was frozen in horror for long seconds. Then she fell to the ground beside Rachel just as her world seemed to explode into a blur of screams, savage cries, gunfire, and the neighing of panicked horses all around her. Frantically, she looked up just as Rachel's father came running across the open space between the wagons.

"Rachel!" he screamed. He was hit by a volley of bullets, collapsing onto the ground in an explosion of dust. "Rachellllll!" he screamed again, reaching out toward her. Then his face sank into the dirt. Rachel's mother shrieked and ran toward him, only to be struck by an arrow halfway across. She sank to her knees, agony on her features, blood staining her dress. Two more arrows slammed into her before she fell forward just feet from her husband.

Ellen was in the grip of panic. This wasn't supposed to be happening! It *couldn't* be happening. She looked down at Rachel.

Rachel was trying to pull the arrow out, as if doing so would somehow save her. Ellen pushed the girl's blood-slick hands away and, in a blind panic pulled hard on the shaft. It wouldn't budge.

Rachel seemed to be fading. Even with the violent chaos swirling around her, Ellen knew Rachel was dying. She lifted the girl's head onto her arm. "Listen to me!" she said, tears flooding her cheeks. "Repeat what I say! Father in Heaven, accept my soul this day!" She shook Rachel as the girl's eyes fluttered. "Say it!"

"Father in Heaven," Rachel slurred. "Accept my—" Her head rolled to one side.

"Rachel!" Ellen shouted. "I believe in Jesus Christ the Savior. Let me be with You this day. Say it!" she sobbed.

Rachel suddenly seized Ellen's dress in a strong grip, looking into her eyes. "Remember me!" she gasped. Then she fell back as her eyes rolled up in her head, and she was gone.

"Rachel! No! No! No!" Ellen screamed, clutching her head in agony.

The wagon shook from heavy blows of combat above. Gunfire and dust and panicked screams filled the air as horses pulled this way and that in fear. She looked up to see Indians everywhere. One of them saw her and immediately pointed a gun at her.

From less than a dozen feet away, he fired.

Ellen felt hot pain explode in her head, and she fell back on the ground over Rachel's body.

It was nearly sunset when a man standing on the depot platform at Elko froze at the sight of a lone woman staggering toward him in the dust. As she came closer he could see blood on her dress, and her hair wildly askew. He ran toward her, and she collapsed into his arms just as he reached her, her face contorted in agony. "Dead," she gasped. "All dead."

A DEADLY SILENCE HUNG HEAVY OVER the carnage of the wagon train massacre as the sun traveled across the clear spring sky. Not a breath of air stirred. Only the buzz of insects provided any evidence of life. The horses were gone; the wagons abandoned, with empty harnesses and yokes piled in front. Bodies lay still, eyes vacant of life among dried blood pooled in the dust.

Two hours after the last of the attackers had disappeared, there was a flicker of movement underneath one of the wagons. An arm moved to brush flies away.

Ellen slowly stirred to life—and found herself staring into Rachel's sightless eyes. Recoiling in horror, she shot upright and slammed into the bed of the wagon above her. Pain exploded in her head and she fell back, unconscious.

When she awoke again, the sun was yet farther along toward the horizon. The full memory of what had happened struck her, and she broke into sobs of grief. She put her hands to her head, and they came away covered in blood. She sat sobbing under the wagon for a long time, staring at the blood in disbelief. Finally she got to her knees and crawled out from underneath, staggering to her feet. She looked around at the silent tableau of death in shock. "Is there anyone alive?" she called softly. "Can anyone help me?" There was no answer.

Like a figure made of wood come to life, she stumbled stiff-legged around the killing ground, her face twisted into a mask of pain. She went to one body after another, calling to them in desperation, sometimes shaking them, hoping desperately to prod them into life. But there was no response. All were dead—except her.

Numb with grief, she returned to Rachel and sat beside her for a while. A mass of dark congealed blood covered the girl's chest. Ellen tenderly stroked the curly blond hair. *I am so sorry,* she thought. *I tried my best to help you at the end. The line between life and death is so thin, so easily crossed. Such a short time ago you were so full of life, so excited to be going west. Now you have crossed over that line. Oh, please come back!* But Ellen knew Rachel would not be coming back. *I hope you are in Heaven now.*

Gradually, Ellen gained the presence of mind to think about herself. *I have to leave,* she thought. *Maybe the savages that did this will be back for me.* She looked down at Rachel one last time, wishing she could do *something* for her—bury her, or say some prayerful words over her. It wasn't right to just leave her. But Ellen's mind wasn't working well enough to think beyond that. "I will never forget you, dear friend; I promise," she said softly into the silent air. It was all she could think of to say. Then, using a wagon wheel for support, she laboriously pulled herself upright. Listlessly, she went again among the bodies looking for water or food. But there seemed none to be found. The Indians had stripped them of anything valuable. They had gone through the wagons too, tearing open the chests and suitcases. Clothes were scattered over the ground around the wagons, along with various other objects the attackers found not worth the taking. At the outskirts of the carnage, she found two of the guards, dead. Of the third, she found no trace.

Finally, Ellen found a full canteen of water hanging from a hook underneath one of the wagon beds. She found three apples under a pile of cast-off shoes and boots nearby. She gratefully scooped them up and put them in pockets of her dress. Then she pulled a bloodstained coat from one of the women's bodies. It took all the courage she had.

She stood up and looked at the sky. From the looks of the light, it appeared to be late afternoon. *I need to leave here,* she thought. *Captain Morrow is north. He can help me. I should head north.* Head on fire with pain, dizzy and on the verge of collapse, it was all the reasoning she was capable of. And so, wearing the bloody coat, canteen slung from one shoulder and diary on the other, she shuffled slowly away from the gathering of death, heading north into the treeless, arid expanse of northern Nevada, into emptiness, into nothing.

A small but heavily-armed party of horsemen set out from Elko at sunrise the next morning. Riding hard, they were at the site in twenty minutes, thundering down into the wash and up the other side. There they pulled to a halt, shocked into silence.

Flies buzzed in the air around the bodies that lay twisted in the final stillness of death. One of the riders, a hard-bitten, sunburned old cowhand, sighed deeply and lowered his head in sadness. For long moments he could think of nothing to say. Then he removed his hat, lips moving in a silent prayer, as one by one, the others did the same.

They rode a slow perimeter around the bodies, especially saddened when they came to two of the guards. "There were three," said the old cowhand. "One of 'em's gone. Might've given chase to the Indians. Two of you ride out and see if you can find him. And be damned careful."

They dismounted, ground-tied their horses, and did a slow walk through the field of death, searching for papers that might identify who was lying there.

"Gosiutes,"[2] said one of the men, holding an arrow in his hand. "I wouldn't have expected this. They were probably out foraging for food and stumbled across the party by accident. Reckon they figured it was just too good an opportunity to pass up."

One of the men stood silently over the body of a young girl with tight blond curls on her head, an arrow sticking out of her chest. Tears rolled down his cheeks. "Same age as my daughter," he said, barely audible, to a man who walked up next to him.

Some bodies had papers; too many did not.

"Can't identify all of 'em," one of the men said when they had searched the last body.

"Do a count," said the old cowhand.

The other who had spoken did a quick scan of the scene. "I make eighteen," he said. "How many passengers made the trip?"

"Twenty. There was the one woman who came back to the station last night. Add her in; that makes nineteen." He stared at the other man. "Somebody's missing."

---

2   Indians of the Great Basin of Utah and Nevada

Liza was sweeping the front porch of the old farmhouse near Salina when a boy came loping down the dirt road on horseback. She recognized him as the telegram delivery boy from town.

"Mornin', Miz Liza," he said genially. "Telegram for you and Miss Nettie." He reached out from the saddle and handed her a yellow envelope as she stepped down off the porch.

Liza fished in her apron pocket and found a dime, which she gave to the boy in return. "Thanks, Jimmy," she said.

The boy grinned, touched the brim of his floppy hat, and turned his horse back toward the road.

Liza looked at the envelope, then smiled. It was from the Central Pacific Railroad, so it must be another telegram from Ellie. The girl must be about to Sacramento by now. Liza pried open the envelope in anticipation and began to read.

Jimmy was almost back to the road when he heard the screams.

Ellen stumbled in shock across the gently rolling, arid landscape, nearly directionless, her only references the horizon ahead and the sinking sun on her left. She stopped periodically to take a sip from her canteen. Twilight came all too soon. She felt the pangs of hunger, and with no thought for how long she had to make her slim supply of food last, ate two of her apples and drank a third of her water. Darkness fell, and she felt incredibly alone. Her head still ached as if it were threatening to split. She sank onto the ground beneath the overhanging branches of a large bush, pulled her legs up as far as she could under her borrowed coat, and, clutching her diary tightly to her chest, cried herself to sleep.

When dawn came, she was up and moving again, mindlessly putting one foot ahead of the other, a numb automaton traversing an empty landscape, the only living human in a barren wasteland utterly disconnected from the world she had known.

Captain Eli Morrow sat in stunned speechlessness as he looked at the telegram in his trembling hands. It had arrived at Fort Walla Walla with the morning express mail rider from the Columbia River, and, busy with drill formations, he had put it in his pocket unread, for almost two hours. Now he sat on a bench outside the barracks, unable to move, heart pounding like it would burst from his chest. Desperately he looked again at the telegram, which had been sent two days earlier from Kansas, hoping to read something new into it that might give him hope:

TO: CAPT E. MORROW
FORT WALLA WALLA , WASHINGTON TERR.
HEARTBREAKING NEWS THIS DAY. OUR DARLING
ELLEN BELIEVED KILLED IN INDIAN AMBUSH AT
ELKO NEVADA. WE ARE OVERCOME WITH GRIEF.
LEAVE ON TOMORROW'S TRAIN TO RETRIEVE HER.
MAY GOD STRENGTHEN YOU. NETTIE O'HARA.

Suddenly he was up and running for the post commandant's office. He burst in the door, strode wordlessly past the commandant's secretary, and walked into Major Riley's office.

Major Riley looked up from the papers on his desk in surprise. He was fortyish, solidly built, with a bald head and a clean-shaven face. He put down his reading glasses. "What is it, Morrow? You don't usually abandon protocol and come bursting in here like this. Good God, man, you look pale as death."

Captain Morrow tried to speak, but words wouldn't come. He gave up and thrust the telegram at Major Riley.

Riley read it and looked up in dismay, eyes wide.

Morrow found his voice. "Major, I request some time off to journey to Elko to investigate. There's a chance she's alive. I have to go."

Riley tapped his reading glasses on his desk, looking once again at the telegram. "I'm profoundly sorry if this telegram turns out to be accurate. I know she was to be your bride. You have my deepest sympathy. But as you know, we've been having sporadic troubles with the Nez Perce over in the Wallowa Mountains. We can't spare you for long." He put down the reading glasses and sat back in his chair. "Be back here in 10 days. Beyond that, I can promise no more."

Eli stood in the dust at the site of the massacre outside Elko. He had ridden swiftly east from Fort Walla Walla into northern Idaho Territory to intersect a wagon road that ran due south to Elko. Hopping a freight wagon , he was there in three days. Nettie and Liza were there waiting for him, as he had dashed off a letter before departure to be delivered to the nearest telegraph office and sent ahead.

Eli found them numb and nearly speechless, not knowing what to do. He was shocked when they told him that the bodies from the massacre had already been buried in the local cemetery. He headed immediately for the train depot. "Why was this done?" he asked the depot manager in disbelief. "How can we be sure who was among the dead?"

The short white-haired man looked up from his desk, frowning over his Ben Franklin reading glasses. "Captain, those poor folks had done gone to meet their reward near twenty-four hours before they was brought here. There ain't an embalmer around these parts, nor ice house neither. Pretty soon they was goin' to be in a state no one would want to see." His features softened momentarily, then took on a grim expression. "Better their families remember them the way they were than how I found 'em. I wouldn't recommend diggin' 'em up. Trust me on that one."

Suddenly overwhelmed with sadness, Eli put a hand to his forehead. "I *have* to know who was on those wagons. Have you got a list?" He leaned over the man's desk. "Please. It's very important to me."

The man shuffled through some papers on his desk, obviously uncomfortable in discussing the tragedy. "Well, we didn't take names before they left on the wagons, but we were able to put a list together by taking an inventory of the passengers who stayed here, and then by looking at the train manifest, figuring out who *wasn't* here." He picked a paper out of a bunch of others and held it out to Morrow. "We think this is right."

Eli took the paper, barely daring to breath, and turned away toward the light streaming in the window behind him. Slowly he made his way down the list, hoping desperately she wasn't on it. But his eyes squeezed shut in grief when he saw the final name:

Ellen O'Hara

His head sank to his chest as he handed the list back to the little man. After a moment he looked up, eyes wet with tears. "I count twenty names on the list," he said, clutching at straws. "Is that how many bodies they brought back?"

The man rested his chin on his hands, seemingly distracted for a second. "No, it ain't. There was one survivor, a woman, who came staggerin' in about sunset the day of the massacre. Add her to the count brought back from the scene, and you've got nineteen."

Eli's heart started to pound in his chest. "So one person on that list isn't accounted for."

The man leaned back in his chair, as if wanting to distance himself from Eli's grief. "It would seem so, yeah. We just don't know who. There were twelve men on the list, and we buried twelve. But there were eight women's names. We buried six. Add the one survivor, and that makes seven women, for a total of nineteen."

Eli turned toward the door, so desperate for a ray of hope he was unable to speak.

"Captain," the man called out to him, getting up from his desk at last and coming around to stand close to him, "I can see how hard this is on you. You want to talk to that one woman who lived to tell the tale, she's at the hotel around the corner. She took an arrow, but it appears she'll make it."

Now Eli stood at the site of the massacre. There was nothing left but pools of blood in the dust. The wagons and their attendant gear had been removed, and all the belongings of the unfortunate souls taken back to town to aide in identification. He had been told the third guard had been found about two hundred yards away, shot full of arrows and very dead.

He had talked to the surviving woman in the hotel room where the railroad had put her up. She was very weak, and pale, but she confirmed that a girl matching Ellen's description had been among the group. The woman had taken an arrow in her side, and had survived only by staying absolutely still as the Indians looted the bodies and wagons. It had taken every bit of will she could muster, knowing if she so much as twitched, she was dead.

"When the Injuns finally left, I went around to see if anyone else was alive. I tried hard to wake 'em," she said, breaking into sobs. "But I couldn't." She hid her face in her hands, tears streaking her cheeks. "They was all dead, includin' the girl you described." She paused, unable to speak. After several long seconds, she put her hands down, and turned her face away. "And includin' my husband. I don't remember much after that. The doc says I lost a lot of blood after I pulled the arrow out." She looked back at him. "I'm sorry. Can't talk no more about it." She turned her face away again, to the wall.

Eli had thanked her and headed out of town to the site, finding it empty. He dismounted and walked around the area, looking for something on the ground that might have been missed. Finding nothing, he mounted up and rode in an ever-widening circle around the scene. The area was a chaos of boot and moccasin footprints. They lessened gradually the farther out he circled.

After an hour, he found what he had desperately hoped for: a single track of shoe prints leading away into the wilderness. Dismounting, he examined them closely. The small size indicated a woman's shoe. Some of the prints had faint drops of blood near them. He mounted up again and followed the prints for half an hour until they petered out. Though he rode back and forth until the daylight began to fade, he couldn't pick them up again. Worse, a stiff breeze was sweeping across the ground, blowing the sandy terrain into featureless dust.

Saddened beyond words, he rode to the top of a small rise, staring out into the distance for a long time. *Someone walked away,* he thought. *A woman. Then she disappeared. Oh God Ellen, are you out there? Or was that woman at the hotel right? Are you buried back in Elko?*

Numb, he turned his horse back toward town.

ELI SPENT TWO HOURS THE next day with Nettie and Liza. He could think of nothing to say to ease their grief. Nettie cried most of the time, and Eli had the feeling she might be blaming him for the tragic turn of events.

Liza took him aside. "She doesn't blame you," she said quietly. "Nobody's to blame, really, except those murdering savages." Her expression turned bitter. "Why did they have to kill them? Why couldn't they just rob them and leave them be?" She put a hand to her chest, face suddenly twisting with sorrow. "Oh, my poor girl. I'm so sorry you didn't get to meet her. She was so excited to be going west—" New tears sprang forth down her cheeks.

Eli put his hands on her shoulders. "I'm so terribly sorry for your loss. I wish there was more I could do." He wanted to look into her eyes but she wouldn't meet his gaze.

He sighed, slowly dropped his hands from her and turned away toward the window, looking down into the dirt street below. "I have to leave tomorrow. I've got just enough time to get back to my post as scheduled. But I spent a lot of time out there yesterday, where it happened. I found one set of footprints leading away. It looks like a woman walked away from the massacre." He turned back to face her. "It could be Ellen. Send me your address when you get settled in Oregon. When I get back, I'm going to request a leave of absence, and I'm going to go look for her. I'll never give up until either I find her, or I know she's buried here."

Liza turned away and sat down, clearly capable of no more talk.

Eli walked to the door, closed it quietly behind him, and left.

The next day, Nettie and Liza departed on the eastbound train for Kansas.

Ellen stumbled across the wasteland, devoid now of both purpose and direction. Drifting in and out of lucidity, she could no longer remember how she got there, or where she was going. Her hair, still matted with blood, was a wild tangle about her head. Exposure was beginning to tell on her. Though it was early spring, the nights were still cold, and she had found it hard to sleep. But something she couldn't remember clearly, some strange drive, kept her putting one foot ahead of the other, drifting north.

The landscape was beginning to rise ahead of her. She was faintly aware of low hills on the horizon. She had been walking for five days, with almost no food for three. She had tried eating new spring grasses she found in patches here and there, but as often as not vomited them up. Infrequently she found small pools of water in bowl-shaped depressions of large rocks, but it was not nearly enough.

Now her hands hung limply at her sides, eyes unfocused, the diary around her shoulders still in place but long since forgotten. She did not realize that the bloody coat had slipped from her an hour earlier, and lay far behind. She swayed slightly from side to side as she walked, near collapse. If it were not for the relatively mild spring weather, and for being a resilient age sixteen, she might well have been dead already. As it was, it could not be far off.

Finally she stopped, unable to move anymore, unable to think of a reason to take another step. A small part of her waning consciousness registered sight of a gathering of gray-white cone-shaped structures off in the distance.

Robbie McIntire put down his pen, hand tired from writing in his notebook, and looked up at the white-haired old woman sitting across from him.

Her eyes glittered in the fading daylight streaming in through the window of the rest home, seeming to be searching his face for something. She put a hand to her chin, one finger along her cheek. "Have I got your attention, young man?" she said.

"Yes ma'am, you do. I couldn't stop now if I wanted to. But I was wondering, why didn't you head back to town after the—the massacre? Why did you walk off into the wilderness?"

She smiled ever so slightly. "I had a nasty head wound, you know. That Indian fired near point-blank at me. His aim wasn't so good. The bullet grazed the top of my skull. It opened quite a furrow. You can still see it if you part my hair right." She looked out the window momentarily. "It wasn't the last bullet I took." She turned back to him. "When I got to my feet, I wasn't thinking too well. It was all I could do to walk. Seems the only thought I had was to get to Captain Morrow. Nothing else occurred to me. So I headed north. I didn't know I was walking into Shoshone[3] country. . . ."

A trio of Northern Shoshone women ambled slowly through the brush in the mid-day sunlight, not far from their spring camp, searching for herbs and berries and checking the rabbit snares set out the night before. One of the women looked up from scanning the ground—and froze in astonishment. The other two saw her stop, and looked at her shocked expression in alarm.

"What is it?" one said to her.

"*Daiboo' wa' aipe'*" she said hoarsely. "*Daiboo' wa' aipe'!*"[4] She launched herself into a run, screaming in fury. The other two woman followed her gaze and saw a heart-stopping sight. A white woman was standing about fifty paces away, looking their way. Boiling over with rage, the other two ran in pursuit.

The first woman reached the intruder, skidded to a halt in front of her, and then backhanded her across the face as hard as she could.

Ellen felt pain explode in her head, and sank to her haunches, unaware of what was happening to her. The other two women had reached her now, and were shouting at her in Shoshone.

---

3   Sho-SHO-nee, sometimes spelled Shoshoni. It means "the valley people".

4   White woman

"White bitch dog!" one of them screamed. "Destroyer!"

"Kill her!" the third woman shouted.

The woman who had struck Ellen took out a skinning knife. "I will!" she shouted, seizing Ellen by the hair and pulling her head back, exposing her throat. She was about to strike when she felt her wrist caught in a vise-like grip; the knife twisted from her hand.

"Stop!" came a loud male voice from behind them.

The women froze, then the knife-wielding woman let go of Ellen and stepped back, breathing heavily, as her wrist was released.

A tall Shoshone man stood glaring at them. He had heard the women screaming in fury and come running. Angrily he waved them away with a muscular arm. Then he looked at Ellen in disbelief. "What is this?" he said to no one in particular.

"*White woman*," the knife-wielding woman said, then spat on the ground near Ellen. "She deserves to die."

The man took a step forward and knelt in front of Ellen, who sat glassy-eyed and trembling on the ground. He looked into her face. "She appears to need little help from you to do so," he said calmly. "She is barely alive." He noticed that she had something slung from one shoulder by a leather strap. He straightened up slightly and examined Ellen's blood-matted hair. "Her head has been badly injured. I do not think she knows what is happening to her. But the wound looks to be several days old. She may have been wandering after her injury for some time, without food. I have heard no news of attacks on whites in our lands recently. If she was the victim of such an attack, it is likely she has walked a great distance over several days."

"But where did she come from, and why is she here?" one of the women said, gesturing angrily at Ellen. "Why has she dared to come into Shoshone lands?"

"I cannot answer that," the man said in his deep voice. "It may be she did not know where she was going. Her mind is likely not working well." He was silent for long moments. "I will take her back to camp." He bent down again and put his arms around Ellen, thickly corded muscles in his forearms standing out as he lifted her off the ground.

Ellen was only dimly aware of what was happening. But feeling the touch of another human after days of unbearable isolation, desperate for survival, she at last let go, gave herself up to the strong arms around her, and sank into unconsciousness.

The man turned away, leaving the women open-mouthed in astonishment.

"Bear Paw!" one of them called out, hustling after the brave, "there will be great trouble if you take her back. The whole camp will be in an uproar!"

The Shoshone man Bear Paw did not break stride. "Then it will be so," he said, walking away.

BEAR PAW WALKED INTO THE camp with Ellen in his arms. As the Shoshone became aware of what he was carrying, chaos erupted, and in seconds most of the camp of over two hundred Shoshone came running at him. Bear Paw ignored the torrent of shouts and headed for his tipi near the center of the camp. But he soon found his way blocked. Seeing the angry crowd was not going to budge, he lowered Ellen carefully to the ground. Still unconscious, she moaned and turned her head slightly.

Several young braves approached. "Let me take her scalp," one said. "I was brave in the last battle against the whites but took no scalps. Give me the honor!"

"If you do not wish to kill her, let me do so," another said loudly. "My knife has not tasted white blood for too long."

"Let us rape her first, then kill her!" shouted a third.

They advanced on Ellen, bloodlust on their faces.

Bear Paw, half a head taller than any other man in camp, stood astride Ellen's body and drew his big battle knife. "If you wish to kill her, you must first kill me."

The advancing men froze and a silence settled over the crowd. Women and children pushed and shoved to get a better view.

One of the young braves was particularly angry. "Bear Paw has no woman, so he brings this *daiboo'* among us. Is this the way of a Shoshone warrior?"

Bear Paw stared at him, massive chest slowly inflating. He stretched out his right arm, knife pointed at the other man. "Black Elk should give more thought to his last words before he goes to the spirit world," he said quietly.

The young man looked at him in disbelief for a moment, then slowly backed away. "You would threaten one of us to defend this white dog?" he said. "I wonder if your mind has gone."

It was only the fear of stepping away from Ellen and leaving her vulnerable that prevented Bear Paw from advancing on him. But those in the crowd who could see his face knew he would not easily forget the insult.

The young braves bent on attacking Ellen did not move, but the rest of the crowd surged forward to get a better look. Many, especially among the children, had never seen a white woman. "She is slender as a stick!" said one. "How could such a creature do a day's work?"

"Where did she come from?" said another. Some reached forward to touch Ellen's dress, but Bear Paw waved them back. One of the older women spoke the words that were already on everyone's mind. "Why have you brought her here?"

"I do not need to explain my actions," Bear Paw said.

"You do!" said the woman. "You are our camp chief. We look to you for guidance. Bringing this white woman here, it is as if you had invited our enemies to sit at our campfires."

Bear Paw sighed. He knew he was fighting a losing battle, that sooner or later—probably sooner—he would have to explain why he had brought Ellen back. But the truth was, he still didn't know why himself. All he *did* know was that as much as he hated and feared the whites, he could not ignore a badly-injured woman's need for help, no matter the color of her skin. In that, he was different from many others, who did not hesitate to kill white women whenever they got the chance.

"If we want to keep slaves, she would make a good one,"[5] he said, stalling for time. He bent down and carefully picked up Ellen as if she weighed next to nothing.

"Fah!" one of the women snorted. "Such a pale and skinny creature could never do the work of a Shoshone woman."

"We will see," he said quietly. He turned to the older woman who had demanded an explanation. "She is badly injured and in need of food

---

5   The keeping of slaves was not unusual among western Indians. The practice had originated in the New World with the Spaniards, and the Indians adopted it. Even after the Spaniards departed, the capture, sale, or purchase of slaves, often whites or Mexicans, flourished well into the 19th century among western tribes.

and water. You will tend to her until she is better. Retrieve your bag of medicines and come to my tipi." With that he walked off.

The woman looked around, searching for support in the faces of the other women, but found none. Bear Paw knew she would obey, grumble as she might. Frowning, she walked off to follow his instructions.

Inside his tipi, Bear Paw laid Ellen down with great gentleness on a bed of furs spread over a buffalo hide. The older Shoshone woman came in and knelt next to him. "Step aside then, and let me tend to her," she groused. With the camp's medicine man having died recently, the woman, possessed of a good knowledge of healing substances, served as a temporary substitute. She examined Ellen's head wound in the light coming in through the open tent flap. "Something struck her a glancing blow," she said quietly. "An arrow or, more likely, a bullet, I would guess. Strike a bit lower, and she would not be here. The wound is bloody, but not deep, and it will heal." She reached into her deerskin bag of medicines and withdrew a storage jar she had obtained from a trader. In it was something she had bought from the Utes to the south at a summer gathering—a salve made from the yarrow plant, used for cuts and bruises. She also took out a patch of clean cloth, which she moistened with water, and used it to clean away the dried blood from Ellen's hair and from around the wound. Then she applied the salve liberally to the wound, finishing up by tying a strip of clean cloth loosely over it, securing it under Ellen's chin.

"I do not have much of these medicines," she said to Bear Paw as she prepared a headache remedy in a wooden cup by mixing powdered Indian turnip with water. "If a Shoshone suffers for lack of them, there will be more anger against you."

"You talk too much, woman," Bear Paw said quietly.

The woman sighed and sat back. "So I have been told. That does not make my words less true. Now, I have done what I can for the wound. If she becomes conscious, get her to drink what is in this cup. It will help her head feel better." She got up. "Have I done what you asked?"

"Yes, that is good for now. You have my thanks. If she worsens, I may have need of you later."

The woman snorted and went out.

Bear Paw looked down at the unconscious white woman, observing her chest rising and falling. *What have I done?* he thought. *I did not think this through before I brought her into camp. There will yet be trouble, and it will be of my own making. Perhaps this was not a good idea. Maybe I should have let the women kill her, or at least turned her around and sent her back into the wilderness. What can be done with a white woman if she stays among us? Will she try to run away? Is Black Elk right? Did I do this because I have no woman?*

Bear Paw's young wife had drowned the previous year, swept into a rushing river by a surge of spring meltwater. Ever since, he had kept mostly to himself, becoming involved with tribal matters only as much as was required. He knew there was talk among his camp that perhaps he would do better to turn leadership over to someone else. There was no shortage of candidates among the younger braves, Black Elk notably among them.

What is this she carries over her shoulder? he thought, reaching out to touch Ellen's diary. *The strap is tight against her; I should remove it so she will breath more easily.* He gently lifted Ellen's head and eased the diary off her body, then stroked errant strands of her wavy light brown hair back into place, assessing her looks as he did so. *She is very young,* he thought, *and badly injured, but still there is a delicate beauty about her, like ice crystals on a winter's day. If she lives and becomes healthy, one could admire a woman such as this.*

Not wanting to face the rest of the camp at the moment, he decided to build a fire and prepare some food. Occasionally he would glance over at Ellen as he did so. Now and then she would moan softly and turn her head a little. While the stew he had put together was warming over the fire, he decided to take a look at the strange object he had taken off her shoulders.

He picked it up and felt its weight in his hands. Whatever it was, it was contained in a sturdy leather case. Loosening the thong ties, he opened the flap and saw that the object inside appeared similar to the white man's Book of Heaven, which in years past had been the subject of much talk among the Shoshone. Could this also be a Book of Heaven? He carefully opened the object. It did appear to be a book, but nearly all the pages hand none of the strange markings the white man used to describe things, as the Shoshone and others of the People did with symbols and drawings. No, only a few pages or had markings, and they did not look like those of the Book of Heaven. This, then, had to be something else.

The white woman continued in unconsciousness.

ELLEN DREAMED OF DEATH. SHE was standing utterly alone on a vast open plain. She looked down, and found an arrow sticking out of her chest. She did not know how it got there. She felt no pain, but was sure she was dying. She grasped the shaft and pulled hard, screaming out into the emptiness for help. But there was no one to hear her.

She felt a surge of dizziness and disorientation as the dream vanished. Her eyes flew open. She saw above her a dark slanted ceiling held up by a framework of straight poles. She turned her head. Someone was looking at her. A man. A large man. Suddenly her mind snapped into focus and she realized what he was.

Ellen shot upright on the furs, eyes wide in terror. A searing pain shot through her head. In a panic, she lurched back against the tipi wall, trying to shrink as far away from the Indian as she could. "Go away!" she screamed. "Leave me alone!" Desperately, she looked around for a way out, but the Indian was between her and the door flap. Then she noticed he was holding her diary. She burst into tears and reached out for it. "Please! Give it to me!"

Bear Paw looked at Ellen, not knowing what to do. The white woman was frantic with fear, like a rabbit caught in a snare. She was shouting, but the sounds were meaningless to him. He did not know what to say to her. She was stretching out her hands to him, and he realized she wanted the object. *Maybe it will make her feel better to have it,* he thought. Attempting to reassure her, he smiled and held it out. She reached out and grabbed the diary, then shrank back against the tipi wall again.

"Please, don't hurt me," Ellen sobbed, clutching the diary tightly to her chest. "Please let me go."

Two people from different worlds stared at each other, one terrified she might be killed at any moment, the other frustrated he could not tell her differently. Ellen continued to clutch her diary tightly, trembling with fear.

Bear Paw tentatively moved toward her, hoping to reassure her with a gentle hand, but Ellen backed away, wide-eyed. "No, please!" she cried, frantic to get away.

Bear Paw thought for a moment, then realized that hungry as the white woman must be, food might be a good thing to start with. He reached over to the fire and spooned some warm stew from the buffalo-stomach cooking pot into a wooden bowl. Then he held it out to Ellen, smiling reassuringly.

Ellen remained frozen for long seconds, staring at the bowl. Still, she would not move, so Bear Paw stretched out his arm and put the bowl on the ground in front of her. Still looking frightened as a startled deer, Ellen snatched up the bowl. After looking at it for a few seconds, she tried a spoonful of the stew. It was unlike anything she had ever tasted, but she found it surprisingly good. She ate quickly, never once taking her gaze off Bear Paw. When she was finished, she put the bowl down between them and clutched her diary tightly again, looking at him sideways as if he might pounce on her at any second.

Bear Paw nodded his approval and retrieved the bowl. Then he stuck his head through the tent flap and called to someone. Ellen could hear the sound of feet running away. A few minutes later, a middle-aged Shoshone woman—unknown to Ellen, the same one who had tended to her head wound—entered.

"Buffalo Calf Woman," Bear Paw said, "show the white woman where she may relieve herself."

"First she should drink what I prepared for her head," Buffalo Calf Woman said. She picked up the cup and held it out to Ellen, rubbing her own head with one hand.

After a moment, Ellen understood and put a hand to her head, becoming aware for the first time of the cloth wrapped over the wound. She started to pull it away, but Buffalo Calf Woman motioned for her to leave it in place. Somewhat comforted by the presence of another woman, Ellen took the cup and slowly drained it.

Buffalo Calf Woman grunted in satisfaction, stood up, and motioned to Ellen to come with her.

Ellen hesitated. The woman motioned again, and Ellen attempted to stand up. Swamped by a wave of dizziness, she fell backward against the tent wall and collapsed on the ground.

"She is very weak," Bear Paw said. "You must help her."

"Already she is troublesome," Buffalo Calf Woman grumbled, but reached down and pulled Ellen to her feet.

Ellen leaned against the woman, fighting to stay upright. After a few seconds her head cleared a little, and she was able to slowly exit the tipi, one hand on the Shoshone woman's shoulder for support.

The two women walked slowly through a gauntlet of curious Shoshone who had stayed near Bear Paw's tipi. The amazement at Ellen's presence, and fascination with what would happen because of it, had not diminished. Buffalo Calf Woman scowled at them as she patiently walked Ellen out to the camp latrine. The crowd followed them all the way, and at that point she had had quite enough.

"Begone!" she shouted. "Even a white woman deserves privacy here. Go away."

Muttering discontentedly, the crowd ambled off, but she knew they wouldn't go far. She tactfully turned her back as Ellen relieved herself. Then she led her slowly back to Bear Paw's tipi.

Ellen balked at the entrance, eyes wet with tears. The press of the Indians around her had frightened her and she longed for nothing so much as to get away from them. But unsure of Bear Paw's intentions, she was afraid to go back in. Buffalo Calf Woman had to put a firm hand on her back and push her into the tipi.

Bear Paw was still inside, partaking of the stew. Ellen retreated as far as she could from him against the tipi wall and sat down.

Buffalo Calf Woman came in and sat a respectful distance away from Bear Paw, who did not offer her any of the stew. "She is like a scared little rabbit," the Shoshone woman said, looking at Ellen. "I do not think she will be of much use here."

"Would you be brave if white soldiers captured you?" Bear Paw countered.

"I would kill as many as I could with my skinning knife," she replied.

"And suppose you did not have your knife?"

"Then I would strike them with my fists, and say it is a good day to die."

"You cannot judge a white woman so," Bear Paw said, putting down his empty bowl. "She was not raised to be a warrior."

Buffalo Calf Woman was silent for long seconds. Then, looking away out the tent flap, she said, "If you keep her here in your tipi, there will be talk."

"There is always talk," he replied, "about something."

"Even so," she said, rising to go, "there will be those who will demand you decide before long what to do with her. Her presence here can only cause trouble." With that, she went out.

THE SPRING DAY HAD GROWN long, and evening shadows were casting their tails across the land. Ellen lay on the furs, periodically dizzy and still very weak. She clutched her diary as if it were the stuffed homemade doll she had slept with as a little girl. Besides the tattered clothes she was wearing, it was the only link to her own world, a world now seemingly impossibly distant. Memory of the bloody chaos of the massacre drifted unbidden into her mind. She saw again Rachel turn pale and tumble to the ground, saw her pull desperately at the arrow. And for the first time, the shocking truth hit her. *That arrow was meant for me. If I hadn't bent over to pick up the water cup, it would have hit me squarely in the back. Oh Rachel, I'm so sorry. If you're looking down from heaven, can you forgive me?* Tears rolled slowly down her cheeks, and she turned her face to the tipi wall and cried until the sunlight faded into night.

BEAR PAW HAD GONE OUT for a while before night fell, but Ellen had not dared to leave the tipi. She didn't have to speak Shoshone to sense there was genuine hostility to her presence in the camp, and not just from the three women who found her. She didn't feel safe either in or out of the tipi.

Bear Paw had come back, looked at her briefly as she lay still with her back to him, and, after stoking up the fire with fresh wood, laid down on his own furs and gone to sleep.

Ellen had a thought as she lay in the silent tipi, listening to Bear Paw's rhythmic breathing. *I have the power to do only one thing: write this down in hopes that someone will read it someday.* She undid the leather thongs from the diary and opened it, relieved to see that her quill pen and precious vial of ink were still in place. She opened the diary to the first blank page. There was just enough light from the fire to write by. Her hand shook so badly she had to force the pen onto the paper.

Date and place unknown—
  Disaster—I am captured! The Indians have me. I don't know where I am or how I got here. I do not know what tribe these Indians are, or what

they may do with me. But most seem angry that I am here. Sooner or later they may kill me. Or if not, I may wish they had.

Everyone that took the wagon detour is dead at the hands of merciless savages. Even my dear friend Rachel, who took an arrow that was meant for me. With her last words she asked me to remember her, and so I shall, forever. I live for you also now, Rachel.

I have been fed and my head wound tended to. But I cannot remain here; I am in mortal danger. I must escape and continue my quest to reach Captain Morrow. As soon as there is the first hint of dawn in the morning, I will try.

ELLEN SLEPT FITFULLY, AWAKENING NOW and then and peeking out the tent flap to see if there was light on the eastern horizon. Finally, there was. Securing her diary over her shoulder and wrapping one of the smaller sleeping furs around her, she exited the tipi noiselessly, leaving a sleeping Bear Paw behind. No one was up and about as she trod fearfully through the quiet camp. Barely daring to breath, in five minutes she had left the outermost tipis behind and was once again walking unsteadily north.

E LLEN TROD DOGGEDLY AWAY FROM the Shoshone camp, fur wrapped tightly around her against the pre-dawn chill. Several times in the first fifteen minutes or so, she glanced back nervously over her shoulder to see if she was being followed. But she could detect no movement behind her. *Will they come after me?* she wondered. *After all the hostility to my presence, I should think they would be glad to see me go.*

The fiery disk of the spring sun peeked over the eastern horizon. In the distance ahead of her, she could see the landscape grow steadily more mountainous. The longer she walked, the more the foolishness of her undertaking settled on her. On her way out of the camp, she had seen several smoked fish curing on a rack, and had taken three, wrapping them in the scarf that had been put around her head by Buffalo Calf Woman. But for that, she was little better off than when the Indians had found her. She had almost no food, and no water.

But how could I stay? she thought. *The big Indian did feed me and see that my wounds were tended to. Still, he is a savage and could mean me harm sooner or later.*

Ellen trudged on, with no thought now other than reaching the man whom she was promised to, and dangerously blind to the fact that she was at the mercy of whatever dangerous wild animals she might encounter.

The sun rose and began a slow traverse across the clear sky overhead. She had been walking less than two hours before her footsteps began to slow, her legs began to feel leaden, and she grew dizzy. Her head throbbed with pain. She realized that she was much weaker than she had hoped. But she could think of nothing other than getting as far away from the Indian camp as possible. *I will rest at the top of that little rise ahead,* she thought. She plodded up the sandy hill, her breathing becoming labored. Finally she reached the top, gasping for breath, bent over. After a few moments she straightened up.

He was waiting for her on the other side.

She stared, slack-jawed in amazement and despair. Bear Paw sat astride a horse, looking at her, face devoid of expression. Ellen put a hand to her face and sank to her knees, clutching her stomach and sobbing with grief. She cried for long moments before she finally looked up again. Bear Paw held out one heavily muscled arm to her in invitation. Clearly he meant for her to mount the horse. Ellen stood stock-still, staring at him, face wet with tears, for several seconds. Then, with no other choice, she wiped her face on the dirty sleeve of her dress and staggered to her feet, then stepped toward him and grasped his wrist. The fish she had been carrying spilled to the ground.

With one powerful motion, he pulled her up behind him astride the horse. He urged the horse into motion, and they turned back the way she had come. Though it repelled her intensely, she soon found that with the swaying motion of the horse, she had no choice but to put her arms around him for stability. Then, suddenly feeling infinitely weary, she closed her eyes and rested her head against his broad back, the fur she had taken around her shoulders. Of three things she was now certain. She was still too weak to walk far. She could not survive in the wilderness on her own. And these Indians, whomever they might be, could easily track her and were not going to let her go.

Captain Eli Morrow stood at attention before Major Riley's desk, waiting for his commanding officer to finish reading the carefully-worded request for his extended leave of absence.

He had arrived back at Fort Walla Walla more or less on time the previous evening, exceedingly travel-weary and saddle-sore. The trip back had been one long episode of agony, knowing he was undoubtedly going farther and farther away from the mysterious white woman who had survived the massacre, then walked away into the wilderness. As he was traveling alone, he had been careful to skirt around Northern

Shoshone territory, and, as he had on the trip south, worn civilian dress to avoid making himself an even more tempting target.

Major Riley at last put down his reading glasses with an audible sigh and looked up at Eli. "This is a terrible tragedy, Eli. Let me say once again how sorry I am your bride-to-be became involved in it. I sincerely hope she somehow survived the massacre." He put Eli's request down on the desk. "But before you left, we discussed the local situation. Things are heating up with the Nez Perce over in the Wallowas. We're having more and more trouble controlling white settlers and their claims on recognized Nez Perce land, and the Nez Perce, not surprisingly, are getting hot under the collar about it. A figure of speech, of course, since their shirts have no collars. But you get the idea."

"Sir," Eli broke in, sensing rejection was coming, "is there any chance this post could be assigned to investigate the Elko massacre?"

"None. Such a task, if it is undertaken, would likely fall to the post at Reno. I'm sorry, it's too far out of our territory." He blew out his breath heavily and stood up, coming around the desk. "Eli, I can tell this thing is breaking your heart. But we can't spare a highly trained officer for an indefinite period of time. I'm sorry, I truly am. But I must deny your request."

Eli looked down at the floor momentarily, then raised his head to look Major Riley in the eye. "I appreciate your consideration of my request, sir. But I must tell you now that in light of your decision, I will consider resigning my commission to go look for her."

Major Riley put a hand on Eli's shoulder. "That would, in my estimation, be a foolish thing to do. You'd be throwing away a promising career. I suggest you rest up for a day and think carefully about it." He paused for a moment. "You may have to let this woman go."

Eli saluted and backed up a step, preparing to go. "Yes sir, I understand." He turned for the door.

"Eli," Major Riley said as Eli put his hand on the doorknob. "Let me know what you decide."

OUTSIDE, ELI CLIMBED TO THE upper parapet of the south wall of the fort, looking out across the landscape in the afternoon light. Behind and below him, a company of men, the men he should be commanding, were marching in drill formation. He couldn't face them. There was an emptiness where his heart should have been, a void he felt nothing would ever fill. Once again, he reached into his coat pocket and took the photograph of Ellen from its slender watertight metal case. Lovingly his fingers brushed over the image of the young girl with long wavy brown hair tied in a thick ponytail. She had managed a genuine smile, no easy task given the long exposure times of studio portraits. Over the weeks, he had grown increasingly in love with her as he had studied the photograph. Her eyes radiated a spark of intelligence, a spirit, that could not be faked. She would, he thought, make a fine companion for the demanding life of the frontier. Reluctantly, he put the photograph carefully back in its case, keeping his face turned away from the troops below. It would not do for his men to see their commanding officer lose control of his emotions. Then his head sank and he wept quietly for what had been lost.

Bear Paw rode slowly back into camp with Ellen. But he did not head for his tipi. Instead, he rode to another area of the camp and stopped in front of a tipi there. He called out to someone inside in Shoshone. After a few seconds, a woman emerged through the door flap.

Bear Paw eased Ellen to the ground and engaged in a brief conversation with the woman who had emerged. Ellen could see the woman was reacting unhappily to whatever Bear Paw was saying. But finally she nodded and motioned for Ellen to come to her.

Confused, Ellen hesitated, but Bear Paw pushed her firmly toward the woman as he gestured toward the tipi. It dawned on Ellen that she was to stay here for now. Feeling marginally better at the prospect of staying with a woman instead of this big Indian, and glad that she hadn't been punished for running away—yet—she meekly followed the woman inside.

Satisfied, Bear Paw turned his horse around and headed back for his tipi. When he got there, he found a small crowd of men gathered, scowling at him. Predictably, Black Elk was among them. He came forward as Bear Paw dismounted.

"So, the white woman ran away," he said, voice heavy with scorn. "Slaves who run away are to be punished."

Bear Paw had grown tired of the man's thinly-veiled challenges to his leadership even before Ellen arrived. He had even less patience for them now. "She is not a slave, and she will not be punished. She desires to return to her own people. Can you blame her?"

"If she is not a slave, then what is she to us?" Black Elk said, ignoring the question.

"That will be settled later. For now, I have asked Rabbit Woman to take her into her tipi. She has agreed. Therefore there can be no talk about her presence in my tipi."

"The whites steal our land and destroy our food, and yet you bring one of them here, and say you do not know what to do with her?" said another of the men. "Why should she be given any of our food?" He took a step closer. "And what if the whites find out she is here? They will come for her, and we will all suffer."

"She may be useful in learning more about the ways of the whites," Bear Paw said, desperately needing some justification for Ellen's presence.

Black Elk snorted. "How can this be? You do not speak the white language, and she does not speak Shoshone."

"I will send for my cousin from the camp to the north," Bear Paw said. "His wife is of the Spokane tribe. She was raised near a white trading post and knows some of their language. She can help me speak with the white woman."

Black Elk's expression took on a look of menace as he too took another step closer. "This is a bad decision. If she stays here, she needs to learn her proper place among us, and what she may and may not do. If she runs away again, I will punish her myself." With that he turned on his heel and walked away.

ELLEN SANK TO THE SLEEPING furs in her new quarters. The woman who had shown her inside said something in her own language and went out, leaving Ellen alone. She drew her legs up under her chin as her head sank, sobbing softly in despair.

FOR TWO DAYS, LITTLE HAPPENED. Ellen was fed, sometimes grudgingly, it seemed, but mostly left alone. She gave no thought of another escape attempt yet, knowing she was still weak. She stayed in the tipi most of the time, except for walks to the camp latrine. During those trips, no one spoke to her or approached her, but she could feel curious eyes on her all the way.

Late in the afternoon of the second day after Ellen's return, the arrival of visitors brought murmurs of interest to the camp. A man and woman rode in on horseback and were welcomed warmly. It was Bear Paw's cousin and his wife, Owl Woman. Bear Paw took them into his tipi for some time, and when he finally emerged, took Owl Woman with him across the camp to Rabbit Woman's tipi.

He paused outside and called out to Rabbit Woman, who invited him in. He entered, bringing Owl Woman with him.

The Spokane woman sat down on her legs and looked Ellen over with considerable interest. "She is very young," she said to Bear Paw. "But quite pretty, as white woman go. How should we start?"

"Ask her how she is called," Bear Paw said.

Owl Woman turned to Ellen. "White woman, how are you called?" she said in English.

Ellen's eyes flew wide in surprise, her hand flying to her mouth. "You speak English!" she said, an enormous wave of relief washing over her.

"Yes. Bear Paw would like to know your name."

Ellen looked at the big Indian who had brought her back to camp. "His name is Bear Paw?"

"Yes. He is chief of this camp, and a man of great importance to the Shoshone, whose lands you are in. Now, what is your name?"

Shakily, Ellen managed to reply, "My—my name is Ellen. Ellen," she repeated.

Owl Woman turned to Bear Paw. "El-len. The white woman is called El-len."

Bear Paw seemed satisfied. "El-len," he said.

Ellen was by this this time fairly shaking with anticipation. "Would you—could you—ask him if he will let me go?"

Owl Woman looked at her for a moment, then translated for Bear Paw, who had no visible reaction. Then she replied, "It would not be wise to bring up this subject now. Bear Paw is most interested in your presence here. He hopes to learn more about the whites from you."

"But—I am to be married. My husband-to-be is waiting for me. I was on my way to meet him when—when I—"

"Were found wandering in the wilderness alone, nearly dead?"

Owl Woman finished the sentence for her. "With no food or water, defenseless against any wild animal who fancied you for a meal? This does not seem true. For now, you should not talk about your white life. There will come a day when you may ask him again. But you are here now, and must live as we do, and learn what you can."

Her sudden hope shattered, Ellen was unable to keep her composure, and began to cry.

Bear Paw seemed embarrassed by her open emotion, and with a few words to Owl Woman, went out, leaving Ellen with the two Shoshone women.

Owl Woman let Ellen cry for a minute, then spoke softly to her. "It is not good for a woman to cry so in front of a man." Suddenly feeling sorry for her, she moved closer. "I am called Owl Woman. I will be here for some time, so that I can understand your words and tell the others what you have said. You are to be Shoshone for now—"

"No!" Ellen sobbed. "You cannot make me one of you!"

Owl Woman moved even closer and put a hand on Ellen's shoulder, which caused the young girl to flinch. "I can see that you are very young, so I will forgive your crying. Know that we do not mean you harm. As a valuable addition to the tribe, you will be well cared for, and will not be punished, as long as you perform the duties expected of you."

Ellen raised her head, wiping her cheeks on her sleeve. "I have family back home—where I come from—they think I am dead. If I write a letter to them, could you see that it gets delivered to a white man who might send it to them?"

Owl Woman shook her head. "This is not possible. War rages all around us. White soldiers kill and burn as they please. None of us would risk their life, even under a flag of truce, to deliver it. And such a letter would certainly bring white soldiers down upon us." She looked into Ellen's eyes. "Your place, for now, is here. I will help you learn what your duties are, and when you are feeling stronger, we will talk with Bear Paw and hear what questions he may have for you."

That night, Ellen wrote by firelight in her diary:

Somewhere in Indian country, date unknown—
They will not let me go! I have no hope of escape anyway. I do not have the strength to walk further across the wilderness, and no weapon to defend

myself against dangerous wild animals, of which I am certain there are many. My heart aches for Nettie, Liza, and Clarence, and most of all for Capt. Morrow, who must know by now that a terrible fate has befallen me. Oh, how I ache to see him! I would rush into his arms and hold myself tightly to him. I am heartbroken for what was to be.

I will hold my diary fast to me in the days to come. It is the one thing I have to connect me to my world now, save the clothes on my back, which I expect they will soon ask me to discard. For they say I am to be one of them. I will resist this with all the strength I have, and live in fear of punishment. For I have no doubt that there are those here who mean me harm. For now, I have little strength to write more, and this dim firelight hurts my eyes.

In the days that followed, Ellen became at least temporarily resigned to her fate. She no longer feared death on a daily basis, although it was clear to her, from the looks she got from some of the young men, that her presence was offensive to them. She took refuge in Owl Woman's ability to speak English, and confided in her that she had been terrified at first that Bear Paw meant her harm.

"You are mistaken in this," Owl Woman told her quietly. "From what he told me when I arrived, he has saved your life twice already. The women who found you would certainly have killed you if he had not stepped in. Then, when he brought you to camp, some of the young men wanted to kill you also, but he challenged them to kill him first. No one wanted to try it."

Ellen was amazed. "I do not remember any of that. I must have been unconscious. Why—why has he not he told me he did this?"

Owl Woman smiled. "You are white. He does not find it necessary to boast to you. He cares little for what you think of him."

After Ellen had rested for three days, Buffalo Calf Woman examined her head wound, and declared it to be healing satisfactorily. "It is time you did some work," she declared. "Everyone, except the smallest of children, has work to do. You will join us in this, though there are many here who think you are weak."

They started her out slowly for two days, going out on short forays to help gather firewood, berries, roots, and other edible items, and to check rabbit snares. Owl Woman was not always along, so the other Shoshone women showed her with gestures what was expected. They were usually gruff with her, and intolerant of her sometimes slow grasp of what they asked her to do. She didn't complain, knowing it was useless to do so.

On the morning of the third day, a woman came to the tipi she shared with Rabbit Woman, carrying a buckskin skirt, cloth shirt, and moccasins. Except for the moccasins, they didn't look new, but were reasonably clean and had been well cared for. Rabbit Woman motioned for her to take off her by-now tattered dress and put on the new garments. Ellen looked at them with great distaste for a moment, then realized she had little choice. The cotton dress she had worn since the day of the massacre was torn in numerous places, and on the verge of destroying her modesty. Reluctantly, she disrobed and put the garments on, then watched sadly as her dress was consigned to the fire. *I've taken another step away from my world,* she thought. But Rabbit Woman seemed pleased with the transformation, nodding her approval at the good fit.

That day, real work began. She was shown how to help stretch out fresh hides in preparation for scraping and curing. If the hide was to be used for everyday garments, flesh and fat were scraped off the inside with bone or wood scraping tools, and hair was scraped off the other side, to eventually produce, when properly cured, a thin flexible sheet of hide that could be cut and sewn into a garment. If the hide was to be used as a heavier garment for cold weather, the hair was left on the outside for warmth.

The women clearly didn't expect her to be able to do her share. But Ellen was a farm girl, and had been working since she was old enough to carry a water bucket. Though more slender than the Shoshone women, she had a wiry strength and great endurance. She could skin game for supper with the best of them, and knew how to sew. Though her head still throbbed with pain now and then, she did not let on, and her ability to keep up quickly won the admiration of the women.

At night, she would write in her diary, fretting at the declining level of her vial of ink, even as she took daily comfort in putting her thoughts and experiences down on paper. *I need to record what is happening to me,* she thought. *When I regain my freedom, if I am able to reach Captain Morrow, he will see these words and know I tried hard to get to him, but failed. I still honor my commitment of marriage to him; I pray he has not abandoned hope for me.*

But as the days turned into weeks and spring eased into early summer, Eli Morrow became caught up with the demands of life on a frontier cavalry outpost, and could afford little thought of Ellen during the day. Relations with the Nez Perce were getting touchier by the month, and it was obvious that before long the tenuous peace might be shattered. Still, there was not an evening that he failed to take Ellen's picture from its case and gently run his fingers over her image before turning down the wick on his bedside oil lamp. Some nights he would lie awake in the darkness, the words of her letters, and her image, floating in his consciousness for too long before sleep would come.

Far to the east in Kansas, Nettie had sold the farm, and she, Liza, and Clarence boxed up what they intended to take west, and boarded a freight wagon bound for the Missouri River, and thence to Omaha. Still in the grip of inexpressible sadness, none of them looked back as the little farmhouse faded into the distance, and was soon swallowed up in the vastness of the Great Plains.

Ellen sadly settled into a routine that varied little from day to day. What would have been unthinkable, horrifying, just months before was now a daily reality: she was living with Indians, as one of them. The curious stares had faded to a certain extent. But she was careful to walk accompanied by other women whenever possible, for fear of encountering Black Elk. His hatred for whites clearly extended to her, even though she had not sought to be in his camp, and had made no secret of her desire to leave. The venom in his expression had lessened not at all, and she was afraid what he might do if he caught her alone.

As for Bear Paw, he had relayed through Owl Woman that he wished Ellen to teach him English.

"You have not taught him?" Ellen asked.

"He has never asked me," Owl Woman replied. "Somehow your presence here has given him the desire to learn. And I will be here only through the warm season. Then I must go back with my husband, to my village."

So in the evenings, she and Owl Woman would go to Bear Paw's tipi, and Ellen began to try to teach the big Shoshone her language. She was not sure how to go about it, and it would have been next to impossible for her, without the assistance of Owl Woman. The Shoshone woman sometimes felt the need to take over the lessons, but Bear Paw clearly did not want her to teach him; he wanted to hear it from Ellen.

Ellen, for her part, was surprised how diligent and patient Bear Paw was in picking up what she haltingly taught him. He was a quick study, and his desire to learn was obvious.

All this did not lessen Ellen's desire to escape again. She had regained her strength, and her head had ceased to throb on a daily basis, though the wound was still painful to the touch. She spent much of each day glancing at the hills to the north, and silently wondering when she could dare to try for them again.

In what she figured to be early June, a decision was forced on her. She woke alone to considerable activity one morning, and soon learned that the camp was being broken down for horseback transport for the annual trek eastward to buffalo country for a hunt. Ellen was disheartened and panicky about being taken even farther from Eli Morrow. *I can't let them take me*, she thought. *I've got to get away, and it has to be now. Maybe with all this activity they won't notice I'm gone for a while.*

She stuffed what food she could surreptitiously take into a deerskin bag. Then, securing her diary across her shoulder and taking Rabbit Woman's skinning knife, she slipped away on the pretext of going to the camp latrine. Once there, she kept walking, again headed ever north.

ELLEN KNEW BY NOW THAT the Shoshone were excellent trackers, and could doubtless find her unless she made some effort to conceal her tracks. So she took every opportunity to do so, wading into any stream she found and walking north up the stream bed for at least one hundred yards before wading out onto the opposite shore. It was tiring, but she felt she had no choice. Whenever possible, she walked on hard ground or stones, where she would leave no tracks.

She walked north with determination, occasionally fingering the skinning knife which she hoped would protect her from dangerous animals. After about an hour, she came to forested country, and walked in among the trees to further conceal herself.

Now and then she had looked back over her shoulder to see if there were any pursuer. Now, shortly after entering the forest, she paused, leaning against a tree trunk, and looked again.

A figure on horseback was coming toward her.

He was walking his horse slowly, looking at the ground. Her efforts to conceal her tracks had not been enough. The man pulled his horse to a halt as he neared the stand of trees, and raised his head.

It was Black Elk.

Ellen recoiled in horror, then darted behind the tree trunk, heart pounding. Her eyes shut tightly, squeezing tears down her cheeks. She was in real trouble now, and she knew it. Black Elk would not hesitate to harm her, or worse.

After staring into the trees for a few moments, Black Elk dismounted and drew a large hunting knife. He began to walk forward slowly.

When he was less than twenty feet away, Ellen panicked and fled deeper into the trees. Black Elk was after her immediately, catching up fast with big strides. She heard him right behind her and drew her skinning knife, whipping around to face him, knowing she knew she had no chance to defeat him, but determined to put up a fight. She slashed at him once, twice. On the third try he caught her arm on mid-air and twisted the knife to the ground. Then he backhanded her hard across the face.

Ellen's head exploded in pain and she fell to the ground. Black Elk pulled her up by her hair. She kicked wildly at him, but couldn't connect solidly. He held her fast by the hair as he withdrew a length of rope from his waist sash. Then he forced her over to a nearby tree and, fastening the rope around her wrists, threw it over a branch above her head and pulled her arms up.

Ellen was by this time crying, and pleading with him not to harm her. He merely looked at her in angry silence and took his hunting knife in hand again. He stepped close to her and raised the knife and sliced a furrow in her right forearm. Ellen shrieked and tried to back away, but the rope held her fast. Then he cut her a second time. Blood ran down her arm and dripped from her elbow as Ellen cried out and twisted in agony.

Black Elk threw the knife to the ground and put his hands on her, groping at her breasts. She could read the lust in his eyes. He slowly reached down and began lifting her dress up above her waist. She knew what he intended now. He was going to rape her.

Black Elk reached down a hand to rub her crotch—then froze as a knife was suddenly at his throat. Black Elk had not been the only one who had pursued her.

Holding the knife was Bear Paw. "Touch her again and you die, Black Elk," he said.

Black Elk's eyes grew large, then his hands slowly fell away. He was pulled away from Ellen, then shoved to the side. He looked at Bear Paw, rage on his face. "Do you not see what the white woman has done to our camp?" he said. "There has been anger among us ever since she arrived!"

"The anger was not of her doing. It was you who have chosen to be angry."

"She is disobedient. She has run away twice!"

"Would you not try to do the same if you were captured by whites?" Bear Paw said.

"Yes. But she is not a warrior, only a servant who does not know her place. She has no respect for our ways." Black Elk was fairly shaking with rage. "She is a thief as well. This time she stole food and Rabbit Woman's skinning knife." He bent over and retrieved his knife from the ground, tension in every muscle.

"I do not think it is her running away and the taking of things that angers you," Bear Paw said calmly. "It is because you do not have her, to do with as you please, to take out your anger against the whites. Know this: this is the last time I will let this foolish behavior go. If you make a move against her again, I will kill you."

Black Elk snorted and slowly stepped away toward his horse. "She has divided us, when we should be brothers, standing as one against the whites." He spat on the ground, then walked away in silence, mounted his horse, and kicked it to a gallop.

Bear Paw sighed and turned to Ellen, who was staring at him, eyes still wide with fear. He reached up and cut the rope that had bound her to the tree branch. Ellen collapsed against him, weak from terror. He gently sat her down on the ground, then walked to his horse and retrieved a length of cloth. He came back to Ellen, who was sobbing, head down. He took her left arm and wound the a strip of the cloth firmly around her wounds. Then he helped her to her feet and led her back to his horse, where he hoisted her up, then jumped up in front of her on the horse. He turned his mount south, and they began to ride slowly away.

Ellen, weak and exhausted, quickly put her arms tightly around him and again leaned her head against his back. Once again, Bear Paw had come to her rescue, and once again he had shown no anger, had not been rough with her, but had reacted with gentleness and patience as before. That was not lost on her, and she felt satisfied to cling to him tightly as they rode back to camp.

BEAR PAW SAID NOTHING ALL the way back. But when they were nearly there, he stopped at a small rise which hid them from view of the camp. He dismounted and held out his arms for Ellen to do the same. Mystified and uneasy, she reluctantly did so, and he gently lowered her to the ground. As she stood there, he took some of the rope Black Elk had used to tie her to the tree and motioned for her to put her wrists together. Wide-eyed, she did. He wound the rope firmly around her wrists, and tied it. Then he took the other end of the rope, mounted the horse, and began to move slowly away. His intent was all too clear. Ellen was to be led back to camp, walking, her wrists bound. Unsettling as it was, she hoped it was all an act. Bear Paw needed to show the rest of the tribe he was punishing her for running away, as they no doubt believed she should be. Perhaps it would mute some of the criticism of her continued disobedience.

She was led into the mostly disassembled camp, feeling eyes of anger and contempt on her. She had delayed the tribe's departure for a day, and they were clearly unhappy about it. Bear Paw led her all the way to Rabbit Woman's tipi, one of the few left standing, where he untied her and motioned for her to go inside. Then he left.

After dark, he was back. Ellen heard him call out to Rabbit Woman for permission to enter. Rabbit Woman gave her consent, and he did so, sitting down ankles crossed before her. Owl Woman was with him.

Bear Paw had learned enough English to converse sparingly. "Rabbit Woman has treated your wounds?" he said.

Ellen lowered her head in shame, unlike her first attempt embarrassed by the trouble she had caused. "Yes," she said softly.

"Good." Then, uncharacteristically, he got right to the point. "I am sad you run away again."

Ellen still couldn't raise her head, and remained silent.

"We treated you well?"

Ellen put a hand to her cheek, and finally managed to look at him. "You have. More than I deserve. I am so very sorry for the trouble I have made for everyone. But what I told Owl Woman is true. I was to be married soon. I wanted to go to my husband."

Bear Paw seemed to think for a moment, as if searching for words. Finally he turned to Owl Woman and said something in Shoshone.

Owl Woman listened a moment and then turned to Ellen. "Bear Paw says that if you try to escape again, he cannot protect you. He says that you are valued here, if you will honor our ways."

She finished and turned back to Bear Paw.

He looked at Ellen, then said, "It would please me for you to stay." Then he got up and left.

THAT NIGHT, AS RABBIT WOMAN slept on the other side of the tipi, Ellen lay on her sleeping furs, head spinning with confusion. It was clear now that she would not survive another escape attempt. She had been dangerously foolish to try a second time. And hard as it was for her to admit it, most of the tribe had been kind to her, especially considering she was white. Bear Paw had been consistently patient and considerate, even with her two flights. And he had now come between her and death three times. But she had no doubt embarrassed him in front of the other tribe members. He did not deserve it, and she couldn't bear to shame him again. *I will not*, she thought. The implications of that decision kept her awake far into the night.

IN THE MORNING, RABBIT WOMAN's tipi was broken down and packed on horseback. The camp began moving slowly east, Ellen walking beside the horses with the other women. She was now going farther from where she felt Eli must be. And she was not only living with Indians, she was moving east with them to hunt buffalo. Though she found it still hard to accept, with each passing day she felt a bit more like one of them.

Stripped of the beautiful romance with which we have been so long willing to envelope him, the Indian forfeits his claim to the appellation of the 'noble' red man. We see him as he is, a 'savage' in every sense of the word; not worse, perhaps, than his white brother would be similarly born and bred, but one whose cruel and ferocious nature far exceeds that of any wild beast of the desert.

When the soil which he has claimed and hunted over so long a time is demanded . . . there is no appeal; he must yield. . . . Destiny seems to have so willed it, and the world nods its approval.

—General George Armstrong Custer

TEN DAYS OF STEADY TRAVEL brought the band to the edge of buffalo country in western Montana Territory. There were a few women who were well-to-do and had horses to ride, but most, like Ellen, walked alongside the pack horses. Along the way, she had met a young girl named Kimama, whose name meant "butterfly". She appeared barely older than Ellen. The two had become fast friends, even without words. Kimama took it upon herself to teach Ellen a little Shoshone, laughing good-naturedly at Ellen's failed first attempts at proper pronunciation.

As she had walked along over the previous ten days, Ellen had tried her best to put Eli into some back compartment of her consciousness. Though she was now resigned to being with the Shoshone for the present, she felt in no immediate danger. She knew a continued sullen and resentful attitude would not win her friends among the women, which she badly wanted. And she had to admit that once she had decided to accept her fate—for the time being—most of the band had been kind to her. Even Black Elk had kept his distance.

Upon reaching buffalo country, the Shoshone paused and rested while scouts rode out far and wide searching for a herd. There was some concern, as finding a sizable herd of buffalo had become increasingly difficult in recent years. Older tribesmen could—and did—tell of times in their youth when the ground had shook with the passage of enormous herds that darkened the hills and plains, and raised huge clouds of dust with their passage, which sometimes took more than an hour. No more.

But good fortune was with them. On the second day, scouts came galloping in from the west at top speed. A herd had been found! The entire camp was galvanized with excitement, and most of the band immediately picked up and began walking in the direction the scouts came from. After several miles, the tribe was motioned to a halt below a large rise. Selected women, including Ellen, walked quietly to a spot just below the top of the ridge. There they lay down flat and crawled to the top, maintaining complete silence. There below was a large herd of the great shaggy beasts, grazing contentedly across the prairie.

The silence was shattered by the thunder of horses approaching at top speed, as hunters, stripped to the waist, swooped in on both sides of the herd, which bolted in panicked confusion. Ellen watched in amazement as they fired arrow after arrow at full gallop, hitting their targets with great accuracy. Some hunters riding in close to the herd hurled sharpened lances. One beast after another fell with ground-shaking impact in an explosion of dust amid the chaos of whooping hunters, running horses, and panicked buffalo.

When it was all over, between twenty and thirty buffalo lay still on the prairie as the rest of the herd thundered off into the distance. The women wasted no time, trotting out to the carcasses and setting to work. For Ellen, skinning the great beasts was only a larger, hairier task than similar work she had done on the farm. Once shown the particulars, she set to work and held her own.

The hides were quickly cut off, and the best cuts of meat were taken. Nothing of the buffalo would be wasted. Every part had a purpose—from ceremonial objects to game pieces, from tools to weapons, from riding gear to clothing or tipi coverings. Glue could be made from the hoofs and hide, tanning agents from the brains and fat, cups and spoons from the horns, fuel from the dung. Just about everything the Shoshone needed to live could come from the buffalo. The same travois that had pulled the camp supplies on the journey were now used to take the harvest back to camp.

When the skinners arrived back to where they had left the others, they found camp set up and help waiting for them. Some started immediately preparing the meat, some of which would be smoked and dried, and some prepared for a feast that night. Hides were stretched and staked out in the sun to dry.

That night, the happy band feasted on buffalo around a roaring fire. Ellen was exhausted, but no more so than the other women. She ate until she was stuffed, then leaned back on her elbows. The teenage Shoshone girls had from the beginning been fascinated with her wavy light brown hair, and vied around the campfire at night to brush it and braid it into a large ponytail or pigtails. Having finished eating, they gathered around her now, attempting to rebraid her ponytail. She was too content to resist, and let them have their way. She saw Kimama looking at her and gave the young girl a smile. Kimama whooped in excitement, drawing the attention of the other women nearby, who all looked at Ellen and nodded, clearly amused. It was the first time they had seen her smile.

While all this was going on, sentries sat at their posts several miles out, on hilltops giving a commanding view of the countryside. The Shoshone were not without their natural enemies, not to mention the risk of a chance encounter with long-knife soldiers. It would not do to be caught by surprise in open country that afforded little in the way of natural protection.

THE NEXT FEW DAYS WERE filled with work. Meat continued to be processed for the trip home, hides were scraped, on one side for making heavy winter garments, on both sides for flexible buckskin to be made into shirts, skirts, and leggings. Ellen wielded her tools with skill and persistence, and won admiring nods of approval from the women working alongside her.

Evenings would bring rest and games for the women, such as the awl game or the button game. Among the children, the girls might play house with stuffed dolls, or enlist their younger brothers and sisters as children in need of mothering. Boys and girls alike might try to throw arrows through a rolling hoop. The men would eventually fall to swapping prized possessions, gambling, or boasting about the speed of their mounts, resulting in races outside the camp. Sometimes, before light faded, virtually everyone would gather for an all-consuming game of lacrosse.

FIVE DAYS AFTER THE BUFFALO hunt, Bear Paw rode up to Rabbit Woman's tipi one afternoon on his favorite mount. Ellen was standing outside. He held out a hand, clearly inviting her to come up. Ellen hesitated, but Rabbit Woman emerged from inside and gently but firmly shoved her in the back. Ellen stepped forward and grasped Bear Paw's muscular arm. With one strong motion he pulled her up behind him, then set the horse into motion, and walked slowly to the edge of the village. Ellen had put her arms around Bear Paw for stability. Now he put his hands over hers momentarily, as if to say, "hold on tight". Then he kneed the big stallion. The horse reared slightly and dug in, then rocketed out of camp like a cannonball. In seconds they were streaking across the prairie. Ellen had never been on a horse going so fast, and she had no choice but to hang on for all she was worth.

They rode out to a rise still within sight of camp. There Bear Paw slowed the horse to a walk along the summit for a few minutes. Then he stopped and slid to the ground, lifting Ellen down after him. He sat on the ground, and Ellen joined him. Far into the distance she could see breezes creating ripples in the grass, like waves on the ocean. The sky overhead was vast and seemed to stretch on forever. She felt very small.

Bear Paw was content with silence for a while. Then he turned to her. "Book you make marks in—it is important to you?"

She turned from her romance with the landscape. "Yes. It is very important."

"What you say in book?"

"I write about the things I see and do each day. I write about how I feel about these things. I write about the Shoshone." *And it helps me stay connected to my world*, she thought.

He looked away across the plain. "You write about me?"

Ellen smiled. "Yes, I do. Do you think I should not?"

"Do if is important to you."

After most of an hour, Bear Paw stood and held out his hands to help Ellen to her feet. He pulled her up but did not let go. Instead he stood close to her, looking into her golden brown eyes.

Ellen didn't know what to think. What was this all about?

After long silent moments, he squeezed her hands gently in his big ones, and she reflexively squeezed back. She was beginning to get uncomfortable when at last he released her, mounted up, and pulled her astride behind him. They rode slowly back to camp, Ellen's head resting against his back as she pondered the meaning of what he had done. They reached camp as dusk was falling, and he rode her back to her tipi. There she slipped to the ground as Rabbit Woman came to meet them. Bear Paw turned his horse away and rode off without a word. Ellen did not see the amusement on Rabbit Woman's face as she watched him go.

Ellen pondered the encounter in her diary by firelight that night. Her mind was tempted to start going in certain directions she didn't want to contemplate, and she firmly squashed the notions. She was more concerned that her vial of ink had run dry, and the only ink left was in her pen. She pressed the tip harder, trying to eke out enough ink to finish for the night—and in mid-sentence the tip of the pen suddenly snapped off. After staring at it in disbelief for long seconds, she tearfully put the broken pen and empty vial away in the diary's carrying case. There would be no more writing. A big part of the white identity she had clung to was gone.

Ellen tried to carry on with her duties the next day but couldn't hide her sadness. Owl Woman asked what troubled her, and she explained. Later, Bear Paw walked by and noticed Ellen was silent and kept her head down as she did her work with the hides.

"White woman seems sad today," he said to Owl Woman. "She mad about ride yesterday?"

"No," Owl Woman replied. She explained about the broken pen and lack of ink. "I think she is greatly comforted to write in her book. It reminds her of her white world, which I am sure she misses. Now she cannot. I think it is a great loss to her."

Bear Paw nodded, lost in thought. Two hours later he had packed a few things, tied them to his horse, and quietly announced to others he trusted in his absence that he would be gone for a day, perhaps two. Then he rode off across the prairie and was soon lost to view.

≋●

A ramshackle peddler's wagon creaked across the rolling prairie, drawn by two horses. Two bearded, weatherbeaten peddlers in strangely out of place battered sou'wester hats sat up front, a faded canvas wagon top over the wagon behind them. The wagon's load of pots, skillets, and other utensils swayed and clanked as it rolled along.

The driver gripped the reins firmly but there was a rifle against his knee. The man riding shotgun carried one across his lap as he constantly scanned the land ahead. Being out on the plains with no military escort was dangerous beyond foolhardy. But times were tough and a living had to be made.

The horses pulled the wagon along a shallow dry wash, then were suddenly jerked to a halt. Both men froze.

An Indian on horseback sat on top of a rise twenty yards ahead, a white flag hanging from a stick across his horse's back.

The driver sighed. "Well, pardner, this might be it," he said. "Always thought we might meet our maker somewhere out here."

The shotgun carrier ran one hand down the stock of his gun for reassurance, then rubbed his beard nervously. "What ya reckon he wants?" he said. "'Sides our scalps, I mean."

"I dunno, but he is showin' a white flag. Mebbe he's got peaceable intentions."

The other licked suddenly dry lips. "Yeah, and mebbe there's forty more Injuns just over that rise, awaitin' fer us."

"Hmm," the driver said. "He could have attacked by now if he wanted to. Could be he wants to trade. And he's blockin' our path, so let's quit jawin' and find out. Just keep a grip on that scattergun." The men warily got down and tried to look friendly, all the while shaking in their boots.

The Indian rode up slowly, hands open and raised slightly to show that he held no weapons. When he was near the wagon he dismounted and walked closer, towering over the peddlers. He waved a hand at the wagon. "Trade," he said.

The driver elbowed his companion. "See? What'd I tell ya?" He turned to the Indian. "Sure thing, Chief! Right this way." He strode back to the wagon and lowered a long panel on one side, revealing a cornucopia of goods—blankets, pots, pans, utensils, knives, bottles of elixir, and a wide variety of other items large and small.

The Indian strode up to the wagon and began perusing the goods, ignoring most of what he could readily see, and poking into small cubby holes as if looking for a specific item.

The two peddlers stood back, watching the powerful muscles in the Indian's broad shoulders working as he moved his arms around. "Look at 'im," the driver whispered. "Gives me the willies. Just as soon slip a blade 'twixt yer ribs as look at ya."

"That's the biggest damn Injun I ever seen," Shotgun said quietly. "If he turns on us, we're done fer."

The silence grew so oppressive the wagon driver spoke up. "Well, Chief, see anything ya like?"

The Indian at last turned to them, a small object in each big hand. The peddlers were amazed to see he held a bottle of ink and a writing pen.

Shotgun gaped in astonishment "A writin' pen, and ink? What's he want that fer? Buck Injuns can't read ner write."

The driver gave him a sour look. "Well neither kin you, so shut up. Chief wants to buy himself some writin' materials, who'm I to say no?" He turned back to the Indian. "Okay, Chief, whattaya got to trade?"

The Indian put the ink and pen on the wagon shelf, walked to his horse and retrieved something, then came back. The men were astonished at sight of one of the most magnificent wolverine pelts they had ever seen. The driver whistled in appreciation and turned to Shotgun. "Why, I could probably get thutty, forty dollars fer that over ta Boise!"

The Indian spoke. "Good trade?"

"Yeah, good trade!" the driver said, quickly making the exchange.

The Indian nodded and turned to go.

"Say, uh, Chief," Shotgun called after him, "if you don't mind my askin', I was just curious—"

The big Indian smiled slightly as he stowed the items away and mounted up. "For my woman," he said, then turned his horse away and rode slowly over the rise and out of sight.

"Phew," Shotgun sighed. "He comes way out here alone, risking gettin' shot, to buy pen and ink. That must be one special woman."

≫◦

Early in the evening of his second day of absence, Bear Paw came riding back into camp. He turned his horse loose with the herd and strode to Rabbit Woman's tipi. There he asked for permission to enter, and was invited in. Ellen and Rabbit Woman were both there, along with Owl Woman, preparing some buffalo meat stew for dinner.

"I am glad to see you have returned," Rabbit Woman said. "Please share our dinner with us."

"I would be most happy to," Bear Paw said, rubbing his stomach. "The trail was long."

They engaged in pleasant conversation over the meal, which was eaten at a leisurely pace. When at last they were finished, Bear Paw turned to Ellen.

"Ellen is well?" he said.

Ellen nodded. "Yes," she said shyly, a little overwhelmed, as she sometimes was, by his presence.

"But you are sad about book? You cannot make the marks."

"Yes," she said, looking down.

He reached into a leather bag tied to his waist. "Be sad no more." He retrieved the ink and pen from the bag and set them before her.

Ellen went wide-eyed in amazement. She picked up the pen and ink bottle, scarcely believing they were real. It was a fine pen, and the ink was just right. She looked up at him, tears of joy streaking her cheeks. "Thank you," she said, clutching the gifts to her chest.

"Gift makes you happy?" Bear Paw said.

Ellen smiled through her tears. "Yes, it makes me very happy."

Bear Paw nodded in satisfaction.

As Ellen examined the gifts more closely, she could see out of the corner of her vision that Rabbit Woman and Owl Woman were trying hard to suppress a fit of giggles.

Then Owl Woman leaned over to her. "You should tell him to go now," she whispered in her ear.

Ellen looked at her in surprise and Owl Woman urged her with a nod. Totally without a clue as to what was going on, she turned to Bear Paw. "I—I am so very happy. Thank you for the pen and ink. I would ask that you go now. I will see you tomorrow."

Bear Paw did not seem in the least offended when Owl Woman relayed her words. He nodded, got to his feet, and went out.

The two Shoshone women broke into poorly-suppressed laughter, trying to hide it behind their hands.

Ellen was by this time annoyed. "What are you two going on about?"

Owl Woman looked at her, face suffused with merriment. "I am sorry. It is time that you know."

"Know what?" Ellen said, vexed.

"He is courting you!"

Ellen's jaw dropped open. "What! Are you sure?"

"There is no doubt. The signs are there. I have suspected it for some time. And the gifts he gave you could only come from a white man, so you may be sure he placed himself in great danger to get them."

Ellen sat in disbelief at the words. This was the last thing she had expected to deal with. As if her life was not already a confused mess. Was it possible that now there were *two* men who wanted her? And that one of them was someone whom she had mortally feared and regarded as a savage only weeks ago? Her mind roiled with confusion. She looked at the two Shoshone women. "I—I don't know what to do," she said, at a loss for any other words.

"I will instruct you in your part in the days to come," Owl Woman said. "This news is enough for one day." She got up to leave. "But know this: you have received a great honor. He is a good man, and many of the women here would wish to have him." With that, she rose and went out.

ELLEN COULD HARDLY WAIT TO open her diary that night and begin writing with her new pen.

Somewhere in buffalo country, late June(?) 1876—

I am being courted! I have attracted the interest of Bear Paw, the very man whom I recently regarded as a savage. I am so confused I can barely write these words. What has happened to me that I do not immediately reject his interest and run screaming into the night? I cannot possibly entertain such a proposal! Oh, how did I come to this, and was any of it my doing? I cannot leave these people at present, but staying with them, warm and comforting as most of them have been, is something I cannot entertain for long. I know my place in the world, and I still believe it is at Captain Morrow's side, and not here. I must find some way to forestall Bear Paw's intentions, and pray my situation improves.

During the next couple of days, Ellen thought she noticed some of the younger women looking at her a little differently. Bear Paw's courtship had not gone unnoticed, and the women smiled at her and giggled to each other as they passed by.

She did not see Bear Paw for two days, which was welcome, as she was still trying to sort out how she would tell him that she could not respond to his courtship, that she remained promised to another man despite her presence among the Shoshone.

But on the third day after the revelation though, he came to her tipi and asked her to walk with him out to the horse herd grazing a short distance from camp. There she found a beautiful paint mare, brown and sparkling white, groomed and brushed to perfection, that had been separated from the rest of the herd and tied to a low bush.

"She is yours," Bear Paw said.

Ellen looked at the mare, wide-eyed. Growing up on the farm, she had long wished for her own horse, a fine, swift animal that she could ride over the prairie. But she had always had to be content with the farm animals—plow horses or wagon horses—that thrilled her not at all. She walked up slowly to the mare and put a hand on her muzzle. The horse did not flinch, but instead rubbed her head against Ellen's chest.

She smiled at Bear Paw. "Thank you. She is beautiful."

"Now we will ride together," he said. He retrieved his horse, put rope bridles on both animals, and he and Ellen mounted up and galloped slowly away from the herd. Once in the clear, he urged his horse into a run, waving for Ellen to join him. Brimming with excitement, she did, and the two horses took off. In seconds she and Bear Paw were streaking over the prairie side by side. Ellen crouched low over the mare's neck, feeling the rhythm of the powerful muscles of the horse beneath her. She breathed deeply of the clear prairie air as it rushed over her; her long brown hair streaming in the wind behind her. She reveled in the warmth of the sun on her face; felt gloriously alive for the first time in longer than she could remember. She looked over at Bear Paw, met his gaze, and grinned.

They rode along at top speed for long minutes, then gradually slowed to a gallop, and finally to a walk. Bear Paw headed for a small ravine just ahead. When he reached it he walked his horse down a narrow trail through low trees and brush that filled the ravine. Ellen followed on her mare, curious about his intent. At the bottom, they came out onto a small open space—and a pool of clear water. A seasonal stream flowed through the ravine, and paused there for a while before moving on.

Bear Paw dismounted and helped Ellen to the ground. He showed her the pool, then picked up something from a log as if he had known all along it was there. He handed it to Ellen.

It was soap root, for bathing. Bear Paw waved at the pool, then at Ellen again. Then he mounted his horse and walked it slowly up the trail and out of sight.

Ellen didn't need any more urging. She had badly missed the opportunity to bathe on the trip to buffalo country. She slipped out of her moccasins and, untying two leather thongs, let her buckskin dress slide from her shoulders. The cool air near the pool felt good; she tingled as it washed over her naked body. Taking the soap root, she waded in, the delicious chill of the water making her shake with anticipation all over. She lathered up with the soap root and washed clean at a leisurely pace, sighing at the sensation of her slick hands moving over her breasts, feeling her nipples erect in the cool water, closing her eyes, mouth open, at the tingle of her hands sliding between her legs for long seconds. Finally she finished and set to work on her hair. When she had washing it thoroughly, she ducked under the water to rinse. After a few seconds, she shot to the surface, breaking into air with a gasp of exhilaration.

Not wanting to test Bear Paw's patience for her privacy, and wondering for a second if she had truly *had* privacy—though she didn't see him anywhere—she reluctantly waded out of the pool and put her dress and moccasins back on, squeezing as much water as she could out of her hair. Then she mounted the mare and ascended the trail.

She found Bear Paw a short distance off, waiting for her. He smiled broadly at sight of her with her wet hair, nodding his approval. She rode up close beside him, and they took off for camp. Some time later, as they neared the camp and slowed to a walk, she angled the mare over close to him and reached out with her hand. He reached his hand toward her and she grasped it firmly. "Thank you," she said with real affection. *I'm supposed to be discouraging him*, she thought. But how can I not thank him for this?

They no sooner reached camp than one of the men came running up to them, trailed by several others. They were considerably agitated. "We have heard word from the sentries," the man said breathlessly. "They encountered an Arapaho rider. There has been a great battle to the east only days ago. A large village of Sioux, Cheyenne, and Arapaho were recklessly attacked by long-knife soldiers. But the great Sioux Chief Tatanka Yotanka[6] was there, and Crazy Horse, and they brought about a great victory! Hundreds of blue coats were killed, wiped out to the last man." The man stepped closer, face flushed with excitement. "We have heard even the Indian fighter Long Hair was killed!"

Bear Paw greeted this news calmly. "Where was this battle?"

"It was at a place to the east the Sioux call the Greasy Grass River," the man replied. "The whites call it Little Bighorn."

Bear Paw was not caught up in the excitement as were the men who had gathered around him, whooping war cries into the air. He raised his hands for silence. When he got it, he spoke solemnly. "White soldiers will be ranging far and wide. They will seek revenge against any Indian they come across. We must leave the plains immediately and go back to the safety of our home. Spread the word around the camp. We leave tomorrow."

Ellen watched the men, Bear Paw included, walk away. Her joyous mood was somewhat deflated. Owl Woman had not been there to translate what had been said, but she could tell it had not been good news. Still, she looked around as the women gathered close to admire her new mount, stroking it and smiling at her, congratulating her on the gift, putting arms around her waist briefly. She was suffused in warmth and friendship such as she could not have expected months ago. As she watched them gather around, so happy for her, a thought suddenly struck her nearly like a physical blow.

She was having fun.

More fun than she had ever had in her life.

---

6   Sitting Bull

*A desperate war of starvation and extinction is imminent
and inevitable, unless prompt measure shall prevent it.*
*—Indian agent William Bent, pleading the
Indians' cause to Congress, mid-1800s*

THE SHOSHONE, ELLEN INCLUDED, WERE up early the next
morning. There was little conversation; everyone set to work with a
quiet urgency. They did not have to be told twice of the danger they were
in, exposed on the plains as they were with their women and children.
Extra horses were put to task as pack animals to help bring the fruits of
the buffalo hunt back home.

The sun was still low in the sky when they started on the trail. Only
then did the group relax enough for conversation. Ellen strode along
by herself, lost in thought. She felt her life was steadily careening off
the path she had set. *What am I to do?* she thought. *If all those soldiers
were killed, including Custer, it won't be safe out here for any Indian, or
anyone wearing Indian clothing. Even if I tried to run away again and found
white people, I might be shot before anyone realized I was white. But staying
here—what will that mean to these people? Will they see it as a sign I am
willing to be one of them, even to marry into the tribe? Impossible!*

After about an hour, Owl Woman strode over to her and walked by
her side. "You are very quiet, Ellen," she said. "Are you still considering
whether to accept Bear Paw's interest in you?"

"I—I don't know what to say to him," she blurted out. "I have my
own world I must return to, my own ways. How can I tell Bear Paw that
what he wants cannot be?"

Owl Woman smiled, looking ahead over the column of pack horses and walking tribal members. "I have a feeling that great forces are coming together in your life. Be open to them, and we will see what path the spirits reveal in the days to come."

Ellen didn't like that answer, but said nothing as they plodded along, their feet whispering through the dry prairie grass with every step.

"For now," Owl Woman continued, "let me instruct you in what you should do to be a worthy member of the tribe. Among us, a woman is valued for her skill with cooking and sewing, preparing hides for use, setting up and taking down the dwellings, and making beadwork for clothing and moccasins. All of the things that are part of these duties belong to her—the tipis, sewing needles, cooking pots and pans, bedding—all these are hers. If she is fortunate and prosperous, she may also own a number of horses. And if she does well with these things, she will be seen as very valuable, and may marry into a good family."

Ellen listened in silence, not really wanting to know how to fit in with a people she had no intention of staying with.

Owl Woman went on. "Now," she said, "you must learn how to be a proper young woman when a man begins to court you. When a man comes to see you at night, do not let him stay too long. That is why I told you last night that you should ask Bear Paw to go. You noticed he was not angry at your request. He knew it was proper. If you let a suitor stay until he is ready to go, he will believe you are in love with him already, and will think less of you. So tell him to go after a short while, but if he pleases you, tell him also that you would like to associate with him in the future. I know that you are greatly fearful of Bear Paw's interest, but do not run away from him, or he will think you are silly, and not sufficiently educated to respect his attention."

"But—" Ellen started to protest.

Owl Woman plunged ahead. "I know that as you came back to camp yesterday, you held his hand briefly. You should not do this for a while yet. You should not exchange too many glances and smiles with a suitor, or he will think you are easy and immoral."

"But why did he take me on the ride yesterday?" Ellen said. "Does he not think that was improper?"

Owl Woman smiled. "Since you are a white woman, he may think the rules do not apply. He may have been testing you to see what you would accept. I do not know what a white woman considers proper.

76

But you must show him that you know what is proper for a Shoshone woman. Remember that if a man touches your breasts, he will think you belong to him. If he then later decides not to marry you, he will tell others what he has done with you, and you will be considered immoral. You then would not have a chance to be purchased and marry into a good family."

"But I don't want to be purchased!" Ellen protested. "No one can buy me! Is there nothing I can do to stop this?"

Owl Woman turned serious. "You can say no. The final choice is always yours." She turned to look at her. "But I hope that will not be your answer. Bear Paw is a good man. I do not think he will make any more improper advances to you, especially after I scolded him about it last night. He is a great warrior, and would be a powerful and loyal protector for any woman. I hope you will honor his interest in you at this time, and let us see what the days to come bring."

Ellen sank into silence, unable to find the words to convince Owl Woman that all of this simply could not be.

THE SHOSHONE REACHED THEIR HOME without incident. Camp was set up and the weary band relaxed for the first time in days. Ellen settled into a routine with the rest of the women, and often, as she went about her duties, mused on her place among them. She kept the ache in her heart for her own world well hidden. Instead, she forced herself to enjoy the daily camaraderie of the other women, and showed appreciation when they instructed her in how to do a task better. The initial bitterness and anger over her presence had long faded away, and they seemed ready to accept her as one of them. Given what she had heard of her own peoples' lies and treachery toward the Indians, she was curious how the Shoshone could so readily take her in and treat her as one of their own. One day she asked Owl Woman why this was so.

"You will notice that there are few children among us, no matter what tribe," she said as they were scraping a hide to make it ready to use for garments. "The spirits do not visit many of our young women with babies. We are few, and with the coming of the white man and all the darkness he has brought into our lives—the sicknesses, the killings, the taking of our food—we are fewer still. So to increase our numbers, we have always been willing to accept anyone, no matter their color, and declare them one of us, if they are willing to live as we do, to honor our ways." She looked at Ellen. "Do our ways please you?"

Ellen was caught off guard, not ready for the question. In truth, the work she was given to do as a woman among them was no harder than the farm work she had done from an early age. And life was certainly much less boring now than at the isolated farm. Still, she didn't want to seem ungrateful, so after an uncomfortable pause, she said finally, "Yes, they please me."

Owl Woman smiled. "You have done well in learning them. But," she went on, "I know you hide a sadness deep in your heart for your white world, and the man who waits for you. But no matter what you decide in the days to come, I will always believe you would make a good Shoshone."

Ellen knew she had received a great compliment, but said nothing. She did her best to be Shoshone from one day to the next, all the while hoping that the long summer would present an opportunity to either leave, or get word to someone outside that she was there.

Owl Woman departed two days later with her husband, Tall Bull, to return to their home. Ellen was sorry to see her go; she had proven to be a good friend.

"One more thing I must tell you," Owl Woman said as she sat on her horse preparing to ride out. "There comes a day for a young maiden when her suitor will present an offer of marriage. This offer will consist of valuable gifts for her family. It may be several horses; if so the number will depend on how highly the girl is valued by her suitor. The gifts are intended to make the girl's family more prosperous. Also, if she is marrying upward in the tribe, it will increase their status to have a daughter married to an important person. You, though, have no family here, so this might be a problem. If Bear Paw pursues you further—and I am certain he will—he will probably consider Rabbit Woman your family, and may make the offer to her. I urge you to let her be your family here. If you accept his offer it will greatly increase Rabbit Woman's status and prosperity among the Shoshone. This would be a good thing, as she is a widow and is quite poor."

Ellen smiled up at her, trying to show her appreciation for advice she didn't want to contemplate. "Thank you, friend, for everything, and most of all, your help with teaching Bear Paw English. He is doing well with it. Rabbit Woman has learned a bit too, and I have learned a little Shoshone. Between us, I think we will soon speak well to each other." She gave Owl Woman's hand a final squeeze, then stepped back as the Spokane woman's horse moved away and began to walk out of camp.

Bear Paw continued to visit her. Sometimes they would go for walks around the village. Two or three times he brought food and water, and they would walk to a shady grove nearby and sit beside a small stream enjoying the day. They did not hold hands; this was not the Indian way. But there was no mistaking his affection—his mannerisms, the way he spoke to her, his thoughtfulness for her comfort and safety—all made it quite obvious. He came now and then to Rabbit Woman's tipi and left small gifts, which Rabbit Woman put away for safekeeping. Ellen accepted them graciously, and tactfully requested of him to leave after a while. Rabbit Woman would nod her approval.

She tried to avoid encouraging him, still feeling all this was futile, but could not help being flattered. He was kind, and quite handsome in a rugged frontier way, she thought. His straight black hair fell to his shoulders, and his facial features were pleasing, his skin smooth, his eyes clear. The powerful muscles working beneath his dusky skin had come to give her a feeling of protection whenever he was around, replacing her earlier uneasiness.

Daily routine was punctuated by warriors departing on raids to capture horses from other tribes, or to go on raids against white property for food or for revenge. Sometimes not all the warriors returned, and there was grief in the camp. Ellen learned such excursions were a regular part of life among the Shoshones. She had long since seen that most of these people, residents of what was mostly an arid and harsh area that yielded food and shelter grudgingly to them, had little in the way of possessions, usually not much beyond what was needed to survive, so she could not begrudge their efforts to acquire more. Still, she grieved with them when a raid brought tragedy, especially when one of the injured or dead was known to her.

It had long been obvious to her that though the Shoshone were poor, they readily shared what little they had with her. She had never been refused food or shelter—or lately, friendship. She wondered at times if her own race would do as well if the situation were reversed.

Her doubt on that subject was strengthened by periodic reports from scouts or sentries of bloody encounters elsewhere between white soldiers or settlers and Indians. More and more pressure was being put on Indians who had not agreed to report to reservations; more and more settlers were claiming tribal lands and either calling on the cavalry to keep the Indians in line, or themselves ruthlessly exterminating any Indians who protested. There were rumors of a gold discovery to the north in Washington Territory, which became a giant magnet, pulling disillusioned ex-miners from the California Gold Rush as well as hundreds of others, into Shoshone lands on their way north.

Ellen could see that her band of Shoshone did not understand the scope of what was happening to them. Though there were very few who still believed the whites were just passing through, most still thought some sort of treaty could be fashioned which would protect traditional tribal lands for all eternity.

Young as she still was, Ellen knew better. She had been hearing reports back in Kansas for years, of murders by whites, broken promises, outright lies, and utter disregard for Indian claims. Sadly, she knew her own race would cast the Indian aside whenever it suited them, under the guise of some sort of mandate from destiny, that it was meant to be, that it was inevitable.

To the Shoshone, Ellen was becoming someone they looked to for answers. They had developed a great affection for her, and thought that since she was white, she could help them understand. At night around the campfire, some women, and a few men, would come to her and plaintively ask what they could do as their world slowly disintegrated around them.

Ellen would look around at the anxious faces full of fear and confusion in the flickering firelight. She always responded to a plea for insight into the ways of the whites, though she knew some of what she said could not be translated, and it frustrated her. She could see that they needed the truth, and it broke her heart not to be able to say it with her limited Shoshone.

Her inability to say everything she wanted was tragically changed with the unexpected return of Owl Woman just two days after she had left. Ellen was shocked to see her condition as her horse walked slowly into camp. She was barely conscious, slumped over the horse's neck.

Blood covered her left side and much of her left leg. She was quickly removed from her mount and carried into a tipi.

Owl Woman was weak and delirious from loss of blood. As several women gathered around her, she seemed at first not to know where she was, and her eyes grew wide in panic. Then she saw Ellen's face, and she calmed a little.

"White settlers," she gasped. "My husband is dead." Then she passed out.

Several Shoshone women set to work cleaning and binding her wound, which appeared to be from a bullet that had struck her in the outer left side below the ribcage and passed out her back She regained consciousness an hour later and the women began giving her small amounts water and thin broth. Though in considerable pain, after a while she was able to tell what had happened.

She and Tall Bull had encountered white settlers barely more than a day's ride from the Shoshone camp. They had tried to avoid them at first, riding calmly ahead as the five whites watched from a low ridge a short distance away. For a minute it seemed nothing would happen. But it was not to be. The whites suddenly drew their pistols and spurred their horses to a full gallop, screaming wildly as they approached.

Owl Woman was terrified as the five rode up and surrounded her and Tall Bull, but still her right hand closed around the handle of her skinning knife beneath her robe.

"Why do you bother us?" Tall Bull said in Spokane. "We wish only to return to our home."

His answer came in the form of a pistol as one of the grinning whites fired from only a few feet away. The shot's impact knocked Tall Bull hard to the ground, but he came up with an arrow notched in his bow. He fired arrows into two of the whites before he was cut down in a hail of bullets. Owl Woman drew her skinning knife from beneath her robe, for she had heard about what whites often did to Indian women. She threw the knife with deadly accuracy, saw it strike one of the whites in the throat; he fell to the ground.

"Damned Injun bitch!" shouted one of the two uninjured whites, and shot her point blank.

Owl Woman felt the bullet hammer into her. She doubled over, clutching her mount's neck. The horse, panicked from the gunfire, turned and bolted away at top speed. Owl Woman could do nothing but hang on for her life.

The man who had shot her fired at her, missing, and gave chase, but his mount was tired and no match her hers. In minutes he gave up.

"The horse seemed to know the way back," Owl Woman concluded. "I tied myself around the horse's neck in case I passed out. I had no strength to do anything but hang on. I knew that if I fell off, I would not be able to get back up." She paused, then continued, tears squeezing from her eyes. "My husband was a great warrior. He died bravely, defending me. I will mourn his passing, and honor his name forever."

Ellen, already distraught, was grief-stricken when Owl Woman translated part of the story for her. The fresh reminder of the mindless savagery her own people could inflict on the Indians sickened her. A woman she admired and respected, a good friend, lay gravely wounded, her husband dead and his body no doubt mutilated and left to rot. Suddenly ashamed of her own skin, she got up, went out, and retired to her own tipi.

ELLEN KEPT TO HERSELF AS Owl Woman slowly recovered over the next few days. She wasn't sure if her imagination was working overtime or if she was right, but she had a feeling that the Shoshone were looking at her with renewed distrust. She was relieved when Owl Woman was finally strong enough to be carried out to a place by the evening fire. If there were any ill feelings toward her, they seemed absent as Owl Woman's presence brought another round of plaintive questions directed at Ellen. Owl Woman could now translate anything Ellen said. And with the needless death of Tall Bull, the floodgates of frustration were opened. The Shoshone pressed around Ellen, some of the men's faces full of smoldering anger, the women's full of fear and confusion.

"How can we fight the white man?" one of the braves said. "We are so few."

"Can we sign a treaty that will protect our lands? Would the white man honor it?" said another.

"Will the whites force us to go to Duck Valley?"[7]

---

7   The Duck Valley Indian Reservation lies in a valley on the Nevada-Idaho border. It was established by executive order in April 1877. The site was selected by a Shoshone leader named Captain Sam. In 1886 and again in 1910 additional land was annexed to provide for the Shoshone-Paiute peoples.

"Why do the whites hate us?"

"How can we survive if they destroy our food and shelter?"

"Will the whites go away some day?"

"Will we ever be as we once were, free to roam these lands?"

Ellen listened to all this with growing sadness. These people she had such affection for were coming to her like frightened children, desperate for a hint of hope, a sliver of reassurance. She knew she had none to give. Ellen felt ashamed now of her trip west. She had come on a lark, a great adventure, never giving thought to the enveloping tragedy around her, the lies, the murder, the deliberate extinction of a people who did not know how to fight the darkness that had come into their lives.

Now she had become part of it, even though she was white. Even though, if she was not the enemy, she *looked* like the enemy. Despite this, the Shoshone needed her, a link to a world they could not understand.

Ellen's heart was heavy as she moved close to Owl Woman and motioned for the crowd to be seated, so all could see her and she could be heard better. Looking out over the assembled crowd, she spoke in a clear, firm voice as Owl Woman translated for her.

"I do not have answers to all your questions," she began. "But I will do my best. Please know that I am very young myself, and not as wise in the ways of the world as you would wish." She took a deep breath and continued.

"The whites are here to stay. They will never leave, and there will be more and more. Their numbers are already greater than you can count." Ellen bit her lip in agony for the news she had to deliver. "The ways of your ancestors are gone forever. No treaty that you can sign will protect your lands. Even if the whites sign it, they will not honor it, and will cast it aside when it suits them. You will be forced onto reservations, there to live your lives as best you can, dependent on the white man's charity." In the darkness toward the back of the crowd, Ellen could see some of the young braves walking away in anger, clearly not wanting to hear such talk. But she could see Bear Paw in the crowd, watching her closely.

A young Shoshone mother with child in tow approached her. "Will there be a tomorrow for my child?" she said.

Ellen fought to control her emotions. "Yes. But it will be different from what you have always known, and it will not be what you would wish for her." She looked up over the crowd and continued. "The whites hate you because you have what they want, these beautiful lands. They do not honor your claim to it. They will take it when they wish, no matter what they may promise you."

There was one question she had not answered yet, one she had pondered herself for a long time, even before she had left Kansas, and more often since she had come to the Shoshone. It would not be easy to explain, but she would try. Taking a deep breath, she spoke to the crowd in a loud voice.

"You ask why the whites have been given so much power. I do not have all the answers. But here is something I know: there is a man in the village near my home who does not hunt, nor does he plant crops. And yet he has no worry about how he will eat."

"How then does he survive?" a brave asked, annoyance clear in his tone.

"He is what whites call a blacksmith," Ellen answered. "This means that he works with fire and iron to make things. Since he does not spend time planting and harvesting crops, or hunting, he can make things for others, such as wagon wheels, swords, knives, plows to prepare the earth for planting. He trades these things he makes to others in exchange for food." Ellen wasn't sure she could explain the concept of buying and selling with money, so she stuck with trade.

"The food he trades for is grown near his house. Since the blacksmith does not have to travel to find food, he can stay in one place and build his family a solid house, safe and secure. And because he has time he can use since he is not hunting or gathering, he may discover how to make something new, such as a more powerful gun that he can trade for still more," she continued. "Not traveling much of the year makes it easier for his wife to bear more children than you do. This is one reason why there are so many whites."

Ellen looked out over the sea of faces, faces devoid of hope, devoid of a spark. With no enthusiasm, she continued. "There are others who do the same, but make other things to trade: clothing, cooking supplies, medicines, furniture, and much more. It is the white man's separation of hunters and food-growers from those who make things that gives him time to invent and build things that give the whites great power, such as guns, cannon, and trains. You, though, spend all your time just trying to stay alive, just trying to fill your bellies. There is no time for anything else. There is no time to create new tools or weapons which would give you more power."

Ellen was by this time weary. She was not sure just how much of what she had said Owl Woman was able to relay to the Shoshone. But a heavy silence had fallen over the crowd. She decided they had heard quite enough bad news for one night. "I am tired," she said. "Please let us have no more talk for tonight. Know that I love you all."

There were quiet murmurs and nodding of heads as the crowd slowly got up and walked away into the enveloping darkness. All except one. The young Shoshone mother with child who had spoken to her earlier remained, edging close to Ellen, eyes wet with tears.

"Will you help us?" she said.

Ellen reached out and put a comforting hand on her shoulder, wanting to give the young mother some ray of hope for tomorrow. "I will try," she said. But she didn't know how it would be accomplished.

As Ellen walked away, the crowd dissipating around her, the thought settled on her again just how much she had become caught up in their sorrow, their tragedy. The joy of fellowship, the shared elation she had felt just days earlier had wafted away like smoke on a breeze. Then something struck her hard. *Eli is part of it too.* She had not felt such a pang of regret about him in weeks. Now her carefully buried desire for him came back to clutch her, and she felt an ache in her stomach. *Dear God, what would he think of me now? I am giving aide and comfort to the enemy-his enemy. I have become part of what he is sworn to destroy. How could he possibly want me anymore?*

Sleep did not come easily that night.

But far to the north, Eli's desire for his lost bride had not diminished. Though others now and then gently suggested that he let her go, he flatly refused. He still kept Ellen's picture in its metal case next to his heart, still made it the last thing he saw before turning down the lamp each night. And he constantly made inquiries about her of troops and civilians passing through the fort. Indeed, there were persistent rumors from Indian scouts employed by the Cavalry that there *was* a white woman living with one of the Northwest tribes. That in itself was not an unheard-of event. But Eli would not let go of the notion that this one could be Ellen.

As the summer progressed, Ellen still thought about leaving, but found herself increasingly attached to the Shoshone. It was clear they did not understand what was happening to them, or how to react to it. She knew there was only surrender in their future. But the younger, hotheaded braves continued to talk of defeating the white invaders once and for all.

Raiding parties continued to venture forth from the camp, sometimes to acquire horses, sometimes for revenge for similar raids inflicted on them, sometimes on raids against white settlers for food. Hunters had usually brought back rabbit and antelope to supplement the buffalo meat they had acquired on the plains. But for several years, game had been ever more hard to find. White colonists moving westward, as well as growing numbers of settlers, had become significant consumers of wild food resources, and the Shoshone found themselves increasingly pushed into areas of marginal food production.[8] Though this had at first been happening farther south in Utah, with the swelling numbers of immigrants choosing the Oregon Trail rather than the road to Sacramento after the California Gold Rush faded, the Northern Shoshone were beginning to turn to attacking farms and cattle ranches as a matter of survival rather than strictly for revenge. Though they had asked for her help in understanding the whites, Ellen was not consulted about the wisdom of these raids. She had no influence with the warriors. She did her best to be a proper Shoshone woman, and that did not include advising the braves on what they should do.

Bear Paw went along on some of them, and when he came back bleeding from an encounter, Ellen did not ask how it happened, but rather treated his wounds in silence. She was trying hard not to become emotionally involved any deeper, or encourage him to do so.

It wasn't working. He continued his courtship, always the

---

8   In 1859, Jacob Forney, Superintendent of Indian Affairs for the Territory of Utah, wrote "The Indians . . . have become impoverished by the introduction of the white population."

gentleman, following the rules that Owl Woman revealed to her, but still persistent.

Ellen wondered how long it would be before he asked for her hand in marriage.

"Courtship among us may go on for several years," Owl Woman told her one day.

"I will not be here that long," Ellen countered. "I am planning to ask him for permission to leave soon."

Owl Woman smiled, a rare event for her lately, after the brutal murder of her husband. "So you keep saying. Yet you are still here."

Owl Woman had a point and Ellen knew it. Every time she became determined that this would be the day she would bring up leaving to Bear Paw, she would go to him, see the smile he never withheld from her, and her resolve would crumble. Sometimes if they were unobserved, he would put his strong arms around her and draw her back into his chest. Ellen knew it was probably not proper, but it felt too good to object to. The truth was that despite herself, she was beginning to feel stirrings of affection for him.

Summer had traditionally been a golden time for the band. The weather was mild, and they dressed accordingly. In the warm weather, Shoshone men wore only a breechcloth belted at the waist. Women wore only an apron. Ellen had to be coaxed at first to wear something that left her breasts bare for all to see. But since the other women did the same, she could hardly feel alone. Even so, she did so only on foraging trips away from the village as she and the other women hunted for pine nuts, berries, and roots. She quickly came to love the new experience of the feel of the sun on her bare skin.

Ellen became distressed to find herself torn between her affection for the Shoshone, their need for her help, and what she regarded as her duty to Eli. It wasn't that she loved him; that had been impossible to know long distance. Nettie's words of advice—"You don't have to love him, child"—came back to her now. Indeed, she had decided to go west on hope and promise rather than love—the hope that Eli was the good man he seemed, and the promise of a new and exciting life in the west.

But now it seemed she was betraying him more with each passing day. He was an Indian fighter. *If I persist in this life*, she thought, *I may end up in his gunsight some day. I have to go before it's too late.*

In what she figured to be late August, Ellen turned seventeen. She felt it was now or never for leaving. She had to get away before the weather became cold. *There is nothing I can do for these people,* she thought sadly. *Telling them the truth will not change the future. I made a promise to Eli to be his wife. And I will keep that promise.*

There was no one she trusted so much as Owl Woman to approach the subject of her leaving. Ellen brought it up to her one evening when they were alone in Rabbit Woman's tipi, where the Spokane woman, now a widow like Rabbit Woman, had settled.

Ellen had asked her earlier why she had not returned to the Spokand.

"There is no one in my home camp I would trust to replace Tall Bull. Therefore I will stay here, and have no man if that is how it is to be."

Owl Woman was surprised when Ellen brought up the subject of leaving again. "Has Bear Paw offended you?" she asked.

Ellen smiled. "No. He continues to be kind and attentive. He leaves me small gifts now and then, but I am always careful to not let him stay too long when he comes to call, as you instructed. There is no doubt he cares for me very much."

"Good," Owl Woman said. "Have we done something cruel to you, then, that you would leave us?" Her expression darkened. "Has Black Elk threatened you again?"

Ellen shook her head. "No to both. I have made so many good friends here. You have all been so kind. And Black Elk has not come near me in months, ever since he learned that Bear Paw is courting me."

"What, then?" Owl Woman said, perplexed. Then she thought of a reason. "Our life is too hard for you."

"Your life is hard, and dangerous at times," Ellen replied. "But no harder than my life on the farm would have been." She reached out and briefly touched Owl Woman's forearm. "I must go because as I have told you, I have made a promise that I would marry a man. I want to keep that promise. I am a woman of my word."

"Everything I know about you says that is so," Owl Woman said. "But I had thought living here might make you forget your promise. I know the whites say they marry for love. Do you love this man?"

Ellen sighed. "No. I was prepared to learn to love him—if he was kind."

"Has he then offered your family valuable gifts?"

"No, that is not what we do. Any gifts would be offered only to me. He has promised me a house, and said that he would welcome children."

Owl Woman frowned. "This does not seem a good marriage. Your family gains nothing."

"Well, they do get rid of me!" Ellen said in jest. "But your way—you make it seem like a business arrangement."

"It is very much that," she said. "Both the bride and groom's family hope to gain in wealth and status from a union."

"Is there no question of love, then?" Ellen said.

"Every bride hopes she will grow to love her husband," Owl Woman said. "A young woman may love a brave, but her family may not approve if he is poor or not of good character. But many marriages are arranged long before they happen; sometimes the bride and groom are matched soon after birth. As I said, each side hopes to gain in standing in the tribe from such a union."

Ellen pursed her lips in thought. "But what if the husband is cruel?"

"Women are not owned by their husbands here. They have equal standing as persons in the tribe. A husband is not to be cruel to his wife. If he is, she may decide to end the marriage and return to her family. Divorce is easy; all she has to do is put all her husband's belongings outside their tipi. Then they are considered divorced. And a woman has her own property, which she may pass down to her daughters if she desires."

Ellen was relieved to hear that; she found the status of women among the Shoshone appealing.

Owl Woman said nothing for a moment. Then she said, "This white man you are promised to—what does he do?"

Ellen had been afraid someone would ask this question sooner or later. Now it had been. Difficult as it was, she would not lie to Owl Woman. Unable to look at her, she said softly, "He is a long knife soldier."

Owl Woman was clearly shocked, silent for long seconds. Finally she spoke. "Tell no one else of this." She picked up a stick from the fire pit and scratched idly in the dirt.

Ellen waited, knowing she had revealed a terrible secret.

Finally Owl Woman spoke without looking up. "You cannot leave alone. It is too dangerous. Someone must escort you to the nearest white settlement. Now that you have proven yourself as a good and honest woman, I believe the Shoshone will honor your request. But first it is proper to seek Bear Paw's permission." She rose and went out, leaving Ellen alone in heavy silence.

TALL, DRY GRASS SWISHED GENTLY around her knees as Ellen strode through a field just outside camp, Bear Paw at her side. She put her hands out palms down, waving them back and forth to feel the grass heads as she walked. It was a beautiful fall day, the bright sun shining down out of a clear blue sky, a slight breeze sighing through a stand of trees nearby. Owl Woman had told Bear Paw that morning, and then left the two of them alone to talk. Between them, Ellen had learned enough Shoshone and Bear Paw enough English that they could converse quite well.

But Ellen had dreaded this time, and now found it every bit as hard as she had feared. She was ashamed of what she was doing, even as she struggled to keep her word to Eli. *This kind and good man by my side does not deserve this*, she thought.

Bear Paw walked beside her, seemingly lost in thought and waiting for her to say something. When she continued to be silent, he finally spoke. "Owl Woman says you made a promise to marry a white man," he said without looking at her.

"Yes," she said, relieved the silence had been broken. "I said this when you first found me months ago."

"Maybe I was not listening at that time. He is good, this man?"

"I hope he will be," she said.

"A promise is a serious thing," he said. "We are people of our word and do not give it unless we intend to keep it. Whites are not like this; they break their word whenever they see an advantage in doing so. But I think you are more like us." Suddenly the control he always seemed to display over his emotions seemed to falter, and Ellen could see real pain on his face as he reached out and grasped her arms.

"I did not think I could love a white woman, but you have shown me that you are worthy of love. Ellen, you are my woman. I would have no

one else but you for as long as I live. When I am with you, I feel strong."
He paused, squeezing her arms gently. "I would give all my horses to buy
you." He sighed. "I am sorry, I know those are not the right words for
a white woman." He dropped his hands, genuine sorrow on his strong
features. "But I cannot stand in the way of your promise. To do that
would be to attack what you are, what it is that makes me love you."
He took a deep breath, then continued. "In the morning, I will take
you in search of whites who will care for you. Then you can keep your
promise."

Ellen began to cry. What she had sought for months was finally
offered. But it brought her no joy, only a mixture of relief mingled with
sadness. She looked up at Bear Paw, cheeks wet with tears. "I do not
care if this is wrong," she said, stepping forward and putting her arms
tightly around him, pressing her cheek against his muscular chest. "I
will never forget you," she said softly. "Nor what you have given me, or
how you have shown me so much I needed to know. A part of my heart
will always be here with you—with all of you."

Bear Paw put his massive arms around her, and they stood in silent
embrace for a long time in the open field as the grass rustled around
them, the breeze played with Ellen's light brown hair, and the world
outside their arms seemed far away and unimportant.

That night, Ellen wrote in her diary.

Late summer 1876, with the Shoshone somewhere in the Northwest—
This may be my last entry written while I am with these people.
Tomorrow it is agreed that I will be taken back to my world. I have wanted
it desperately for so long, and now that it is here, I did not expect to feel such
sadness. I could not have imagined this months ago, so frightened was I. But
now I cannot help but feel ashamed to leave. These people have little, yet
they have shared all they have with me. They have taught me how to live as
they do, a necessity here. Even more than this, they have embraced me as a
friend, and trusted me to share what wisdom I may have about my people.
I have wounded Bear Paw grievously, I am sure, but the union he wants is
something that can never be.

Most of them do not fully realize it yet, but there is only darkness ahead
for the Shoshone. I cannot stop what is to come, and I do not want to be a
witness to it. I must go. I must go.

EARLY THE FOLLOWING MORNING, ELLEN packed what little she intended to take with her, along with her diary. She walked with Rabbit Woman through the village, still quiet in the crisp morning air. A few people were up and about. No one spoke to her. Men showed a quiet contempt on their faces, the women sadness. Before long, Ellen could not look at them, and kept her eyes on the ground.

The two women walked out to the edge of the horse herd. Bear Paw stood waiting, having put bridles on his horse and her paint mare. She couldn't speak to him, couldn't look at him. Wordlessly he helped her mount, and she took the reins in hand. She turned her horse—and found a sea of faces looking up at her. While she had walked, looking at the ground, an increasing swell of villagers had silently begun to follow her.

Now they pressed close around her. One of the braves moved through the crowd to the front. It was Black Elk.

He looked up at her. "I was wrong, Ellen," he said in Shoshone. "You have become a good Shoshone woman. I would be pleased for you to stay."

Ellen was moved. She knew it must have been difficult for him to say this in public. Not caring if she was committing a breach of etiquette, she reached out and laid her left hand on his arm. "Thank you, Black Elk," she said, speaking in Shoshone. "I am pleased to count you as a friend."

Rabbit Woman, who had said not a word so far, stood crying in front of her. Also in tears next to her was Otter Girl, a young teenager Ellen had befriended over the summer. Other women in the crowd were quietly sobbing as well.

"Ellen, what shall we do?" Rabbit Woman said, wiping her cheeks. "We do not know how to protect our land from the whites. We do not understand how to make treaties with them, or what to do when they do not keep their word."

"We need you to teach us," said another woman. "We are few, and much blood has been spilled. We hear talk we will be forced to go to a reservation. We do not know what to say to the whites, how to tell them we will not go. Please, Ellen, you must help us!"

It was obvious to Ellen that much of what she had told them around the campfires had not been absorbed. It only confirmed her belief that she could not help them. She dismounted and hugged Rabbit Woman and Otter Girl tightly. Kimama was there too, and Ellen embraced her long and hard. "I am sorry, my good friend," she said. "There is no more I can do." Fighting back tears, she mounted up by herself and stared at her horse's mane as Bear Paw led her slowly away. The cries of the women behind her stung like wasps; she covered her ears to drown them out.

She and Bear Paw were joined by Owl Woman, who rode up on horseback beside them. "I will go with you a short way," she said.

The trio of horses walked slowly away, ever farther from camp, until distance drowned out the wails of the women behind them. Ellen rode with her head down, silent. They walked up a gradual slope to the top of a rise. When they went down the other side, the camp would be lost from view.

Ellen's horse lagged behind, as if itself reluctant to leave. They reached the top. She suddenly pulled her mare to a stop. She got off, and walked a few steps away, standing with her back to Bear Paw and Owl Woman, staring at the land ahead. She stood in silence, fists clenched, breathing hard.

Owl Woman dismounted to go to her, but Bear Paw held up a hand to stop her. They waited, watching, for long minutes, the only sound the sigh of a breeze through the grasses.

Ellen stood wrestling with herself, her mind a cauldron of emotions she couldn't control. *What are you doing, you coward? You are needed here, you are looked up to here, and you abandon these good people for your own selfish interests? You would leave them when they are desperate?* She stopped, struggling for direction. *I have crossed over some invisible line, and I do not know how to go back. I am no longer the girl Eli proposed to. I am the enemy now. Maybe he would better off without me. Some day I swear I will go to him, if he will still have me. But for now, I cannot turn my back on what I have become. I cannot walk away from the cries of people whose lives are about to be shattered forever. I cannot prevent it. But I must do what I can, or never find myself worthy of Eli—or any man.*

Ever so slowly, Ellen turned and walked back to her mare. She jumped up onto the horse's back and turned it toward the Shoshone camp. Bear Paw and Owl Woman followed in silence.

THE WHOOPS OF JOY STARTED when they were still a short distance away.

A frenzied group of women came running at her as she dismounted, smiling. Otter Girl, young and quick, reached her first and leaped at her. The rest of them surged around her horse, nearly frightening it into bucking. Ellen was mobbed by crying women, hugged so hard she could scarcely breathe.

Ellen walked back to camp with the Shoshone, still feeling that she was straying farther than she could ever have imagined from her original path. *The train has taken a side track,* she thought, *and is plunging recklessly ahead—toward what, I do not know.*

Unknown to her, events had been stirring to the north that would take her even further from the world she had been born to, and from her prospects as Eli's mail-order bride.

Our nation is melting away like the snow on the sides of the hills where the sun is warm, while your people are like the blades of grass in the spring when the summer is coming.
— *Oglala Sioux Chief Red Cloud*

ELLEN SETTLED IN WITH THE Shoshone as fall progressed and winter approached. She ached to somehow get word to Nettie and Liza that she was alive, but was certain they had left Kansas and had not had a chance to send word of their new address before Ellen disappeared. All had assumed they would arrive at their chosen destinations and contact each other. Looking back, it was a bad assumption.

The Shoshone looked to her for wisdom more than ever now. Even some of the hotheaded young warriors were not ashamed to ask questions of her, though she professed that she was merely a young girl, and not a military strategist. This did not deter them. *You are white; you know how whites think*, they would say. Some of them asked her how to defeat the soldiers. Much as she wanted to help them she was unwilling to say anything that could lead to white soldiers dying. So she tactfully skirted the issue and gave them only advice she thought might help the braves return safely.

There seemed to be a growing feeling in the camp that the whites would force them onto the Fort Hall Reservation rather than Duck Valley. No one in the camp was willing to go; there was much blustery talk among the warriors that they would resist unto death. And Ellen knew if that was what it came to, the whites would say *so be it*. She couldn't bear the thought of losing any more of her adopted brothers and sisters.

She saw Bear Paw on a regular basis. But he acted a little distant now, and seemed to have stopped courting her. The thought that she had disappointed him was a burden on her heart. Rabbit Woman also seemed unhappy at times, but Ellen didn't know why.

As the weather grew cold, Ellen was surprised how snug and comfortable the tipis were. They were covered for the season by buffalo hides with hair left on the outside, providing excellent insulation. She also gained new respect for the quality of the Shoshone diet. They were experts in preparing a variety of wild plants—roots, berries, acorns and other nuts—in many ways to supplement the fish and small game they regularly brought in. Necessary starch, sugar, and fats were obtained from chosen plants. To supplement the buffalo meat obtained during the summer journey, braves turned to deer, elk, and antelope—when they could find it, which was increasingly difficult. All in all, Ellen felt it was superior fare to what she had been raised on. But now there was not enough of it.

Reports coming in from outlying areas about white predation got worse, and fear about removal to Fort Hall became more prevalent. Almost daily, Ellen wrestled with the desire to make a dash on horseback for the outside to try to get the whites to back off, to stand down, to give the Shoshone breathing room. But she knew it wouldn't work. Her white brethren had their eyes firmly fixed on Shoshone lands, and were beyond reason, or guilt, or compassion. *And they would no doubt regard me as an Indian now,* she thought. *God only knows what reception I would get. I cannot stay, and yet I cannot go. It is only a matter of time until these people are forced onto a reservation. I must do what I can to keep as many as possible alive when that day comes. I always wanted to do something important. For now, this is far more meaningful than simply being the wife of a soldier.*

OCTOBER ROLLED INTO NOVEMBER, THEN December, and snows came. In that month there was a particular incident which disturbed Ellen greatly. White Deer, an old war chief, had courageously ridden out, along with a number of other braves, in hopes of meeting with white soldiers to broker a peace. They had indeed met, and talked for a while with the *toquashes,* as white soldiers were called. White Deer came back full of optimism—and with a gift. "The whites have given us flags of protection," he said, dismounting and pulling two items of cloth from his horse's back. He unfolded them and held them up for all to see, one draped over each arm. They were an American flag, and a white flag of truce. "They have told me to fly these flags over my tipi," he said. "This will give us protection. It will give us peace."

Ellen watched sadly from the fringes of the crowd that had gathered around him. She said nothing, unwilling to deflate the mood of relief that settled over the camp. Instead, she turned away, head down, and retreated to her tipi.

That night, though, she went to Bear Paw and sat with him inside his tipi. After they had exchanged pleasantries and warming drink over the central fire for a few minutes, she changed the subject. "The gifts the whites have given to White Deer are a trick," she said. "They will not be honored. More likely they were given to keep you quiet, to make you think you will not be attacked. Do not believe this."

Bear Paw was silent for long moments. Finally he spoke. "I feared that this is so. Yet it is not my place to tell White Deer that he has been tricked. I must be more watchful than ever for an attack. I am pleased you have chosen to tell me this, that you have gone against your white brothers to help us."

Ellen grimaced and let out a sigh. After a long pause, she looked down and said softly, "Sometimes I feel like they are no longer my brothers." And with that she had crossed another line.

Bear Paw's eyes widened in surprise in the flickering light from the fire. "Ellen—can this be?" he said. When she said nothing, he continued. "Ellen. I wish to know why you are still here."

Ellen wrestled for long seconds with what she should say, how much she should tell him about what she knew was coming. Finally she decided to soften the truth as much as possible. "I have grown in friendship with all of you. You have been so kind to me, so willing to make me one of your own. You have denied me nothing. And now you ask me for help. I cannot refuse it." She took a deep breath. "The day is coming when the white man will give you no more choices. He will give orders and you must follow. Some of you will not, and will die. I have chosen to stay so that when that day comes, more of you will live. On that day I will speak to the whites on your behalf. I will do my best to protect you, to see that you are given what you need, that you are not deceived. This I must do for my friends."

Bear Paw was silent, pondering what she had said for an uncomfortably long time. Then he nodded, as if he had known all along what was going to happen. "And when that is done—what then, Ellen?"

"Then, I will return to my world, and to the man who waits for me," she said. "If he would still have me." Suddenly she was overcome with a surge of sadness and, unable or unwilling to stop herself, moved close, leaned into him and put her head against his chest. "But for now, I am here," she whispered.

THE WINTER WAS LONG AND hard, filled with uncertainty about adequate game, sightings by scouts of more whites moving into the area, and sometimes violent encounters with white settlers. One brave on a hunting expedition was slain by whites in a dispute over a kill. His companion was wounded and barely escaped with his life. A solemn party of braves retrieved the body the next day and brought the warrior back to camp in a sad and silent procession. More deaths occurred when braves went out to recapture a group of Shoshone horses stolen by whites. Ellen's bitterness about what her own people were doing grew as she listened to the wails of the women grieving in the winter snow. With each new incident of the whites' callous indifference, she felt herself drifting steadily away from her birthright, and the memory of a white farm girl from Kansas receded ever further toward the back of her consciousness.

OVER THE WINTER ELLEN GREW strong in the ways of the Shoshone, fluent in their language, and became a substitute mother to some of the teen girls like Otter Girl, and others. They would ply her with questions as they gathered in the tipis on long winter nights, sequestered against the cold with little to do when not sewing garments but play games, tell tales of legends, or ask about the white world. Ellen was patient with the girls, and did her best to satisfy their curiosity. She was joyful when Kimama, the young girl she had befriended on the previous spring's trek to buffalo country, married and became pregnant. But fear for the Shoshone was always present in her mind.

SPRING APPROACHED AND SHE KNEW it was nearly a year since the Elko massacre. Ellen felt it was time to take some action, to intercede for the Shoshone if she could before it was too late. A minor opportunity presented itself when a party of braves prepared to depart on a trip to trade with a white settler some distance away. It had been a lean winter for game, and for several weeks there had been little to eat except the last stores of jerked meat, roots, and berries. The people were hungry enough to risk an attempt to trade with whites for fresh meat.

Ellen asked to go, suggesting that she might have more luck talking with the settler. Some of the braves were offended, but to her surprise Black Elk, who was one of the party, spoke up and said that she should come. "She will be useful in talking to this white man," he said. After a few moments of silence, it was grudgingly agreed that she could go.

Upon learning of her inclusion, Bear Paw immediately decided to join the party. "This is too dangerous for you, Ellen," he said. "I would have you stay, but if you are set on going, I will ride by your side."

They rode out shortly after sunrise, headed north, horses plodding through a blanket of snow from a late spring snowstorm the night before. The winter sun offered little comfort, and the air was biting cold. Ellen, like the rest, was bundled up in rabbit fur pants and jacket, overlain with a buffalo-skin cape. They rode across the gently rolling landscape for an hour, through periodic clumps of scrub bushes and willow thickets.

Finally they paused on a rise. Below them near a stand of pine trees was a crude log cabin with a compound on one side made from thin pine tree trunks, inside which were a milk cow and two scrawny beef cattle. Smoke poured from the cabin's chimney. As the party slowly descended the hill, no sign of life was visible. But as they approached Ellen could see a rifle barrel poking through a window slit.

There was no sound or movement until the party was only steps from the fence. Then a loud male voice called out from the cabin. "You Injuns clear off! We got nothin' you can have!"

Ellen spurred her horse forward a few steps. Bear Paw immediately rode up protectively beside her. "Hello the cabin!" she called out. "We mean you no harm. Will you come out and talk?"

After a few seconds, the rifle barrel withdrew from the window and the cabin's wooden door creaked open. A burly, bearded man emerged, firmly gripping the rifle he now leveled at the party. "Who said that?" he shouted, walking slowly forward.

"I said it," Ellen called out. "Please, come and talk with me. No harm will come to you."

The man's jaw dropped open; his eyes widened in surprise. "You don't sound like an Injun," he said. Curious despite his fear, he approached Ellen's horse and stopped about ten feet away. But he did not lower the rifle. "You a white woman?" he said, brow furrowing in disbelief as he took in her light brown hair done up in pigtails down her back, and her golden-brown eyes.

"I am," Ellen said. "It is cold, so let me speak plainly. These people and their families are hungry. It has been a hard winter. Game has been scarce." Behind the settler, she could see three large racks of elk antlers hanging on pegs along the roof eves of the cabin. "We have come to trade with you for one of your cattle." She couldn't imagine how he had kept the cattle alive in the confined space through the winter, but somehow he had, though they were none too fat.

The man's nervousness appeared to increase. "Can't spare it," he said. "I got a family to feed too."

"We have brought good items to trade," Ellen said, ignoring his refusal. "Our offer will be generous." At that Bear Paw turned and motioned to one of the braves, who moved his horse forward, dismounted, and from his horse's back took several fine beaver skins and two lynx pelts and draped them across an upper fence rail.

The settler looked at the offerings in disbelief. "We can't eat those!" he nearly shouted, then turned back to Ellen. "What's a white woman doin' sidin' with these redskins?"

Ellen sighed. "There is no time for this. Please, we want only to feed our families. We are greatly in need. I came along in hopes that a white person could talk more clearly with you."

"Clear off, I say!"

Ellen couldn't hide her disappointment. *Perhaps I can appeal to his sense of charity, if he has one,* she thought. *Or perhaps I can shame him into it.* "It is you and others like you who have brought these people to this," she said. "You hunt game that was theirs, put up fences on their land, as if they did not exist. When they protest, you kill them, or demand that the cavalry do something to enforce your claims to land that was not yours to take. These men have women and children who are hungry because of what you and others like you have done. Can I not appeal to your Christian charity?"

"No," he said. "You people hungry, it ain't my concern."

Ellen's expression hardened. "I am ashamed this day to be white," she said.

The settler glared at her and spat on the ground. "You ain't white no more. You done turned Injun. You're prob'ly some buck's woman now, ain't fit to be called white." He raised the rifle barrel higher, pointing it right at Ellen. "You all clear off! I ain't talkin' no more." With trembling hand, he pulled back the hammer on the rifle.

Bear Paw knew Ellen had been insulted. Quivering with anger, he moved his horse between the settler and Ellen.

Ellen hung her head in sorrow. She had failed utterly. Worse, she could tell that the man, despite his bluster, was badly scared and on the edge of panic. He had probably never confronted Indians at gunpoint, and that made him unpredictable. "We are in great danger," she said to Bear Paw. "We must leave."

But as she started to turn her horse away, it was already too late. She heard the noise of movement behind her and looked up just in time to see one of the Shoshone, a brave named Lehi, jump down from his horse, knife in hand. He had had enough talk.

"Give us one of your cattle or we will take it!" he shouted in Shoshone, jumping up on the bottom rail of the fence to intimidate the man, brandishing the knife.

"No!" Ellen screamed at the settler. "He will not harm you!"

But eyes wide, the settler took a quick step backward and fired. The blast caught Lehi in the chest and blew him off the fence onto his back in the snow, the front of his shirt a mass of blood.

The settler backpedaled as he cocked the rifle and fired again, looking right at Ellen, an instant before Bear Paw's arrow struck him squarely in the chest, followed by another from Black Elk into his right arm. Still, they were a fraction too late; the bullet struck Ellen in the shoulder and spun her off her mount onto the ground.

The settler staggered around and ran for the cabin. He got three steps before he collapsed in the snow. There was a hysterical scream from the cabin and a woman came running out to him. Black Elk and another brave notched arrows and leveled them at her as she sank to the ground at the settler's side.

Bleeding freely and clutching her shoulder, Ellen staggered to her feet, putting herself in front of the fence in their line of fire. "No!" she screamed again, holding her arms out wide as crimson dripped from her shoulder onto the pristine snow. "Enough!" she said in Shoshone. "There is nothing for us here. Please, let us go back to camp!"

Bear Paw shouted for the braves to lower their bows, and they did. Black Elk went to Lehi. He was dead. Wails of anguish from three of the braves filled the air.

Bear Paw went to Ellen and wrapped a strip of cloth around her shoulder over the wound. Then he lifted her back onto her horse as two others picked up Lehi's body and draped it over his horse's back. All of them galloped off quickly through the snow back the way they had come, leaving the settler's wife wailing into the cold air as she frantically tried to get her husband to respond.

THEY HAD NOT GONE FAR when Ellen began to weaken. From what she could see from briefly pulling aside her cape and undergarment, the bullet had passed through her upper shoulder. But the bleeding had not stopped. Through her pain, she grieved for Lehi and for his widow, sick over his needless death. But even that could not put out of her mind the memory of the hate-filled heart of one her own people, nor the haunting words he had leveled at her: *You ain't white no more.*

Ellen soon became dizzy, and nearly tumbled off her horse, caught just in time by Bear Paw, who had ridden close beside her, watching intently. He put her on his horse in front of him, where he could support her. A few minutes later, she lost consciousness and grew limp in his arms. Bear Paw told the others to come as they could, and spurred his horse into an urgent run for the camp.

Thirty minutes later, he burst into camp, slid off his horse, and called out loudly for Buffalo Calf Woman as he carried Ellen rapidly through the snow to his tipi. A wave of shocked murmurs swept through the Shoshone in his wake as they saw the blood on her garment and her limp form. Inside, he gently lowered Ellen onto his sleeping furs.

Buffalo Calf Woman was there in minutes. She had brought her supplies of medicine, and unlike the first time, she used them now without hesitation or complaint. "She has lost much blood," she said as she worked. "But she is lucky. The bullet missed any bones, and merely pierced her flesh and went out. I think she will recover."

Bear Paw looked somewhat relieved as he hovered over Ellen.

Outside, as the rest of the party arrived, Lehi's widow collapsed wailing beside his horse. Then before anyone could react, she took her skinning knife and cut off her left little finger. After that, she was left alone to grieve as she would.

Ellen drifted in and out of consciousness the rest of the day as crowds of Shoshone sat outside her tipi praying and waiting for news. By evening, she was lucid but very weak. The next day she could sit up and began taking thin soup for nourishment. After that she was gently transported on a litter to Rabbit Woman's tipi. By that evening, she could sit up and was carried by Bear Paw out to the campfire. A sitting place near the warming flames was quickly cleared for her, which she gratefully accepted. She had barely sat down when a procession of Shoshone approached and wordlessly left small gifts at her feet. Puzzled, she turned to Owl Woman, who sat next to her.

"They consider you a warrior now," she said, smiling.

"But—but I failed!" Ellen protested.

"Yes. But you tried, and put yourself in danger to do so. You were wounded for them. That is important to them because you are white."

At least one man did not think I am, she thought as she graciously accepted the gifts, smiling at each presenter. That night, she kept them near her bedside.

WORD CAME IN FROM SCOUTS that white reaction to the settler incident was swift and angry. The Shoshone were blamed, of course, and there were shocking rumors among settlers that a white woman had been involved. There were new calls for Bear Paw's band to be forced onto the Fort Hall reservation.[9] It was also heard that there were rumblings for the arrest of Bear Paw himself—and the white woman.

Ellen was profoundly distressed by the incident. She had hoped to begin an intermediation role for the Shoshone, but her first tentative effort had brought only death for a young brave, and grief to his widow.

---

9   Fort Hall was established in 1863, and was located in what is now southeastern Idaho, on the Snake River Plain north of Pocatello.

She felt sorrow for the settler's wife, who had played no part in causing the violence. But she felt no sympathy for the settler, who had refused to share what he had, gunned down a Shoshone out of irrational panic, and had three antler racks on his cabin that bore mute witness to his part in creating the Shoshones' hunger.

Buffalo Calf Woman's ministrations had stopped Ellen's wound from bleeding, but she had considerable pain at times, and still felt weak. She spent most of the days to come sleeping. A week after the incident, Bear Paw came to Rabbit Woman's tipi. He sat down with Ellen, who was alone, worry heavy on his features. "Ellen, you are better?" he said.

"Yes, thank you. Buffalo Calf Woman has treated my wound well. She hopes that in time I will be able to use this arm as well as the other. Please thank her for me."

"It is good," he said. "I will do so. The first day I feared that you were badly hurt." He was silent for a moment, as if contemplating his next words. Then: "Ellen. You were very brave. I am proud of you, as are many others."

Ellen blushed. "Thank you," she said softly.

He looked at her, eyes shining. "You are Shoshone," he said quietly. Then he rose to go. "Tell Rabbit Woman I will call on her in the morning," he said, and went out.

Ellen silently thought about what he had said. She knew he had given her a great honor, one not given lightly to a white woman. All the rest of the day she pondered its implications—and puzzled about why he had asked her to tell Rabbit Woman he would return in the morning.

THE MORNING BROUGHT AN ANSWER. Rabbit Woman was called outside not long after sunrise by Bear Paw's voice. Sleepily she stumbled up out of her sleeping furs and went outside.

Bear Paw stood before her. He held the bridles of five of his best horses.

Rabbit Woman gasped. She knew what this meant.

"Rabbit Woman. I ask for Ellen's hand in marriage," he said. "Will you accept my gifts?"

Rabbit Woman's hand flew to her mouth, eyes wide. "I am greatly honored," she said. "I will return shortly." She dashed back into her tipi.

Ellen was just stirring awake. "What is it?" she mumbled.

"Bear Paw asks for your hand in marriage. He offers me five good horses!"

Ellen was momentarily speechless. She had thought that this might be coming if she stayed long enough, but still didn't know how she would handle it. After a moment she spoke. "What do you wish to say to his offer?"

Rabbit Woman hung her head, unable to look directly at her. "If you were my daughter, I would accept it at once. It is a fine offer from a man of good character."

"But?"

"But you are not my daughter," she said, sadness evident in her tone. "I cannot speak for a white woman."

"I see," Ellen said. She looked at Rabbit Woman, whose distress was obvious. She had come to know the Shoshone woman well over the past year, and knew that with the death of her husband she was poor and of low status in the tribe. And with fewer and fewer single braves left in the camp, her prospects for remarriage were small. It was traditional that if a man died and left a widow, the man's brother would marry her. But her husband's only brother was also dead. Such a gift as Bear Paw offered would instantly make her a woman of means. Ellen knew she desperately wanted it. Even so, Rabbit Woman would not answer for her.

Ellen laboriously got up, pushing on the ground with her good arm. She took Rabbit Woman's hands firmly in her own. "Yes, you *can* answer for me, dear friend. I do not want to shame you in front of the tribe. I would be proud to be your daughter. I will make the decision, and you can tell him. Please tell Bear Paw that you will carefully consider his offer, and that you will give him your decision tonight at campfire."

Rabbit Woman's eyes grew moist and her lower lip trembled. "But—but what if he changes his mind and takes the offer back?"

Ellen smiled reassuringly. "He will not. You must trust me in this."

Rabbit Woman bit her lip. "Very well," she said so softly Ellen could barely hear her. "But first know that I must give him a valuable gift in return. And I have nothing to give."

Ellen pondered for a moment. "Nor do I."

"But you do. There is hardly a day gone by that you do not hold it and look at it."

Ellen looked blank for a moment. Then she knew.

ELLEN STRODE SLOWLY AROUND THE perimeter of the camp, her injured shoulder in a sling, her mind flooded with emotions at war with each other. When she found a flat rock to sit on, she opened her diary and began to write. Rabbit Woman observed her at a discreet distance, making sure that nothing befell her.

Spring 1877, With the Shoshone, location unknown—

How did I come to this? So much has happened in one year. None of it could I have foreseen. I was promised to marry—but not to this man. What of Eli? I cannot imagine he would want me now. Even if he did, I would only bring shame to him. I have lived with the enemy. I have become the enemy. These people hated me at first, and I feared them. Now I see that they are not so different from us. They fear for their children, guard their daughters' virtue, and raise their sons to be strong and brave. They are generous and forgiving. Yes, they have their faults, their human frailties. In all that, how like us they are! And I love them for it.

They have made me one of them—and yet I am white. Can I really live as they do? Can I turn my back on all that I was born to? I do know I can no longer accept without protest or be a part of what my brethren are doing to these good people. The hatred and fear of the settler was only a small example. I cannot count myself among white people any more, lest I be ashamed of my own skin.

Is there a purpose behind all of this? I did not ask for it. It was thrust on me but I cannot turn away. The Shoshone do not quite believe it yet, but their world is soon to change. They will not know how to live in a white world.

But I do.

On she walked, the spring sun warming her back. After nearly another hour, she had made her decision.

THE SUN HAD JUST SET when Ellen and Rabbit Woman made their way slowly toward the camp fire. Ellen carried her diary under her good arm. She was somewhat taken aback when they came in view of the fire and found not only Bear Paw but the whole camp there. *I did not want to make this a public spectacle*, she thought. *But I should not be surprised that they are here.*

She walked with Rabbit Woman up to the fire and stopped. The crackling of the flames was the only sound in the oppressive silence. Ellen found herself unexpectedly nervous. Rabbit Woman was tense as she turned to the crowd. "Bear Paw has asked for the hand of my daughter in marriage," she said, voice quivering slightly. "I accept his offer of five horses. I offer a gift to him now." She turned to Ellen.

Ellen slowly opened her diary folio, reached in, and withdrew a worn letter from its hidden compartment.

It was Eli's letter of proposal.

Rabbit Woman took the letter as Ellen offered it to her. Then she turned to the fire. "This is my gift," she said to the crowd. She held it above the flames for a moment. Then she opened her hand. The letter fell, and was quickly consumed. She turned to Bear Paw. "Does Bear Paw accept my gift?" she said.

"I accept it," he said, looking only at her.

"What has the white woman done?" whispered Kimama to Owl Woman as both stood close by.

"She has made a decision," Owl Woman said. "It was hard, and took great courage, and there is no going back."

Rabbit Woman took Ellen's hand and moved her so that she stood next to Bear Paw. Bear Paw unfolded a large woven blanket from his shoulder, and put it around both Ellen and himself. Then Rabbit Woman took Ellen's braids and moved them from her back to the front, on her chest.

And as simply as that, they were wed.

10

Damn any man who sympathizes with Indians! I have
come to kill Indians and believe it is right and honorable
to use any means under God's heaven to kill Indians.
—Colonel John M. Chivington

But what shall I do with the Third Colorado Regiment if I make peace?
They have been raised to kill Indians and they must kill Indians.
—Colorado Governor John Evans

THE **S**HOSHONE **ERUPTED IN CHEERS** and celebration as Bear Paw and Ellen were mated. Ellen shyly buried her face against Bear Paw's chest and put her good arm around his waist. After congratulating Ellen, a gaggle of squaws surrounded Rabbit Woman asking to see her newly-acquired horses. She smiled broadly and was only too happy to comply.

Ellen still tired easily, and when Bear Paw noticed, he declared to all that it was time to retire to his tipi with his bride. With that, he scooped Ellen up in his arms, and they left the crowd behind.

The entry flap beckoned invitingly as Bear Paw carried her inside his tipi and gently set her down on his sleeping furs. Ellen sat primly on her legs and smiled up at him. Bear Paw sat cross-legged before her and added a few sticks to the central fire. He smiled back at her, then poured tea for both of them and gave a cup to her.

Ellen took a sip and set her cup down on the ground before her. "One year ago I could not have imagined this," she said quietly.

"It is the same for me," Bear Paw replied. "My woman is white. Such a thing seemed impossible then. You have taught me that a good heart can beat in flesh of any color. But even before I learned this, I desired you, even from the first time I saw you, injured and weak as you were. I told myself then that it was foolish and dangerous, yet my heart urged me to take the chance. I chose to follow it. Now I am glad I did, for you are all that I could wish for in a woman. There is only love in my heart for you, Ellen."

Ellen reached out and laid her hand on his arm, eyes shining. "You and the others have shown me that you are not savages, that you are a proud people, generous with what little you have. But even as much as I have come to love you all, even as I fear for the Shoshone and hope to intercede for you, it would not have been enough to keep me here, if not for you. You are my protector, my guide. I feel safe with you and know in my heart that you care for me deeply. A woman cannot ask for more, and so I am proud to say that I love you." With that she moved gingerly close to him, careful to not brush her injured shoulder against his body, and leaned her back against his chest. She warmed to the feeling of his powerful arms around her. They sat in silence for a while, drinking their tea and speaking to each other without words. Ellen felt his lips nuzzle her neck, his big hands slide gently over her body.

At last, he broke the silence. There is something I must give you now," he said softly. "A Shoshone woman needs a name. A good name tells something about what a woman is. Let me tell you a true story. When I was a small boy, my mother and father and I were camped one day on a hillside where I could see far across the land. The sky was filled with clouds; rain seemed certain. I looked out across the land—the prairie, the streams, the arroyos. Beyond all that, what seemed far away to a young boy, I saw a high hill through the clear air. The clouds were gathering thick and dark, yet a bright shaft of sunlight fell on the top of that hill. I was sure that there I could see long green grass rippling in the breeze, there a herd of buffalo grazed peacefully as hawks swooped high overhead. It was the most beautiful sight I had ever seen, and I imagined that I must be looking through a door into heaven, the sunlight revealing a place with no darkness, no fear, where game is always plentiful, where the hunt is always good. Where the people could live in peace in the old ways, and there is no sorrow."

"I have longed for such a place all my life, but with the coming of outsiders to our lands, it seems ever farther away as the years pass." He tightened his arms around her and put his lips next to her ear. "But you have brought the vision of that place back to me. You are my light in the darkness, my peace, my hope. So you, my Shoshone woman, shall have this fine new name: *Manakwa Noovigaded Pa' a Taviduaga*. It means 'Light on a Distant Hill'. Carry this name with pride, and know that you have brought that light into my arms, and into my heart."

Ellen was a little overwhelmed and didn't know what to say, so she asked Bear Paw to repeat the name for her. He did, and she tried to match it. After several attempts, she got it right, haltingly, to his obvious pleasure. "I am pleased and honored to be given a name that means so much to you," she said. "It recalls a grand vision, and I pray that I can live up to it."

Bear Paw stroked her hair down the left side of her head. "You already have," he said softly, nuzzling her neck again.

Ellen shifted in his arms and, pushing gently against him, slowly extricated herself. Rising on her good arm, she laboriously stood up. She stepped away from him and turned around. "I am ready for you," she said quietly.

Bear Paw looked at her face, serene and beautiful in the flickering firelight, framed by her light brown braids running down the front of her chest. There was love in her golden-brown eyes. But he was surprised by her words. "Ellen, it is but seven days since you were badly injured and I feared for your life. I want to lie with you more than I can say, but I do not think you are well enough yet."

Ellen smiled. "Your words are like strong arms around me," she said. "They tell me I have made a good choice in a mate. Yes, I am not well yet. Yes, I still have pain in my shoulder. But you are my husband now, my love, my man above all others. Tonight I can deny you nothing." With that, she reached behind her neck, undid the leather thongs holding her dress, and let it slide off her shoulders onto the ground.

Bear Paw stared at her, momentarily forgetting to breathe. Except for the dressing on her wounded shoulder, she was flawless. Modest but beautifully shaped breasts sat high on her chest. His gaze traveled slowly down over her taut stomach, down to the light-brown delta of hair between her thighs, down her smooth slender legs, and finally back up. Despite his determination to be careful with his wounded bride, he felt his body responding. "You are truly beautiful, as I could not have imagined," he said, voice husky with desire. "Let us find a way, then, so that you are not harmed." With that, he stood up and removed his shirt, tossing it aside.

In the firelight, Ellen could see several faint scars on his muscular body from knives or arrows, or perhaps bullets, marking a history of battles won, and maybe lost. She moved to him and ran her hands over his torso, fingers tracing over the scars. "Such a hard life," she said softly. "I feel sad seeing the signs of it on your body."

"Do not be sad, Ellen," he said, looking down and taking her head gently between two big hands. "It is our life, as the Creator gave it to us. We accept it."

She looked for a moment into his dark eyes, then stretched herself upward on tiptoe, and placing her hands on his cheeks, kissed him long and tenderly. He responded by massaging her back, carefully pressing her close to him. She slowly ran her hands down his chest, over his flat stomach, and down between his legs, feeling his body stir at her touch.

He stepped backward and loosened his breechclout, letting it fall to the ground.

Ellen was transfixed as his member seemed to take on a life of its own and swell between them. She had never been with a man, so she couldn't judge how relatively large he was, but it seemed a match for the rest of his oversized body. She trembled at the thought of him inside her. "I have not lain with a man before," she said. "I will follow your lead, but we must go slowly."

Bear Paw smiled at her. "That you would accept me as the first is a great honor, Ellen," he said. "Come, let us lie together." He took her hand and eased her down as she reclined on the furs, then he stretched out beside her. Propped up on one elbow, he kissed her gently, tenderly, stroking her cheek.

Ellen looked into his eyes, feeling his love, his tenderness. *This man will never hurt me*, she thought. She reached up her good arm and put her hand on the back of his neck, drawing him close to her, then felt him probing at her lips. She opened her mouth to him, feeling his tongue slip inside and caress her own. A warmth from deep inside suffused her body, and she gasped as he drew back from her mouth and slid his head down to her left breast, gently squeezing, then taking it into his mouth. She could feel her nipple rapidly become erect under the swirling embrace of his tongue. She arched her back, mouth open in soundless pleasure as she felt his hand move down her chest and stomach, then gently onto the silky delta of hair over her mound. His fingers probed for her opening, then found it and began to slide gently up and down.

Ellen's breathing became deeper, more rapid. She covered his big hand with her own and pressed it down against her as she opened her legs to make the way easier for him. Then she reached down between his legs and took his erection into her hand, squeezing and stroking. She reached lower and encircled his scrotum, massaging and pulling gently for a minute, then returned her attention to his engorged shaft. "Bear Paw," she gasped, "the time is now; I must have you inside me." She felt his hot breath on her cheek as he removed his hand from her triangle and grasped her head between both hands, gazing into her golden-brown eyes. "Yes, Ellen, yes," he said, voice heavy with desire. "But I cannot lie on top of you; you would be crushed." That much was true; he undoubtedly weighed more than twice her 110 pounds. "And I do not think you can support yourself on one arm if you are astride me."

She smiled and rolled over on her left side, back to him. "This will work," she said glancing over her shoulder, her smile a beguiling invitation.

He stretched out behind her and drew close.

She could feel his erection probing between her thighs, drew her upper leg forward to ease the way, and reached between her legs to guide him. He found her opening and ever so carefully pushed into her, working slowly so as not to harm her. She was tight, but his gentle persistence flooded her vagina with wetness as she rocked forward and back a bit to help him enter.

He came up against her maidenhead, and spent long moments pushing gently, knowing this was where he must be patient.

Finally he broke through, and Ellen gasped as he thrust fully into her. They lay in silent ecstasy, fused into one being, wordlessly speaking joy to each other.

After long minutes of embrace, as his hand reached over her body and enveloped her right breast, thumb roving over her nipple, he began to move inside her. Ellen felt a fire spreading through her loins as he thrust in and out. She felt closer and closer to some inner edge of control, some limit of all she had known before as for long glorious minutes he moved deep within her and then out, clutching her tightly, his breath on her neck. He thrust faster, and she was suddenly over the edge, crying out as waves of ecstasy rolled over her. Then she felt him shudder against her, moan, and cry out her name as he released his seed deep within her. He continued to thrust in and out of her for a few minutes, then his grip on her breast gradually loosened as, completely spent, he relaxed behind her and was satisfied just to hold her closely. There they remained in perfect silent contentment, intertwined in pleasure Ellen did not want to end as she gradually drifted off to sleep in his arms.

Sometime in the small hours of the night he awakened her as he probed again between her legs. This time she rolled over on her back as he straddled her, keeping his weight suspended above as he entered her and brought her to climax once more with his body and with the fierceness of his desire.

Ellen gradually rose to consciousness the next morning as the gray light of an overcast spring day penetrated into the tipi. She found herself still in Bear Paw's arms. When she turned over to face him, he was fully awake, looking at her, eyes gleaming.

He had been watching her, content to do nothing more for long minutes as her small frame lay nestled against his large one. Then he had gently removed the sleeping fur from her and softly run his hands over her womanly contours, taking in the smooth mounds of her breasts, the silky stretch of her skin over her hips, her sheer alien *femaleness*. "I need nothing more than to watch you asleep, to see your chest rise and fall with each breath," he said, "to marvel once again at your beauty and what you have given me. I am content."

She leaned close and kissed him. "Good morning, my husband," she said sleepily. "I would stay here in your arms all day, but I suppose we had better rise. People will be expecting us."

She was right about that. When they emerged from the tipi together a short while later, Ellen was embarrassed to find a considerable crowd nearby, who erupted in shouts of celebration and congratulations, as well as a little teasing. Red-faced, she turned into Bear Paw's chest for a few moments until she regained her composure.

"This is Manakwa Noovigaded Pa'a Taviduaga," Bear Paw announced loudly to the crowd. "Remember her name, and honor her. For she is my wife, a Shoshone woman."

Ellen opened her good arm in welcome and they came forward. She accepted the embraces of her best friends, including Kimama and Otter Girl. It was obvious that the camp chief's new wife met with the approval of them all.

That night she wrote in her diary.

Summer, 1877—with my husband. Location unknown.

And so I am wed. My mind is still in a whirl. How did this come to be? I am not sure. Bear Paw is a good man; I love him, and I have no regrets. But sometimes it seems like I am being pushed along by forces I cannot see, demanding ever more of me. Something has chosen a different path for me. Where is all this leading? I do not know. But there is great danger on the horizon, and I cannot escape it. May God give me strength and wisdom to do the right thing.

THE CAMP LIVED IN PEACE, as did Bear Paw and Ellen, into early June. Ellen rejoiced daily in her husband's embrace, exulting as they made love in a meadow not far from camp, his shaft like a missing puzzle piece inside her. She felt secure inside his arms, and more content than she had ever hoped to be with the Shoshone, more at ease by the day with her decision to stay—and to marry.

But game continued to be scarce, and there were periods of hunger in the camp. Ellen had been prepared to accept the hardships of the new life she had chosen, and did so now.

The camp knew that it was past time to pack for the annual trek to buffalo country. Ellen quietly and privately advised Bear Paw against it. "There is great danger if you make this trip now. You will all be open to attack at any point along the way, not just by other tribes but now by whites as well. And you may come back to find your lands taken over completely by whites, and nothing left for you but the reservation. We need to stay, and protect what you have until we can sue for peace."

Bear Paw listened intently, nodding in agreement with her as she outlined the dangers of leaving even for a couple of months. He said nothing, and left after she was through. She did not know if what she had told him would sway the others.

While they were pondering the situation, an ugly incident threw everything into chaos. Several braves had gone out far from the camp in search of game. They had come across white hunters doing the same.

Tempers flared on both sides; shots were fired. A full-fledged fight, stoked by Shoshone anger over white invasion, and by whites caught up in their own arrogant belief in destiny, erupted. The braves rode hard back to camp, one of them bleeding from a bullet wound. Three whites were killed, they reported. One other was wounded but escaped. The horses of the three dead white men were taken.

Ellen was present when the braves came riding in, exhausted, their horses blowing hard. They yelled victory shouts and waived their weapons in the air. She heard the story and turned away, grim-faced.

Bear Paw noticed and took her into their tipi. "You know how the whites think, Ellen," he said. "We must be ready. What will they do?"

Ellen looked at him, sorrow on her face. "They will be coming," she said.

MOUNTAIN MEADOW REST HOME, OREGON COAST
1930

ROBBIE MCINTIRE SLUMPED BACK IN his chair, exhausted, right hand cramped from writing. After five days, he no longer had words for what he was hearing. Shock, amazement, disbelief—all seemed inadequate.

Ellen looked at him with her piercing gaze that seemed to cut right through any false front he might have thrown up. He would have no secrets from this woman. If he flatly didn't believe her, she would know. But he *did* believe her, and that made the writing he had filled several notebooks with all the more astounding.

"I hope you aren't scandalized by the choices I made, young man," she said with a faint smile.

"Uh, no ma'am," Robbie replied vigorously. "Amazed, yes. But scandalized, no. I let go of any such notion days ago."

"There has been no shortage of people who *were*," she said. "Some later condemned me for marrying Bear Paw, and deciding to live with the Shoshone. In their ignorance, they thought I had chosen to live with savages, charmed by some svengali buck who wanted nothing more than a white woman for a trophy. But it wasn't that way. The Shoshone were an imperfect but beautiful people, as I hope you know by now. Bear Paw truly did love me, and it was obvious he would give his life for me. Every day I spent with him deepened my belief that I had made a good choice, and that I needed to stay with these people to see them safely to whatever destination the cavalry chose for them. I knew there was nothing I could do to help them beyond that. But if I could make a difference in their fate, if I could do something that would be remembered to their children, if I could serve someone besides myself, then I would not shrink away from it."

A look of sorrow settled on her features, an expression Robbie had seen too often in their days together. "But it was not to be," she said quietly. "Events beyond our control were pushing us toward the crossroads of history. . . ."

FORT WALLA WALLA
WASHINGTON TERRITORY
JULY 1877

ELI MORROW HAD BEEN SUMMONED unexpectedly to the Post Commandant's office. Major Riley was seated behind his desk, waiting for him. "You wanted to see me, sir?" Eli said.

"Yes," Riley answered. "A messenger rode in earlier this morning from Fort Lapwai. It seems the Nez Perce have fled the Wallowas and are on the run. As you know, General Howard had ordered them to report to the Fort Lapwai reservation by June 14th, or be forced onto it by his troops. Hah!" he snorted. "I'd like to have seen them try. You ever seen the Nez Perce in action, Eli?"

"No sir, I have not had that privilege."

"A privilege it is, Captain. They're the finest horse warriors in the west. They can shoot arrows or guns from horseback at top speed with deadly accuracy. And their horses are far superior to the Cavalry's, being as the Nez Perce are the best horse breeders in the west. I know this is a fight Howard didn't want. His troops are mostly civil war leftovers—poorly trained, poorly equipped, and untested in Indian fighting. The Nez Perce would make hash of them in a fair fight. And that's where you come in, Eli."

"Sir?"

"Howard needs officers with leadership skills to organize that rabble and get them motivated to go after the Nez Perce. I really hate to lose you for an extended period, but I have orders. You're to ride out to Fort Lapwai as soon as possible, and report to Howard. He'll assign you to accompany his other officers on the pursuit." Riley rose to his feet. "Good Luck, Eli. See if you can bring the hostiles back as quickly as possible. I've heard they're responsible for a rash of murders, rapes, and robberies all over the Camas Prairie. They need to be brought in."

"Yes sir," Eli said, saluting and leaving the office. Outside, his mind whirled. This was unexpected news. But there was one good thing about it. Stuck at Fort Walla Walla, he had just about exhausted his sources for any news of Ellen's existence. This would get him out and about where he could send out more feelers for information. He quickened his stride toward his quarters.

SHOSHONE CAMP
SOUTHERN IDAHO TERRITORY

An increasing feeling of unease pervaded the Shoshone camp as summer progressed. Sleep for most did not come easily. Ellen was surprised that, as they reached late July, no strike had come. The number of outlying sentries was increased, and word was received that white forces were gathering just over a day's ride away. The Shoshone numbers too were swelling, as panicky small groups came in from the surrounding country to swell the camp to about 400.

During her monthly "unclean" time, Ellen retreated to a private lodge with other menstruating women, as was the custom. There she would stay for four days until her time was over. This was done because it was believed that to touch a menstruating woman was to invite disaster, as they were thought to be possessed by evil spirits during this time. No one, especially the warriors, wanted to risk a chance encounter. But this ritual did not last long for Ellen, as during the first week of August, she discovered she was pregnant.

What should have been a cause for joyous celebration was instead yet another worry. "This is not a good time for this," she told Bear Paw. "There is so much danger in the air."

"I agree, my love," Bear Paw said. "Perhaps we should have thought of that and taken steps to prevent it. But what is done is done."

"Yes." She looked at him with a penetrating gaze. "My heart tells me we will be attacked soon. What of your weapons?"

"We have a few rifles but little ammunition for them. We do not use them for hunting buffalo; many people are still attached to the traditional ways. Of bows and arrows there are plenty. Our best battle horses are kept close at hand now."

Ellen fell silent, looking at the ground inside the tipi. After long moments she looked up. "I must do what I can to stop this," she said. "I must go out and meet with the *toquashes*."

"I forbid it," Bear Paw said sternly. "It is too dangerous. The whites are in a frenzy; they would shoot you on sight."

"I *must* try," Ellen insisted. "You depend on me for knowledge of the whites. Now you would turn away from it? If there is a chance I can prevent this, I have to try."

Bear Paw was silent and grim for a few seconds. Then he spoke slowly. "Very well. I will go with you. We will take five of our best warriors, under a flag of truce. But if I think it is too dangerous to talk, we will return to camp immediately. Do you agree to this?"

"Yes. I will obey any decision you make." She moved over close to him and snuggled into his arms. "As I always will."

JUST BEFORE SUNRISE THE NEXT morning, the small party mounted up and headed out of camp. They rode in silence, the six warriors forming a loose cordon around Ellen's mount. They reached the crest of the first hill, where Ellen had made her decision to stay with the Shoshone. All was silent across the land, the wild grasses rustling in a slight morning breeze. They rode on slowly, headed for the next rise a half-mile away, as a thin sliver of sun appeared behind it. They reached the top—and stopped short in shock. Two Shoshone sentries were racing toward them, tearing across the dry ground, urging their horses on at top speed. They spotted Ellen's small party. "*Toquashes!*" one of them screamed. "They come! They are many!"

Ellen and Bear Paw looked away into the distance and heard the rumbling of many hooves, then could see a dust cloud in the air against the rising sun. That was all Bear Paw needed. "Go!" he shouted. "Return to camp!"

Ellen looked at him, wild-eyed, her horse dancing nervously

underneath her. She looked toward the rising sun, longing to charge desperately forward to meet the foe, to implore them to stop, to beg for mercy. "Let me go to them!" she screamed.

Bear Paw could feel she was about to bolt, and quickly put his horse in front of hers. "No; it is too late! Run for camp, now!"

Dejected, Ellen whirled her horse away and kicked it into a run for the camp, Bear Paw at her side.

Behind them a swiftly-moving river of dark figures surged over the far ridge like a wave and thundered toward the Shoshone camp.

BEAR PAW, ELLEN, AND THE rest tore into camp in a tornado of pounding hooves and dust, then spread out, shouting at everyone to get up and prepare for battle. The camp erupted in chaos, then quickly, carefully-planned procedures took hold. Bear Paw barked orders as the warriors ran to him. "Women, children and old people to the river!" In truth, it was more creek than river, but its banks were the only place to find refuge near the camp. Bear Paw looked at Ellen, who did not move. "Ellen, you must go with the women!" he shouted above the din.

"My place is with you, my husband," she replied.

"Not in war. It is too dangerous, and your presence would tie my hands in battle. Now, go! I will protect you."

Ellen looked unhappy, but nodded and whirled her horse away toward the creek, stopping at her tipi to leap off her horse and retrieve her diary.

Bear Paw turned his own horse around toward the approaching army. The ground was beginning to shake. All around him warriors were taking cover behind whatever defenses they could find. Skilled as they were at horseback warfare, western Indians did not fight well from stationary defensive positions. It was alien to them, and something they did not do willingly. But now they had no choice.

Bear Paw vaulted from his horse and took cover. He could do no more.

The mass of mounted soldiers surged out of the rising sun. The Shoshone could hear their screams as they approached, but could not see them clearly in the sun's glare. A vanguard of riders materialized out of the glare at full gallop, their horses pounding into the outer perimeter of the camp. The crack of gunfire suddenly filled the air, punctuated by the screams of combat. The camp erupted with desperate battle as soldiers raced in. The Shoshone began firing with deadly accuracy, sending soldiers and their mounts to the ground. Shots were fired point blank as combatants tumbled, dust and the smell of blood heavy in the air.

The soldiers were in a killing frenzy, beyond the control of their commanders. White Deer's flag of truce was torn from his tipi and trampled in the dirt. When he saw it gave him no power, no protection, he stood with arms folded, singing his death song. He was cut down, riddled by bullets.

Before long, the Shoshones' ammunition ran out. Then the massacre began.

The warriors did their best to protect the women, fighting valiantly in the swirling chaos, giving more than they got. The women and children were screaming and crying along the creek as the warriors were forced back toward them, some falling along the way as they fought on with bow and arrow. In the creek bed Ellen did her best to keep the women together, but some were bolting and running for their lives toward a grove of trees about one hundred yards away. Some were cut down as they ran, along with their children.

It was now more of an Indian hunt than a battle. Women tried to hide in clumps of willows along the creek bed. It was in vain. As soldiers approached, five women burst from hiding to show that they were squaws, not warriors. The soldiers shot them all. A larger group of thirty or forty women sent out in desperation a girl of about six, waving a white flag on a stick. She was slain in a hail of bullets. The message was clear: there would be no surrender accepted. And there would be no mercy.

Soldiers continued to hunt down the Shoshone women in the creek bed. Those that were found were shot at close range while they begged for mercy. Ellen found herself wedged inside a tight mass of hysterical women, felt the thud of bullets into their bodies, became trapped beneath them as they fell.

The warriors near the creek were being cut down. Some who could close on the soldiers killed them until they themselves were shot, usually from behind. Trapped in her hiding place, Ellen could see Bear Paw making a heroic stand, leaping at soldiers on horseback, dragging them to the ground, throwing himself at others before they could react, slashing and stabbing, leaving carnage in his wake. Two soldiers on horseback charged him, and he retreated, sprinting through the creek just yards from Ellen, and bursting out the far side, which had been free of combatants. The soldiers tried to force their mounts through the heavy willow clumps but could not, and dismounted, charging through on foot.

From her hiding place Ellen could see the battle. She watched as the first soldier through was struck in the left side by Bear Paw's knife. He gasped and fell to the ground in agony, clutching his stomach. The second raised his pistol and fired point blank at Bear Paw. The gun clicked on a dud round, and Bear Paw leapt at him. Both tumbled to the ground. Frantically fighting off the big Shoshone in a desperate bid for survival, the soldier tried to roll away as Bear Paw's hands closed around his throat. Unseen behind them, the first soldier staggered to his feet and picked up the malfunctioning pistol. With no time to investigate the cause of the misfire, he swung the pistol hard at the Indian's head. Bear Paw jerked violently and fell on his back, lifeless.

Ellen clamped a hand over her mouth to stifle a scream as she saw him fall.

The soldier who was being strangled struggled to a sitting position, rubbing his neck. "Damn Injun near kilt me!" he rasped. "Good thing you got up." He laboriously staggered to his feet. "We oughta finish 'im off."

"Forget it, Luke," said the other, bloody hand still clutching his stomach. "I'm bleedin' like a stuck pig. He looks kilt enough to me. Help me get back to the doc 'fore I pass out."

The two staggered away, leaving Bear Paw lying on the ground.

Hiding in the willows, Ellen was consumed by grief and shed silent tears. She could smell smoke in the air and hear the crackling of flames, and knew the soldiers were burning the tipis. A half an hour went by as the screams of the wounded and dying and the frantic cries of mortally wounded horses gradually diminished. Ellen knew she had to get to Bear Paw. She tried to get the others to move, then realized they were all dead. Tearfully she pushed and shoved her way out from under the bodies. Then she stumbled out of the creek bed and over to Bear Paw. They were alone on the far side of the creek bed, hidden from view from the main camp by the thick willows. The right side of Bear Paw's head was a mass of blood. At first she thought he was dead, but she saw the slight rise and fall of his chest and could feel a faint pulse at his throat. Her tears fell on his face as she frantically tried to rouse him to consciousness, calling his name over and over. He moaned and stirred slightly, but did not open his eyes. Unable to get more from him, she pulled her shawl over her head and sat at his side, hands clutching her head, crying and rocking in grief.

She had been there a few minutes when she heard the voices of white soldiers approaching from behind.

There were two of them, walking around looking for someone to rob or kill. "We still ain't found that white woman," said one.

"You mean the white Injun," said the other. "I get hold of her, she'll rue the day she ever became a buck's wife."

"Hey, look over there!" said the first, stopping short as he spotted Bear Paw and Ellen. "Lookit the size of that Injun! I'm gonna get me a nutsack what'll make a fine tobacco pouch."

"We gotta get that squaw away from him," said the other as they drew close.

"No problem," said the first. He closed on Ellen and reached down and seized her by the hair. "Get off that Injun, squaw! I'll tend to you shortly."

"Not 'til I have a go at her," said the second.

Ellen had found Bear Paw's knife on the ground near her and picked it up. Her man was near death. All desire for peace was swept away. She was trembling, gripped with a ferocity such as she had never known, the wrath of a wounded Shoshone warrior. As the soldier bent over and grabbed her hair, she whirled and with all her strength shoved the big knife between his ribs and into his heart. *"Are you looking for me?"* she snarled, face contorted with rage.

The soldier's eyes bulged in shock, then rolled up in his head as he fell on his back, dead.

Ellen got to her feet, advancing on the other soldier, bloody knife held out in front of her, her face a mask of vengeance. The man stumbled backward in terror, all his bravado and bluster gone. For the first time he was on the receiving end of the carnage. Panic took hold and he reeled away in terror, shrieking as if being pursued by demons.

Ellen watched him go until he disappeared into the creek willows. She knew she must try to find two horses she and Bear Paw could escape on—if she could get him off the ground. She also knew now the soldiers were looking for her. With her shawl still over her head to conceal her light brown hair, she walked steadily but carefully across the creek and into the remains of the camp she had called home for more than a year. She could see what survivors there were numbly drifting into a group to await their fate. The smoking remains of tipis and flames from burning food caches filled the still air with haze. There were bodies everywhere—braves, women and children, and dead horses and dogs. She saw horror and savagery she could not have imagined. Several women had been raped and then shot point blank. There were warriors—and women—with their genitals sliced off. She saw a pregnant squaw, dead, her stomach cut open and her baby dead on the ground beside her. Dead infants littered the camp. Ellen could see that the soldiers had grabbed the babies by the heels and swung their heads into whatever hard object they could find. She didn't see Rabbit Woman, and hoped her friend had been able to escape on one of her horses. But she found Owl Woman, dead. Ellen had to fight hard to stay on her feet, fight the overwhelming urge to collapse in inexpressible grief. But though she wanted so badly to know if Kimama and Otter Girl were among the survivors, she had to keep going.

She came across Black Elk, his sightless eyes staring at the sky. There were five dead soldiers close by. It looked like he had given a good account of himself. She knelt at his side and closed his eyes. "Farewell, brother," she whispered. "You are with the spirits now. May your hunt be forever good." She rose, afraid of attracting attention. Turning away, she saw her beloved paint horse and one other, wearing rope bridles, standing not far off. She walked slowly over to them, afraid with every step that someone would notice her. But none did, and she reached the horses safely. Speaking softly to them, she led the horses as quietly as she could to the other side of the creek. She reached Bear Paw and knelt at his side. Long minutes of massaging his chest and shoulders and calling his name quietly through her tears was rewarded as his eyes finally fluttered open. He smiled when he saw her looking down at him, but did not speak.

"We must go, quickly," Ellen said. "I have horses." It took all her strength to raise him to a sitting position. She could see how bad off he was, but there was no time to waste. Pulling hard on his arms, and with uncoordinated help from him, she managed to get him to stand, leaning against one of the horses. He stood panting for a minute as she urged him to mount. He raised his left leg and Ellen cupped her hands under his foot. He was far heavier than she would ever have been able to lift under normal circumstances, but this day she would not be denied. Straining with all her might, her wounded shoulder on fire with agony, she was able to get him high enough, as he pulled with his arms across the horse, for him to swing his leg over the horse's back. He collapsed against the animal's neck, barely conscious but mounted at last. Ellen clutched her stomach—slightly swollen with child now—briefly, then mounted her own horse, and with her leading Bear Paw's horse behind her, they began a slow walk away from the field of death. She prayed that the trees and clumps of willows in the creek bed still shielded them from being seen by the soldiers on the other side. In a few minutes during which she barely dared to breath, fear gripping her with her horse's every step, they were at last out of sight in a grove of trees and away, walking aimlessly northeast.

*What voice was first sounded on this land? The voice of the
red people who had but bows and arrows. What has been
done in my country I did not want, did not ask for it; white
people going through my country. When the white man comes
in my country he leaves a trail of blood behind him.*
—*Red Cloud, Sioux Chief*

Ellen led Bear Paw's horse slowly through the trees. She knew the soldiers were looking for both of them. It wouldn't be long before they realized they were not among the living or the dead at the camp. Would they come after her? She didn't know. But she did know she couldn't outrun them. Bear Paw was barely conscious.

She stopped periodically to check on him. He had managed to stay on his horse but was unresponsive. She grew increasingly worried as the afternoon wore on, but was afraid to stop. Finally, in early evening, she halted at a depression in the ground beside a stream.

Ellen reviewed their circumstances and found them not good. She saw no shelter for the coming night. The land itself offered them nothing. They had no food, no blankets for cover from the night air. But at least there was water here. She helped Bear Paw down off his horse and carefully to the ground, finding the softest spot available. There she helped him to stretch out, then took off a shawl she had wrapped around her neck and spread it across his chest.

He opened his eyes fully and focused on her face. "Ellen—I love you," he whispered.

"And I you," she replied, putting on a brave face and lightly stroking the uninjured side of his head. "I saw you today. You were magnificent. You gave all you had to protect me and the other women."

"Where are we?" he said, barely audible.

"I do not know. I thought only to get away unseen, and the cover of trees lay to the north. Here I thought it time to stop for the night. We have no food or shelter. And I have no medicine to treat your wound. We must make do with very little."

He smiled and squeezed her arm. "You are Shoshone. You will find a way."

She bent down and kissed him, then tore a small strip of cloth from her shawl and walked a few steps to the creek. There she wet the strip thoroughly then returned to him. Carefully brushing his long hair aside she examined the wound closely, thinking she might clean it. At the roots of his hair, the skin was broken and blood still oozed from the wound. She pulled his eyelids open and looked at his pupils. The left eye's iris was open noticeably wider than the right. *He may have a fractured skull,* she thought. *This is not good.* With no medicine to treat the wound, she thought it best to keep his head cool but otherwise leave the wound alone and let his body do what it could.

Ellen looked up at the sun's position and figured she had little more than two hours of good light left. She took Bear Paw's knife, sharpened a stick she found to a point, and walked along the creek, looking for edible plants. It took only a few minutes to find tall slender stems topped with bluish-purple flowers arising out of a nest of long spiky leaves that marked a patch of camas plants. Digging out the roots with the stick, she carried them back to Bear Paw. Then she again brought the stick to a sharp point with the knife and went hunting at the creek. Walking slowly along, she eventually spied small trout here and there where shallow pools formed. She felt fortunate to spear one after several tries, and just plain lucky when she got another one a bit later. After that, the fish were too spooked to make themselves visible.

She then went to the creek and cleaned the camas roots she had found. Returning to Bear Paw, she wrapped the roots as best she could in damp green grass harvested from beside the creek, then covered them with a thin layer of soil in an area she intended to use for a fire pit. It was not the best baking method, but it would have to do.

She rooted around for twigs and sticks to build a fire. She knew there were firestones in the small bag Bear Paw always had at his waist, and reaching in, found them. She struck them against the tinder of dried leaves and grass she had gathered, and soon had a good fire going. She wouldn't waste time worrying about the fire being spotted; they needed it. If it was, it was. But as they were in a small depression beside the creek, the flames were not likely to be seen, and the dimming light would soon make the smoke invisible as well.

She then found two larger sticks with forks at one end where branches had angled away, and rammed the other ends into the sandy earth on both sides of the fire. Then she placed a crosspiece on the forks. With practiced hands, she gutted the fish quickly with Bear Paw's knife, and placed them over the fire on the crosspiece.

When the fish were well baked, she fed Bear Paw one of the fish a piece at a time, then slowly ate the other. With nothing to hold water, she brought it from the creek in her cupped hands and gently poured it into his mouth. The camas roots usually took twenty-four to thirty-six hours to bake, but they would get twelve at best before she and Bear Paw had to move again. But she would try to keep the fire going strong throughout the night, and eat them in the morning if they were edible.

Bear Paw looked up at her, pride mixed with love on his features. "You are my Shoshone bride," he said, voice a bit stronger now. "I have been blessed beyond measure. If I die tonight in your arms, it will be well."

"You must not talk so," she admonished him with a smile, gently running her hand over the top of his head. "You must be strong and heal so the day will come again when you can care for and protect me. But until then, I will do that for you."

He expressed a need to relieve himself, so pulling with all her strength, she helped him to his feet and he leaned on her as they walked slowly in among nearby bushes. She turned her back until he had finished, then steadied him as he stepped painfully back. After he was down once more, she stretched out beside him, snuggling up close and putting her left leg across his. "It has been a day I hoped I would never see," she said softly into his ear. "But now let us rest and gain strength for tomorrow. We will need all we have." She did not mention the searing pain in her shoulder.

At mid-morning the next day, they were up and away again. Ellen rode beside him, watchful for any sign he might fall off. "Is there a direction you wish to go?" she asked him as the horses moved away from the creek.

"One direction is as good as another," he said. He was able to sit up astride the horse now, but still slumped forward, head down. "As long as it is away from the soldiers. We will go north until we find someone who can help us."

The following day proved uneventful. Having long left the trees behind, they suffered the August sun beating down on them as they traversed the arid countryside. Ellen longed for the cover of trees but saw only solitary willows and pines here and there. Bear Paw continued to be weak and unsteady on his feet whenever they dismounted, and mostly silent, content to let Ellen lead them where she would. They saw nobody, white or Indian. It was as if they were the only people in the world. *That would be enough for me*, Ellen thought.

Toward the evening, she could see rain clouds gathering above them. "We must find shelter now," she told him. "We may have rain soon." She slightly quickened their pace when she saw a large stone cliff looming ahead in the fading light. When she reached it, she turned and rode along it until she saw what she had hoped to find—a large shelter under a rock overhang. It was not deep, but it would do. The back wall was partially covered with the soot of countless fires. It had obviously been used many times before. *Probably for centuries*, she thought. As she dismounted, she felt the first drops of rain. "We must take shelter quickly," she told Bear Paw, eyeing the dark clouds massing overhead. "Rain is coming." She reached up to steady him in dismounting. He slid down, put one foot on the earth—and fell on her. Ellen was slammed to the ground under his 200-plus pounds. She screamed as her shoulder erupted in pain, and her right arm went numb.

She was momentarily trapped beneath him. He had blacked out, but came around a few seconds later and managed to roll off of her. Still gasping for the breath that had been knocked out of her, she tried to drag him forward with her left arm as he crawled on his knees underneath the overhang. In considerable pain, she stumbled out to the horses and got them under too—just as the skies opened up. A torrent of rain pelted the ground in front of the shelter as lightning flashed and thunder boomed seemingly right overhead. Ellen dashed out into the rain in a desperate grab for firewood before everything got soaked. She snatched up an armload of whatever sticks she could find nearby and turned for the shelter. Abruptly she stopped and doubled over as cramps clutched her and a stabbing pain seared her belly. She staggered forward into the shelter; the armload of wood spilling to the ground as she collapsed.

Ellen cried out minutes later as her belly convulsed and her fetus was ejected onto the ground, along with a considerable amount of blood. Stunned, she gasped in agony, stared at it in stupefaction for long moments, then realized it was dead. She cried for the child that would never be. After about ten minutes, she tenderly picked up the fetus and, disregarding the pain, stumbled out into the rain. A few steps out she sank to her knees, put the fetus down, and began to tear at the wet earth with her bare hands. Rain pouring down on her, she clawed at the muddy soil until she had dug a depression about a foot deep. It quickly began to fill with water. Then she placed the fetus at the bottom and shoved the saturated earth over it until the hole was filled. She sat in the rain, looking down at the ground, numb. Then suddenly boiling over with rage and grief, she raised her face to the black sky. *"God, where are you?"* she screamed against the rolling thunder. *"Where are you!"* Sobbing uncontrollably, she pressed her forehead to the wet earth over her baby's grave.

Ellen's tears were lost in the rain.

THE HORSES HAD BECOME LEADERS of the journey. Ellen no longer had strength to direct them for more than an hour at a time. Little food and water had been found in the three days since departing the shelter. Bear Paw was improving, but he had not had the rest he should have had since the head injury. Now they were both weak. Ellen was beginning to think they would either die in this wilderness, or at best be at the mercy of anyone who found them—if anyone did.

They had stopped to rest whenever they found the shade of a tree. Ellen lay in her husband's arms, taking what strength she could from his embrace.

"Are you sorry you have cast your lot with me?" Bear Paw asked her on the second day as they lay together, trying to deny the hunger gnawing at their stomachs. "All that you must have hoped for is gone, broken. I fear that I have brought great sadness into your life."

Ellen slowly turned her face to him and smiled. "I have not regretted it for a moment. I am content, for I have found a purpose, and a great man to love. I could ask for no more." She clutched his arm fiercely. "Even if we die together."

Bear Paw was silent for long moments, as if searching for the right words to say something. Finally he spoke. "Ellen, we must return to our camp. Some of our brothers and sisters fled into the woods. They may be injured or starving. I need to bring them together, to protect them if I can. To help them stay free."

Ellen had been expecting this at some point, and she had prepared a response. "My love, you were badly injured, and you are still weak. We are both wanted by the white soldiers. I have no doubt they would hang you immediately if you are captured. They might hang me as well. I know your desire to return is strong, as is my desire to be with you. But we must wait until our bodies are strong once again. To go now would be to invite certain death, and that would not help our brothers and sisters."

He was silent again, looking out across the landscape. Then he turned to her and said, "It shall be as you say."

After they slept for a while, they laboriously mounted and gave the animals their head. The horses plodded on.

ELLEN WAS DIMLY AWARE THAT the horses had stopped. She opened her eyes, her head resting on her horse's neck. Were the animals waiting for something? She pushed herself upright and saw that Bear Paw was close by, slumped over his horse. She thought she heard a faint rumbling, and looked to the northwest. Something very large was coming, raising a great cloud of dust. As it drew nearer, it transformed itself into a vast body of people and horses. They were coming straight at her.

The more we can kill this year, the less will have to
be killed the next war . . . they all have to be killed
or be maintained as a species of paupers.
    —William Tecumseh Sherman, Civil War hero and
    chief military officer of the High Plains

THE TALL, HANDSOME NEZ PERCE chief known to his people as
Heinmot Tooyalaket (Thunder Rolling Over the Mountains),
and to whites as Chief Joseph, rode forward to the front of the great
body stretched out behind him on the dusty plain. As a camp chief in
charge of the welfare and safety of the women, children, and elderly, he
customarily rode with them near the front, where they were protected
by warriors from attack at the rear, but now he moved up to the very
apex of the great assemblage, anxious about what lay ahead.

Behind him was a vast body of 800 Nez Perce men, women, and
children, plus 3,000 horses. The Nez Perce were the finest horse
breeders in America, their magnificent stock the envy and desire of both
other tribes and whites. The horses, more than anything else, were their
identity, their pride, their badge of accomplishment.

It had been over two months now since they had seen no other choice
but to flee their beloved homeland, the Wallowa[10] Mountains in the
northeast corner of Oregon Territory. Since then, pursued relentlessly
by the U. S. Cavalry under General Howard, their lives had become a
continuous nightmare.

It had started inauspiciously enough. They had for years been

---

10   Wal-LOW-a ("low" rhymes with cow).

increasingly pressured by white civilians, and later the Cavalry, to abandon the Wallowas and move to a reservation near Lapwai, Idaho Territory. The Wallowas, wild, rugged, inaccessible and beautiful, were increasingly coveted by white settlers. It didn't help when disappointed gold seekers drifted north from the California Gold Rush into the area, seeking better luck.

Despite Nez Perce claims to their traditional homeland, there had been increasing conflicts with white settlers staking claims, increasing incidents of thievery and killings the Nez Perce were always blamed for, and increasing calls for the army to do something to protect the white invaders.

The smoldering resentment among the Nez Perce had been very difficult to contain among young hot-headed warriors eager for revenge after seeing relatives killed over trifling conflicts, or their women raped. Each time all-out war threatened, Chief Joseph had pleaded for calm, and through the sheer power of his eloquence, powerful personality, and respected leadership, he had prevailed.

But one day a young brave named Wahlitits was goaded once too often to avenge the death of his father, who had been killed when he complained about a white man's fence through Nez Perce territory. This time, a brave name Yellow Grizzly Bear pushed him over the edge, chiding that he if he was a real Nez Perce warrior, he would avenge his father.

Wahlitits rode out that day, and did.

Other young warriors, emboldened by the action, finally could not be held back, and erupted into rides of vengeance over years of abuse, humiliation, and lies from whites. White settlements were burned, and widespread rape, robbery, and murder erupted.

At that very time, the Nez Perce were actually enroute to the Lapwai Reservation. Heartsick, Joseph had finally given in. When Joseph heard the news, he was gravely troubled. He had ample experience that the white man tended to blame all Indians for the actions of a few, or even one. He knew that the cavalry response would be merciless now, and that the women and children in his charge were in great danger. The war chiefs White Bird and Looking Glass were in agreement.

There was no recourse but to flee the Wallowas.

Now the sadness seemed to have no boundary. It was endless, all pervasive. The shattered survivors of three battles stumbled along, numb and confused. It was as if they had descended into hell. Three times the cavalry had caught up with them in their flight, and three times the soldiers had attacked without mercy, killing indiscriminately. Each time the Nez Perce warriors had been able to repel the attack, giving the main body a chance to flee again. But too many bodies were left behind.

They could not imagine what they had done to be so relentlessly hunted and slain. It was clear to them now that surrender would not be sufficient for the white soldiers. If they were caught, they would all be killed. There would be no mercy—not for the children, not for the women, not for the sick and elderly.

Their fine clothes, like their horses the envy of many, were in ruins now. Some were gone, left at the battle sites. Much of what they had left was torn up to bind wounds, or was ripped and dirty. Most of their food—including the supplies they had purchased at the white settlement of Stevensville—was gone too, abandoned as they fled the sight of the last battle, as were lodge poles used for tipis and many of the buffalo robes they used for cover.

They now passed through the Big Hole plain under a sweltering August sun. Joseph, feeling more dead than alive, rode alongside Springtime, his wife, who had been wounded in the last battle. She cradled his infant daughter, who suffered terribly in the heat. Earlier, he had watched as his brother Ollokot's wounded wife, Fair Land, faded away to death, powerless to help her.

The injured cried in agony as the travois poles bounced across the rough ground. Wounds opened, broken bones jostled against each other, bullet holes dripped blood. Before long, there was no one not personally acquainted with death. When the old and injured could no longer bear it, they implored to be left behind. Joseph insured they were given food, water, and blankets. It was a pitiful farewell for their families, who knew as they watched them fade into the distance that it was a death sentence. They would either die of their wounds, or be found and killed by warriors of other tribes, white soldiers, or settlers. The ones left behind knew it as well.

Looking Glass, who had led the flight so far at a deliberate pace, was

135

now a pariah. The people were furious at him for his refusal to speed up. They blamed him for being surprised by the soldiers at the last attack, so he was removed as leader and replaced by Poker Joe, who knew the land, was part white, and could speak a little English. He might then know something about how whites think, which could be of help in decision-making in the days ahead.

Poker Joe got the group moving at a rapid pace. It was no longer a journey, but a flight. A large group of scouts went out far and wide in all directions, assuming there might be soldiers just beyond the nearest ridge. The people rose early, ate a hurried breakfast, and traveled without stopping until late morning, when they paused to eat the only meal of the day they dared to build fires for. They started out again in early afternoon and continued into darkness, sometimes traveling until nearly midnight. Without lodge poles once again, the new ones they had cut laying burned and broken at the battle site, they were reduced to draping skins over bushes for shelter.

The heightened pace was too much for many. Some of the weaker ones died on the trail and were buried in shallow graves. There were fewer Nez Perce with each passing day, and with each one who went to the spirit world, the mood of the survivors grew more despondent.

It now became impossible to control the rage-filled young warriors, who had failed in their attempt to burn soldiers who had taken refuge in a pine grove back at the last battle site, known as the Big Hole, and who had held back their wrath for so long. They rode out daily on raids, sometimes capturing large quantities of alcohol and becoming raging drunk. They were beyond the influence of even Joseph and the other chiefs, who pleaded for restraint to no avail. Whites were killed, houses were burned, horses were stolen.

Because he had been an eloquent spokesman for his people in earlier fruitless negotiations with General Howard, Joseph was seen by the public as the leader of the fleeing band, even though he was not. Now stories of terror and savagery at the hands of "Joseph's Indians" spread panic throughout the west by telegraph and newspaper. Whites were frantic for protection, and they saw the cavalry as being incompetent bunglers unable to catch Joseph, the cunning "Red Napoleon", whose men were murdering white civilians and going unpunished.

But in truth the pursuing soldiers were severely undermanned.

Colonel Gibbon, the architect of the Big Hole massacre, had fewer than 150 men.[11] General Howard's men, farther back in pursuit, had almost no food, and some of what they did have was, shockingly, non-perishable rations left over from the Civil War.

The fleeing group was falling apart internally. Traditionally friendly tribes they had counted on for assistance turned against them. The people suffered terribly from the heat in barren country. Different factions sprang up, each with its own opinions of what should be done. Even killings within the group began to happen.

The rolling tragedy stumbled on, dragging sore feet and unwilling bodies across the blazing, powder-dry landscape, clinging desperately to exhortations from the leaders that they would before long be near buffalo country. Ever south they went toward the place of the geysers—toward Yellowstone.

AT EARLY EVENING OF THIS day—one more in an endless succession of tears, pain, and fatigue—Joseph looked through the slanting late-day sunlight and suddenly called a halt. He had seen something in the path ahead. It looked like two figures on horseback. Several of the young warriors followed his gaze, then urged their tired mounts into a full gallop before he could stop them.

Joseph followed at a slower pace. He saw the warriors leap from their horses and approach the two on horseback. Quickly the scene turned ugly as the warriors suddenly dragged both from their horses and threw them to the ground, screaming in fury. Knives were pulled. Joseph spurred his mount toward them and arrived just in time to fly off his horse and tackle one who had raised his knife and was about to strike. The man was one of the hotheads that had ridden out from the group on alcohol-fueled raids against any whites they could find. Joseph slammed into the brave, driving him off his feet and into the dust. The brave came up spitting and screaming, ready to bury his knife in the attacker. Until he saw who it was.

Joseph was known for his reason and calm demeanor, but it could leave him if the situation required it. He advanced on the young man,

---

11 The Cavalry boasted that 89 Nez Perce were killed during that battle. What wasn't mentioned was that more than 50 of them were women and children.

glaring, knife held at the ready. The moment seemed frozen in silent time. No one wanted to challenge him.

"What do you do?" the brave finally screamed. "See what we have found." He pointed to the two strangers. "A Shoshone, and a white woman! A horse thief and a murderer! I will kill them; do not stand in my way." The screaming emboldened him and he took two steps forward, knife poised. Joseph parried the knife arm, smashed him in the chest with a swinging forearm, and the man was down again, Joseph's knife at his throat. He was fairly trembling with rage. "I have had more than enough of your drunken savagery," he said. "You have caused more trouble than anyone else. Do not test my patience further. Yes, Shoshone are horse thieves and whites are murderers. But not all of them. You will not harm them now." He turned to the others. "Release them."

Ellen had been dragged off her horse by her hair. She felt the brave holding her let go and scrambled to Bear Paw's side, hovering over him protectively, eyes wide with fear. He seemed incapable of getting up.

"All whites deserve to die!" shouted one of the men.

"All Shoshone as well," spat another.

"All of the People are brothers now," Joseph said calmly, never letting his gaze wander from the hostile faces before him. "We are all united in pain and death. If we do not stand together, we are worse than they. Let us not be so quick to kill one of the People who may be a victim of the whites as well."

"Then let me spill this white woman's blood!" shouted the brave whom Joseph had collided with. "What reason is there to keep her alive?"

Joseph looked at Ellen closely for the first time. He saw a slender young white woman, probably still a teenager, doing her best to protect one of the biggest Shoshone braves he had ever seen. She looked very weak and was clearly exhausted, the hollows around her eyes dark with fatigue. If the braves had not pulled her from her horse she might have fallen off on her own.

"You will not do so," he said firmly. "The white woman might prove useful. If we have put our faith in Poker Joe because he is part white, might there not also be something to be gained from this white woman as well? We must know how they came to be here, near death as they seem. They will come with us. Tonight we will hear their story in council, and then we will decide what to do. And for now," he said, glaring at them, "any brave who raises a hand against them will feel my knife at his throat."

Consumed with disgust, the braves mounted and sped off, expressing disdain at Joseph's commands, though not so loud that he could hear them. It was clear they would give him no help in getting the two strangers back on their mounts.

Joseph stepped over to Ellen and bent down close to her. She flinched as he reached out to her, eyes darting with fear, and attempted to cover Bear Paw with her small body. Joseph couldn't speak Shoshone, but he did what he could to merit her trust by looking into her eyes and laying a gentle hand on her shoulder.

Ever so slowly, he could see that she began to believe him.

ELLEN AND BEAR PAW WERE given small amounts of water and a bit of jerky to chew on. Then the procession began to move again. Ellen was deeply frightened by the venomous looks she saw every time she dared to peek at the Nez Perce. It was worst from some of the women, who glared at her and drew a finger across their throats.

They stopped late that night and set up camp, which took nearly no time at all as there was almost nothing to set up. There was just enough light from a full moon to see each other in the dark, and a council of chiefs gathered around Bear Paw and Ellen, sitting on the ground around them.

White Bird was full of anger at Ellen's presence, and of a mind to exact his revenge on her then and there. Toohoolhoolzote, another prominent brave legendary for his physical strength, wanted the pleasure of vanquishing Bear Paw, weak though he obviously was. Joseph insisted the strangers' stories be heard, and for once he was listened to.

No one spoke Shoshone, and so with his limited English Poker Joe asked Ellen to tell her story. She talked for a long time, occasionally taking a sip of water. Finally, after nearly an hour, she stopped. The chiefs looked at each other in silence for a moment. Finally Joseph spoke. "It seems as if these strangers have suffered as much as we have at the hands of the whites. My heart will not let me turn them aside or see them come to harm."

Toohoolhoolzote, who could see the way things were going, relented on his lust to kill Bear Paw. "Shoshone warrior," he said, "if we let you come with us, will you fight the white man alongside our warriors?"

"Yes," Bear Paw said. "To the death."

Toohoolhoolzote saw the opportunity to add a capable warrior to their numbers, and a very large one at that. "Then let them stay," he said to the others. "But the white woman must be willing to help us escape the soldiers."

Poker Joe looked at Ellen. "Will you do this?"

Ellen nodded. "I will."

It was agreed by all. The two new arrivals would stay.

THEY STRUGGLED ON SOUTH THROUGH the heat, tired, thirsty and hungry, and bereft of any purpose other than to stay alive one more day. They found a crossing point through an otherwise impassible ravine at which there was a shack whites had built as a freight station for supplies brought up the adjacent Corrine Road wagon trail. The road brought supplies north from the Union Pacific Railroad in Utah. Debilitated as they were, it took them nearly five hours to make the crossing.

WHEN THE NEZ PERCE CUT the telegraph wire at the crossing, panic erupted in the surrounding countryside. No one was sure of where the Indians were, or their intentions. Howard, who had pursued them from Fort Lapwai to the point of exhausting his soldiers and horses, bungled the chance to cut them off at the crossing site and ended up camped forty miles north. Pushing his worn-out men—tired to the point of falling out of their saddles—and mounts relentlessly, they managed to close within eighteen miles of the Indians. Here they could go no farther, even though Howard knew the Nez Perce were only a half-day ahead. Instead, he though he knew where the Nez Perce were headed. To this end, he sent forty men ahead to prepare an ambush at a spot he was sure the Indians would pass through. But, finding no one, and believing they were following orders, the men returned to camp before the Nez Perce arrived. Once again, it seemed Howard he had been outsmarted.

Nez Perce scouts detected their presence, and were puzzled by Howard's decision to make camp though he was only a half-day behind. Truly, this white soldier was beyond understanding. It was decided the warriors would try a nighttime raid with the purpose of capturing the soldiers' horses. They did indeed capture a number of animals, but it was too dark to see them clearly. The braves discovered upon returning to camp, to their disgust, that they had captured mules. The warriors were embarrassed, but the raid was not a complete loss, as Howard's men, now without their pack mules, were slowed still further. And the ease of the raid—captured mules or not—had once again shown them that Howard's troops were disorganized and poorly trained. With that sliver of respite, the Nez Perce set up camp near a high mountain lake. But high country nights were getting colder, the days shorter. Pursued and pursuer were both suffering as the weather turned against them.

Howard's troops were nearly at the end of their rope. Their clothes had long since seen better days; some soldiers did not even have winter coats, suffering through the cold nights in nothing more than their uniform jackets and pants. The miserable food was driving them crazy too. With the loss of the mules, they were more disheartened than ever.

As if things could not be worse, Howard's untrustworthy Bannock scouts continued to be just that. He knew they were butchering the old and sick Nez Perce they found left along the trail, and stealing horses when they could.

Out of a sense of growing desperation, Howard telegraphed General Sherman for more supplies. Sherman, stung by the continued derision heaped on him and on Howard's troops in the press for their failure to capture the Nez Perce, angrily dismissed Howard's request. He questioned Howard's commitment and capability, even suggesting he might want to turn over command of the pursuit to someone else. Howard would get no help from him, or anyone else in the western chain of command.

Eli Morrow, who had caught up with Howard three days' ride out from Fort Walla Walla, was suffering along with the rest. He was more fortunate than most in that, having been stationed at Ft. Walla Walla for a good length of time, he had acquired cold weather clothing, which he had had the foresight to bring. But he still had to share the same pork fat and hardtack biscuits the rest had to eat. The biscuits were so hard they were often soaked in water overnight to make them soft enough to fry.

He had begun to question the wisdom of this whole enterprise. Certainly these renegades had to be collared and held to account, but this—was it worth pursuing them if the troops died trying? He had heard the report about Gibbon's Big Hole Massacre, and it had shaken him profoundly. Chasing outlaw warriors was one thing, but running women and children into the ground was something he hadn't signed up for.

He went to Howard the morning after the pack mules were stolen. Eli saluted and got right to the point. "General Howard, I'm beginning to have doubts about the wisdom of this mission," he said. Women and children are being slaughtered. That was never something I wanted to be a part of. Some of our troops are wrapping rags around their feet because their shoes have disintegrated. If we continue much further without adequate winter clothing, we may start losing men to death or desertion. Wouldn't it be more prudent to abandon this chase until next spring? The Nez Perce can't hide for long, no matter where they go. We could find them where they've settled, and arrest the warriors. Let the women, the children, and the elderly live; they're not combatants. Must we pursue them until either they're all dead, or we are?"

Howard had listened to this in silence, his expression giving up nothing. He was still stung by Sherman's rebuke over the request for supplies. Finally he spoke. "Eli, I'm glad you've joined us. The men like you; you've given them a dose of leadership and purpose they badly need. I don't have to be told what bad shape they're in. I see it every day. But the last thing I need is to have *you* lose heart for this task. As you know, Sherman refused us any assistance. What you don't know is that he said, in so many words, that I'm a coward and a bungler, perhaps not capable to finish the job. He even suggested that I should turn over command to someone else. In that he was doing no more than repeating the opinion of the western press."

Howard turned away, looking out across the land lit by the dim morning sun. "Captain, secretly I am in accord with your concerns. I never wanted to come on this journey in the first place. But I have my orders." He turned back to Eli. "And orders, Eli, are something I have always followed. That's why I have this insignia on my uniform." He pointed to his general's stars. "Sherman is already dealing with bad press on this issue, as am I. He does respect the military skill of these Indians, but he won't allow the Cavalry to become a laughingstock by terminating the chase until next year, or giving other tribes false hope that they can defy us, temporary though that hope would certainly be. No, Eli, as much as I think this is a fool's errand, we will continue. Sherman has ordered me to pursue them to the death, and pursue them to the death I will. And so will you."

IN THE NEZ PERCE CAMP, as Ellen cared for Bear Paw and saw him slowly grow stronger, Ellen was still trying to lessen the hostility of the women. Once she regained a bit of strength, she pitched in to the women's work with a fervor. The throat-slashing gestures quickly faded, but there were still resentful looks at meal time. She was someone who shouldn't be there, and was taking precious food.

The Nez Perce, deeply fatigued, were not sufficiently rested by their short stay at the meadow they had camped at. Even the water and good grazing could not rejuvenate the horses. Nevertheless, they packed up and moved on, deeper into the bizarre and dangerous Yellowstone countryside, southward on a less-well known trail.

SUMMER WAS NOW DRAWING TO a close. An approaching winter was on the wind. Each day the trees shone with more yellow and gold, and the creeks were coated with a thin layer of ice in the morning. The people were weary in heart, mind, and body as they pushed on ever harder to reach Crow country. The children suffered constantly from the cold and could not be comforted. They had lost nearly 150 people since the flight began. There was not a day now that one of the elders could carry on no more, and asked to be left behind.

Desperate for an advantage over the soldiers they knew were relentlessly pursuing not far back, the Nez Perce decided to try a ruse. They would split into two groups. A contingent of warriors—there were little more than one hundred left now—would mill about along one route, dragging branches along to raise a large dust cloud they were certain would attract the soldiers and convince them the Indians had chosen that route. Joseph, overwhelmed with the suffering, spoke against the plan. He was by this point thinking about surrender, if only the horrible agony of his people would be over. But he did not carry the day; others felt that Crow country—and freedom—was near. Poker Joe led the rest across one trail while the warriors attracted attention on another. Poker Joe's group descended through narrow, rubble-strewn crevasses on hillsides so steep it was easier to slide than walk. Finally, bone-tired, with people and horses scraped raw and bloody, they emerged onto the valley floor.

Howard took the bait offered by the warriors, and sent men ahead to block the way. But he arrived to find he had chosen the wrong canyon. The Nez Perce were gone; they had outsmarted him again. Fuming, he turned to Eli, who was riding beside him. "I tell you, Eli, these Indians seem to have a knack for staying one step ahead of us. They seem to know what we're thinking. It's almost as if they had a white man along, guiding them." Unwilling to talk any longer, he turned his horse away.

Eli was left alone, observing the pass that had been blocked for nothing. Howard's words came back to him, and suddenly his thoughts froze. *It's almost as if they had a white man along, guiding them,* Howard had said. Heart suddenly racing, Eli dared to entertain another thought: *or a white woman.*

HAVING ONCE AGAIN GAINED BREATHING room from the pursuing soldiers, the Nez Perce debated their next move. Looking Glass had returned from a trip to meet the Crow, with tragic news. Like the earlier encounters with the Bannock, the Crow were afraid to take them in, having heard that whites were fearful that the Nez Perce planned to join with Sitting Bull to foment a great Indian war. *No,* they said, *if we take in our brothers now we may be killed as well.* The Nez Perce had traveled and struggled for weeks to reach sanctuary with their friends and allies. And once again, it was denied.

The news was devastating. There were no poles to make shelter from the coming winter, the horses were sick and injured, some people were ill and could go no farther, and now their last ally had turned against them. They found themselves in danger now not only from whites but Bannocks and Crows as well.

Meeting in council, they came to the conclusion that their only chance for survival lay to the north with Sitting Bull in the Old Woman Country.[12] The trip would be fraught with danger. They would be moving into Sioux country, and though there was a pact of peace with the Sioux, who knew if it would hold when so many others had turned against them?

Joseph said little. He knew that too many would not survive the

---

12   Canada; the reference is to Queen Victoria.

journey through the increasing cold. Many of the sick and elderly had already been left behind, waiting for death. Poker Joe, still in command, insisted the people must go, and quickly, even if it meant that some of them would die so that others might live.

And so, with little food, or clothing to protect themselves from the cold rain and snow, heartsick and riddled with injuries and crushed by fatigue, the people, with Ellen and Bear Paw, turned north toward the distant Old Woman Country.

*We have come to the point in the history of the country
that there is no place beyond population to which you can
remove the Indian, and the precise question is: Will you
exterminate him or will you fix an abiding place for him?*
—*Senator Lot M. Morrill to the U. S. Senate*

THE COUNTRY THE NEZ PERCE, plus Ellen and Bear Paw, were
passing through now was relatively flat, offering them little in the
way of cover or refuge should there be a battle. Worse, it was flanked
on both sides by high hills. As they continued north, it soon became
obvious that they were being watched. More and more, Indians were
seen riding through the trees on those hills, flanking their movement.
Some of the chiefs and warriors rode out to confront them. Surprisingly,
they turned out to be Crow, who professed they meant no harm. But the
Nez Perce knew better. Such accomplished horse thieves were they that
it was well-nigh impossible to stop them.

And to the Nez Perce, horses were life. As their horses went, so went
the people. Horses were their wealth and their future, their strength in
hard times. If there was any spark left in them, the loss of their prized
horses would surely put it out. Pursued by merciless soldiers, betrayed
by every tribe they encountered, there was nothing they could do as
the opportunistic Crow and Bannocks and others shadowing their
movement steadily pecked away at their once-magnificent herd. Each
horse that was taken was a wound, a cut that bled the People of their
shredded resolve. And they could not stop it.

THE ENDLESS FLIGHT CONTINUED NORTHWARD, passing through rolling hills across a barren landscape. Begun in the spring, it now extended into early winter. With each passing day, snow seemed to descend further down the flanks of the mountains visible in the distance. The weak sun provided no comfort on the infrequent occasions it appeared through gray clouds heavy with the threat of rain or sleet.

As she had with the Shoshone, Ellen soon won over the Nez Perce women with her hard work, her willingness to do whatever was needed. Her skinning and sewing skills surprised them, and she did what she could to comfort the children, who found her white skin and brown hair a distraction from their pain and sorrow. She badly wanted to be with Bear Paw, but since he was stronger now and could walk about and ride for short distances, his place during the day was with the warriors and not at her side, and she accepted that.

As she trudged along with the rest, often cold and hungry, she fell in with a young girl who looked about twelve. Through gestures and body language, they became friends, clearly glad for each other's company. One night after they had made camp, she led Ellen to Joseph himself, where Ellen learned she was Joseph's daughter, whose Nez Perce name translated to Noise of Running Feet.

Over the next several days, they quickly became close, and Ellen also found herself at the center of a large gaggle of children walking with them, curious about the white woman and how she came to be with them, and thankful for her attention.

In Joseph, she had found a man who projected calmness and warmth. From their first meeting on the trail days before, she had seen a gentleness in his brown eyes. She was deeply impressed with his steadiness and dedication to his duties as camp chief in the face of unrelenting agony. She had seen from a distance his compassion for the suffering of parentless children and the sick and elderly, and watched as he saw to it that they were as well cared for as possible under the circumstances. His composed demeanor spread to others around him as well.

The procession had divided into several groups, traveling separately but coming together into one at the end of the day. Smaller groups made hunting easier, and would mystify any soldiers that came upon them. But it also escalated the divisions that had been festering among them. Through it all, Joseph stood as a unifying influence, refusing to let the procession disintegrate into warring factions, as his steady spirit won new respect throughout the group. His earlier frequent pleas to return to their own country—impossible now—seemed wise indeed in the looking back. Joseph had quickly taken a liking to Ellen, and did not fail to put a gentle hand on her shoulder whenever they met. He could see that her heart was good, and was sure she would keep her end of the bargain to help them in their flight if she could.

A HUNDRED MILES BEHIND THEM, Howard's men struggled in pursuit. The horses were in such bad shape that the mounted cavalry was now walking with the infantry, leading their mounts behind them. Eli walked along with them, having the good fortune, unlike some of the rest, to still have boots and socks on his feet. Howard was one of the few still riding, and at one point Eli walked up close to the general's horse. He had been wanting to talk to Howard for several days, and was waiting for a good opportunity—and a little courage.

"General Howard, do you think we'll catch the hostiles before they reach Canada?" he began.

Howard spoke with eyes still ahead on the endless trail. "I'm not optimistic at this point, Captain."

Eli was nervous about broaching the next subject. "General, I know you're aware of how the men are suffering. They won't complain to you about the food and the bad water that's making them sick. But they do complain to me." Eli took a deep breath. "We've been out here for months, and most of the time it seems like we're chasing ghosts. We haven't had a sniff of the Nez Perce for days. For all we know, they may already have crossed the border. Some think it would be better to pursue the hostiles just to push them into Canada, rather than fight them again. Most of the troops just want to go home. They don't want to be out here when winter hits hard, and it will before long. Many of them just don't have the heart for this anymore. Some have even confided that they feel sorry for the Nez Perce." Eli held his breath waiting for Howard's reaction.

Howard smiled wryly. "They are not alone in that, Eli. Dispatches I have received recently tell me the country is now divided into two camps regarding this campaign. There is one side still lusting for blood, of course. But a great many Americans now favor the Nez Perce, and wish we would just let them escape into Canada." He turned to look at Eli. "Secretly, Eli, I don't want to fight them either. The courage of those people has moved me greatly. There has been far too much blood spilled on both sides along the way. I would rather see them simply leave the country, and have done with it." He looked ahead again. "But as I mentioned earlier, I swore to Sherman I would pursue them, and I intend to. But you may tell the men that before long those who wish to return home to their posts will be able to do so. Colonel Miles and his contingent are marching hard from Tongue River to intercept the Nez Perce somewhere ahead. I hear his troops are exhausted as well, but in just a little bit better shape than ours, which will allow our own troops to be relieved. As for what else we've discussed here, Eli, keep it to yourself."

Eli angled off into the crowd, leaving Howard in solitude.

The weary general looked ahead, and saw, as he had for days, only an empty landscape. "God, I hope they make it to Canada," he whispered.

IN ELLEN, ELI WAS GIVING his theoretical white advisor guiding the Nez Perce too much credit. She knew nothing about military strategy, and was consulted by the chiefs only when they thought it advantageous to know what the whites might do next. At such times they would call her into council, where she felt very much intimidated. Bear Paw was not allowed into the council circle so he stood nearby, hoping his presence would give her strength. She gave what advice she could, but too often it was just an educated guess, though she did not tell the chiefs that. These incidents began to dwindle as the Nez Perce became convinced the pursuit was weakening. Crow and Bannock raids on the horses had become slowly more infrequent. The rearguard scouts saw no evidence of soldier activity behind them. It seemed the procession was once again alone on the empty buffalo plains.

Even so, Poker Joe refused to slacken the pace.

THEY STAGGERED AT LAST TO the Missouri River. The whites called this country the Missouri Breaks. It was a chaotic welter of hills descending for miles down to the brown, silt-laden Missouri below. The Nez Perce were familiar with the area, and had established a favorite crossing place there. White travelers favored the place's shallow crossing as well, and when the procession finally made its way down to water's edge, they found a huge pile of supplies on the far bank, which had been brought upstream by riverboat. It was guarded by a few soldiers. There was also a heavily-laden wagon train laboriously moving up the slope away from the river, on the far side.

An advance group of warriors crossed the river and stationed themselves between the hunkered-down soldiers and the People. No battle was sought, and silence prevailed as everyone crossed. When all had made it across, the chiefs went forward to ask the soldiers for food from the towering cache. Surely a small amount could be spared. But the soldiers refused, saying it was not theirs to give. The Nez Perce displayed gold and silver, saying they would pay. Even that did not sway the soldiers beyond a grudging gift of a bag of hardtack and one of bacon.

The warriors, upon seeing the niggardly gift, were incensed. This would not feed 650 hungry people. So they strategically moved into a position that would cut the soldiers off from the cache and allow the people to safely take what they wanted. And they did. After everyone was satisfied, the warriors set fire to the remainder. Fortunately no one was killed.

The Nez Perce moved on up the far slope the next day at first light. In early afternoon, they came across the wagon train they had seen ascending the hill on the far side of the river. Surrounded by hundreds of Indians whose intent they could not be sure of, the drivers of the thirteen wagons were extremely nervous.

Poker Joe, seeking to avoid violence, talked to them in a civil manner. He made up a tale that his scouts had seen a large contingent of Sioux warriors not far away, and it would be better for the wagon drivers to hide themselves before the Sioux arrived and killed them all. Fearing for their lives over Poker Joe's phantom Sioux, the drivers heeded this advice and went off to hide nearby for the night. In the morning, they returned to find the Nez Perce warriors stripping for battle, and the whole group packing for departure. Convinced the Nez Perce meant to kill them, they fled again. The warriors set the wagons on fire.

But it was not the wagon drivers that aroused the warriors to prepare for battle. The rear scouts had seen a new contingent of soldiers making its way up from the Missouri River. They had held them off with rifle fire from the heights while the People once again put distance between themselves and these soldiers, whoever they were.

Even with this close call, many had had enough of Poker Joe's rapid pace, which he did not favor slowing, knowing the white man as he did. After lengthy and thoughtful discussion in council, the lead was given back to Looking Glass. Poker Joe had relented, but continued to insist disaster was on the wind, and that they would all be caught and killed.

With Looking Glass once again setting a slower pace, the people moved out into broad plains. The weather was constantly against them, as they slogged on, often through strong winds and heavy rain. Most of the time they were wet, and their clothes now ragged and dirty. They were forced to make camp at night with even their meager shelter coverings wet. Moccasins and gloves, for those who had them, could not be dried, forcing them to start the trail each morning with wet, cold feet and frigid hands. There was no relief.

They moved on northward and steadily upward to the buffalo plains. Despite their weariness and the constant chill of winter in their faces, they had reason to feel confident, with just a shred of optimism. The Old Woman Country was surely only a few days ahead. The land they were passing through, difficult as it was, was familiar to their buffalo scouts, and hunting began to improve. General Howard was believed to be far away, struggling through the breaks, and the People had adequate camping supplies and foodstuffs taken from the cache at the river.

What they did not know as they drew ever closer to sanctuary was the presence of an unknown army, led by Colonel Nelson Miles, bearing down on them from the east.

MILES' MEN WERE FARING LITTLE better than the Nez Perce. They too were suffering from the wet, cold weather. Their tents were far behind in supply wagons still struggling through the breaks. There was no wood to build a fire, only wet buffalo dung they had no skill in using, preventing the preparation of any hot food. They marched for hours with wet boots. Despite all this, Miles drove them with unrelenting fervor, sometimes on as little as three hours' sleep per night. The glory that would come to him with the capture of "Joseph's Indians" would be worth it, he thought.

ELLEN AND BEAR PAW SUFFERED along with the rest. He came to her each night when they made camp, wrapping her in a cloak he had obtained from the freight cache they had burned at the Missouri River.

She accepted gratefully and hugged him tightly, putting her head against his chest.

"I am sad, Ellen," he said, looking down into her golden-brown eyes. "This is no kind of life for a Shoshone bride. I am ashamed that I have brought you to this."

She attempted to smile at him, but it came out only as a tight-lipped grimace. "Husband, we are taken along this path by forces bigger than we. I pray daily this path has a purpose. I pray that I may yet be of use in helping these people—and yours. But I am ready to die. If it comes, let it be in your arms; I would wish for no other end. If the soldiers catch us, fight like the warrior I know you are. But if we are to die, come to me and hold me tight as we are cut down. I love you."

"If the end is upon us, I will come to you, Ellen. If we die together, I will have one last happiness." He stroked her hair and smiled down at her. "You are my bride forever; I will love you in this world—and the next."

Five days past the time they had looted the wagon train, the Nez Perce could see in the distance the low hills known to them as the Wolf's Paw. Just beyond that they could see the line of mountains they knew marked the border of the United States. And beyond that was Canada—and freedom.

THEY CAME TO A PLACE well-known to buffalo hunters as the Place of the Manure Fires. It was a large depression on the plains. Surrounded on three sides by bluffs, it provided shelter from the constant wind. There was good water available and plentiful buffalo chips for cooking fuel. Indeed, advance scouts had killed several buffalo here and left them for the people when they arrived. There was also good grazing for the horses. The weary people were desperately in need of such a place, and Looking Glass announced they would camp here for the night to recuperate.

Not all were happy with this decision. The weather worsened as they set up camp, and a pelting rain turned to snow, falling until there was several inches on the ground. The moisture was making the buffalo dung too wet to build a cooking fire with. More worrisome to the warriors was the fact that the surrounding bluffs made a perfect place for soldiers to fire down on the encampment, trapping the Nez Perce in place. They had willingly abandoned the high ground.

Most of the people no longer worried about Howard, convinced he had given up. But scouts had seen a group of dots far to the east. It was too far away to determine if they were soldiers, Indians, or large animals. But their presence was unsettling, and angry debate erupted among the chiefs about the wisdom of pausing with Canada so near. Poker Joe was still supported by some, and others still doubted Looking Glass's wisdom. The final decision went to Looking Glass, who was supported by Joseph, characteristically concerned with the women, children, and the sick. They would stay the night.

Miles' men were at this point but fifteen miles away, camped and thoroughly miserable and just as thoroughly wet, being still without their supply wagons. Miles woke them at 2 a.m. and had them on the move by 4:30 a.m. without a warm breakfast. The ground was a muddy slop of icy mud, as a change in the wind had melted much of the snow.

They had had reports the night before that their Cheyenne scouts had located the fleeing tribe, just as they had doubted whether they would ever see the enemy again. This fresh hope was tempered by the knowledge that they were marching dangerously close to Sitting Bull and his two thousand Sioux warriors, whom they devoutly did not want to encounter. Still, they quickened their pace.

A chill morning drifted slowly into the Nez Perce camp. Tantalizing smells of coffee and roasting buffalo meat drifted through the air. There were already signs of activity in preparation for moving. The packing was going smoothly, and the spirits of the people were high in anticipation of one final push to freedom.

But unexpectedly a strange mournful shouting was heard. It was Wottolen, the visionary who had foreseen in dreams the soldier attacks at the Big Hole and the Clearwater during the flight. He was ignored then, even though his tragic foreboding had proved correct. Now he was shouting that his vision in the night told him death was imminent for all, the skies would soon be filled with the smoke of battle, the creek red with the blood of the Nez Perce.

Looking Glass once again refused to give in to such a dire warning. He shouted for the people to build fires, cook breakfast, let the children eat. Afterward, they would move on. But just as he was doing so, two scouts came galloping into camp. They had just seen buffalo stampeding not far away. "Soldiers are coming!" they shouted.

Immediately some of the people gathered up their camp goods and hit the trail northward. Others refused to be rushed, uncertain of what to do. The camp was quickly descending into bedlam. It erupted into full-scale pandemonium when another scout from the south came streaking into camp. He paused on one of the hilltops and fired his rifle while he rode in a tight circle shaking his blanket. There was no confusion about this sign. An attack was at hand.

Like the Battle at Big Hole during the flight, the people were confused as to who these soldiers were and where they had come from. But there was no time to think about it. Those who were fortunate enough to have horses in camp grabbed what they could, shouted for their children to come to them, and headed north up the gullies. Joseph shouted for the herd to be safeguarded. Without the horses, the people would be defenseless in this open country.

Over the screaming chaos, a sound like thunder began to fill the air. Suddenly the ground itself was shaking. Puzzled, Joseph looked around just in time to see a giant wave of blue-coated soldiers erupt into view around the base of the southern bluff, headed for the horse herd. Joseph ran back toward the herd. He found Noise of Running Feet, whom he had sent a short while before to bring his family's horses back across the creek to camp. She was panic-stricken and frozen as chaos swirled around her. Horses reared in confusion and fear as Cheyenne warriors allied for profit with the Cavalry and painted for war, and soldiers firing their guns, charged into the herd, slapping at the horses, trying to scatter them in all directions. Joseph ran up to his daughter and thrust a bridle rope into her hands. Collaring the first horse he could, he threw her on its back and slapped its rump. "Go!" he shouted. "To the Old Woman Country!"

Joseph watched her speed away and again became aware of the hell around him. The air was heavy with the screams of terrified infants and their mothers. Acrid, eye-stinging gun smoke drifted over the battle. Flashes from the southern bluff top revealed rifle fire coming down on them. He had to get back to his wife and infant daughter. He jumped on his own horse and streaked across the camp to the creek as bullets cut through the air all around him, some even cutting through his clothing and searing his flesh in a glancing blow. His horse was hit, but he was not, and miraculously made it to the creek. His wife handed him his rifle and exhorted him to join the fight, then retreated to her shelter with their daughter screaming in fright.

In the maelstrom of battle, Bear Paw hesitated for a brief second. He looked at Ellen, fear for her life written on his features. She ran at him and leapt against his body, arms around his neck. Then she pulled back and grabbed his shirt. "Go!" she pleaded. "Join the warriors! They need you. Your duty is to them now." She kissed him hard and deep, pouring her love into him in a desperate flash of passion. "Go now! Fight for your life, for *our* lives. If all is lost, come to me; I will be waiting."

He nodded, face alive with the fury of combat, then jumped on his horse and galloped away.

THE CARNAGE LASTED NOT QUITE an hour. Battle smoke hung over a camp littered with debris: camp supplies, dolls, pots and pans, all strewn about in chaos. The soldiers had been forced back, but they held the high ground. The precious horses were mostly gone, scattered by the soldiers and the Cheyenne. Some of the people had gotten away toward the north and freedom; the rest now were stuck to the earth of the campsite as surely as a butterfly specimen fixed to a display board.

Like the rest of the women and children, Ellen had retreated to a deep pocket in the hillside on the north end of the bowl-shaped campsite. Periodically a hail of bullets would rain down on the camp from one of the bluff tops, and small groups of soldiers would try to storm the camp. The warriors shot most of them, and none made it into the gathering of survivors. Joseph and some others frantically threw up a barrier of saddles and anything else they could hide behind for defense.

Darkness fell, and the surviving warriors—including Bear Paw— filtered back into camp, some wounded, all of them suffering from the cold, as they had hurriedly stripped for battle when the attack began. Bear Paw ran to Ellen, taking her gently to the ground and wrapping their sleeping furs around them. It was only then that she saw that he had suffered a cut in his side from a grazing bullet. She wrapped it as well as she could with strips of cloth from a shawl she had taken from one of the dead women.

Some of the warriors had retrieved what supplies they could from the creek side campsite and brought them in. Women were hurriedly hacking and scraping at the frozen earth with knives and skillets to create firing pits for the warriors. Ellen joined the other women, walking out onto the battlefield to tend to the injured and retrieve whatever the warriors may have missed from the dead soldiers.

They could hear a badly injured soldier crying out for water. In a characteristic display of compassion, the Nez Perce brought him water and placed a blanket under his head.

When all were once again together, sharing what little food they had left, they received an accounting of the casualties of the day. The news could not have been worse, and only added to the paralysis they were all feeling. Ollokot, Joseph's younger brother, was dead. So too were Toohoolhoolzote, Pile of Clouds, Lone Bird, and Poker Joe. There was still no information on the fate of those who had managed to flee to the north, no news of Noise of Running Feet, nor of the hunters and women who had left camp in the early morning to hunt, before the attack. And so the shocked survivors, numb and directionless, waited out the night, certain that the dawn would bring a new attack.

The soldiers that had attacked them were still a mystery. The winter coats and boots they were wearing made it certain they were not Howard's ill-supplied forces. But whose then? Like the troops at Big Hole, they seemed to have come from nowhere.

Morning revealed the hopelessness of their position. The wounded soldier they had given water and comfort to the night before lay dead under several inches of new snow. Soldiers looked down from the bluffs that surrounded them on three sides. The view out to where their treasured herd had been showed that most of the horses, the heart of their tribe, were gone. There were few of the People left alive to fight. Most of who *were* left were women, children, and the elderly.

In council, Joseph advised surrender. He saw no way to keep fighting, and the People could not flee now. But there was a slim hope, some countered. Several riders had been dispatched during the night to slip through the enemy lines and try to reach Sitting Bull. His large force would certainly turn the tide of battle. No one knew if they had succeeded. But on this slender thread of desperate hope, the prevailing opinion was that they should hold their ground, little protection though it gave. And so they waited, huddled on the frozen ground, their food dwindling, as were their spirits.

UP ON THE SURROUNDING BLUFF tops, Colonel Miles fared little better. He had lost seventy men, which might have been acceptable if they had won, but all they had accomplished was to put the Nez Perce under siege. No one else had done this, to be sure, but it was not something certain to win him glory—or a promotion. He, as well as his troops, feared the possible arrival of Sitting Bull and his two thousand merciless warriors. What they did to injured white troops was known all too well from reports of the Little Big Horn battlefield. The pretentious posturing of days before about avenging that battle were gone now. Now they had spent the frigid night on the ground. Too many of them, especially the injured, did not make it to sunrise.

And so the stalemate went on into the day. There had been sporadic rifle fire during the night and it continued now. Miles' troops were badly frightened when they saw how incredibly accurate the Nez Perce warriors were with their rifles. Even the briefest exposure from cover could result in a bullet in the head. On the other side of the battle lines, Looking Glass was killed in this way when he stood up to see if any relief was approaching from the north.

Bear Paw, exhausted and sore from the bullet that had grazed his ribs, was trying to sleep when he was shaken awake by one of the women. She pointed urgently outward. He looked, and saw a sight that chilled him to the bone.

Ellen was walking out into the open with a white flag on a stick.

He stumbled to his feet, fighting stiffness, and sprinted after her. Just before he reached her, he heard the crack of a rifle shot, and saw a round dig into the earth near her feet. He tackled her and carried her back to camp as quickly as he could.

"What are you doing?" he said, voice raspy with fatigue.

Ellen looked down as if she had shamed him. "I—I thought that maybe I could make peace with the soldiers, that maybe they would listen to me if I tell them how we are suffering, since they are of my people."

Bear Paw shook his head. "No, I forbid it. They are beyond that now.

You would be shot, or if they captured you, hung as a traitor. They are not your people anymore. You must remember that you are Shoshone now. You must not go."

Ellen looked up at his battle-worn features. "You are right, my husband. They are no longer my people. I am sorry. It shall be as you say."

THE WEATHER WORSENED. MILES KNEW his troops did not have the resolve or the numbers for another attack. So he ordered a newly-arrived Hotchkiss gun—similar to a howitzer—to be put into play. Because of its mounting, all it could do in this situation was lob shells into the air over the Nez Perce. It caused no physical damage, but the wear on the nerves of those below was debilitating.

Miles eventually sent word to the Nez Perce that he would like to meet with Joseph. Some of the People were against this plan, and mystified about why he had chosen Joseph. He was not a war chief. But after considerable discussion, it was agreed that Joseph would go.

They met on a rise halfway between the battle lines. Joseph kept his rifle with him. He shook hands with Miles, and then walked with him up the hill. As they did, people from both camps warily moved out onto the field of battle to brush away the snow from the wounded and the dead, and drag them back to camp.

More snow continued falling, wet and heavy. Out on the battlefield, it covered the corpses of men and animals alike, transforming them into fantastical shapes on the barren ground. Joseph was held prisoner for a day in a soldier tent, then finally exchanged for a junior Cavalry officer who had foolishly entered the Nez Perce camp and found himself hostage.

THE DIVISION BETWEEN WHITE BIRD and Joseph grew stronger as the people grew more desperate. White Bird still favored a run for Canada; Joseph still favored surrender. He could not bear to see the People, whose well-being he had been in charge of for so long, face what he felt was annihilation.

The decision was made. They would wait one more day for Sitting Bull.

That day went by in agonizing slowness. The Hotchkiss gun had been moved to where it had a direct line of fire into the camp. Though some shells continued to explode overhead with terrifying effect, others now periodically landed right in the camp, killing indiscriminately whomever had the misfortune to be at the spot. Women, children, the elderly—it did not matter to the white soldiers.

The next day dawned with no sign of Sitting Bull and his warriors. But scouts spotted the arrival of Howard and a few of his officers. The rest of his beat-up troops could not be far behind.

When he arrived, Howard was astonished at the pitiful remnant of the mighty group he had been chasing for months. So many were no longer there. Miles' fear that he would be robbed of the capture was put aside as Howard graciously agreed to see that he and his men got credit. This decision was met with considerable anger by his troops, who had endured hell on the trail for so long, and had in fact chased the Nez Perce to this spot so Miles could capture them so easily. But Howard's decision did not change.

Howard sent two treaty Nez Perce he had brought along down toward the camp as emissaries. Their presence pleading for surrender provoked fierce debate. Some of the warriors favored fighting on; Joseph clearly did not. After several hours and back and forth trips between camps by the emissaries, Joseph carried the day. He called the two treaty Nez Perce emissaries to him and addressed them in a formal manner:

"Tell General Howard that I know his heart. What he told me before, I have in my heart. I am tired of fighting. Our chiefs are killed. Looking Glass is dead. Toohoolhoolzote is dead. The old men are all dead. It is cold and we have no blankets. The little children are freezing to death. My people, some of them, have run away to the hills and have no blankets, no food; no one knows where they are—perhaps freezing to death. I want to have time to look for my children and see how many of them I can find. Maybe I shall find them among the dead."

Then, as some of his people behind him prayed to their *wayakin* for deliverance, as others sang their death songs, as the children who could not be comforted cried from the hunger and cold, he turned to the other remaining chiefs, White Bird, Yellow Bull, and Husis Kute. "Hear me, my chiefs. I am tired. My heart is sick and sad. From where the sun now stands, I will fight no more forever."

And finally, it was over. It was over after a journey of fifteen hundred miles that had begun in the spring and ended in the winter. It was over after a trail that brought unimaginable suffering to Joseph's people, a journey on which scores of the wounded and elderly could run no more, and were left behind to die. Sitting Bull had not come. Every friend and ally they had counted on had turned against them. It was evident now that they had been alone on this flight from the start.

Most of the warriors lay dead. The band's greatest asset, their horses, was largely gone. Now the remaining people were wet and freezing in the snow, with too many of their children dead or terrified and hungry, and most of the adults nearly hysterical with grief and fear, their will to fight vanished. It was over.

White Bird protested, still favoring making a break for it to try to fight their way out. *Better to die like a wolf than a sheep,* he spat. But it was too late.

Joseph's memorized words were delivered to Howard and Miles by the emissaries, and written down verbatim by a Lieutenant Wood, recorded for future generations to hear.

Miles, Howard and Joseph met on neutral ground on a buffalo robe spread out between the camps. Miles made assurances to Joseph's demands that all the Nez Perce were welcome to as much food as they needed, and that the Nez Perce would be allowed to return to the reservation that had been prepared for them, and that they would not be punished for crimes of the past. Joseph did not know the latter two promises by Miles were not his to make. But after lengthy discussion, all stood and shook hands.

Not long after, Joseph rode up out of the camp to the bluff top and surrendered his weapon to Miles. Seeing this, most of the remaining people began coming forth from their pits and gullies on the freezing ground. The morning winter mists drifted across the battlefield as the surviving Nez Perce wearily climbed the hill to the army encampment. They were a pitiful sight—dirty, with ragged clothes, many wounded. Some were blind and unable to walk without guidance; many were of advanced years who needed to be supported as they struggled up the hill. Children came, shoeless and mute with fatigue and fear.

The soldiers stood silently watching them come. This was their victory, this was the glory they had sought for so long. Eli could barely stand to look at the pitiful remnants of what had been a proud, prosperous people only months before. After a few minutes, he turned and walked away in shame. He had become part of an unspeakable tragedy that he could not escape, could not deny that he had played a part in bringing it to pass.

HOWARD'S SUPPLY WAGONS HAD FINALLY caught up, and there were tents, winter clothing and boots for the soldiers, as well as plentiful food. At another time they might have been dancing in glee over the fresh supplies, but what they had brought about sobered them all. It seemed now like a pyrrhic victory. The ragged, weeping women, the frightened children, the humbled but still proud warriors—all seemed as if awaiting death—overwhelmed any thought of boasting or pride about what they had done. Particularly shamed were the troops among them that had long ago begun to sympathize with the Indians, and wished themselves somewhere else.

ELI RETREATED TO HIS FRIGID tent, overwhelmed with sorrow, and for the first time looked down at his uniform with shame, fighting the urge to rip it off.. Not wanting to step outside, he finally did upon hearing a voice hail him. Pushing the tent flap aside, he buttoned the top button on his winter coat as he stepped out.

There was a young sergeant waiting for him. He saluted upon sight of Eli. "Captain Morrow?"

Eli grimaced as duty presented itself "Yes, sergeant?"

"Sir, General Howard wishes me to inform you that the pris—the hostiles have all been rounded up."

"Do they look at all hostile to you, sergeant?"

The young soldier turned a little red. "No sir, not at all. The doc is tending to those with injuries over at the surgical tent. He's working through them as fast as he can. General Howard would like you to assist in getting the wounded to the tent."

Eli grimaced. "Very well. Show me the way."

The sergeant didn't move. "Sir, there's one more thing I thought you should know. There's a white woman with 'em."

Eli's heart started to pound in his chest. *No, it couldn't be. Not here. Not now.* He fought for calm. "Did you get a name, sergeant?"

The sergeant looked apologetic. "No sir, that's just it. She won't talk to us. She just sits and stares at the ground, and if she speaks at all, mumbles some Indian lingo. One of the Cheyenne scouts says it sounds like Shoshone."

Eli sighed. "Lead me to her, sergeant."

"Yes sir, right this way." He set off and Eli fell in beside him. "She's up there on that rise, sir. You can see her from here."

A short distance away, Eli could see a small cloaked figure seated on a rock.

"I'd be real careful with this one, sir," the sergeant continued. "She tried to stab Private Collins."

"*What?*"

"Yes sir, she did. She must have found a knife on the ground. None of us knew she had it. Private Collins put a hand on her shoulder to move her along, and she whirled and stuck him in the chest with the knife. It was his heavy winter coat that kept it from penetrating. That, and the fact there wasn't much force behind it. I think she favors her right shoulder, sir. She might be injured."

Eli's heart sank. *Tried to stab one of the soldiers? It wouldn't be her.*

They approached the woman from behind. "Leave us, sergeant," Eli said.

"Yes sir." The sergeant saluted and walked off.

Eli approached slowly. The woman remained motionless, head down. He walked around to one side. Her face was hidden by her buffalo robe cloak, which she drew around her tightly with white-skinned hands. Her posture made her look very small and frail. He approached closer, to where she could certainly see his cavalry trousers in her field of vision. Still, she did not move.

He reached out slowly, carefully, and pulled her cloak aside so he could see her face, thinking as he did that this sullen, uncooperative woman, this woman who spoke only some strange Indian tongue, who had tried to stab one of his troops, could not possibly be the bubbly sixteen-year old he had proposed to less than two years before.

But she was.

Eli felt like his heart had suddenly stopped. He had memorized every line of her face over the past months, every freckle, every tiny feature that had made her Ellen, and there was no doubt. He began to shake, tried to speak, but his throat seemed paralyzed. Still she would not look at him. With trembling hands, he withdrew the protective tin containing Ellen's photo from his inner jacket pocket. Then he took out the photo and slowly placed it on her lap.

Ellen remained frozen for long seconds, fingering the picture. Then she looked up at him briefly, eyes wide. Her head slowly sank to her chest and she broke into heavy sobs, her whole body shaking.

Eli let her cry, afraid to touch her. How could this be? How could so much have happened in less than two years? What had become of the girl who had answered his ad seeking a bride?

Ellen slowly raised her tear-stained face to him, still crying.

"Why are you crying?" he said softly, finally finding his voice.

"Because it is too late," she sobbed. "Oh, I am so sorry." She could barely speak as she looked away. "Too late, too late."

The bottom had dropped out of Eli's world. He had never felt such a loss. Nearly speechless, numb and stiff, he slowly bent to one knee to be level with her face. She was still crying, her face turned slightly away as if ashamed to look at him. "I never gave up hope that you were alive," he whispered, voice raspy with emotion. "I went to Elko to look for you, I was in agony to know whether you were alive or dead. I never forgot about you, or put away my desire that you would be my bride. I searched for you for months every chance I had, spread the word to others and set them to the task. And now I find out that I've been following you for weeks." He straightened up, fighting for composure. "I refuse to accept that it's too late for us." He paused for a long moment, gathering himself. Then he knew what he wanted to say, *had* to say. "We will see what the coming days offer now that you're back in the white world."

Ellen finally got hold of herself and stood up, briefly looking at him straight on for the first time, then turned away. "I am Shoshone," she whispered.

Eli's head sank, feeling like a knife had been plunged into his gut. *Could she be right? Is it too late?* With a heavy sigh, fighting for control, he looked at her. "Is there anything I can do for you now?"

"Yes, Captain Morrow," Ellen said softly. "Restore my husband to me."

Eli suddenly did not have the strength to stand as he sank to the cold ground and lowered his head between his knees. Shock upon shock, beyond all possibility. Ellen had put him into some kind of frozen hell. He sat for a minute, then slowly found the strength to stand. *If I can be of aid to her,* he thought, *she might yet be turned around.* "Yes, I will see to it."

"Very well," she said softly. "Now, I would be pleased if you would help me find him. He is injured."

Following his lead, Ellen walked a few paces away from him as Eli strode across the encampment to the area set up for treatment of the wounded. They were almost there when he realized Ellen had stopped. He turned to see her staring down at the frozen battlefield below, littered with the corpses of humans and animals, where the desperate Nez Perce, where she and Bear Paw, had fought so hard just to stay alive.

He came up beside her, not knowing what to say now to this strange woman who was once his mail-order bride.

She was seemingly lost in thought. Finally, she spoke, still staring at the battlefield below. "Captain Morrow," she said, barely audible, "were you part of this?"

Eli could say nothing, not wanting to speak the truth he could not deny.

She suddenly whirled, face contorted with rage, and pounded her fists into his chest. "*Were you part of this?*" she screamed.

Eli could barely recognize her. She had become like an angry animal, inhuman, alien. "God help me," he said. "I was."

I think you had better put the Indians on wheels,
and you can run them about whenever you wish.

—*Sioux chief*

A DAZED AND SADDENED ELI LED Ellen slowly to the medical tent. It was larger than most of the others.

Ellen looked around, making a slow circle of the tent and looking down the line of Nez Perce waiting for treatment.

"Do you see him?" Eli asked.

"No," she said dejectedly.

"Maybe you missed him. There's quite a lineup here."

"No," she said, turning to him. "You cannot miss him. Trust me in this."

"Could be he's inside the tent," Eli replied. "Come, we'll take a look." He stepped forward and pulled back the tent flap.

The interior of the medical tent had warmed considerably from the weak winter sun, making the temperature tolerable inside. Eli held the tent flap for Ellen. She saw four cots, all with occupants. On one of the back cots was Bear Paw. "There," she pointed, enormously relieved. "That is my husband." Eli's gaze followed her pointing finger as she moved toward the cot. He could see why she had said "*you cannot miss him*". He was looking at one of the biggest Indians he had ever seen. He was so tall that his feet stuck out over the end of the cot.

At sight of Ellen Bear Paw bolted upright and got to his feet, glaring at Eli, who had stepped up close behind her.

Eli was tall and robust himself, and had not shirked from close combat during his cavalry career, but he involuntarily backed up a step under the ferocious gaze of the Shoshone warrior.

Ellen jumped at Bear Paw, pressing her hands hard against his chest. "Do not, husband," she pleaded as Bear Paw seemed about to move toward Eli. "He is a friend." When she was sure he would stand fast, she turned to Eli. "Captain Morrow, this is my husband, Bear Paw." She turned back to him. "Has your wound been treated?" she said.

"Yes, it has been cleaned and wrapped. I will be healed." He scowled murderously at Eli. "Who is this white soldier, and why is he standing close to you?"

Ellen took a deep breath and let it out. "I must tell you sooner or later. This is the man I was promised to marry, before I came to you."

Bear Paw's eyes widened in shock. "Can this be true? You were promised to a long knife soldier?"

"Yes," Ellen said softly, looking down. "Please do not think ill of me."

Bear Paw seemed to deflate slightly. "Did you plan to meet him here?" he said gruffly.

"No," Ellen said quickly, shaking her head. She could feel his tenseness. "His presence here was a great shock to me. You must believe me in this." For the first time in longer than she could remember, she couldn't read his expression.

He gazed at her for long moments, his big hands on her arms. Then his shoulders slumped. "Will you go with him now?" he said, a deep sadness settling on his face. "Is our marriage at an end?"

Ellen leaned against him, wrapping her arms around him tightly and pressing her head to his chest. "No, never, my husband," she said fiercely. "I never want to be apart from you! I am your bride always. Always!" She pulled back and stretched as far upward as she could to kiss him.

Eli watched in private agony, almost unable to look, as they conversed in a strange language.

Ellen separated from Bear Paw after long uncomfortable moments, murmuring something to him as she did so. Then she turned to Eli. "I owe you an explanation," she said.

"You do owe me that much," Eli said, voice roiled with emotion. "Can we talk in private?"

She turned to Bear Paw and said something. He glared at Eli once again, but then nodded his assent.

Bear Paw sat back down on the cot as Ellen and Eli went out into the cold air. She walked a few paces away from the tent, Eli beside her.

Suddenly he could keep silent no longer. "That brave in there is your husband? *I* was to be your husband!"

Ellen choked back a sob, tears suddenly streaking her face. She didn't speak for long moments, looking out across the wintry landscape. Finally, she began. What she told him then was a tale he would not have believed if it had come from anyone else.

"The men said you favor your right shoulder," Eli interrupted after several minutes. "Was it injured?"

"Yes," Ellen said testily. "I was shot."

"By an Indian?"

She turned to look at him. "By a white man."

After that, Eli didn't interrupt.

When she was done after what seemed a long time, he had no response at first. Then he looked away into the distance. "Do you love him?" he said quietly.

"Yes. Very much. He—" She stopped and broke into sobs again, hand covering her mouth. "Oh Captain Morrow, I am so very sorry!" she gasped. "You have done nothing to merit this. You deserve so much better. Perhaps I am not the woman you hoped I would be." She couldn't look at him. "You must be very disappointed." Then she turned back to him, cheeks wet with tears. "Please, if you can, find it in your heart to forgive me someday."

Eli fought an overwhelming urge to embrace her, crush her against him, tell her that he loved her still. Standing fast was one of the hardest things he had ever done. "Ellen I—I cannot fathom what you went through. It's amazing you're still alive." He paused for a moment, then went on. "You ask if I'm disappointed in you. Ellen, I have more admiration and respect for you than ever, now that I know more about you. Disappointed? No, never." He fell silent, wanting to say so much more, but convinced it was useless.

"What will happen to us now?" she said.

Eli shook his head. "I'm not sure. Colonel Miles has sentiments that may not be honored by General Sherman. And it will be Sherman who calls the shots."

"Bear Paw and I have traveled, and struggled, and fought alongside the Nez Perce for weeks. They are our brothers and sisters. It breaks my heart to see what they have endured—and are yet to endure. If I thought I could change anything—" She was silent for a moment. "But our fate is not intertwined with theirs. We are Shoshone. Bear Paw is well now, and for some time he has talked about returning to his village—what *was* his village—to find the scattered remnants of his tribe, if he can. Will we be allowed to go?"

Eli frowned. "There may be trouble. Even though you're not Nez Perce, your presence with them at this final battle will probably mark you as combatants. To most white men an Indian is an Indian, regardless of tribal affiliation. Some here will lump you together with the Nez Perce."

Ellen moved a step closer to him. "I have no right to ask this, but I must. Can you help us?"

Eli looked into her eyes, trying to convey the truth of his compassion, his affection, at the same time wrestling with his raging need to tear Ellen away from this Indian she called her husband. He sighed. "I will do what I can. For now, I ask only one thing in return."

"What is it?" Ellen asked, apprehension clearly in her voice.

"That you would please call me Eli."

She gave him just the smallest of smiles. "It shall be so," she said, again using that phrasing he had heard from her that a white person would not likely use.

Unexpectedly she moved forward and put her arms firmly around him. "I am so sorry," she murmured into his chest. "I cannot say it enough. You are such a good man. May God give me the chance to somehow set this right some day." She pulled back. "I would ask two more things, if you will grant them to me. Can you get word to Nettie and Liza that I am alive?"

Eli nodded. "Yes, I can do that. When I went to Elko to search for you, we met briefly. We exchanged addresses, and promised to notify the other if either of us learned you were alive. They have settled in Portland. But what will I tell them about your return to them?"

"Please tell them that I am well, and that I love them and Clarence very much. And that I will see them when I feel the time is right."

"They will find this all very hard to understand." *As do I*, he thought.

Ellen smiled wryly. "Yes, I know. I do not mean to cause them more pain, but there are some things I must do first." She paused. "For now, please send my love." She looked down, seeming embarrassed to ask him for so much. "There is one other thing." She opened her cloak, and for the first time Eli could see that she had a leather case hanging by a strap from one shoulder. The case and the strap were worn and battered, the strap on the verge of falling apart. She lifted the strap off her shoulder and held the case out to him. "This diary means so much to me. I have carried it for hundreds of miles. If I am fortunate enough to have daughters some day, it will be my gift to them. Would you please keep it safe for a while? I fear it may not survive much longer. Someday I will come for it."

It was those last words that sealed the bargain for Eli as he accepted the case. *I will see her again*, he thought, pulse quickening. *She will come for the diary*. "Yes, I will keep it safe," he said, smiling ever so slightly at her as he took the leather case. "You may be sure of that. When you come for it, it will be there."

They talked for a while longer, then parted.

ELI WASTED NO TIME IN going to Colonel Miles to discuss the fate of Ellen and Bear Paw. Now as he stood at ease in Miles' tent, he fought to remain calm. For the first time, he might have to lie to a superior officer.

"What can I do for you, Captain?" Miles asked as he looked over papers at a makeshift desk fashioned from a sheet of tin resting on an empty cot.

Eli took a deep breath and began. "Sir, I wish to know if you have made a decision on the fate of the white woman and the Shoshone Indian she is with. They are clearly not Nez Perce and thus not involved with the incidents back at the Lapwai. I would think that perhaps they could be allowed to return home."

Miles sat back in his camp chair and regarded Eli closely. "Well, yes, they're not Nez Perce. Joseph has told me as much. But the woman appears to have been among the Indians for some time. And she shows no inclination to act like a white woman again. So it's hard to separate her from the combatants. There's no reason to believe she was not involved in the resistance we encountered. And her companion was clearly seen engaged in firing on the troops. At this point they both must be regarded as hostiles. And that means they'll undoubtedly have to be taken to Fort Keogh along with the rest. Perhaps there we can make a better decision as to their fate."

Eli's heart sank, though he had tried to prepare himself for such bad news. He desperately wanted to get Ellen out of this dangerous environment, but if he argued too vociferously, his motive would be suspect. Though he wasn't privy to Sherman's ultimate plans for the Nez Perce, he had little hope Sherman would be merciful. He would have to find a way for Ellen and Bear Paw to slip away during the night. He licked his lips nervously. "When will we depart for Fort Keogh, sir?"

"Tomorrow. General Howard is eager to get moving out of this godforsaken frozen wilderness. I know it will be hard on everyone, but we're going nonetheless." He paused for a moment, contemplating. "You've spent some time with this white woman. Is she the one you've been searching for, for so long?"

Now the hard part. If he admitted that she was indeed the one, he would be watched, and thus hamstrung in any escape effort he could fashion undetected. Now he used the crushing disappointment he felt upon seeing Ellen's astounding transformation. "No sir, regrettably she was not."

"A shame," Miles said. "Maybe it's time to give up on this quest. It's dogged you too long."

"I agree, sir. Perhaps I should let it go."

Eli left with the small satisfaction that in a very real way he had told the truth. The innocent teenage girl he had proposed to no longer existed. And the woman who had taken her place he had yet to know.

THE SOLDIERS CONTINUED TO BE surprised by their captives. Here were not the legendary warriors they had feared for so long. Here were not the wily adversaries that had outsmarted them again and again, leading them on a months-long chase across the northwest. What they saw now were a people very much like themselves—hungry, cold, wet, exhausted, and fearful of what the next hour might bring. And there were only 418 of them now, out of the 800-plus who had started.

Surprising too was the compassion of the Indians during the battle toward white soldiers. Rather than being tortured and mutilated as they had expected, fallen soldiers were comforted and given water and blankets as they lay on the field between the battle lines. In this the Nez Perce had had more honor than the soldiers.

The calming influence of Joseph as he walked among his people, doing his best to lift their spirits, won deep respect too. This was not the savage "red Napoleon" they had expected, but rather a dignified man who did not waste his time on hatred of his captors, but constantly saw to the physical and spiritual needs of his people.

Thus the capture had at last put a very human face on their adversary—and the soldiers could see themselves reflected in it. Even so, they remained puzzled by and contemptuous of Ellen. How could a white woman voluntarily live with Indians? To the soldiers it seemed degrading, and they wrote her off as no longer white.

COLONEL MILES AND JOSEPH SPENT considerable time together, walking across the hills around the camp and talking with the aid of a translator, forging a mutual respect for each other and their respective sides in the battle.

Ellen had asked Eli if he would give her insight into what the white chiefs were thinking about the fate of the Nez Perce. Now she saw Joseph and Miles conversing and knew she needed to talk to Joseph.

She found him in the afternoon alone near the edge of camp. He was wrapped in a warm blanket provided by the soldiers, who had kept their promise to provide winter garments, clothing, food, medical treatment, and comforting fires to the Indians. She approached Joseph with some hesitation, reluctant to disturb his rare solitude.

Joseph saw her coming, and a warm smile spread across his face. He reached out and embraced her arms in greeting, then motioned for his translator to join them.

"It is good to see you, Ellen," he said, relief visible on his face. "I feared for your life during the battle. You are well?"

"Yes, I am well," she replied. She took a deep breath and continued. "I have seen you talking with Colonel Miles. I do not want to intrude on your privacy, but I would like to know if he has promised you anything."

Joseph turned reflective, looking away across the hills for a moment, then back to her. "I do not mind. It is good that you are here to help me understand what the whites are telling me. Too many of them speak one thing and do another. Yes, he has promised great things. Can you help me in this?"

Ellen did her best to give him a smile. "It would be my pleasure," she said. "I have grown to love you, all of you, for your bravery, your generosity, your courage. I want so much to make things better for you if I can."

Joseph nodded. "During our talk about the surrender, Miles promised that we will be returned to the Lapwai reservation, and that we will not be punished for past crimes. Now he says we must first travel to a place the soldiers call Fort Keogh, and stay until the spring when the weather will be better. Then we will return to the Lapwai."

"I do not know what General Howard is thinking, but I have been told he will let Colonel Miles make most of the decisions here. Do not believe what Colonel Miles tells you. He is a good man, I think, and means well for you and your people. But he will not have his way. His and General Howard's chief is a man called Sherman, and I know of him. He is ruthless, cold-hearted, an Indian hater. He will show no mercy to you or your people. And what he tells Miles to do with you, Miles must do."

Joseph was silent for a long uncomfortable moment. "We have no choice but to obey. Our power is gone, and Miles will not return our weapons."

"Yes, that you can be sure of. But believe nothing else Miles promises you. He wishes to do good for you, but in the end it will be the great chief Sherman who speaks your fate. Knowing this will make no difference in what happens to you, but I do not want you to place hope in promises that will almost certainly prove false."

ELI HAD TO WAIT UNTIL dark to make contact with Ellen without being seen. He found her among the Nez Perce, huddled around a fire in Bear Paw's arms. The sight of them together was still like a knife to the gut.

But getting her away from here, he thought, *is the first step to someday getting her back.*

She saw him on the edge of the crowd in the dim light and rose to join him. Bear Paw kept his place but his eyes were on them.

"What have you learned?" Ellen said.

"Bad news, but it was not unexpected. The cavalry and the Nez Perce are leaving tomorrow for Fort Keogh. Howard is anxious to get away from here. I think he's still worried about Sitting Bull and his warriors showing up. I tried to convince Miles that you and Bear Paw should be let go to return to your home. But as I expected, he wasn't buying it. He regards both of you as combatants, and wants to take you along to Fort Keogh to have more time to sort out your fate. The longer you stay with the Nez Perce the harder it will be to separate you both from them."

Ellen looked crestfallen. "Then we must escape. And it must be tonight."

Eli's face twisted in torment. "I've searched for you for months. And now I've found you. I still can't understand what drove you to do what you did. In that I'm sorry. But even finding you as you are, I don't want to let you go." He drew a deep breath and let it out. "But I can't bear to see you caught up in this either. When the camp is asleep, slip away to the base of this hill near the battlefield. I'll be waiting for you." He walked away into the darkness.

ELLEN SOUGHT OUT JOSEPH IMMEDIATELY. She found him near one of the campfires with his wife, Springtime, and their infant daughter. Springtime was still healing from her wounds suffered earlier. Ellen was warmly welcomed into the fire circle and sat next to Joseph.

"We must leave tomorrow, Ellen," Joseph said, looking into the fire. "It will be a hardship on our women and old people. Some will not survive." He turned to look at her. "It would be a great thing for the spirits of the People, especially the children, if you would come with us."

"I am honored that you would think I would lift your spirits, Joseph. I would be pleased to go with you. I have grown very fond of the children. But Bear Paw has a great hunger to seek his scattered people, and help them if he can. He is my husband, and my place is at his side. I also have dear friends among the Shoshone. Some of them may be starving in the woods, or gravely injured. I would like to find them if I can, and see if I can help them. We must go, and it must be tonight."

Joseph understood this commitment very well, and respected her decision, though not without regret. He nodded, looking back into the fire. "Then go, Ellen. May the Great Spirit guide your steps to your homeland. I will pray that we meet again some day."

"I will pray for this also," she said, standing to go. "Farewell."

Far into the black winter night, Ellen and Bear Paw slipped away from the camp as quietly as ghosts and made their way down to the base of the hill. At first there appeared to be no one there, but then Eli emerged out of the blackness. He was leading two horses. Ellen's paint mare had disappeared in the battle, but these would do.

"These horses are in fairly good shape," Eli said, barely above a whisper. "I've given you extra blankets and a small cache of food. Walk the horses away for a bit to keep silence. I don't know if anyone will come after you, so when you mount up, ride as quickly as you can in the darkness. Now go."

Bear Paw took the reins to both horses. His face was no longer full of anger, but instead showed a grudging respect for the white soldier. Both of them started to walk away, but Ellen suddenly whirled, came back, and threw her arms around Eli. "How can I ever deserve this?" she murmured. "You are all the man I hoped you would be. Thank you, thank you for this. It will never be forgotten." She slowly released her arms from him and stepped back. Surprisingly, Bear Paw moved forward and extended his arm. The two men, met over a small woman only one could have, clasped arms briefly, firmly.

"Keep her safe," Eli told him, voice distorted with emotion.

"I would give my life for her," Bear Paw replied.

"I believe you."

Ellen and Bear Paw turned once again to go.

Eli could contain himself no longer. "Ellen, I love you!" he called after her.

She turned to him one last time. "I know."

Then they were gone.

It didn't take long the next morning for the soldiers to conclude that Ellen was gone, and with her her Shoshone husband. Eli found himself summoned to General Howard's tent.

"The white woman and her husband are gone," Howard began. "Colonel Miles tells me you inquired of him yesterday as to what would be done with them. He thought you didn't appear too happy to learn they'd be taken along with the rest. Do you know anything about this disappearance, Captain?"

Eli had by this time grown considerably sour not only on this tragic campaign and its result, but his whole military career as well. When he had signed on to help keep peace in the west, he didn't intend it to include murderous campaigns against women and children, the sick and the elderly. He had lately begun to second-guess the cavalry's entire mission in the west. So it didn't bother him to compound his earlier lie to Miles and do so again now to Howard.

"No sir, I don't," he replied.

Howard regarded him silently, as if seeking to read his mind. "Hmph," he finally said. "Well, personally the loss of one man and one woman from this group doesn't bother me that much. A few others have disappeared as well. But Miles is in a lather, so I suppose I shouldn't be cavalier about it. On another subject, it's time to return you to your unit. You were on loan to us from Fort Walla Walla, to assist in the capture of the Nez Perce. Now that has been accomplished. Anyway, I've noticed your enthusiasm for this pursuit has waned considerably over the last several weeks."

"As has yours, sir," Eli put in.

"Yes, well, in reality I had no heart for it from the start. But I did my duty. Now, I'm going to send you back to your post. You may leave today if you like. I'll get a messenger off to Fort Keogh to telegraph Fort Walla Walla that you're on your way." He rose and put out his hand. "Good luck, Eli. And, since Miles suspects you had something to do with their escape, if you should encounter the missing couple somewhere in your travels, it would be well for your career if you could bring them to justice, if you catch my drift. That will be all."

Eli saluted and left, feeling a small sense of relief for the first time in weeks. He wasted no time saddling up the best horse he could find, grabbing a supply of trail food and winter gear, and heading west.

Eli had been gone less than an hour when a courier arrived with a packet for Colonel Miles. Miles took the packet and shuffled through the stack of papers inside. Two caught his eye, and he was suddenly up and trotting to Howard's tent. "Sir, you need to see this," he said, after pushing aside the tent flap, saluting, and offering the papers. "You know those two who disappeared last night? Back in Idaho Territory there are wanted posters out for both of them."

*The Indians should be "made to work, sow, and do
all that is necessary and to adapt to our ways."*
—*Christopher Columbus*

THE REVEREND JEDEDIAH "OLD HELLFIRE" Jamison skewered the flock of his Pocatello, Idaho Territory church with the burning gaze of a missionary on fire with divine purpose. "Brothers and sisters, the Lord's providence has put opportunity in our reach!" he shouted, brushing back his long silver hair. "Our destiny is at hand!" He paused for effect. "Now you know, as I have told you," he continued, "that the Indians around these parts are hungry for the word of God.[13] And it is our duty to bring it to them! For the Lord commanded us through his Manifest Destiny to spread forth across this great continent and subdue all that is within it—savage beasts and savage peoples alike. This was ordained by Almighty God himself."

"And having conquered this great land, we cannot shirk from our divine purpose now!" he roared as his congregation nodded their heads in affirmation. "Let us be mindful of the plight of the Indian, for the Lord has commanded us to bring these poor ignorant peoples to the Word, to turn away from their false gods, from their sinful lives. Yes, the Good Book itself warns us that the heathen shall be judged also, for they know

---

13   The appearance of Nez Perce in tribal dress on the streets of St. Louis in 1831, purportedly seeking the Christian gospel, caused a sensation among would-be missionaries. Here was proof the Indians were receptive to the Word, ripe for conversion. In reality, the Nez Perce had sent a few of their number east in hopes of learning how to obtain the power the Book of Heaven seemed to have conveyed on the whites.

the difference between right and wrong. Brothers and sisters, we must not let these people suffer the Lord's judgment of eternal damnation!"

"Amen, brother!" shouted several in the congregation.

"We're ready, preacher," shouted another. "Lead the way!"

Jamison looked down from his pulpit in satisfaction. "Here is our opportunity to do the Lord's work. The Fort Hall Indian reservation is nearby, as you know. Its population has recently increased, now that the Shoshone have been brought in. Here are souls waiting for the Word! And it is our duty to bring it to them. The grown-ups are set in their ways, but we can start with the children."

"Hallelujah, preacher, when do we leave?" came a shout from the back pew.

"Soon, very soon, now that we're finally ready to start our own Indian school here. We need young impressionable minds ready to see the wisdom of the white race, and to hear the word of God. We will take in these children, give them Christian names, and teach them what they should know about farming, about the divine wisdom of the Founding Fathers, about prospering in the new world visited on this continent. Let us go forth to the reservation, and fulfill the destiny the Lord has given us!"

Old Hellfire nodded in satisfaction as his flock came to their feet, shouting and stomping, ready to follow him to the gates of Hell itself—or at least to the gates of Fort Hall.

Ellen and Bear Paw rode southwest, careful to not cross over into Blackfeet country. They encountered isolated groups of Flatheads, who took them in, giving them food and respite from the bitter cold. Part of the friendly reception they got was because of Ellen. If Bear Paw was merely tolerated, she was received warmly. Word about her had spread among the northwest tribes—about her marriage to a Shoshone chief, about the soldier she had slain to protect her husband, about her steadfast support of her tribe. Many pressed forward to touch her, with pleas to hear her tales around the evening campfire. She patiently obliged each time.

The Flatheads told them that the Shoshone who had survived the massacre were taken to the reservation at Fort Hall. There they were living under the white man's rule. They were beaten down and heartsick for their homeland, but were receiving food and medical care. They were alive, though some continued to think it not worth even that price. Ellen and Bear Paw took in these reports with great interest. Then, fed and rested, they continued on.

She and Bear Paw strengthened their bond even further as they made their way to what had been their home. At night they would melt together under the sleeping furs, she finding warmth and strength in his powerful arms, he enchanted, as always, at the delicate curves of her body, the graceful femaleness that hid her unbreakable will. They were two become one, souls united in purpose, lives irrevocably intertwined.

As they rode south, Ellen asked Bear Paw about his intentions for any survivors they might find.

He was silent for a few moments. "I have given this much thought," he said slowly. "There is no good path for them. Some of them must certainly think the white soldiers are still roaming about, seeking to kill the last Shoshone. They are afraid to come out. But if they stay in the woods, they will die, or be killed by other whites. If they come with us, we can lead them to the reservation, where they may live, according to the white man's will. Some will say they will die before they accept this." He paused, letting out a long breath. "My heart tells me it is a sad thing to bring them to the white man. I do this against all that I have been taught, all that we lived by. But I cannot bear to let the winter kill them. I would wish for them to see their brothers and sisters again, to be fed and have their wounds tended to, to see their children with full bellies and given the chance to grow before they decide whether they should live or die. In the end, it is the children among them I will do this for."

"Will you—will we—stay on the reservation?" Ellen said quietly.

Bear Paw looked at her as they rode along side by side. "They will expect me to stay. If I go, others will follow, and this tragedy will grow larger. More will die. So I will stay."

He suddenly dismounted and walked a few steps away from his horse. He turned in her direction, but it seemed his eyes had trouble meeting her gaze. "You must decide on your own whether to go or stay. I cannot force you to live as we will, or endure as we must."

Ellen was aghast at this remark. She slipped from her horse and ran to embrace him. "But I am your wife! Where you go, I will follow. Do you not believe this by now?"

Bear Paw pulled her back and looked into her face. "Even now sometimes I am not certain what you will do. Please forgive me for doubting you."

Ellen clasped his hands firmly, eyes brimming with tears. "I do forgive you, my love. It is surely hard to be married to a white woman in these times, when the Shoshone are betrayed by whites. But remember, I am Shoshone now. Where you go I will follow. It shall always be so."

IN FIVE WEEKS, THEY WERE there, riding out of the trees in mid-morning into the clearing where the village had stood. Ellen looked over the site, grief stricken. There was nothing left to show it had once been a thriving and happy settlement. A thin layer of snow covered the trampled earth, broken by scattered piles of scorched tipi poles, fragments of hides, the remains of campfires, broken cooking utensils. The skeletal carcasses of horses and dogs gave the place an air of death. A burnt smell lingered. All was silence.

Bear Paw said nothing. After a few minutes, he dismounted and began to walk slowly across the site. Ellen dismounted and walked beside him, mute as she numbly shuffled through the remains of the village, fighting to contain her tears. Her effort failed when they came to the creek, where she and the other women had huddled, frantic to stay alive, desperate to protect their children, and screaming for mercy.

There were five skeletons in the creek bed.

Ellen broke down and sank to her knees, sobbing. Bear Paw looked at the remains in grim silence. There were no words that would do. Then he knelt and put his arms around his wife, pressing her head into his cheek. They sat for long moments as Bear Paw gently rocked her back and forth, calling out the short version of her Shoshone name softly to her: "*Taviduaga*", meaning Light from Above.

They sat for a while, with no sound but the rustle of a slight breeze in the dry winter grasses. Then Ellen finally spoke. "There was evil here," she said without looking at him. "We must do what we can for the dead."

Bear Paw nodded and stood up, limbs stiff in the winter cold. Using whatever they could find for digging tools, they doggedly hacked a grave out of the frozen earth. By afternoon, it was deep enough to hold all the remains. They reverently gathered up what bones they could find, most of which were in a jumble, arms and legs intertwined in death as they had been in their last moment of life. One of the skeletons was that of a child. They placed the remains in the pit they had dug. Bear Paw performed a short ceremony to speed the victims on their way to the spirit world. Then they scooped the frozen soil over the grave.

Afterward, they rode about a mile away and camped in a grove of trees at a place that offered shelter from the wind. Neither of them had wanted to spend the night where too many of their brothers and sisters had been so mercilessly slain.

LATE THE NEXT MORNING, THEY began a slow circle of the campsite, riding in ever-widening arcs looking for survivors who had fled to the woods. They did not find anyone for two days. Then, on the third day, Bear Paw spotted a thin column of smoke coming from beyond the next ridge. They rode slowly up and over the ridge, and had no sooner topped it than below them about one hundred yards away, the smoke evaporated at the source, as if a fire had been hurriedly doused. Bear Paw looked briefly at Ellen, motioning for her to stay put, then slowly threaded his horse down slope through the trees toward the spot he had last seen the smoke.

He had disappeared from view when Ellen heard him loudly call out a greeting in Shoshone. There was silence for a few seconds, then she heard him call her to come forward. She guided her horse carefully through the brush and deadfalls around the standing trees. Finally she emerged into a small clearing in front of a large rock about twenty feet tall which had a cave-like depression at its base. Standing with Bear Paw before the rock, around the remains of a smothered fire, were a man and a woman. They were a pitiful sight, gaunt and tired-looking, and appeared to be in shock over their visitors. The woman did not look well. At sight of Ellen, she let out a wail, staggered forward, and embraced her, tears streaking her cheeks, as Ellen dismounted.

Ellen had forgotten their names, but she had seen them on numerous occasions around the village.

"This is Many Horses," Bear Paw said, indicating the gaunt warrior. "And this is his wife, Hawk Woman."

Ellen disengaged herself from Hawk Woman and bowed slightly to the man.

Bear Paw looked over the man's poor condition and ragged garments. "You will die in these woods, alone and far from your brothers," he said. "Many of those who survived the killings have been gathered up and sent to the white man's reservation at Fort Hall. There they receive food and medicine from the white soldiers."

Many Horses mustered enough energy to raise himself up straight and show contempt for this news. "And you believe this?" he said.

Bear Paw looked at Ellen, who stepped forward. "We believe," she responded. "We have heard this from our brothers the Flatheads."

"Even so," the man said, "I would rather die on my feet than live on my knees. It saddens my heart to hear Bear Paw say we should live under the white man's rule."

Bear Paw knew the man was summoning a last desperate show of Shoshone defiance, probably because his wife was present, so he did not respond to the insult. "I would ask you to think of your wife. I can see she is not well. If she is here much longer, she will surely die."

Many Horses deflated considerably. "Game is scarce. I cannot provide proper meals to strengthen her. And we suffer from the cold."

"The game will get ever more scarce as more whites come into the area," Bear Paw replied. "Some day a white man will come to you and say, 'This is my land, you must move'. If he does not shoot you first. Come live with your brothers and sisters at Fort Hall. You say you would rather die on your feet, but there is no honor in starving to death alone in the woods, watching your wife die before you. You must think of her now. This is your duty as a Shoshone man."

Many Horses looked down at the ground for a moment, shoulders slumped in defeat, pride shattered at last in the face of looming death. Then he looked up at Bear Paw and nodded his agreement. "There are others," he said, "scattered through the woods."

OVER THE NEXT THREE DAYS, with Many Horses for a guide, they found scattered knots of survivors huddled in the woods. Tragically, there were some children with them. All the holdouts were in a bad way to varying degrees, and Bear Paw could see that their condition, especially that of Hawk Woman, made it imperative that they abandon further search and get this group to Fort Hall.

So Ellen and Bear Paw led a small group of fifteen out of the woods, moving only at the slow pace the survivors could muster. Bear Paw let them rest when they asked for it. Their mood had not improved since leaving the hiding places. The men continued to be wearily defiant, claiming that in the woods at least they were free.

Bear Paw grew sad over these continued objections, and at times secretly longed to say, "yes, let us go back, and be free until we are dead". But he had seen so much of the white man's power and mercilessness that he could not stand to see his people die, even in freedom, if there was a chance they could live. They did not realize there were no choices left for them except the reservation or death.

Even so, he could not bear to be the one to lead his people into something he knew only what he had been told of. So as they rested one evening at the Snake River, he addressed them.

"Brothers," he said, "our camp is gone, too many of our people lie dead, unburied and dishonored. The great wheel of life has turned around to a new time for the Shoshone. The old ways mean only death for us all. I am trusting our brothers the Flatheads that they have told the truth about the reservation. I wish only that you may live. Still, it is not my place to take you where you do not want to go. You must think now not only of yourself, but of your wives, your children and a future for them. Maybe we will find such a thing at Fort Hall. Maybe we can call into being a new way of life for the Shoshone. We must know if the Great Spirit has plans for us. We do not honor him by starving in the woods, our families with us in death. Let us stand on what little ground the white man has given us, and be proud of who we are—and who we were." He paused, looking out over the ragged group, the weary warriors still defiant but drained of power. "I hope you will come with me. But I say to you now, anyone who wishes to return to the woods and go into hiding, let him do so. I will not stop you. If any of you wish to go back, let him stand now."

No one did. So in the morning, the whole group continued on. They arrived at Fort Hall in the afternoon, four days later.

THEY CAMPED WITHIN SIGHT OF the fort, apprehensive about going further without more information. Toward dusk a lone rider came loping out to meet them. He proved to be a warrior named Eagle Feather, whom Bear Paw knew and trusted.

Eagle Feather was shocked to see Bear Paw. "We thought you were dead!" he said when he had recovered. He walked forward and embraced him. "Brother, it is good to see you. The *toquashes* looked for you for a long time, but you were not found. I thought you might have been badly wounded and gone off into the woods to die." His gaze turned on Ellen. "And I see Taviduaga is with you. This will be a great blessing to all of us here."

"The People are well treated?" Bear Paw asked.

"It is as always with the white man. Some words are kept, others are not. But we have shelter, food, and medicine." His expression turned somber. "What we do not have is our land. We live by the white man's will on this patch of ground. We are beggars, waiting for the white man's hand to bless us with what we need to live." A spark flared in his eyes. "But some of us are waiting, gathering strength for the time when all the tribes will unite in a great last battle to rid this country of the white man forever."

Bear Paw fought to avoid showing his sadness at this declaration. He would let Eagle Feather and the other braves hold on to this notion for a while; it was all they had left of their manhood.

"You must not go in with the others," Eagle Feather continued. "The white soldiers think you may still live, and they wish to capture you. You cannot hide on the reservation for long, and if you are caught, they will kill you." He turned to Ellen. "You may hide your presence for a short while, but there is great danger for you as well. Perhaps you should let me take these people in, while you ride on."

Ellen and Bear Paw turned away and talked privately for a few moments.

"He is right, husband," Ellen said quietly. "Knowing the white man as I do, I have no doubt they blame you for every bad thing that has happened in this area over the past few months. If you are caught, they will give you a trial that will be a joke, and then they will hang you."

"I have brought these people this far, at times against what I believe is best for them," Bear Paw said. "I would not wish to send them in without seeing what their fate will be. This is my duty as camp chief." He put his arms around Ellen. "We will go in, and at least for now, we will stay."

"It shall be so, husband," Ellen said.

LATER THAT DAY, BEAR PAW and Ellen led the small band into the reservation at a spot where no white soldiers could be seen. Word quickly spread of their arrival, and Shoshone came running with shouts of joy, eager to see if there were relatives or friends among the newcomers. And there was a great commotion when Ellen was spotted. The women pressed close around her, weeping and hugging her. She embraced each one tenderly, and whispered her love. Then the newcomers were quickly absorbed into the surging mass, and taken to the village in celebration.

Though the Shoshone had not known what had become of Ellen and Bear Paw, word had spread among them, in part through overheard white soldier talk, of Ellen's brave defense of her man at the massacre. The act had given her an exalted status. "We have never seen such a white woman," one of them said. "You have paid the price to be Shoshone."

It was abundantly clear to Ellen that, as Eagle Feather had predicted, her presence greatly buoyed the spirits of the downtrodden people. As more and more of the tribe came in at word of her presence, she was overjoyed beyond words to find Kimama among them. Ellen threw her arms around the young girl and hugged her tightly for a long minute.

Kimama drew back with tears in her eyes. "I despaired that you were dead," she sobbed. "I have missed you so much. The spirits have blessed us with your presence."

Smiling, Ellen put her hands on Kimama's arms, reluctant to let go. "I am so pleased to see that you live, dear friend. It is you who bless *me*." She paused. "What others are here?"

Kimama's face grew downcast. "Not many. Some who were wounded did not live long enough after the murders to make it here. But there is one who needs to see you, who needs your presence in her tipi. Rabbit Woman is here."

Ellen gasped and put a hand to her face. "My Shoshone mother! Is she well?"

"In body, yes. In her mind, no. Come, let us see her and she will explain."

The two went off hand in hand, walking across the ground to a tipi apart from the others.

"She does not come out much," Kimama said. "Perhaps that will change now." She called out to Rabbit Woman when they reached the tipi.

There seemed to be no answer for a few moments, then Ellen heard faint sounds inside of someone moving around, and the tent flap was throw open. Rabbit Woman came out and stood blinking in the sunlight for a moment, then her eyes focused on Ellen and widened in disbelief. She fell to her knees and began a wail of celebration.

Ellen had to go to her and lift her up to get her off her knees. She gently stroked Rabbit Woman's hair and hugged her tightly as the older woman sobbed.

Rabbit Woman at last drew back, and tearfully looked at Ellen in disbelief. "Is it really you? My daughter has come back to us?"

"Yes, it is really me," Ellen said, smiling and still stroking Rabbit Woman's hair, which now manifested a touch of gray. "It is good to see my Shoshone mother. But Kimama tells me you are sad. Can you tell me why?"

Rabbit Woman looked away. "All the People are sad now," she said, sounding a bit defensive. There is much to be sad about."

"Yes, there are many reasons for sadness," Ellen said. "But somehow I believe that with you there is something more." Ellen put her hands on Rabbit Woman's arms. "Can you confide in your daughter?"

Rabbit Woman looked down, silent for a few moments, as if ashamed to speak. "My—" she began haltingly—"my horses are gone. All were taken." She broke into sobs again.

Ellen looked at Kimama in distress. "This is true? Do you know what happened to them?"

"No," Kimama replied. "When the white soldiers collected us all at the camp and ordered us to start walking to Fort Hall, few horses were with us. I think white soldiers took many of them."

Ellen turned back and embraced Rabbit Woman once more. "I am blessed to see you again. We will talk more of your horses. For now please, for me, come to the fire circle tonight. The others have requested that I tell what has befallen me and Bear Paw these many months. There is much to tell." With a final hug, she slowly let her go, and turned away, walking off with Kimama.

"I love her dearly, but she is such an insecure woman," Ellen muttered. "It seems she thinks she is nothing without those horses."

"With us, there is some truth in that, as surely you know" Kimama said. "Horses are wealth, and for a brief time she could forget she was a poor widow, with no dowry to attract a new husband. Now she is a poor widow once again. Many understand and feel sorry for her. But there seems to be nothing we can do."

"We shall see," Ellen said.

THAT NIGHT AROUND THE FIRE circle Ellen told the people her tale of what had befallen her and Bear Paw since they were last seen at the campsite massacre. They listened with rapt attention, often nodding knowingly, as if not surprised to hear some parts of the cruelty visited on the Nez Perce. Ellen looked around at the ruddy faces in the flickering firelight, the crowd transfixed by her words. Knowing how they had already suffered so greatly, it was difficult for her to tell everything, and she deliberately left out some of the worst parts, concentrating when she could on the warmth and generosity of the Nez Perce people, and Joseph in particular.

OVER THE NEXT FEW DAYS, Ellen and Bear Paw tried to settle in with the others, but Ellen could tell that despite his brave speech to the survivors on the way in, he was not taking it well. He was used to being a leader and decision maker. "You are quiet, my husband," she said one day, trying to draw him out. "What troubles you?"

He put an arm around her as they walked about. "What purpose does life have here? Shall we try to make choices, when we do not know what plans the white man has for us? How can the People help their children prepare for tomorrow, when we do not know what tomorrow will bring, when it may be different from any we have known? How can I lead these people when I do not know where we are going?"

"I know, my love," Ellen said. "But many of the other braves are dead. You are all the leader they have. You must find a way to fight for them, to give them a tomorrow if you can."

"How can I fight a battle that is already lost?" he said.

"You talk like an old woman!" she said sharply, turning his big body to face her. She had never spoken to him in such a tone before, and his eyes were full of surprise. "Do not talk so; else I will think you are a spineless imposter who has secretly taken the place of my husband. I will hear no more of such talk. It is up to us to *find* a purpose here."

Two days later, she did.

THE REVEREND JAMISON STOOD AT the gates of the Fort Hall reservation, tingling with excitement. Behind him were a small group of his followers, hand-picked for their zeal to the purpose at hand. Old Hellfire turned and addressed them. "We are here!" he said loudly, belaboring the obvious as only he could. "We have been given permission to enter and make a visit. Now, let us go forth into this godless congregation and fulfill our destiny." The group surged forward toward the gate.

Jamison and his flock had met with the commandant of Fort Hall, one Lieutenant Colonel Adams, who, upon seeing they had brought quite an array of foodstuffs the Shoshone were not likely to get from the military—pies, cakes, bread, fresh vegetables and even some fruit, which the congregation had spent considerable time preparing and collecting—had given them permission to make entry for a limited time to deliver them. Jamison talked with fervor about the Indian school he and his congregation had prepared, and their hope of attracting a group of Indian youth who were receptive to education and learning the white man's ways. The commandant quickly warmed to the idea. *Such a project might be well-received back in Washington,* he thought. Now that he had the Indians on the reservation, he was under pressure to pacify them and keep them that way. The school might be a start; perhaps it would keep their minds off revolt. He made it clear though, that Jamison was there at the pleasure of the Shosone, and he would not sympathize with him if he and his flock were not welcomed with open arms.

Old Hellfire mentioned nothing to him about his mission to further the call of Manifest Destiny.

THE MISSIONARIES ENTERED IN A tight group, nervous about the stone-faced Shoshone around them. Some of the missionary women were frightened, though they tried to put on a brave face, and silently marched in a short distance with their two wagonloads of gifts trailing along behind. There Jamison called them to a halt, and ordered the supplies uncovered.

The reaction from the Shoshone was considerably more low-key than he had hoped for. They cautiously crowded around the wagon, examining the foodstuffs, but did not pick up anything. Jamison was surprised, and asked a brave whom he had overheard speaking a little English what the Indians were thinking.

"They want to know what is the price for these things," he replied, frowning.

"Why, they are all free!" Jamison replied, smiling. "They are gifts for your people."

The man's frown darkened into a scowl. "With the white man, nothing is free. There is always a price."

"Well, ah—" Jamison stuttered, "we—we bring good news with these gifts! We have established a new school just for the Shoshone, south of here in Pocatello. We are ready to receive some of your children, and educate them so that they can be make a living in this new world." He might have added *and give up their heathen ways and cleave to the one true God*, but he thought better of it.

"Is there a chief among you I can speak with?" he said.

The brave snorted and walked off, leaving the women, observing some unseen signal, to finally start taking food from the cart.

Jamison thought he had been rebuffed, but minutes later, the brave he had spoken with returned, and motioned for him to follow. They walked across the camp for a couple of minutes, then approached a small group of Shoshone and stopped. "Chief," said his escort.

If Jamison was nervous before, he was downright scared now, as he found himself face-to-face with a Shoshone warrior who towered over him. The man approached him and stopped less than two paces away. He did not look happy. *Relax; they look that way all the time*, he chided himself.

"White man, how are you called?" the man said.

Jamison forced a smile. "Why, I am the Reverend Jedediah Jamison. I'm pleased to hear you speak English."

"I speak some," the man said gruffly. "You are preacher of the Book of Heaven?"

"Yes, I preach the Gospel of salvation. I have a church down in Pocatello. I have brought some of my congregation—my followers— with me today. If you don't mind me asking, who taught you English?"

"My woman taught me," Bear Paw replied. "You wish to take some of our children to your school?"

"Yes, I do," Jamison said, licking his lips. He knew the man could break him in half without raising a sweat if he chose to. He would have to choose his words carefully.

"Why?" Bear Paw said, voice heavy with suspicion.

Jamison began to sweat. "Well, now that you see we have the white man's civilization in this land, it is good for your children to learn the white man's ways, to become educated, to learn how to survive and prosper. We will give them good schooling, and teach them how to do things they should know for this new world."

Bear Paw's eyes narrowed still further. "What they do for this?"

"Why, they will learn how to dress as whites do, and learn how to farm. They will need to do this to prosper. And they will be given Christian names and be taught from the Book of Heaven."

"And the white chief Adams has said this should be? He says we must do this?"

Jamison paused ever so slightly. He was not averse to lying if it would further the task the Lord had set before him. After all, it was for a righteous cause; there were souls at stake. What could be more important? He plunged ahead. "Yes, Colonel Adams has given his approval to this plan. He told me that the children should, nay, *must* attend this school, that they will profit from it."

"I seriously doubt he said that. And in any case, it will not be hard to find out the truth."

The words came not from Bear Paw but from someone behind him. Jamison jumped and turned to see who had spoken. He saw a small slender woman in Shoshone dress. He was shocked as he realized she was white. "Who in God's name are you?" he said, supremely annoyed and frustrated.

"I am Manakwa Noovigaded Pa'a Taviduaga. It is a long name, so you may address me simply as Taviduaga."

Jamison felt a prickling of unease on the back of his neck. This was not something he was prepared to deal with. He was counting at least in part on the Indians being sufficiently docile from their impoverished state to sign off on most anything he laid before them, if they were plied with enough gifts. Now he had a white woman in Indian dress before him, and the creature sounded anything but compliant. Attempting to gather his resolve, he drew himself up taller and said, "I presume you have a Christian name?"

"Yes," the woman said. "I was called Ellen O'Hara."

"You *were* called Ellen O'Hara?" he said, mustering a bit of righteous anger. "Have you no shame, child? You have chosen to cast your lot with these heath—with these people, and forego your Christian heritage?"

Ellen walked around him and stood next to Bear Paw. "I would choose my words carefully, Reverend. This is my husband, and he takes a very dim view of those who insult me."

"Your husband!" Jamison barked. He had heard once or twice of white women who had taken up with Indians, but had never met one. The very idea was incomprehensible to him. But he knew when he was in danger, and it was prudent to retreat. One wrong move or word and this woman would probably set her enormous husband upon him. He winced at the thought of the results.

"I'm going back to my congregation now," he said, backing up. He turned to go, then looked over his shoulder in defiance. "But I'm not going away! I am on a mission from God and I will not shirk from it!"

Ellen watched him go, unease settling into her mind. "I should have expected to see this here at some point," she murmured. "I should talk to the white chief Adams. This man should be watched. There is more to this than schooling."

"If you do this," Bear Paw cautioned, "your presence here will become known. This is very dangerous."

"I know," she said.

JAMISON STALKED AWAY, GRUMBLING TO himself. *I won't let this fallen woman deter me*, he thought. *The Lord has set me to this task, and it shall be done. We will teach these heathen children, and they will know the true path to salvation!*

Old Hellfire walked back to his congregation, which was overseeing the distribution of the last of the gifts from the wagon. The Shoshone who had accepted the gifts, mostly women, seemed pleased as they walked away. There were smiles all around. The men were less pleased and made no secret of it. He would have to gear his next approach toward the women.

He gathered his small flock together. "We will spend the night here. Colonel Adams has promised the use of an empty barracks for one night," he told them. "In the morning, we'll come back and see who is receptive to the Word." With that, they all crowded into the now-empty wagons and rolled away.

IN THE EARLY HOURS OF morning, Jamison and his flock re-entered the reservation. He hadn't bothered to ask permission of Lt. Colonel Adams again; as far as Jamison was concerned he had enough trouble on his hands already. He could apologize and ask for permission after the fact if he had to.

Before long, a considerable crowd drifted in to surround him and his companions. *They are undoubtedly curious to see if we brought more gifts* he thought, and knew they might drift away quickly if he did not seize the day. Finding a large rock with a flat top, he jumped up as his church members surrounded him at the base, as if to protect him. In truth, they were still nervous about the crush of Shoshone around them, and could have done nothing of a protective nature anyway if it came to trouble.

Old Hellfire looked out over the crowd, barrel chest inflating with deep breaths as his excitement rose. *This is just like standing in my pulpit back home*, he thought, unbridled enthusiasm starting to grip him. Just the thought of the mass of souls before him waiting to be saved gave him a fresh burst of energy. He spotted the brave who spoke English that he had met the day before.

"Brother, I wish to speak to your people here. Will you relay my words to them in Shoshone?"

The man scowled as before, but nodded and climbed up on the rock with him.

Old Hellfire smoothed back his luxuriant silver hair and took hold of his coat lapels, nearly vibrating with energy. He was truly in his element now, ready to fulfill his task.

He took a deep breath. "Brothers and sisters!" he shouted. "Our new Indian school awaits only good children to fill it! We need children who are eager to learn, to grow, to prosper. We can teach your children to do the things they will need to do for this new society. We will give them food, clothing, and a place to live. They can pass on to you what they learn. I know you want a future for your children, a better future than life on the reservation can provide! We can give them that future. Bring the children unto me here, now, and see if we do not keep our word on this." Jamison paused. There was no way for him to know if his translator had accurately relayed what he had said, or had urged the crowd to hang him on the spot. In truth, the man's expression had grown steadily angrier as he went along, but he seemed to have finished the task.

There was low-key mumbling throughout the crowd. Word of Jamison's school had spread throughout the camp the day before. Word had also spread that the white chief Adams had said that they must do this. Many were unhappy at the thought of sending their children to a white man's school even though it was not far away. But with their villages, their very culture, destroyed, they were desperate for some ray of hope, some sign that *anyone* in the white world cared about them now, that anyone could offer their children a brighter future than the demeaning reservation life. And since they had been told Adams directed it, and since they were afraid that if they resisted they would be punished in some manner, many of them sadly nodded assent to the offer. Those that had brought their children to hear the speech now quietly moved them forth near the front of the crowd. Some had tears in their eyes.

Jamison beamed a broad smile as he saw the children gathering near. He ignored the distressed look on their mothers' faces and alighted from the rock, opening his arms to the children. "Let the little children come unto me!" he said, imitating Jesus' words as he was sometimes wont to do.

They crowded around him, fearful, tentative, pushed forward by their mothers. At this point he felt he had succeeded. But he was interrupted by a loud voice from behind him.

"Shoshone!" came the cry.

He whirled to see who it was.

Ellen was standing on top of the rock he had just come down from.

The heathen woman! She's dangerous; I must not allow her to take control now, he thought. Turning his back on the children, he leapt back up on the rock. "Godless woman, what do you do here?" he spat.

Ellen fixed cold eyes on him. "I am here to tell these people the truth," she said. "They have no idea what they are getting their children into." Before he could protest further, she turned to the crowd.

"Shoshone!" she said again. "Hear me! This man is not what he seems. I plead with you to keep your children close at hand. Do not send them to this school."

Jamison gasped as the sea of faces turned their eyes to her. He could feel his victory slipping onto uncertain ground.

"I have seen the white man's schools," she continued. In truth, she had, back in Kansas. And even then, as a young girl, she was nauseated by what she saw. "He will make them into little brown-skinned white men. He will put white clothes on them, and make the young men cut their hair. He will give them Christian names, and forbid them to use the names you have given them. He will tell them that the spirits you pray to are false, and that his is the one true god. He will try to make farmers of them. But when they are finished with this school, your children will be no more welcome in the white world than they are now. Acting and looking as whites do will not lessen the hatred many whites feel for them."

"You lie, fallen woman!" Jamison screeched. "I seek only to give them tools to become more successful in the world they are now in."

"A world you and your kind created," Ellen shot back.

"But it was all ordained by God himself!" Jamison shouted, wild-eyed. "He commanded us to go forth and conquer these lands, to convert the people to the Christian way. It was our destiny, made manifest in His word!"

Ellen glared at him and moved a step closer. "Did that destiny include destroying whole civilizations, murdering thousands of native peoples, promising much and delivering nothing? Did it include a campaign of lies, treachery, and theft against people who wished nothing more to continue to live as they had done for thousands of years, to raise their children in the ways of their ancestors? Did your commandment encompass all that?"

"You are a fallen woman and a tool of the devil!" Jamison shouted, desperate now as he could sense the crowd turning against him. Some in the crowd who could speak a little English were quietly translating Ellen's words as she spoke. "God sent me to deliver these people from eternal damnation!"

"That is what this is really all about, is it not?" Ellen countered. "You are more interested in seeing how many of these people you can convert than in schooling them, aren't you?"

"Yes, for the glory of God!" Jamison said, nearly out of control with rage now.

"Is it for God's glory or for yours?" Ellen said. "I believe that these people are far more spiritual than you are. They see spirits everywhere and they live their lives as a continuous prayer to them, and their Creator. They believe themselves part of their world, not apart from it. They give thanks for its blessings, and do not seek to dominate or conquer it. They are not saints, but they know their place, and honor it with their lives. The whites have taken everything from them. They are so beaten down that they do not know what they can safely refuse. Allow them at least the dignity to live in their traditional manner on this small piece of land that is all they have left. You would take the children and force them to forgo their rich heritage. You would force the young men to cut their hair. A brave cuts his hair only when he is in mourning. To do it any other time is a great insult." She moved a step closer. "You will *not* take their children."

The crowd below her was growing angry. Some of the braves were running hands across their knives and glaring at Jamison.

Ellen turned to the crowd again. "I have talked with the white chief Adams," she shouted. "He did not say that your children must attend this school. Even here, you have rights. And those rights include the privilege to raise your children as you desire. Keep your children here. Raise them in the traditional way. Teach them to honor their ancestors. If you have nothing left, remember always that you are still Shoshone!"

The crowd did not know Jamison. But they knew Light on a Distant Hill, and knew her heart. They erupted in shouts of praise—and anger, and surged forward toward Jamison.

Terrified, Jamison saw women advancing with murder on their faces. He jumped down from the rock, desperately searching for the rest of his flock. But they were already beating a hasty retreat toward the gate. In a panic he ran after them, coattails flying, hotly pursued by women brandishing sticks and knives. At the gate he turned to Ellen once more, rage on his face, and threw caution to the winds. "Daughter of Satan!" he screamed. "You haven't seen the last of me! No, by God, not the last of me!"

16

How Like Us They Were!

ELLEN WATCHED HIM GO, THEN jumped down into Bear Paw's arms. He gave her a big smile and hugged her tightly. She returned the embrace, then led him away from the noisy crowd to a quiet spot.

"The whites will know that I am here now," she said. "This was a great risk. But it was one I was willing to take for my people."

"I am ready to flee with you if you wish," Bear Paw said. "We can go to the mountains."

"No," Ellen said. "I am so tired of running. I am worn out from running. Let us make a stand here, come what may. Perhaps they wish only to question me." She looked into his eyes. "I will need you beside me."

Bear Paw looked at her, his expression grim. "I will kill anyone who tries to take you."

She knew he meant it. "Let us hope it does not come to that."

The Reverend Jedediah Jamison rode away from the reservation trembling with rage, trailing his followers as they headed back to Pocatello at a brisk pace. The treasures he had hoped to store up in heaven by converting the Indian children were now beyond his reach. When he finally got back to town, he sat fuming for a long time on the steps of his church. Finally, he got up and walked down the dirt street toward his customary afternoon visit to the general store, where he could usually find a sympathetic ear in the owner, and unburden himself.

When he got there, he was about to go through the front door when a poster on the wall to his right caught his eye. He drew closer and read it with growing interest. It was a wanted poster. Before he was done, his mouth fell open in disbelief. Then it curled into a smile. His chance to bring the Indian children to his school might be gone for good. But by God's grace, at least he would have his revenge. *And the reward will make a nice contribution to the church coffers,* he thought. He tore the poster off the wall and strode down the boardwalk to the sheriff's office.

THE SHERIFF WAS, BY GOOD fortune, in when Jamison came through the door. He looked up to see who his visitor was. Jamison was standing in front of his desk, eyes alight, with a large piece of paper in his hand.

Samuel Broward, a big man with a bushy mustache and piercing eyes, looked at him with annoyance. Whereas he was amiable with most of the townsfolk, Jamison was someone Broward merely tolerated. The man was a pompous blowhard. Sighing, he put down his paper and reached for his cup of coffee. "What brings you in, Reverend?" he growled.

If Jamison detected the sheriff's disdain, he didn't let on. Instead, he plunked the wanted poster on the sheriff's desk, nearly knocking over an inkwell. "You want to get credit for bringing this criminal in?"

Broward looked at the wanted poster. It read in part:

WANTED

WHITE WOMAN LIVING AS INDIAN.
SEEN IN COMPANY OF SHOSHONE CHIEF.
MAY ALSO BE WITH NEZ PERCE BANDS.
SOUGHT IN CONNECTION WITH BATTLE
WITH NORTHERN SHOSHONE SO. IDAHO TERR.
AUGUST 1877.

REWARD

There was more in small print. He read it and looked up. "Reckon

I would," he drawled. "Why? You get a tip from God as to her whereabouts?"

Jamison smiled. "You might say that."

The sheriff reached over to his left and threw another piece of wood in the nearby Franklin stove and leaned back in his chair. "And what do *you* want out of this?" he said.

"A share of the reward, of course," Jamison said. "*And* to be there when you bring her in. You see, I know just where to find her."

It DIDN'T TAKE LONG TO get the sheriff riled up enough to head out to the reservation the next morning, with two deputies and Jamison in tow. Broward had been amazed to find out this widely-sought woman was not far off.

Now they were seated in Lieutenant Colonel Adams' office on the Fort Hall reservation. Adams was not happy to see them. "Jamison," he barked, "you caused a peck of trouble here yesterday. Shoshone drums were going half the night. I don't need more of that. These Indians are just too unpredictable."

"Don't lose sight of the fact you're harboring a wanted criminal," Broward put in. "Maybe two of them. There's a poster out for a big Shoshone too, and word has it he's usually found with her."

Adams shoved the wanted poster they had presented across the desk away from him and leaned forward. "And don't *you* lose sight of the fact that you have no authority here. This is my jurisdiction. I can't account for every Indian on this reservation. It's a pretty big chunk of land. *If* she's here, I'm not about to let you two come in and try to take her out. I could have a full-scale rebellion on my hands."

"Then what can we do?" Jamison put in, frustrated.

Adams frowned. "If she's here and she slips away from the reservation, she's fair game," he said. "Do what you like. But I've heard about this big Shoshone you say is with her. If you try to capture her, I have a feeling you'd better have some serious help with you."

Ellen was determined to find a way to restore Rabbit Woman's horses to her. But she could find none on the reservation she could acquire. "Let us leave while we can, and search for horses," she told Bear Paw. "Then we can bring them back to her."

Bear Paw looked closely into her face and smiled. "You are no more content here than I am," he said. "But there is danger in this. We are not safe outside the reservation."

"We have not been safe anywhere for months," Ellen countered. "Is there anywhere left where the Shoshone are safe, even here? Come, help me do this one thing for my Shoshone mother. Then we can come back and see what tomorrow brings."

Bear Paw could not refuse her, despite his misgivings about the idea. "We shall go. Let us see if we can gather some things to trade from the people for fine horses."

They set about the task that day. The Shoshone had very little of value left other than the clothes on their backs. But with a quiet campaign of soliciting, and with the widespread love for Light on a Distant Hill, they found people willing to donate some items that might purchase one horse, or perhaps two. It would have to do. Having gathered these, they slipped away from the reservation early the next morning.

ELLEN KNEW THERE WAS LITTLE chance they would find one of Rabbit Woman's horses, though the woman had put her mark on them. She might find them among the soldiers' horse herd, but examining that was too dangerous, and would probably put them right back on the reservation if they were discovered. Trying to spirit them away at night could lead to being caught as horse thieves, with fatal results. No, they would have to range through the countryside, hoping to find horses running free, or buy some if they could from white settlers.

Bundled against the winter cold, they set off through arid country dotted with patchy snow and low scrub-trees that were more large bush than tree. After several hours they had seen nothing. The countryside seemed deserted. Ellen was discouraged as they stopped for a meal at mid-day. She built a small fire and broke out some cakes and dried berries to eat, and water to drink.

"My legs have grown stiff from riding in this cold weather," Bear Paw said. "I will walk to that hilltop, and see what lies beyond."

"Very well," Ellen said. "Please keep me in sight."

"I will," he promised, turning and walking away up the slope.

Ellen set out the cakes and berries for his return. She felt they had been too optimistic about their chances. In truth it was unlikely they would find horses running free that bore no mark. Horses were of such value on the frontier that few remained unclaimed for long. They would have to risk contact with a white settler if their search was to bear fruit.

She was musing on the discomfort of talking with white strangers when she heard the crunch of a boot in the snow behind her. She turned and found herself staring into the barrel of a Colt .45.

SHERIFF BROWARD AND THE REST had left the reservation after the fruitless meeting with Adams, and headed back to Pocatello. But Jamison wasn't ready to give up.

"We shouldn't quit when we're so close to getting that reward money!" he pleaded as they rode along. "She's there, I tell you! You don't know what she looks like, but I do. We can go back and keep a lookout for her and that husband of hers. If they wander off the reservation, you and your deputies can grab the both of them."

Broward frowned at him, breath blowing clouds of steam into the chill air. "Preacher, you're damned loco," he said. "Me, I'm headed back to Pocatello where I got a nice warm stove waitin' for me in the jailhouse. You got me to come out here once in this cursed cold and it didn't pan out. You want to go back and keep watch, that's your business. You see her, come and get me. But it'll be the last time I come up here."

Eyes gleaming with zeal, Jamison let them go and turned back toward the reservation. He would have his revenge, no matter what it took. God would provide.

ANY WHITE MAN WITH AN ounce of sanity would not have considered spending an Idaho Territory winter night out in the open. But Old Hellfire, gripped with righteous indignation he wore as a suit of armor, was prepared to put his body to the test in pursuit of his sacred goal. That determination lasted just about as long as it took for the sun to go down and a cold wind from the north to spring up. Jamison headed for the gates of the fort and waited for any soldiers that might be returning late. He found a small group of three and begged them for a night on the floor in their barracks, preferably near the stove.

"Can't turn down a man of God, can we boys?" said one, a corporal.

"Reckon not," said one of the others. "Come on, Preacher, I guess we can spare some floor space for the night."

Jamison spent a night in the barracks, and by then had worn out his welcome. He departed early the next morning without breakfast, afraid to push his luck that far. Beaten down and cold, he had been on his way back in the general direction of Pocatello to rethink his plans for acquiring Ellen when he had spotted her and Bear Paw making their way through the low hills outside the reservation boundary. He couldn't imagine what had prompted them to leave, but he didn't care. After shadowing them for a while to determine their general direction, he had quietly put some distance between them and himself, then spurred his horse for Pocatello.

ELLEN'S BREATH CAUGHT IN HER throat at site of the big pistol pointed at her from less than ten feet away, then she cursed herself for her inattentiveness. Bear Paw would never have allowed someone to get that close. Where was he? If he had seen the intruder, she knew he could put in an appearance at any second—when the time was to his advantage.

The gun was held by a big man with a thick moustache and a day's growth of stubble on his cheeks. He was wearing a thick winter coat with a sheepskin collar. A stained light-colored hat sat low on his forehead, and he held the Colt rock-solid in his right fist.

"Ellen O'Hara?" he said in a low growl.

Ellen knew it was useless to play games with her identity at this point. "Yes, I am she," she said.

"Sheriff Broward of Pocatello," the man said. "Ma'am, I have a warrant for your arrest. I'd appreciate it if you'd come peaceable."

Ellen didn't want men to die because of her, but there was little she could do to control what was going to happen. She stood up slowly, stalling for time. Two other men emerged into the clearing. One was wearing a deputy's star, and he had a pistol trained on her as well. The other, she now saw with disgust, was Jamison.

Jamison came forward, eyes gleaming. "Didn't I tell you?" he said, oozing satisfaction. "Didn't I tell you you hadn't seen the last of me? The Lord has delivered you into my hands."

"She ain't in your hands, Preacher," Broward growled. "So back off on the gloating." Despite his advantage with the gun, he looked uneasy as he turned to the deputy. "Where's Samuels? I sent him into the trees to check our backside."

"I don't know," the deputy answered. "Maybe he stopped to take a leak."

Broward's eyes narrowed. "Not likely at a time like—"

He didn't finish the sentence as something very large came flying through the air and smashed into the deputy, knocking him off his feet. It was the missing man. Both men tumbled to a heap on the ground, the deputy trapped underneath. The deputy tried to push the other man off and found his hands covered with blood. Samuels was dead. The deputy's eyes widened in revulsion and he tried frantically to get out from under. Broward whirled around in the direction the body had come from, but he wasn't fast enough. Jamison, eyes bulging with fear, had a large knife at his throat and an arm around his chest. Holding the knife was Broward's worst nightmare.

Ellen screamed to Bear Paw in Shoshone. Then she switched to English. "Please, nobody move!" she yelled. "He would kill all of you to protect me!"

Broward hadn't become sheriff by showing indecision in a crisis. Ignoring Ellen's cry, he took one big stride forward, grabbed her arm, and put the Colt to her head. "Your move, Injun," he said to Bear Paw.

Ellen was in tears. "Please, no more blood," she pleaded.

"Get him off me!" Jamison pleaded to Broward in panic. "Save me!"

"Preacher, you ain't high on my savin' list," Broward said coldly. "You got us into this. This pistol's for me more'n you." He looked at Bear Paw. "Now, I mean to take this woman in, one way or another." He looked down at Ellen. "You got any ideas?"

Ellen was crying as she looked at her husband. "Please, my love, you cannot win this fight," she pleaded in Shoshone. "Let the preacher go, and run. I do not want to see you die here." She spoke to Broward. "If he releases the preacher, will you promise to give him safe passage?"

Broward looked around. One man was dead, the other too far from his gun to change anything. "I will," he spat. "That's a promise." He turned to the surviving deputy. "Let him go if he backs off," he said. "We can pick him up later." He turned back to Ellen. "Now, can you deliver your end of the bargain?"

Ellen faced Bear Paw, anguish and longing on her face. She knew he was in a killing rage, and she wanted desperately to run to him, to feel his big arms around her one more time, to feel his love flowing into her—maybe for the last time. But she knew he could not reach the sheriff before the man cut him down—and maybe her as well. "Husband, please," she pleaded. "One or both of us will die here. You must live to fight for me another day. Please, let him go, and run. I ask this as your wife."

Bear Paw loosened his grip ever so slightly.

"I love you now and forever," she said in Shoshone, tears streaking her cheeks. "I *will* see you again."

Bear Paw backed up a step, his face a mask of both rage and resignation. He nodded, then backed away. "You are my light always," he said softly in Shoshone. Then he took two steps into the woods and was gone from view.

The surviving deputy sprang to his feet and snatched up his gun.

"Stow it, Reuben," Broward said. "A deal's a deal, even with an Injun. And I don't reckon you want to end up dead too," he added, looking over at the body of Samuels. "One was too much."

Ellen was silent as Broward gently bound her wrists in front of her.

"I'm real sorry about this, ma'am," he said.

"What is this about?" she said, as he hoisted her onto her horse. "Do you need questions answered about that settler who was shot with arrows at his cabin many months ago?"

Broward looked at her in surprise. "No ma'am, it's not about that. I heard about that one. That was one tough settler; he survived the attack. Last I heard, him and his wife pulled up stakes and moved back east. Reckon they'd had enough of frontier life. No, this is about the death of a cavalry soldier during the battle at that Shoshone camp not far from here. Ma'am, I hate to be the bearer of bad news, but this poster—" he unfolded a piece of paper he took from an inner pocket and held it out before her—"this poster says you're wanted for murder."

ELLEN WAS TAKEN BACK TO Pocatello, where she was held in the jail under 24-hour guard. She was treated with deference if not dignity, but remained silent and uncooperative to whatever questions were asked of her. Sadness gripped her at the knowledge that she had failed in her attempt to restore at least some of her Shoshone mother's horses. Gone too were the precious treasures she had collected on the reservation to accomplish the task. She had asked the sheriff if he could try to return them to the reservation, but had not received a reply.

Some of the proper ladies from Jamison's congregation came to gawk at her, especially those who had not been on the expedition to Fort Hall. They were curious about the white squaw who had single-handedly sabotaged their minister's plans. She ignored them. Jamison himself did not show.

Sheriff Broward had sent a telegram off to the cavalry as soon as they had reached town, and three days later, he received a reply. Word had already gotten around among the tribes in the area about Ellen's capture, and it was spreading into the Northwest. War drums were heard on the Fort Hall reservation. General Howard knew there was trouble in the offing if she was tried in Idaho Territory. Fearing he might have another Indian rebellion on his hands, he telegraphed an order for her removal to Portland, Oregon to face charges.

Sheriff Broward met with her in private when the cavalry detachment arrived. He seemed apologetic. "Ma'am," he said, "I felt real bad when I had to tie your hands and bring you in here. I don't like to see a woman in jail. There's always more to the story. I've been out here on this frontier some thirty years, and I've seen some strange things happen, unexpected things. People get caught up in some situations they didn't see coming. Sometimes they have to do some things to survive that get pretty ugly, and pretty strange to them folks back east resting in their parlors. I have a feeling something like that might've happened to you." He moved a little closer and sighed. "I don't know what's going to happen in Portland, but I just wanted you to know before they take you, that I wish you the best, and that those things you had with you when we found you, well, I've seen that they were returned to the reservation." He fell into an uncomfortable silence for a moment, then looked behind him as one of the cavalry detachment officers knocked on the front door of the jail and stuck his head in. It was time. He turned back to Ellen. "Is there anything else I can do for you now?"

Ellen raised her head and looked at him squarely. It was the first time she had done so since she had been put in her cell. She could see that he meant what he said. "Sheriff, thank you for your kindness in returning the items to their owners. The People have almost nothing else, so I know how much it means to them to get the gifts back." She paused for a moment, then took a deep breath and continued. "I know I haven't the right to ask for a big favor. But there is one thing that would mean so much to me, if you are willing."

Broward looked at her. "What is it?"

"I am in need of five horses."

ELLEN WAS TAKEN TO PORTLAND by stage, accompanied by a heavily armed escort of thirty mounted cavalry. She knew Bear Paw was shadowing them from some unseen vantage point, and she prayed that he would not try to rescue her. The soldiers had no doubt he was there too, and always traveled at least in pairs, if not more, with eyes constantly on the landscape.

The trip took just under a week. When they arrived, she was shown to a private cell, and assigned a lawyer, a Captain Olsen, from the cavalry officer corps. He seemed experienced and determined to do his best for her but she remained mostly uncooperative, and would barely look at him. The next day she made her initial court appearance, where the judge explained the charge against her. At the end, he declared that she would stand trial. He ordered her held indefinitely until a jury was selected.

Rabbit Woman was startled from her tipi by a considerable commotion outside. She emerged blinking into the sunlight and stood with a hand at her forehead to shade her eyes. An amazing procession was coming toward her. Many of her Shoshone friends were walking her way, and by their pace and loud conversation, seemed considerably agitated. Merely curious at first, she became instantly uneasy when she saw that a mounted white lawman was trailing them. In her experience, no good thing had ever come from an encounter with a white lawman.

The crowd grew near and gathered around her, then parted to allow the lawman to approach. He rode his horse close, then dismounted and walked up to her. His size and the big gun on his hip frightened her and she stepped back.

She saw that Dull Knife, a Shoshone brave and friend who spoke some English, was with him. Dull Knife smiled at her. "Do not fear, Rabbit Woman. The white lawman has not come for you. He has brought you gifts." With that Dull Knife and the lawman stepped aside, and the crowd also parted wider. Rabbit Woman peered at what was behind them, and was suddenly weak in the knees.

There were five horses tethered on a long lead to the lawman's horse.

Rabbit Woman walked closer to them, eyes growing ever wider. She saw the horses were of good quality.

"These horses are a gift from your white daughter," Dull Knife said. Then he turned to the crowd. "These are Rabbit Woman's horses!" he said loudly. "Come forward and see what good stock she has."

Rabbit Woman put a hand to her mouth, eyes filling with tears. Then she sank to the ground at the side of the closest horse, put one hand on its left foreleg, and broke into sobs of joy. Some in the crowd came forward and put hands on her back, then after a moment lifted her gently under the shoulders to her feet, and embraced her. The rest gathered close around to inspect the fine new horses.

"See what my white daughter has done!" Rabbit Woman cried to the crowd, tears streaking her cheeks. "See what the white lawman has done! It is a great day!"

Sheriff Broward faded away toward the back of the congratulatory crowd, and mounted his horse. He smiled as he untied the lead from his saddle horn. He didn't mind if Ellen got the credit for giving the horses. He was just glad he had gotten lucky and acquired them cheap. Now as he looked at the crowd, he reflected that it had all been worth it. He had never seen the Indians this way before, and he was struck by how familiar the emotions he was witnessing were. Rabbit Woman was the center of attention. Dull Knife had told him how much the horses would mean to the impoverished woman. He saw her broad smile of joy at this considerable gift, the congratulations of friends, the admiration for her new horses. Maybe for the first time, he saw the People as the humans they were, and not the wild children of nature he had always thought them. *They don't look any different than us*, he mused. It was a thought he would carry all the way back to Pocatello.

Ellen sat disconsolately in her cell, her back to the bars and feeling very much alone, helpless to influence anything that was happening to her.

She had already decided she would deny nothing regarding the charges against her. She would then leave her fate to those in power who held her life in their hands. She had seen far too much of the white man's "justice". She no longer recognized its power to judge her life, and she would not beg for mercy before it.

She ached for Bear Paw. *Oh husband, will I ever see you again?* she thought sadly, hands twisting her leather skirt. Despite her brave talk as Broward held the gun to her head when she was captured, she was not sure she ever would. *I need your touch,* she thought, *your big arms around me, whispering my name and telling me that all will be well.*

She heard the sound of approaching footsteps behind her, but did not move. She had been there three days and had had few visitors other than her lawyer, but was already tired of looking into the faces of the curious who came to gawk at this strange creature who was once a white woman.

"Ellen," someone called softly.

The voice sounded familiar, and she turned slowly. Standing outside her cell were Nettie, Liza, and Uncle Clarence. She gasped, and putting a hand to her mouth, stood up and walked up to the bars.

Nettie was looking at her in disbelief, while Liza stifled tears and Uncle Clarence did his best to smile at her. It was he who had called her name. "We came as soon as we got word you were here," he said.

Nettie looked unsure of who she was gazing at. "Ellen? It *is* you, isn't it? It really is you?"

"Yes," she answered. "Please forgive me if I seem slow; I have heard that name very little until I got here."

Nettie's lip trembled. "We thought you were dead!" she sobbed. "We got a telegram from Captain Morrow some weeks ago with the news that you were alive. At first we were overjoyed, but then we took to grieving again. We don't understand. If you have been alive all this time, why didn't you come home? And what are those strange clothes you're wearing?" She stifled a sob. "What in God's name happened to you?" she cried as she covered her face with a handkerchief.

"I am so sorry for the pain I have caused all of you," Ellen said softly. "I can never set it right."

Liza and Nettie seemed too distraught to talk further, but Clarence moved closer to the bars. She had always liked him; he was calm when others were not. "Can you tell us what happened, child? It would be a great comfort to know."

"You will need some chairs from the jailers to sit in," Ellen said. "It will take a long time to tell."

Chairs were acquired, and Ellen began to slowly and deliberately unwind the incredible story of what had happened since her disappearance at the massacre near Elko. Nettie and Liza listened with a mixture of disbelief and astonishment. Ellen spared them little except some of the details about the bloodier encounters she had witnessed. She withheld nothing about her love for Bear Paw. Her description of their relationship seemed to shock Nettie and Liza further yet, if that was possible.

When she was finally done, Nettie and Liza were speechless. Uncle Clarence silently nodded, affirming that he believed what she had said.

Nettie finally found her voice. "We have settled here in Portland," she said, voice distorted with emotion and looking down at her lap. "When are you coming home to us?"

The question told Ellen Nettie still didn't grasp what she had gone through—or what she had become. "I do not know, Nettie," Ellen said. "Oh, how cursed I am for the pain I have caused you! Now my life is in the hands of others. I am to stand trial for murder."

"But surely you didn't—" Liza began.

"I *did*, Liza," Ellen replied. "I killed a man. I killed him to save my husband. And I would do it again."

At that Nettie rose to go, followed by Liza and, reluctantly it seemed, by Uncle Clarence. "I fear you are lost to us, child," Nettie murmured. "We will pray for you."

With that they were gone.

ELLEN FELT MORE ISOLATED THAN ever. Was there anyone in the entire city who was sympathetic to her, she wondered, who cared what had brought her to this point? She doubted it.

She had had her arraignment, where the charge against her was restated, and, disdaining Captain Olsen's advice, pled not guilty, but insisted on a jury trial. A trial date was set, just five days away. There was no escaping it now.

Her attorney filled her in when he came to visit. Captain Olsen was trim and distinguished-looking, fair-haired with touches of gray at the temples. He was first-generation American, the son of Swedish immigrants who had settled in Minnesota. Olsen had gone west as soon as he finished law school, and joined the cavalry, eventually ending up in Washington Territory. Ellen was not sure whether he really cared about her case, or whether he was just doing the job that was assigned to him.

Now he sat with Ellen in her cell. He had brought a formless package wrapped in paper with him, which he laid on the floor near his chair. Ellen sat primly on the edge of her bunk, hands in her lap, and as usual, said little.

"We've got less than a week to prepare for trial," he told her as he shuffled through some papers. "Frankly, you haven't been much help so far. You've told me you did kill this man, and intend to own up to it in court. That alone could sink us. I don't think the jury will buy negligent homicide, so if things are looking bad I think our best bet would be for you to change your mind and plead guilty to manslaughter."

"What—what does that mean?" Ellen asked.

"Manslaughter means that though you do admit to killing this man, you did it in the heat of passion. I'm sure we can muster ample cause for passion. Or we could go a step further and plead insanity, that you were not in your right mind at the time. You did suffer a bad head injury at Elko, after all. We could plead it severely clouded your judgment when you stabbed Bailey."

Ellen looked at him directly with her piercing eyes. "I will never do that, Captain. To throw myself on the mercy of this court by pleading that I was insane at the time would dishonor every choice I have made over these last difficult months, everyone I have cared and fought for, and most of all the man I love. I *did* mean to kill him, Captain. I wanted to make sure he died, so I stabbed him in the heart. And I would do it again to protect my husband."

Captain Olsen grimaced and looked away for a moment. "So much for that idea," he said morosely. Then he looked at her, anger on his face.

"Damn it, woman, you're on trial for your life! Are you going to put up a fight or not? I can't do this all by myself! If you won't plead that the injury you suffered clouded your judgment, it doesn't mean that I won't pursue it."

Ellen said nothing for a moment. Then: "From what I have seen of the white man's justice, I doubt it would do any good."

"Fine," Olsen said with a sigh. "I've got a job to do, and I'm going to do it as well as I can, with or without your help. Maybe I've got to save you from yourself. Now, are there any witnesses we can bring in who can attest to your character during this long and trying period?"

Ellen smiled. "There are many, but they are all Shoshone or Nez Perce. Even if you could get them here, would they be listened to?"

Captain Olsen grimaced. "Probably not."

"There—there is one white man," Ellen said reluctantly. "But I have hurt him deeply, and I don't expect he would ever testify for me. Besides, I would rather not have him dragged into this."

Olsen was grasping at straws. "Was he there at the massacre?"

"No."

The captain sighed. "I'll take what I can get. Tell me where I can find him."

Ellen grimaced. "His name is Eli Morrow, and he is a captain in the cavalry. He is stationed at Fort Walla Walla."

Olsen wrote the name down. Then he looked at her sternly. "I'll fire off a telegram with a subpoena immediately, but we may not get him here by the time the trial starts. In the meantime," he said, reaching for the package at his side and unwrapping the paper, "you'll stand a better chance of favorably impressing the court if you look like a white woman again. I've brought you a dress to wear at the trial. Try it on; I'm told it should fit quite well. Now," he said, rising to go, "I'll be back for you the morning of the trial." He pointed to the dress. "And by God, you'd better be wearing that."

THE REMOVAL OF THE TRIAL to Portland did not entirely eliminate the gathering of Indians to its location. A steady stream of members of various tribes, men and women, drifted into the area and settled down around the outskirts of town. The good citizens of Portland grew more nervous with each passing day at the sound of drums in the distance and the sight of columns of fire smoke out in the woods. They appealed to local law enforcement, but the sheriff was helpless to make that many Indians leave. He was about to request the presence of a large cavalry detachment when he decided to visit Ellen. He had had the foresight to ride out to one of the circling encampments first and request someone who knew Ellen to come with him.

ELLEN WAS OVERJOYED TO SEE Many Horses, the brave with the sick wife whom Bear Paw had convinced to come out of the woods, standing outside her jail cell, even if accompanied by the local sheriff. She surged forward to the bars and gripped his arms, smiling broadly. "It is good to see you, Many Horses," she said in Shoshone. "I fear for you; it surely was not safe to leave the reservation."

"It is a small thing," he said. "It is good to see that Taviduaga is well, though she is not free."

"Your wife is well?" Ellen asked.

"Yes, she improves daily. Soon she may be strong enough to bear a child."

"I am glad."

"They have not harmed you?" Many Horses said.

"No, though I fear they do not know me. They will put me on trial as a white woman, not as Shoshone."

Many Horses nodded in understanding. "It is to be expected."

Ellen moved closer to him so she could speak softly. "Do you have news of Bear Paw?"

"Yes, I have seen him He is not far, though he keeps well hidden in the forest. He speaks daily of coming to rescue you."

Sorrow settled on Ellen's face. "Please tell him that I love him but I beg him not to try. He will be killed if he does."

"I will tell him this for you," Many Horses said.

Ellen glanced over at the sheriff and continued speaking in Shoshone. "Why has the white lawman brought you to me?"

"There are many of us here, outside the white city," he said. "Not just Shoshone, but also Flathead, Spokanes, Lemhi, Cayuse, even a few treaty Nez Perce, and others. They have come from many tribes near and far when they learned you were to be put on trial. Your story, and the honor you have brought to your tribe, has spread to many of the

People. The white lawman has brought me here because he is afraid we will try to take you away from this place and dare the whites to take you back if they can." He grew closer to her and spoke in a low voice, eyes gleaming. "Taviduaga, our camps ring the city. We are great in number. At night our campfires are like the stars in the sky. You have only to say the word, and we will storm these walls and take you away."

Ellen gripped his sleeve tightly. "I am honored to be so highly thought of among the People. You all are forever my brothers and sisters. But I love you too much to see any of you come to harm. I am captive to the white man's justice. Please spread the word that I feel the presence of all of you in my heart day and night, and that I ask you to stay nearby until the trial is over. Please, do not risk your lives for me. I have seen too much innocent blood spilled. If there is any more to be spilled, let it be mine. I killed a white man to save my husband, and I am ready to meet whatever punishment is to come. Please, Many Horses," she pleaded, "do this for me. Tell the people they will honor me best by not coming to rescue me."

Many Horses smiled and put his hands through the bars onto her shoulders. "You are a Shoshone woman. Someday I will tell my children about the time I knew you. Your story will be sung in fire circles for generations to come." He stepped back. "But I will honor your request. I will spread the word among the People that Taviduaga wishes them to spill no more blood, to be at peace."

"May the spirits bless your house, Many Horses. Go now, and spread the word."

He smiled, and preceded the sheriff out the door.

Ellen sank back into depression after he left. The trial was only two days away.

SHE SAT IN HER CELL, silent and alone. The trial was to begin the next day. It was comforting to know that so many of the people were near, but when she stepped into the courtroom, she would be on her own before the judge and jury. Except for her lawyer, of course, but he didn't really know her. He was proceeding by the book, and not by his heart, as he should be.

An untouched dinner sat beside her on the bunk. She had lost her appetite. Tomorrow she would go on trail for her life, and she had no husband by her side, no man to protect her, to fight for her. She would be alone deep in a world she no longer felt a part of, her life dependent on decisions made by people she no longer felt a kinship with.

She heard footsteps behind her outside the cell. She turned—and felt as if her heart stopped.

Eli was standing before her.

He was freshly shaven and handsome as ever, his uniform clean if a bit rumpled.

Ellen put a hand to her face. On shaking legs she stood up and walked slowly forward to the bars. "I did not think you would come," she said. "Not for me."

Eli smiled broadly at her. "I couldn't stay away. The post commander didn't want to let me go, but a subpoena is hard to ignore. Good thing he saw it that way; I was ready to resign my commission if that's what it took to get here." He brought forth the arm he was holding behind him. "I brought you something."

It was her diary.

Ellen's eyes lit up and she gave a low gasp. She reached slowly through the bars, tenderly grasped the diary and drew it to her, clutching it under her chin. "Thank you," she said, eyes shining. "I sometimes despaired of ever holding it again. It means more to me than you can know."

"I figured," Eli said. "I'm glad I could bring it back to you."

"How did you get here so quickly?"

"Modern transportation," Eli said. "Fort Walla Walla isn't far from the Columbia River. I rode down to the river and caught the first riverboat downstream, staying on board for the whole trip. We got into Portland in about a day and a half."

Eli looked at her closely. "How have you been? Have they treated you well?"

"Yes," she replied. "I have adequate food—except that tonight I seem to have lost my appetite."

"Have they respected you as a woman?"

Ellen sighed. "It is hard to know. I have a feeling sometimes that they do not regard me as a woman anymore. To them I am—something else. A strange creature they do not understand. A traitor. An Indian."

Eli hung his head for a moment, then looked up at her. When he did his face was full of emotion bursting to come forth. "Ellen, I—there's something I want to tell you. That I need to tell you."

She reached throught the bars and put her fingers gently to his lips. "Eli, there is one more thing I am." She turned and walked back to her bunk, sitting down on the edge. "I am another man's wife."

Eli's face sobered, and slowly he straightened up to his full height. He seemed to deflate ever so slightly. "Is there anything I can do for you?"

Ellen stifled a sob. "For tonight, no. But it would please me to see you in the courtroom tomorrow."

"You will," he said. Then he was gone.

Ellen could contain her tears no longer, and sat on her bunk and wept long and hard. For it was the unspoken truth that stepping back from the bars was one of the hardest things she had ever done. What she could not tell Eli, what she could not speak, was that over the months since she had first seen him, and now in seeing him again, that her desire to be in his company had grown stronger. She could no longer deny that her heart was at war with itself.

She opened her diary. Her pen and vial of ink were still in place. She opened to a new page.

February 20, 1879—Portland, Oregon

I am to be tried tomorrow. They say I murdered a white soldier. But did I? What is the definition of murder? All I did was to protect my husband when his life was threatened. I did not ask to be in that place at that time. I did not ask to be required to take a life. It gave me no pleasure to do it then, nor does it now as I look back. I have been carried this way and that for months into events I hoped never to be a part of. My life has been in constant danger, and there are many times I should have been dead.

Now I am here, and my life is in danger once again, but this time in a more civilized manner. They will listen to the evidence, and then they will find me guilty. If I am guilty of anything, it is that I have loved a man, a wonderful man who would give his life for me even now, and I for him. It fell to me to protect him, and I did without hesitation. I would do it again. I am guilty because his skin is red, because he is the lie to all that the whites hold true, all that they believe God has destined for them. So they must find me guilty, or deny all that they have done on this continent for over a century.

Perhaps I shall be hanged. If that is to be, I accept it proudly, and I will not bow my head to their judgment—or to the noose.

The crowd began lining up early outside the courthouse. Most of them were bored citizens with a taste for scandal; others came with the fire of righteous indignation, longing to see one of their own punished for her scandalous ways. By this time all of the Northwest had heard of Ellen and her trial, and even the eastern newspapers were following the story. There was little doubt in the minds of most of the public that Ellen was guilty. How could anyone have faith in the character of a white woman who had taken up with Indians? The unspeakable horror of such a choice was unsettling in the extreme, especially to the women, who were repelled by the very thought of sleeping with a red man. Since she was now an Indian, she surely killed the soldier without mercy. The only remaining question was what her sentence would be—a long prison term or the noose? All this had made finding twelve unbiased jurors very difficult, and Captain Olsen was still not convinced that they had.

A murmur of excitement ran through the crowd as Ellen walked in clutching her diary, escorted by Captain Olsen. She had given in to him and donned the dress he had provided for her. That morning he had also begged her to get rid of her braids. Reluctant at first, she gave in to his pleading and removed them, then combed out her long hair, which cascaded down her back once again. She turned her head slightly left and right as she walked down the center aisle, and was surprised to see the Reverend Jamison in one of the back rows. She did not at first glance see Eli. Nearing the front rows, she looked to her right and found Liza and Clarence smiling reassurance at her. But Ellen was sad to see that Nettie had not come.

By the time the bailiff declared that court was in session and ordered "all rise" for the judge, the courtroom was packed, and the overflow faced standing-room only around the back of the room. More would-be listeners milled about outside.

Judge Mason, a large squarely-built man on the far side of fifty with a clean-shaven face and short gray hair, made the introductory remarks about the case before him and brought the crowd to order, which took several blows of his gavel. He made the preliminary introductions of prosecutor and counsel for the defense.

"Major McGuire," he said, looking at the prosecutor, "you may begin."

The prosecutor was a middle-aged army officer with a hawk-like visage and piercing eyes. He rose, pulled down on the bottom of his uniform jacket to smooth out the wrinkles, and stepped forward in front of the jury. "Gentlemen of the jury," he began in a booming voice that belied his thin frame, there being no ladies among the jurors, "we will show that army private Ronald Bailey was viciously murdered, with malice aforethought, by the defendant Ellen O'Hara during the United State's Cavalry's campaign against the troublesome Northern Shoshone during the Bear River engagement some two years ago."

"Objection!" Olsen said loudly, standing up. "Prosecution's opening remarks are prejudicial in describing the Northern Shoshone as troublesome."

"It is an established fact—" began Major McGuire.

"Objection sustained," said the judge, looking at the prosecutor. "Major, try not to stray too far from the case at hand in your opening remarks."

"But your honor, we need to remind the jury that these hostiles—"

"*Sustained*," replied the judge. "The jury will disregard the remark. Proceed, Major, and use caution."

Olsen sat down. He had won a small victory that might restrain McGuire's rhetoric later on. But he knew that after this victories would be harder to come by.

McGuire finished his opening remarks and sat down. Captain Olsen stood up and strode to the jury box. "Gentlemen of the jury," he began, "there is more here today that merits your careful consideration than the issue of who killed Private Bailey. We must also consider in what context it occurred, and what influence that context had on his demise. We will ask you: were there other choices that could have been made, or were no other choices available? We will consider the mission of the cavalry in the massacre and how that might have played a part—"

"Objection!" shouted McGuire. "Defense counsel's description of the campaign as a massacre is prejudicial and inaccurate."

"Overruled," said the judge. "I have made a study of this campaign, and there is no shortage of reports describing it as a massacre. Gentlemen, we may never get past the opening remarks if both of you engage in such inflammatory rhetoric. I caution both of you to use restraint and stick to the case."

Olsen finished his preliminary remarks and sat down. The tack he would take in the trial was now clear. Ellen sat primly next to him at the defense table, diary in her lap, resisting the strong desire to turn around and look for Eli.

"Major, your first witness," the judge instructed.

"The prosecution calls to the stand Corporal Ephraim Hackett, U. S. Cavalry," McGuire said.

A young man in uniform with a shock of sandy hair rose from the benches and took the stand. He was sworn in and took a seat on the witness stand.

McGuire approached him, hands on the lapels of his uniform. "Corporal Hackett, would you describe to me the events of August 20th, 1877?" he asked.

"Yes sir. Well, we were engaged in a battle with those Shoshone hostiles in Idaho Territory."

"And why had you been sent into this battle?"

"Well, I wasn't really too sure. Colonel Connor, he said they was troublemakers, refusing to go onto the reservation, and wanted in the deaths of some settlers in the area. They was stealin' cattle and threatening homesteaders too. Or so the Colonel said."

"And how did the death of Private Bailey come about during this campaign?"

"Well, the battle was mostly over, and he and I were walking around behind the main camp, on the other side of this creek where some of the Injuns took cover, and we seen this squaw sittin' on the ground beside one of the biggest Injuns I ever seen. Only as we found out, she weren't no squaw."

"Continue."

"We approached the squaw, and Ronnie—that's Private Bailey—he reached out to pull her away from the Injun so's we could see if he was the Injun we were lookin' for. We had orders to look for one Injun in particular, a chief named Bear Paw. We thought it might be him. We knew if we found him, well, it would be a big feather in our caps."

"And what happened when Private Bailey reached out to the squaw?"

Hackett's eyes grew moist. "Her back was to us. She whirled around and—and she stuck Ronnie in the heart with a big knife! Ronnie, he fell back on the ground." He began to cry, his face sinking into his hands. "I—I could tell right away he was dead."

"And then?"

"The squaw, she stood up and came at me with the knife. And that's when I seen she was white. She had crazy eyes. Lord, she meant to kill me too! I ran. By the time—"

"Objection," Olsen said. "The witness is speculating as to her intent."

"Overruled," said Mason.

"Continue, please," McGuire said.

"By the time I could bring someone else back, she and the Injun were gone."

"And do you see the woman who stabbed Private Bailey in the courtroom today?" McGuire asked, turning to the audience with a flourish as he did so.

"Yes sir, I do," Hackett said, wiping his eyes. "That's her sitting over at the defense table."

A murmur spread through the crowd, and the judge banged his gavel.

"Let the record show that the witness has identified the defendant as the person he saw kill Private Bailey."

"Thank you, Corporal," McGuire said. "There will be no further questions at this time," he said to the judge. "I reserve the right to recall the witness later."

Captain Olsen stood up and approached the witness box, fire in his eyes. "Tell me, Corporal, what was the objective of your cavalry unit in attacking the Shoshone camp that day? What were your orders?"

Hackett twisted his cap in two hands. "Well sir, we was told to show 'em no mercy, that they were to be wiped out."

"And did you?"

"Yes sir, I'd say we did a pretty fair job of it," he replied, voice roiled with emotion and barely audible. "There weren't many survivors."

"What made it possible for you to be victorious that day?"

"It—it was mostly that the Injuns only had a few rifles. When they ran out of ammo, well, we overran 'em pretty quick."

Olsen turned to a sheaf of papers he was carrying in one hand. "Yes, you did. As a matter of fact, according to the United States Cavalry's own record of the event, dated January 5, 1878, over 200 Shoshone were killed that day, including women and children. It is the largest mass slaughter of Indians in the west to date. Your Honor, I'd like to submit this report as Defense Exhibit A." He handed the report to the bailiff, who gave it to the judge. Olsen turned back to the witness stand, leaning close to Hackett. "Isn't it a fact, Corporal, that according to eyewitness accounts of the battle scene, women were slain as they begged for mercy and some of them had their genitalia cut off, babies were swung by the heels against rocks, their brains bashed out, warriors were castrated, pregnant women were killed, the babies cut from their bodies and slain?"

"Objection!" roared McGuire.

Olsen ignored him and plunged ahead. "Isn't that the way it was, Corporal? And didn't you in fact see these things being done?"

"Yes sir, I did," Hackett said, lip trembling.

"Objection!" McGuire shouted again. "This line of questioning is irrelevant to the trial before this court!"

"On the contrary, Your Honor," Olsen said. "As I indicated in my opening remarks, I believe the context in which Private Bailey's death took place is entirely relevant."

The judge looked at him sternly. "I'll overrule—for now. But I caution you, Captain, you'd better be heading somewhere with this."

Olsen turned back to Hackett and moved in for the kill. "And didn't you and Private Bailey in fact *take part* in some of these atrocities?"

Hacket hung his head, unable to speak.

"The witness will answer the question," the judge said.

Hackett's face twisted in pain and his lip trembled. "Yes sir, we did." He broke into sobs. "God help me, I haven't been able to stop the nightmares ever since."

Olsen wasn't proud of what he was doing, but he knew he had Hackett just where he wanted him. "Combatants on both sides of these Indian wars are known to castrate or mutilate fallen combatants and take scrota and female genitalia for tobacco pouches or war trophies." He leaned close and loomed over Hackett. "So didn't you and Private Bailey approach the big Indian with the idea of castrating him?"

"No! Not me," Hackett said, shaking his head, his jaw set in denial. "But—but Ronnie did."

Olsen backed up a step, as he could sense McGuire was about to accuse him of badgering the witness. He turned toward the jury and spoke in a soft but intense voice. "And isn't it also possible, Corporal, that the squaw you approached knew that these things were being done that day, and that she feared for her husband's life?"

"Objection," said McGuire in a loud voice. "Counsel is leading the witness."

"No further questions at this time, Your Honor," Olsen said, striding quickly back to the defense table. He had accomplished his mission to severely undermine Hackett's and Bailey's character and intentions. But he hated what he had had to do. And when he glanced at Ellen, she looked unhappy too.

"Court will recess for ninety minutes," said the judge. "We will resume at 11:00 o'clock."

"All rise," intoned the bailiff as the judge got up and walked through a door at the rear of the courtroom.

Ellen turned and sought out Liza and Clarence. They met her halfway as she walked toward them. Without hesitation, Liza wrapped her arms around Ellen, hugging her fiercely. Then she drew back, tears in her eyes. "Oh child, this all sounds so horrible for you. I can scarce believe what I'm hearing. How is it possible you could be mixed up in all of this? Surely this is a case of mistaken identity!"

"Aunt Liza, it is not, unfortunately. I am the one the Corporal spoke of. But where is Nettie?"

She refused to come," Liza said. "She thinks you have turned into someone very strange indeed. We tried to convince her to be here, that you need her support, but she says she will not do so until you come home and give up your Indian ways."

Ellen was downcast. "I cannot do so, not right now. I have crossed over a line I could not see, Liza. And there is no going back. Not completely. Perhaps one day I may straddle that line. It is the best I can hope for."

"Well," Liza sniffed, wiping her eyes, "we were worried sick that you were dead. Now that we see you're alive, I'm more worried than ever."

Ellen attempted a reassuring smile and reached out to touch Liza's arm. "I am so sorry, Aunt Liza. You don't deserve this. If the trial is too much for you, you have my blessing to go home."

Clarence put a hand on Ellen's shoulder. "Whatever happens, child, we're behind you all the way. We love you."

Ellen started to respond, but something captured her attention and she looked away. Eli was standing at the rear of the room. She disengaged and walked over to him. "I am blessed to have you here," she said, smiling, "but at the same time I am sorry to see it."

"I hope I can contribute to your defense. Captain Olsen says he plans to put me on the stand when we resume."

Ellen frowned. "I am opposed to this. He has plunged ahead with it anyway."

Court was back in session at the indicated time, and Olsen did indeed call Eli to the stand.

"Captain, are you acquainted with the defendant?" he began.

"Yes sir," Eli said.

"And do you have knowledge of how she came to be with the Shoshone?"

"Yes, I do. She was part of a party of travelers who were attacked by Gosiute Indians at Elko, Nevada. She was one of only two survivors and the only one not accounted for among the living or dead at that time. No one knew what had happened to her. As I later learned, she suffered a bad head injury and wandered off into the wilderness. After several days, she staggered, near death, into a camp of Northern Shoshone."

"So is it possible that this head injury affected her future judgment?"

Eli paused. He had heard Ellen's story when he rediscovered her and believed she had overcome her injury, and made her choices with a clear mind. He could see she had in fact been toughened beyond imagining by her ordeal and had grown into a mature and rational woman. He was therefore reluctant to provide her with an excuse he didn't believe for defending her husband. But he also knew Olsen had put him on the stand to help her. Reluctantly he replied. "Yes sir, from what I know a bullet fired at close range glanced off her skull. It could have affected her judgment for some time."

"Perhaps even to the point of clouding her mind when it came time to defend her husband?"

Eli nearly bit his lip trying to hide his discomfort. He was convinced with every fiber of his being that Ellen had been perfectly rational, if intensely distraught, when she stabbed Bailey. "Yes sir, I believe it could have."

"Thank you, Captain. No further questions at this time, Your Honor," Olsen said, walking away.

"Major McGuire, do you have a cross?" the judge said.

McGuire rose and strode to the witness box. "Captain, do you have medical training?"

"No."

"Then your opinion regarding the long-term effect of the defendant's head injury is strictly that of an uninformed amateur, is it not?"

"Yes, it is," Eli said, taking a deep breath.

"Then would you tell us, please, how you presume to know the defendant's state of mind when she killed Private Bailey? Were you there?"

"Objection," Olsen said. He was grasping at straws now. "Prosecutor is assuming it has already been determined that the defendant was in fact the one who stabbed Private Bailey."

"Overruled. You may continue, Major, but watch your assumptions."

"I ask again," McGuire said. "Were you there?"

Eli hesitated and gathered his thoughts. "No, but I have talked with her about what happened during the massacre that day."

"I see," McGuire said, sensing the opening he was looking for. "And tell me, Captain, what is your relationship to the defendant that she would share such information with you?"

At the defense table, Olsen grimaced. He had known there was a risk when he had chosen to put Eli on the stand. Now his fears were at hand.

Ellen leaned over, glaring at him. "I am most unhappy that you put him on the stand!" she whispered. "I do not want to see him embarrassed."

"I'm sorry," Olsen whispered back. "I was looking for anything that could bolster your defense."

"This is a price I am not willing to pay. He is too good a man to be made a fool of by that vile prosecutor."

Olsen sighed, exasperated with his client's unwillingness to act in her own defense. "I'm sorry, but it's out of my hands now."

Prosecutor McGuire was prodding Eli again. "Captain, will you please answer the question?"

Eli was clearly unhappy. "I—"

McGuire cut him off. "Captain, isn't it a fact that the defendant was your fiancée before she disappeared into the wilderness, that she was coming west to marry you, and that we should therefore question the objectivity of your judgment regarding her state of mind at the time of Private Bailey's murder?"

Eli was shocked. How could McGuire know?

"Isn't that so, Captain?"McGuire shouted. "How can we trust your judgment if it's colored by the defendant's being your bride-to-be?" McGuire didn't wait for an answer, but strode away to the prosecution's table. "No further questions, Your Honor," he said to Eli's back.

At the defense table, Captain Olsen's head sank ever so slightly. Just as he himself had torpedoed Hackett, McGuire had now torn down his only witness for Ellen's defense.

"I'd like to see both counsels in my chambers," the judge said.

Olsen and McGuire rose and followed the judge into his private room at the back of the courtroom.

"Do either of you have any other witnesses to call?" the judge asked when he was seated behind his big desk.

Olsen shook his head no.

Major McGuire said, "I'm holding Colonel Connor, the commander of the unit that carried out the mission against the Shoshone in reserve, to testify if necessary."

"To what end?" said the judge.

"I'd like him to testify as to the necessity of the action against the hostiles."

"I'll tear him apart, and you know it," Olsen said quietly. "Given the bad press that's resulted from news of the nature of the massacre, and the tone of the army's own report, I doubt he wants to restate what he though was necessary at the time, and what the actions of his troops led to. If he takes the stand, I'll make him relive it in every bloody detail."

"I've already sustained an objection to taking testimony as to the cavalry's intent," the judge said.

"Never mind," McGuire said, smiling. "I don't really need him."

"Captain," the judge said, turning to Olsen, "do you plan to put Miss O'Hara on the stand?"

"No, Your Honor," Olsen said, sighing. "She hasn't been very cooperative, and I'm not sure she would help her cause in the witness chair."

The judge leaned back in his chair and put his hands over his expansive stomach. "Then I take it there is no more testimony to be given. That being the case, if there are no objections, we will hear final arguments tomorrow."

They got up and left the private chambers. The judge returned to his seat and declared that court was adjourned until 10:00 a.m. the next day.

Eli walked slowly over to Ellen.

She was looking at him with confusion and disappointment on her face. "How did the prosecutor know about us?" she said.

Eli looked sorrowful. "I don't know."

"I might," Olsen said. "When McGuire found out about your appearance as a witness for the defense, he probably became curious as to your connection to the case. He may have shot off telegrams to Fort Walla Walla asking for information. Was your relationship to Miss O'Hara a secret there?"

"No," Eli said, silently kicking himself. "It was known to a very few that I had found my missing bride-to-be. I'm sorry, Ellen, I just couldn't face it alone. I needed someone to talk to."

"Do not be ashamed, Eli," Ellen said. "The shame it brings me is the pain I have caused you—and still am causing."

"Miss O'Hara, from the start I've been unsure about what you want from this trial," Olsen said. "Tomorrow is the final day. Care to enlighten me?"

Ellen gave him the faintest of smiles. "Tomorrow you will know," she said.

ELLEN SPENT THE EVENING IN her cell, rereading parts of her diary until it was late. Eli came to see her. She went to the bars and put her hands in his.

"Your hands are cold," he said.

She chuckled, smiling, then released her hands from his and put them in the pockets of her dress.

"Tomorrow it ends," Eli said. He looked closely into her face, trying to fathom what she was thinking. "It could be a very tough day. Are you up to it?"

Ellen started to nod, but suddenly put hands to her face, sobbing. "Oh Eli, I am scared. I thought I could be brave for all of this—"

Eli smiled and reached toward her through the bars. "It's hard to remember sometimes that you're only seventeen. But right now I'm reminded of it. Don't carry this burden alone. I'm here; lean on me."

Ellen stepped forward into his arms and did her best to press her head to his chest. Eli could feel her shaking.

"I will," she said quietly. I promise. Now, you should go. I will see you in the morning."

After Eli had gone, Ellen sat on her bed and, opening her diary once again, wrote a long entry before asking the guard to turn down the lamp for the night.

If the trial crowd had been huge and boisterous before, it was even more so the next morning. People started lining up for a seat inside the courtroom in the pre-dawn darkness, huddled against the morning fog, and at the same time nervously glancing toward the outskirts of the city, many of them convinced the Indians were massing for a last-minute rescue of Ellen. They had respected Ellen's request, however, and though the sound of drums sounded most of the night in the woods about the city, they had not moved.

The courtroom was packed when Ellen made her entrance at Captain Olsen's side. She looked about and found Liza and Clarence still there, and so was Reverend Jamison. Eli was seated in the first row behind the defense table. She gave him a nervous smile as she was seated.

Prosecution, and then defense, made their closing arguments. There had been no corroborating testimony to Corporal Hackett's claim that it was Ellen who had stabbed Private Bailey, and there was precious little to go over. Most of the arguments were merely a summary of the inquiries and answers they had garnered the previous day.

Olsen returned to his seat at the defense table when he had finished. He leaned over to Ellen and whispered, "I've done the best I can for you. It's in the jury's hands now."

Excited chatter erupted throughout the crowd. The judge banged his gavel for order. Then he looked at the jury and gave them final instructions. "Court is in recess until the jury reaches a verdict," he declared.

Few went anywhere, not those in the benches nor those outside. Eli reached forward and squeezed Ellen's shoulders. She briefly reached up a hand to cover his.

BARELY AN HOUR LATER, THE jury sent word that they had reached a verdict. The bailiff declared that court was once again in session, and the jurors filed silently into the jury box.

"Has the jury reached a decision in this case?" the judge inquired.

The jury foreman stood up. "We have, Your Honor," he said, handing a folded piece of paper to the bailiff, who walked over and presented it to the judge. The judge unfolded the paper and studied it for a long moment. Then he looked up. "The defendant will rise."

Ellen rose from the defense table, and Captain Olsen rose beside her.

The judge looked at her, his face a mask of ill-concealed pain. "Ellen O'Hara, the jury finds you guilty of murder in the second degree."

*I thought God intended us to live, but I see I
was mistaken. God intends to give
the country to the white people, and we are to
die. It may be well, it may be well.*
—*Standing Bear of the Poncas*

THE COURTROOM ERUPTED INTO CHAOS. In the third row, Liza sobbed and buried her face in a handkerchief as Clarence wrapped an arm around her. Reporters ran for the door. At the defense table, Captain Olsen looked down, the fingers of each hand on his forehead. Ellen sat expressionless and silent.

She spoke to Olsen, still looking ahead. "It was nothing less than I expected from the beginning."

She looked around to see Eli standing in the aisle just behind her.

"I'm so very sorry," he said, fighting for composure. "I will stay with you all the way."

They were interrupted by the banging of the judge's gavel. After a few seconds, he was finally able to quiet the crowd. "Court will re-convene tomorrow morning at ten o'clock," he said, "at which time sentence will be pronounced. Until then, this court is adjourned."

A ripple of murmurs spread across the room, and the judge reached for his gavel.

"Give him the diary," Ellen whispered urgently to Captain Olsen.

"What?" he said in surprise.

"*Give him the diary!*"

Olsen shot from his seat. "Your Honor! As mitigating evidence in determining the defendant's sentence, we would like to offer her personal diary for your examination."

Judge Mason looked at him in surprise, then over at Major McGuire. "Does Prosecution have any objection?"

McGuire smiled. Ellen had already been found guilty, so he saw no harm. "No, Your Honor."

The judge nodded, and Olsen approached the bench and laid Ellen's diary before him.

Ellen slowly rose to her feet, numb. She turned and saw Liza and Clarence standing nearby. Liza appeared near collapse, with nothing to hold her up except Clarence. "Oh, child," she sobbed, "what will become of you?"

"Tomorrow we will know, Liza. I beg you stay nearby until then."

JUDGE MASON TOOK ELLEN'S DIARY home that night. Once there, he changed into comfortable clothes, sought out his favorite chair, and turned up the lamp on the nearby table. Putting on his reading glasses, he opened the diary and began.

At 3 a.m. he was still reading.

ELLEN WAS RESTLESS IN HER CELL. Eli had come to comfort her as best he could through the bars. After about ten minutes, she asked him to go. It was just too painful to see the distress on his face. Liza had not come, but Clarence showed up in the early evening. "Liza's too distraught to face you," he said. "Truth to tell, it took all the courage I could muster to get myself here." His pursed his lips, struggling to hold back the pain he felt. "Child, this could be the last time we can get close to you. Or even the last time we see you. If the sentencing goes bad tomorrow, Liza has told me she can't stay. I'm afraid I'd have to go with her. We can't bear the thought of seeing you—" He couldn't finish, his head sinking nearly to his chest.

Ellen reached through the bars and grasped his hands tightly. "I would want you to go," she said. "I would not have you see me hanged. Now, please go, and give my love to Liza."

Clarence left, and she sat alone on her bunk, unable to think of anything except the next morning. Fear began to seep into her mind, and she wished desperately for Bear Paw to be there, his big arms around her, taking her away to someplace safe. She was suddenly sorry she had sent word to him not to attempt her rescue. Right now, she wouldn't object. If he could break her free, she would go with him, would fly across the hills and into the mountains, to live life on the run and free, as long as that might be until the relentless white soldiers found her and brought her back.

She was preparing to bed down and turn out the lamp when she saw she had yet another visitor. Many Horses was back, and with him was a wizened little Indian woman she had never seen.

Ellen was overjoyed at his presence. "What news of Bear Paw?" she said.

"I have seen him this day," Many Horses said. "He is waiting for tomorrow. He has not said what he will do if you are to be put in prison or sentenced to death. There will be no stopping the People if they decide to free you. What they decide to do, will be done."

Ellen looked down and clasped her hands together. "I know," she said. "I pray there is no more blood spilled on my account. But who is this you have brought?"

Many Horses brought the stranger a step forward. "This is Waits for Her Husband." he said. "She is Shoshone. She traveled far to be here, and she asked to bring you something for tomorrow."

Ellen looked at the small woman. Her face was lined with age, and her hair was gray, woven into a single large braid.

She smiled at Ellen and brought her arms up. In them was a magnificent buckskin garment, nearly pure white. It looked like it had never been worn. There was delicate fringe on the sleeve cuffs, along the bodice, and across the upper back, as well as around the hem. "This is for you, Taviduaga," she said. "When you face the white man's justice tomorrow, let it be as a Shoshone. Wear this, and let them know how proud you are to be of the People. Show them the courage you have shown us so often."

Ellen reached through the bars and gently took the garment into her hands. It was amazingly soft, and had obviously been worked for many hours. "Did you make this?" she asked.

The old woman smiled and nodded.

"This took a very long time. And it looks as if it has never been worn. Who did you make it for?"

Waits for Her Husband smiled, but Ellen could see there was pain behind it. "It was to be my daughter's wedding dress," she said. "But she will never wear it in this world. Two years ago, she was killed by white settlers who found her gathering food in the woods." Her eyes grew moist. "They had no mercy on a young girl. I put the dress away, determined that it would not see the light of day until I found someone worthy of wearing it. I have."

Ellen held the garment tightly against her chest. "I am honored, Waits for Her Husband," she said softly. "I will wear it with pride tomorrow. But since you have come, would you do one more thing for me?"

"Name it, child."

"Would you braid my hair?"

The old woman smiled and nodded. Under the watchful eye of the ever-present guard, Ellen backed up to the bars and sat on a stool as Waits for Her Husband lovingly braided Ellen's hair into twin braids. When she was done, she placed the braids in front, signifying her as a married Shoshone woman.

"ALL RISE," SHOUTED THE BAILIFF over the raucous crowd. "Court is in session, the Honorable Judge Reginald Mason presiding."

The judge strode in with Ellen's diary under one arm. He sank into his chair, put the diary down and banged the gavel twice. The raucous conversation slowly faded away.

Judge Mason glared at the crowd until the last voice was silent. "Ladies and gentlemen," he began, "sentencing will be postponed briefly while I address all of you for a few minutes." He paused and seemed to gather himself. "A great tragedy has unfolded before us during this trial. Unfortunately, it is only one of many such episodes that have occurred across our land. Most of them are still not fully known to the public. If ever there was a case crying out for full disclosure, for tolerance and understanding, it is this one. If ever there was a case calling for all of us here to re-examine our purpose in what we have brought forth on this continent, it is this one. For this is a tragedy for both sides. It is a tragedy of destruction and death for the conquered. It is a tragedy of character for the victorious. It was not only calamitous that we went forth across this land, destroying native cultures as he went. What is unforgivable is that too often it was done under the banner of God's will, as if God was sympathetic to the whites, was the God of the whites alone, and not a God of the Indians. Some of us claim—without a shred of proof—that He meant for us to conquer these peoples. Some of us claimed it was all in the cause of saving heathen souls, as if the beliefs the Indians hold about their Creator were not worthy of consideration. In the Bible, Jesus commands his disciples to go out into the world and spread the good news of salvation. He did not command them to go forth and put other peoples to the sword while doing so, to sweep aside all who where in their way. And he did not command them to do this while flying the banner of a righteous cause, of a Manifest Destiny."

The judge paused to catch his breath, then continued. "What we have done on this continent cannot be undone. The great tragedy we have visited on these peoples will live forever, and their children will inherit it. We will live comfortably in our cities hewn out of the wilderness, and the former inhabitants of this land will be conveniently forgotten on patches of the land that was once theirs, to fend for themselves, or live as beggars off the white man's reluctant charity."

"I have read the defendant's diary of her experiences over the many months she was forced into running for her life. The pages smell of blood. It is a tale of murder, starvation, and endless flight, of bodies buried in shallow graves along the trail, of children suffering and dying for reasons their mothers could not explain to them because they themselves did not understand, could not know what they had done to merit such relentless and merciless tyranny."

"My sympathy for the defendant is strong. I cannot fault the choices she made when, not of her own choosing, she was thrust into a world dying around her. I question whether any of you would have made different choices." He paused for a moment and sighed. "Yet I am constrained by the law. A verdict of guilty has been rendered, and a sentence must be applied." He looked at Ellen. "Will the defendant please rise?"

Nervous muttering ran through the crowd as Ellen rose to her feet in her beautiful buckskin dress, her braids resting on her chest. Captain Olsen put his arm around her.

"Ellen O'Hara, the jury has found you guilty of murder in the second degree. Do you have anything to say before the court passes sentence on you?"

Ellen slowly rose from the table. "Your Honor," she said, "with your permission I would like to address the court on my behalf."

Captain Olsen sighed. He had done all he could for Ellen, but she was determined to have her way.

"You may do so, Miss O'Hara," the judge said.

Ellen approached the bench. "May I, Your Honor?" The judge nodded, and she took her diary, holding it against her chest. She looked over at the jury briefly, then turned around and faced the audience, holding out the diary. "This book is a personal diary I have kept since I left Salina, Kansas over two years ago. I have done my best to accurately record what I have experienced over that time. My husband and I, after leaving the Nez Perce band following their capture by General Howard's men near the Canadian border, journeyed back to find the home we were so cruelly torn from." Ellen opened the diary to a page she had marked. "I wrote this entry last night from my memory of our arrival."

What I think is February, 1878—near what was our Shoshone camp in southern Idaho Territory.

We returned yesterday to the village we had called home. It was a good camp, full of people mostly happy, doting on their children, instructing the youngsters in how to succeed at the tasks they would inherit according to their sex, as it had been from time beyond knowing. There were marriages, buffalo hunts and games, joy and pride at skills improved or perfected. Through the sad times, the hungry times, there was support and comfort for new widows, and elation as a new Shoshone entered the world. I was a part of all this, as I had become one of them, sharing their triumphs and their tragedies.

It was hard to hold back my tears as we rode into camp, and saw what had become of all this. Bear Paw was silent and numb. The happiness we had known here was gone forever, replaced by cold, heartless death. We dismounted and walked among the ruins. Through the snow on the ground, grim shapes arose, the skeletal remains of horses, dogs—and Shoshone, frozen in death. The charred remnants of tipi skins and their lodge poles, the smell of their burning was still in the air. Belongings formerly cherished were strewn about, broken and rusted. All was silent.

We walked over to the creek bed where I and a group of Shoshone women had huddled, desperate to protect the children, hoping the white soldiers would not find us. The remains of the child who had been sent forth with a flag of truce lay nearby, where she had been shot down. At that I could no longer contain my tears.

There were five skeletons in the creek bed. One of them was that of a child. It was here that we had made a final stand, screaming for mercy as the soldiers gunned us down, I protected only by the bodies of those who fell around me.

We gathered what things we could find to dig with, and with much effort scraped a grave out of the frozen earth. There we reverently placed the remains of those from the creek bed, and scraped the cold ground over them. Bear Paw performed a brief ceremony to speed them on their way to the next world. Then we went to our horses and left. Neither of us wanted to spend the night on this killing ground. There are still ghosts in the air.

Ellen closed the diary slowly and looked up. "We were attacked without warning or mercy. The soldiers had one clear instruction: they were to wipe us out, man, woman, and child. When the braves were no longer able to defend their camp, the slaughter began. It continued until nearly all were dead. Some of them lie there still."

"What was their crime? They wanted only to raise their children in the only way they knew, on the lands their Creator had given to them. In the beginning, they did not seek to raise their hand against the white man, but in time they were given no choice. The way they lived their lives was unacceptable to whites. They were to be pushed aside, their villages destroyed, to make room for people who had no mercy for the ones they inconveniently found on land they now claimed as their own."

"You view me as sick and twisted, perhaps even a traitor. I am strange to you, because I married the wrong man. But what in truth is my crime? For me, I married the right man, the man I needed. I have no regrets. Few of you have any idea of what these people are like. Sometimes you refer to them as noble savages, wild children of nature, and thus forever apart from you. But they are neither noble nor savage. They argue, they gamble, they are jealous or prideful. They make war on each other, sometimes only to gain honor, sometimes for no reason at all. Some of them keep slaves. They have shown the same kind of brutality in warfare against whites that white soldiers have against them—rape, kidnapping, the taking of scalps, murder. I ask you how much of that was forced on them by whites who gave them no other choice but to surrender the life they had always known, and whose own merciless brutality served as an example for their response?"

"These people you think are wild beasts fear for their children as you do, work hard to raise them well, and jealously guard the virtue of their daughters. They laugh, they cry, they support those in need. If necessary they will give their lives for their loved ones. You would find their cares, their concerns, their triumphs very familiar. Beneath the garments they wear, behind the lives you find so strange, how like us they are! This, above all, is what I want you to know."

Ellen paused for a moment, then continued. "You have put me on trial for the murder of Private Bailey. I will make things very clear to you now. Yes, I did kill Private Bailey. I meant for him to die, that is why I stabbed him in the heart. I had seen the blood, heard the screams throughout the camp. The intentions of the white soldiers toward my husband were clear. They would torture him, mutilate him, kill him and be proud they had done so. When he was struck down, it fell to me to defend the man I love." Ellen paused, making eye contact with the jurors. "I killed the soldier that day," she said. "I would do it again." Then she turned and walked back to the defense table and sat down next to a morose Captain Olsen.

"I've done all I can for you," he said. "You were determined to have it your way. I hope it has done you some good."

"This is all I ever wanted," she replied. "I have had my say. If my life is the price, so be it. I have little else left."

Judge Mason banged his gavel for order. Then he looked at Ellen and gave her the faintest hint of a smile. "Will the defendant please rise?"

Ellen did so.

"Ellen O'Hara, you are hereby sentenced to time served, and this court orders your immediate release. You are free to go, and this case is closed."

The courtroom crowd exploded in pandemonium. People sprang to their feet, some yelling approval, others cries of outrage. The latter included many of the women present, who had wanted to see Ellen punished for falling in with heathens. Some shouted abuse at the judge. He ignored them.

Over at the prosecution's table, Major McGuire looked off into the distance for a few seconds, then nodded his head ever so slightly in approval, a tight smile on his face. At the defense table Ellen's stone wall of stoicism collapsed, and she fell back in her chair sobbing with relief, hands to her face. Captain Olsen hugged her tightly until Eli reached them and put a protective arm around her, his face a mask of anger toward the courtroom crowd.

Ellen buried her face in Eli's chest for long minutes, and when she finally stepped back, she saw Clarence standing there.

"It's a good day after all, child," he said, smiling broadly. "I can't wait to get the news to Liza and Nettie." He moved closer. "Now I know things are pretty unsettled right now, but they are certain to ask me when you're coming home."

Ellen wiped away tears and smiled back at him. "I cannot say, Clarence. It may not be soon. There are things to sort out, and it will take time. But tell them they have my promise they will see me at their home, in time."

"That will not make them happy," Clarence said. "I don't think they understand the change you've been through. They don't understand why you can't give it all up and behave like a white woman again."

"I am sorry, Clarence. I don't want to hurt them and you again. But the truth is I am not a white woman anymore, not in the sense that I was. When I can find a middle ground to survive in, then I will see them, and you, again."

Clarence nodded. "God bless you, child, and go with you always." Then with a parting hug, he turned and walked away."

"He does, Clarence," she whispered after him.

When she turned around, Olsen handed her her diary, having retrieved it from the bailiff.

Olsen suggested it was time to go. With he and Eli flanking Ellen protectively, they made their way down the aisle and out the entrance into the sunlight. Crowds of people were waiting, not all of them charitable. "You'll pay for this on judgment day!" somebody shouted. "Murderer!" shouted another as the three walked the gauntlet of people. But there were shouts of encouragement too. "We love you, Ellen!" shouted several, all women. "You are so brave!"

They got nearly to the end of the line when Ellen heard a familiar voice call her name. She looked around for the source.

It was Reverend Jamison. He appeared embarrassed—and contrite.

Ellen approached him, not knowing what to expect.

"Miss O'Hara, there's something I need to tell you. I—I journeyed here to see justice done. I had vengeance on my mind. But somewhere between Pocatello and Portland, God touched my heart. Today I did see justice done—and I am so very happy for it. You are free, and that is a blessing." He stopped for a moment, barely able to keep his eyes on her, then continued. "You see, you shamed me that day you were captured. I might be dead now if it wasn't for you. I will never forget what you did for me, someone who defied you, tried to deceive your people." His chin trembled. "I prayed for forgiveness for calling you a Daughter of Satan. I think on that day, you were closer to God's will than I was. I am so ashamed." He took a deep breath. "Please, will you accept my apology?"

Ellen was deeply moved. This was something she would never have expected. "Yes, Reverend Jamison, I will. God has brought us together today for a purpose, and it is a good one."

Jamison appeared truly relieved. "Just one more thing, Miss O'Hara. We *will* have a school for the children. But they will be invited to come, to accept or not, as they choose. They may keep their Indian names, and will not be asked to cut their hair or dress as white children. We hope to serve them in this way, knowing that *that* is truly God's will."

Ellen reached forward and gave him a brief hug. "You have made me truly happy." With that, she turned and walked on.

At last they were clear of the crowd, where they could talk.

"What will you do now?" Eli asked.

"I am so very tired," Ellen said. "I would like to stay somewhere nearby for the night, and I will leave tomorrow to seek Bear Paw. I have need of my husband."

Eli said nothing, but nodded. "I'll arrange quarters for you."

AFTER ELI SAW ELLEN COMFORTABLY settled in a private room for the night, he went for a ride out of town to clear his mind and think about what he should do now. Ellen was free, but she was not ready to return to the white world. She would go back to her husband. He had not thought this far ahead, he realized, and it left him in a quandary.

As evening approached, he dismounted and made a small fire for coffee. He was seated near the fire enjoying his first cup when he heard a noise and looked up.

Bear Paw was standing ten feet away.

Eli nearly dropped his cup, breath caught in his throat. This was the last person he expected to see now. He had not worn his pistol on the ride, and his rifle was in its scabbard on his horse fifteen feet behind him. He was defenseless before a man who in the past would not have hesitated to kill him. He looked his visitor over closely. Bear Paw appeared completely unarmed. No bow, no rifle, no knife. *At least that I can see*, he thought.

Bear Paw spoke. "White soldier, I watch for you. I see you leave. I follow, come to you. We share fire, talk."

Eli, eyes never leaving Bear Paw's face, took a deep breath, slowly nodded, and bade him come forward. He picked a spare cup out of his small pack and poured coffee for his visitor.

Bear Paw settled on a rock next to the fire, then reached out with one big hand and took the cup. He took a sip of the coffee, silent.

Eli was immensely relieved. It seemed the big Shoshone had not come to fight. He knew that Bear Paw's command of English was limited, and so he would simplify his words accordingly. "Yes, we will talk."

"Taviduaga is well?"

"Yes, she is well." Eli hadn't heard the shortened version of Ellen's Shoshone name, but he had no doubt about whom Bear Paw was referring to. "She rests tonight, then she said she plans to seek you tomorrow."

Bear Paw spoke again. "One small woman. Two men. Different worlds," he said, a wry grimace on his face.

Eli nodded. "Two men," he agreed.

"Not enough woman for two," Bear Paw replied. "Taviduaga can't live in two worlds."

"No," Eli said. *Where is he going with this?* he thought.

"For long time I am angry she promised to white soldier."

Elil chuckled. "For a long time I could not understand why she married you. But I believe you are a good man." He grimaced. "Worthy of her love."

"Never meet good white soldier," Bear Paw said. 'But you good man also. I see how she could love you."

"And we are back to where we began. One woman, two men. Do you trust her love for you?"

Bear Paw hung his head. "Not always. Sometimes I think someday she go back to you. I shame her."

"She will not come back to me," Eli said bitterly. "You can trust her to keep her vow to you."

Bear Paw grunted in satisfaction. "She is good, this woman. Another day, I seek to kill you. But not this day."

"And I would seek to kill you. Ellen is not even here, but she has brought us together. We who have long been enemies sit and talk. No weapons, no anger. She is powerful, yes?"

Bear Paw nodded. Then: "You still love her?"

Eli hesitated. Conversation with a mortal enemy was one thing, but baring his soul? Slowly, he responded. "Yes, I stil love her, more than ever. I always will. Like you, I would give my life for her."

Bear Paw nodded and was silent, listening to the crackle of the fire and sipping his coffee.

The moments stretched on as Eli watched the flames dance above the wood. He pondered the strangeness of it all, to be seated having a civil discourse across a fire with a Shoshone warrior, neither one armed, neither one seeking an advantage, both trying to deal with the fact that they loved the same woman. He began to wonder if Bear Paw had more to say.

Finally the big Shoshone spoke. "Do you know the big hill that sits on the shore of the bitter water, toward the setting sun? It is west as the crow flies."

"Yes, I know the place. It has a rounded top with a meadow among a scattering of trees. The front face is a straight drop to the water far below, where the waves lap against the base."

Bear Paw nodded. "Yes, that is the one. Do one thing for me, white soldier. Go to Taviduaga tomorrow morning, and guide her to that hill. Tell her that I will meet her there, at the top. But tell her also to climb to top alone. You do this for me?"

"Yes, I will do this. You have my word. But why do you go there?"

Bear Paw stood. "Do not let go of your love for her. Taviduaga may have need of it." With those cryptic words, he turned and left, vanishing into the trees.

Eli sat by the fire for almost an hour afterward, trying to decipher the meaning of what Bear Paw had said.

ELLEN WAS PLEASED TO SEE Eli waiting for her the next morning when she emerged from her lodging, diary across her shoulder. But she was amazed when he told her why he was there.

"Is my husband well?" she said.

"Yes, he appeared well, if a little somber."

"How incredible that you were able to sit and talk with each other, with no weapons, no rage, only words. It is more than I could have hoped for."

"It wasn't easy," Eli said. "He sent me to guide you to him. The place he chose is due west about three days' ride."

"He is that far?" Ellen said, amazed. "Why?"

"I don't know; he wouldn't say. But his instructions are very clear. I am to take you to the coast. There is a large hill at water's edge. He waits for you at the top."

ELI ARRANGED FOR A HORSE for Ellen, and they set out at midday, riding west. Ellen had packed away her white dress, substituting garb more suited to a long ride, but she had it with her. They rode at an easy but steady pace, and camped when night fell. Neither said much during the trip. Eli did not trust himself to engage Ellen in extended conversation without losing control and begging her to leave her Indian life and cleave to him. He had promised Bear Paw to bring her safely to him, and he would keep his word out of respect for Ellen, much as it hurt him to do so.

Ellen was largely silent, lost in thought about what her husband was preparing for her, wondering endlessly why he had not simply waited in the hills outside of Portland for her. Perhaps it was because he was still a wanted man, and feared capture. She did not know.

THEY ARRIVED IN LATE MORNING of the third day. "He said he'd wait for you up there," Eli said, pointing upward. "But he made it clear you are to go alone."

Ellen looked up at the sharply-sloped mountain. It must have been two hundred feet or more high, and looked much like a loaf of French bread stood on end. Its lower slopes were covered with trees and festooned with ferns and other greenery. Higher up, the vegetation began to thin out, giving way to bare walls of granite in some places. She saw a faint trail through the trees at the base of the hill to her right.

They sat in shade and rested, eating a light meal from the food Eli had brought. Then Ellen rose.

"It is time," she said to Eli. She moved forward and embraced him tightly.

He put his arms around her. "I'll be waiting here," he said, "as long as it takes."

Ellen let go and slowly walked to the trailhead. It wound through the trees, and once begun, she found she had to step around exposed tree roots and brush aside ferns and other shrubbery. The temperature in among the trees was a little warmer than where Eli was camped as it was sheltered from the ocean breeze, but still very pleasant. Insects buzzed in the shafts of sunlight poking through the canopy, and she could faintly hear the roar of surf from around the front side of the hill.

Ellen climbed steadily, her shoes crunching along the sandy soil. She stopped when she grew weary, at places along the narrow path where water trickled from the cliff face. There she scooped up some of the cool liquid with her hand and took a drink, gazing out at the incredible view to seaward. Waves rolled in along an endless beach that was devoid of human life. *Maybe this was how it looked ten thousand years ago*, she thought. *I wonder if it would be better that way. We have brought so much pain to this land.*

She was weary and her footsteps slow when after nearly half an hour she sensed she was near the top. A wiff of fire smoke came to her. Her heart began to pound, but not from the exertion of the trail.

BEAR PAW SAT IN THE sunlight on the summit of the great coastal hill. Ocean breezes periodically found their way up the sheer western face of the hill, bringing the scent of sea spray to his nose. He had gathered rocks to form a small fire pit, and found enough tinder to start a fire, then added larger pieces. A skinned pheasant roasted on a crude spit above the flames. As he sat, he worked with a scribing tool on the polished surface of a thunder egg which had been sawed in half. Suddenly he stopped, senses tingling. Slowly he stood up and turned around.

Taviduaga was standing thirty feet away.

Bear Paw put the thunder egg and the tool down. Slowly he walked toward his wife, a smile on his face.

Ellen couldn't stop herself, and launched into a run, then slowed and melted into Bear Paw's big arms. She began to cry, her face pressed to his chest.

Bear Paw held her tightly and whispered to her, "Taviduaga. My wife. My love. You are free now."

"I missed you so," Ellen said, more subdued now. "There were nights I would have given anything to be in your arms as I am now. I was not sure I would see you again, ever."

"We are here now, together," Bear Paw said, drawing back slightly so he could see her face and gently wipe away her tears. "Come, there is food and drink, and a place to rest."

They walked over to the fire, where Bear Paw gently sat her down on a flat rock he had brought to the fire circle. The pheasant was done, and there was coffee as well. They ate in silence for a while. Finally Ellen spoke. "I am joyous to see you, my husband. But why did you not wait for me outside the city, after you learned I had been freed? This spot is truly beautiful, but I do not understand its purpose."

Bear Paw put down his cup and turned slightly to face her straight on. "In the woods, I was in a rage while you faced the white man's justice. There were times when it took strong talk from others to keep me from coming for you. Many Horses knew where you were held, but he made me see that the time was not right, and that such a thing might cause more pain and would not stop the whites from wanting to punish you. I did not want to stoke the fires of their hatred, and so I waited and watched, strong in the feeling that at some time I would have to come for you. Then Many Horses came with the news. I have never been so happy."

Ellen could not sense where his words were leading.

The light from his face vanished, and his look grew somber. "Taviduaga, you are free now," he said, looking into the flames. The whites will have no more claims against you, no more reason to seek you." He paused for a moment. "But I am not free. They seek me still. Where can we go to be together?"

A look of pain settled on Ellen's face and her head sank.

"It breaks my heart to see my words bring pain to you," he said. "But there is no place for us anymore. The whites seek me. They will always seek me, until I am dead. In truth, I am already dead. I am a walking ghost. Can you not see that?"

Fresh tears tracked their way down Ellen's cheeks.

"I would not have you see me as the whites would make me—if they do not hang me, I will be put in prison. If I am freed someday, it will be to a small patch of ground they have left us. I will grow old; my hair will turn gray, and I will grow ever weaker until someday I will take my last breath. I will die as a beggar, hand out to the white man for what he is willing to give, powerless to demand what he will not. I will have long since been shorn of my lands, my hunting grounds, my pride as a chief of my people, for there will be few left to lead." He looked off into the distance. "Once I wondered why the white man was so determined to destroy us. I thought at times he must hate us for some reason I cannot know. Or maybe because he has no soul, and does evil things without thinking. But now I know the reason is not so good as that. No, it is not because the white man hates us, or because he cannot stop himself from doing evil. It is because he believes his God gave all these lands to him. And we are simply in the way." He looked back at Ellen. "When I am old and poor, if I live that long, I will have no power to protect you. I would not have you see me like that."

Ellen turned pale, knowing now where his words were taking her.

"No," he continued, "I will not go to the spirit world as a beggar. There is only one place left where the whites cannot touch me, where I can live strong and free, as I am now." He paused for a moment, then continued. "It is there."

Ellen raised her head, and saw that he was pointing out to sea, to the sky, to the clouds.

"I love you with all that is in me, Taviduaga. You must know that my words are true. But we cannot live in peace in this new world the whites have brought upon us. If we are together, they will find us soon, and then they may be angry at you and seek to punish you again. I will not let that happen."

He stood up and helped her rise, suddenly weak in the knees as she was, then put his arms around her, strong and gentle all at once. They stood in silence for several minutes, she sobbing quietly into his chest as he stroked her hair. "Can you see any way this cannot be, Taviduaga?"

"We—we could go to the Old Woman Country," she said in desperation.

He shook his head, trying to keep a smile on his face. "No, even there we would live in poverty, outcasts from our world that is gone forever. With every passing year, there will be more whites, and fewer and fewer of the People. Our legends, our stories of the great warriors of the past, our tales of our ancestors, their great deeds—all will be forgotten. For our children's children, even the memory of what was lost will be lost. They will grow up in a world they were not made for, and do not understand." He stopped for a moment, his voice heavy with sadness. "I will not put my woman through this, a strong woman who has suffered so much already, to my shame."

"It was of my choosing," Ellen said. "Where my man goes, I will go also. This is the price of my love."

"It is time to stop paying that price, my wife. You can live a free life now, without me to give you pain. I would have you remember me as I am this day—strong and free to choose how I will meet tomorrow. But if you would have me, I wish to leave you with something of me, something no one can take from you." He stepped back and removed his shirt, then his moccasins. Lastly he loosened and let fall to the ground his leggings and his breechclout, standing naked before her.

Ellen knew in her heart that he had spoken truth to her. The whites would never stop pursuing him. It would not matter whether he was innocent or guilty; their lust for vengeance would never die. There was nowhere for them now, no peace they could find. All that was left to them was this moment.

That realization was like a knife in her gut, but slowly she reached to her shoulders and untied the top of her dress so that it could slide off her to the ground. She stepped out of her shoes, the whole of her body caressed by the sunshine; her nipples erect in the slight breeze playing around the hilltop.

Bear Paw came to her and took her hand. "Come," he said softly, "I have prepared a place for us." He scooped her into his arms and walked to a spot with long soft grass. He had strewn wildflowers around where they were to lay. Gently he lowered her to the ground. She laid back on the grass, signaling that she was willing to receive him. He stretched out beside her and took her in his arms. They lay together for long silent moments, their bodies reveling in each other's touch. He kissed her mouth, then went down to her nipples and did the same, taking each one briefly in his mouth while his right hand caressed her downward to her silky mound. She shuddered at his touch, her body arching upward to him as she kissed his cheek, his mouth, his neck.

At that he raised himself above her, his erect member probing between her legs. She reached down and helped guide him into her. Ever so gently he entered her, she moaning softly as his fullness penetrated to her last secret place. She stroked his hair and commanded him with her eyes to continue.

He began to thrust, slowly at first, long strokes in and out that sent waves of ecstasy through her. Soon he reached his peak and shuddered above her as she felt him release his seed deep within her. She clutched his shoulders and pressed him to her, crying out in wordless ecstasy as the earth spoke to them. Spent, he lowered himself onto her. He did not see her face, and so he did not see Ellen's silent tears. They would be her last for him.

Knowing his great weight was a burden to her, he soon lifted himself off, and they lay together in silence for a long while, she feeling his heart pounding in his chest against her, he running his hands up and down her, caressing her smooth skin, reveling in the feel of her naked body and its curves. Then without speaking he got up and walked to the fire. He picked something up and brought it back to her. "This is for you," he said. "Keep it always as part of me given to you."

Ellen looked down at what he had placed in her hand. It was a round rock that she recognized as a thunder egg, one side flat and polished to a high gloss. Inscribed on that side was the imprint of a bear's paw.

He knelt in front of her and kissed her long and deep. "I will wait for you on the other side," he said. Then he rose, and without another word, sprinted away from her toward the edge of the hill. She watched his powerful calf muscles propel his body ever faster, long strides eating up the space. Then he reached the edge, and with a great lunge forward, arms spread, launched himself into eternity.

ELLEN DID NOT GO TO the edge of the hill. She lay in the grass in silence for a very long time, drifting in and out of lucid thought. In all the long months on the trail, fleeing for their lives through brutal weather, through the savage fights as bullets tore the air around her, over the too many times she helped bury a dead child alongside the trail, she had done all her crying.

Finally, as the shadows of afternoon began to lengthen around her, she rose on stiff legs, put on her dress and boots, picked up the thunder egg, and slowly, haltingly made her way down the trail to the bottom where Eli was faithfully waiting, to tell him Bear Paw was gone.

ELI KNEW AS SOON AS he saw Ellen approach through the trees that something momentous had happened. She was not the same woman who had walked to the top.

Ellen walked slowly up to him and leaned gently against his chest. "He is gone," she said softly. "Forever."

Eli knew nothing he could say would comfort her now, so he was content to hold her until she finally backed away.

Then he prepared their mounts, broke camp, and they rode in silence back toward Portland.

THEY ARRIVED THE MORNING OF the third day. Ellen said almost nothing the entire trip, and Eli did not press her. But now that they were back, the buildings on the outskirts of Portland laid out before them, he knew it was time.

"What will you do now?" he said as they dismounted. "It would seem a good time to go back to Liza and Nettie."

Ellen looked at him directly for the first time since they had left the coast. "I cannot go now. I have been suspended between two worlds for so long. It will take time to sort things out."

"I'd worry about you," Eli said, trying to mask his disappointment. "How can you be safe?"

Ellen managed a small smile. "There are many of the People here who will care for me," she said.

Eli sighed. If there was one thing he had learned about Ellen so far, it was that she would not be swayed from her chosen path. "After what you've been through the last two years, I reckon you can handle just about anything. And as for me, I've got to get back to my post as soon as possible. It's going to be hard enough to explain to my superior that the trial ended six days ago. I just wish I knew when I could see you again. Or even *if*."

Ellen smiled and put a hand on his arm. "Dear Eli, you have been so amazingly understanding and generous for so long. I have asked you for so much, none of which I deserved. I do not know what the tomorrows to come will bring. But I feel in my heart that we *will* meet again. I am so sorry that this is all I can give you now."

Eli sighed. "I know you well enough to know when your mind is made up. But at least take this with you." He reached into a jacket pocket and withdrew a folded slip of paper. "Before Liza and Clarence left after the trial, they asked me to give you their address. You can go there when the time is right."

Ellen took the paper and tucked it away in her diary case. Eli had carried the diary in his saddlebags for her during the trip to the coast. "Thank you, Eli. I should be going. I am very confused right now, and I need time to think."

Eli grimaced, fighting the urge to throw his arms around her. "Very well. Please be safe."

With that she walked away toward the trees and was soon lost from view.

He knew it would be counterproductive to shadow her, and with her heightened Indian senses, she would probably discover him before long. *Women*, he thought. *Why does it have to be so complicated? I know exactly what should happen next.*

ELLEN BEGAN TO WALK THROUGH the trees, her diary slung across her shoulder. The white settlements thinned out the farther she got from Portland. She was confident some of the Indians who had gathered for the trial had not left the area yet. By mid-afternoon, she was proved right. She came across a small encampment of treaty Nez Perce. They erupted with whoops of joy when they saw her walk in. The language barrier did not prevent their obvious pride at seeing her in their camp. They rushed to give her food, and when night fell, a sheltered place to sleep.

She spent several days with them, mostly silent and lost in thought, though not failing to be gracious for their hospitality. They made no demands on her, and mostly did not bother her. Her deeds had become almost the stuff of legend, and their pleasure at playing host to Taviduaga, the Light on a Distant Hill, was enough.

After about a week, she could see that they were preparing to depart. *No doubt they have worn out their welcome around here*, she thought. *The whites will be pressuring them to leave.* She thought of what she could give them in return for their hospitality. It quickly came to her. Like so many other camps she had come across, she knew that they were eager to hear some of her stories of her long journey with Bear Paw after the camp massacre, and especially of the time they fled with the Nez Perce into the depths of winter. She sat down with them that night around the campfire. She had found one of them who knew just enough Shoshone to relay the gist of what she said to the rest.

There was a heavy silence all around the campfire when she told them Bear Paw had gone to the spirit world. She talked until the fire waned as it consumed the last of the wood. When she was done, she turned to her translator and asked him one question. "Does anyone know what has become of Chief Joseph and his band?"

When he translated her words, there were somber looks and heads shaking all around. "None of us know," the translator said. "We know that they were taken somewhere by the bluecoats from the place of surrender. From there, we have heard nothing. This was a long time ago. It is as if the earth swallowed them up." A silence settled in around the fire, broken only by the pop and hiss of burning embers. Ellen was sorry she'd asked. "I think it is time for sleep," she said. "Tomorrow you must return to your homes, and I must go also."

ELLEN WENT HER WAY IN the morning, as the treaty Nez Perce did theirs, but she was surprised to find herself with an escort. He, she was made to understand, would stay with her until she reached the next Indian village safely, then he would rejoin his tribe. Evidently his task was a great honor.

He spoke little as they rode along, intent on full awareness of his surroundings. He looked like a good protector to Ellen, and she relaxed as they rode. Ellen herself said little as well, lost in thought about her place in the world without Bear Paw at her side. She ached for the touch that she would never feel again.

After two days they came across a small camp of Northern Paiutes, who had gathered for Ellen's trial and were now journeying back home. They were astonished when she rode in and they realized who she was, and fell all over themselves in providing hospitality. Her escort stayed one night, then departed the next morning as Ellen thanked him warmly.

A large campfire was lit in her honor that night. The Paiutes gathered close around her, mostly silent but expectant. Ellen did not want to talk about the horror of the last two years, but she felt obligated to talk to them. After a while she began to speak, slowly, haltingly, to tell parts of her story. She left out much.

She finally could not continue, and fell silent. The Paiutes were wise enough not to press her further, seeing the pain on her face, and drifted off to their shelters. Except one, a wizened old woman who had been looking at her most of the evening. When she was finally alone with Ellen, she shuffled her bent old body over to Ellen and sat down, resting one hand on a cane. Then, smiling, she turned her deeply lined face to Ellen, and unexpectedly reached out a hand and placed it flat on Ellen's chest below her bust.

Ellen was startled but did not move as the old woman slowly took her hand up, down, and around, head cocked as if listening or searching. After a minute she stopped and her eyes looked up with a merry twinkle. "I have great news, Taviduaga. You are with child. You will have a daughter."

Ellen looked at her in disbelief. With child! How could the old woman know? Her eyes grew moist as the thought and she put a hand to her lips, then to her chest. The old woman put her hand over Ellen's and pressed gently. Bear Paw had indeed left her with something of himself, something that could not be taken away.

Her mind roiled with emotion. She had been thinking lately of Fort Hall, where her brothers and sisters lived in poverty, and that she might return there to be with them. But it was not that simple. Somewhere out there was another man who loved her. And now this. That she was carrying a girl made her decision simple.

Nettie sat in the parlor of the Portland home she shared with Liza and Clarence, sewing on her treadle machine in the midst of a sunny April day. She hummed as she pushed the fabric forward under the moving needle, her feet working the treadle in perfect rhythm.

Her neighbor, eleven-year old Samantha, sat in the bay window looking out, as she sometimes did when boredom brought her over for a visit. Liza and Clarence were away in town.

Samantha suddenly stopped her roving eye and called to her. "Nettie! There's an Indian coming to your door!"

Nettie never missed a beat on the sewing machine. "Nonsense, child," she said in dismissal. "Are you sure it isn't your little friend Lucy? I hear she got an Indian outfit for her birthday last month."

"No ma'am, it's not Lucy. This is a real grown-up person."

"Well, child, I don't see how it could be a real Indian here in the middle of town. After all, it's 1879; these are modern ti—" Nettie froze in mid-sentence and turned pale. "Oh my God," she gasped. She rose on shaking legs, her piece of fabric falling to the floor. She tottered across to the bay window, hand to her mouth, and looked out. Her eyes flew wide. "Ellen!" she got out in a tortured voice. She tore across the room to the front door and flung it open.

"Hello, Nettie," Ellen said. "May I come in?"

For a moment unable to speak, Nettie opened her arms and rushed forward, gripping Ellen in a tight embrace. "Oh dear girl," she said, finding her voice, "have you come home to us at last?"

"Yes, Nettie. It was time."

Wiping away tears, Nettie guided her inside. Ellen still had her diary slung firmly across her shoulder. Nettie felt a need to sit down, and took Ellen into the parlor, where she couldn't stop gushing about Ellen's return. She squeezed Ellen's hand, but gave a dubious eye to her fine white buckskin dress. After she calmed down a bit, she said, "But you're still dressed as an Indian, dear."

"Yes. I am Shoshone," Ellen replied.

Nettie stiffened ever so slightly. "Well, I shall search about for some more suitable clothes for you. I'm sure I can come up with something."

Samantha, who had been forgotten in the fuss, but had stood back at the entrance to the parlor, now approached, wide-eyed. "Are you a real Indian?" she said to Ellen.

"Samantha dear," Nettie admonished, "such questions aren't appropriate at this time—"

"I do not mind," Ellen interrupted. She looked at Samantha. "I am a white person who became a woman of the Shoshone tribe."

Samantha was clearly impressed. "Do you have an Indian name?"

"Yes. I am called Manakwa Noovigaded Pa'a Taviduaga. It is a long name, so you may call me simply Taviduaga. It means 'Light from Above.'"

Samantha was fairly bouncing with excitement, her long auburn curls jumping around her shoulders. "Can you tell me some Indian stories?" she said.

Ellen smiled. "Yes, I can tell you stories of the good times we had."

"Now, enough of this," Nettie broke in. "Samantha dear, Ellen and I have so much to talk about. Now shoo, and you can come back perhaps tomorrow."

"A real Indian!" Samantha called out as she skipped away.

"Yes, but now she's going to be a white woman again!" Nettie called after her.

Ellen said nothing.

THEY SAT IN THE PARLOR and talked, Nettie a bottomless well of questions, and thinly-veiled comments disparaging of Indian life.

Ellen sighed. Would her aunt ever understand? She had serious doubts.

An hour later, Liza and Clarence came through the front door. "Anybody home?" Liza called out.

"In the parlor," Nettie replied in a loud voice.

Liza and Clarence came into the room. Liza's eyes went wide in shock, and she collapsed to the floor, suddenly sobbing. Clarence reached down and, after a minute or so, managed to lift her up onto a sofa as he looked at Ellen, a broad smile on his face.

"Are you really here?" Liza said, voice trembling. "This isn't some kind of temporary visit?"

"No, Aunt Liza," Ellen said, reaching out to touch her arm. "I'm here to stay, I hope in this house for a while, if you will have me."

"But—but what of your husband?" Liza said, still unsteady and reaching out to Ellen to touch her and make sure she was real.

Ellen hung her head. "Bear Paw has gone to the spirit world."

Liza's face took on an expression both of pain and relief. "He is dead then?"

"To us, he is, Liza. It was his choice. The only one left to him."

Liza seemed satisfied. "Well then, my dear, there's no reason to keep up this romance with the Indians. You can be our white niece again."

Ellen bit her lip at the insult. It was as if all the Shoshone, Nez Perce, and others of the People she had met, become friends with, fought alongside, comforted through endless travails, and considered brothers and sisters didn't exist, as if were it not for Bear Paw, none of the last two years would have happened. *This is going to take a while,* she thought.

Liza jumped to her feet, all a-twitter. "Well, this is all too wonderful! What a dinner conversation we shall have tonight! Come, Nettie, let us go and prepare the spare room for our niece, once lost but now found."

Later that night, long after dark, Nettie and Liza had retired at last. Restless, Ellen was still up. She found Clarence in the parlor. The spring night still offered a chill, and he had built a fire in the fireplace.

"Come in, child, this fire is for you," he said to her when she hesitated at the doorway.

Ellen was weary, and sank into a chair opposite Clarence, staring into the fire for long minutes. Clarence said nothing, but she knew he was observing her. "Thank you, Uncle Clarence. There were many nights when I was desperate for such a fire."

Clarence reached out a hand to her own, smiling at her. "I have no doubt, child. None of us can imagine what you went through in the time you were gone."

Ellen smiled. "Dear Clarence," she said, "you have always been so steady and practical. Nettie and Liza will fly off into histrionics at next to nothing, but you are so calm and accepting. I need that right now, more than I can say."

Clarence chuckled. "Yes, well, I already overheard Nettie telling Liza to be on the watch for any wild Indian behavior. She said she won't tolerate it. I think she's surprised you can still use a knife and fork."

"Change is hard for her, I know," Ellen said.

Clarence was admiring her buckskin dress. "That's a beautiful dress, child. I've never seen one like it."

"Thank you, Clarence. It was to be my hanging dress. Fortunately it was not necessary. I decided to wear it when I came home in honor of the people whom I was once part of."

Clarence put his hand under his chin, looking thoughtful. "I always thought you'd come back, Ellen. I never lost faith, even when the other two thought you were dead." He paused as if gathering courage to say something. "But I wonder, child, why now? Why return at this time after so long away?"

"Because Bear Paw is dead, Uncle. And I carry his child. Were it a son, I might consider returning to the Fort Hall reservation, and raise him among my many friends, and try to teach him what I could of the ways of a Shoshone warrior. Perhaps his children would carry on the tradition. But a girl—no, I cannot raise a daughter among such poverty and despair. She deserves better. She deserves to know her white heritage. I will bring her forth in this world, and I will give it to her."

Clarence whistled softly. "Nettie and Liza will have a collective heart attack when you tell them you're pregnant."

"I am sure. On that day, I will need to lean on you."

"Child, will you be able to tell us anything of what happened to you these last two years?"

Ellen grimaced. "Some of it, Uncle Clarence. But there are some things that I can never tell. The pain I carry is a great burden. I do not wish to see others burdened with it as well."

Clarence moved forward in his chair and embraced her. "A wise choice, child. We here can all make do without knowing about some of the things that torment you still. I'll respect whatever you choose to tell us in the days ahead. And don't worry, I'll make sure Liza and Nettie do too." With that, he dropped his arms from her and slowly stood up. "Well, it's late and it's been quite a day for all of us. I thank a merciful God you're back. Tomorrow we'll begin the task of bringing you back into the family. Sleep well."

Ellen looked up at him. "Thank you, Clarence. I am tired as well, but I think I will sit here and enjoy this wonderful fire for a while longer."

When the fire had died down to glowing embers, she finally got up and went to the bed her aunts had prepared for her, a soft bed, a real bed, such as she had not slept on in longer than she could remember.

ELLEN AWOKE JUST AT DAWN the next morning. Sleep had not come easily. The unfamiliar softness of the bed had kept her awake for a while, wishing for a bed of sleeping furs. Looking out the window, she could see the great orange sun starting to clear the horizon, under a deep blue sky.

The house was quiet as she rose and slipped on a light gown Nettie had hung over a chair for her. She stretched her arms for a moment and then went to the small writing desk in her room and sat down, looking out at the approaching day once more. Then, opening her beloved diary, she took a pen from the inkwell, opened to a new page, and began to write:

April 15ᵗʰ, 1878—Portland, Oregon

I have returned to the white world. This may be the last entry on the pages of this diary, this faithful book which I have carried for so many hundreds of miles, its pages redolent with sweat, blood, joy, tears—and grief crushing beyond description. It is my gift to what children may come, that they may know what formed me. Perhaps then they will think kindly of me when at times I am different from what they expect. For I was set adrift between the world of my birth and a world I could not have imagined.

Is there a hand unseen, guiding me still, toward a destiny I cannot know? I dare not say no. But here I will stay, and discover what I have become. For I am someone different now. I am white. I am Shoshone. I am both. I am neither.

I grieve in secret for the nameless child who will never draw breath, buried in a muddy grave somewhere to the east, at a spot I can never find again. A part of me remains there.

I loved a man and he loved me. I love him still. What more is there? We are lost to each other now, and yet always together in our hearts.

What was lost, what was gained—these I will weigh against each other, and keep to myself. The things I have seen, the things I have done—some of them I will reveal, for there is much that others should know—must know. Some of what I have seen—would that I had not—I can never speak of, even in the pages of this diary, for they are a burden too great for me to bear. I would not wish them on anyone else. No, never. These things I will keep in a small and dark corner of my heart, a separate place that will forever claim a piece of my soul.

And though the past will always be with me, I will live each new day to the fullest for the task I have taken on. For new life swells within me, a girl whom I shall call Rachel (Yes, dear friend, I remembered you).

Ellen paused and looked out the window, feeling the soft breeze drift in. The morning sun shone down on new grass, pale blossoms richly adorned the apple tree in the yard, and she could hear the songs of birds calling forth their good will toward the new day.

The pen began to move, and she wrote her last line: *It is a fine day, rich with the promise of spring. And I am content.*

18

TWO DAYS LATER, ELLEN WAS dusting when she heard a knock at the front door. She was alone; everyone else had gone into town on errands. She put down her dust rag, ran hands quickly through her hair, went to the door and swung it open.

Eli was standing on the porch.

She leaned lightly against the door frame, the faintest of smiles on her face. "Hello, Eli."

He was as handsome as ever, his hair freshly cut, his clothing new and well-pressed. But he appeared nervous, fingers gripping the hat in his hand tightly. "Hello, Ellen. I'm glad I found you home."

"You are not in uniform," she replied calmly, looking over his civilian dress.

"No. When I got back to my post after the trial, I resigned my commission."

"I hope it was not on my account."

"It was, partly," he said. "But it had been coming for a while. I couldn't be a part anymore of the movement that visited such limitless grief on your people, and all their brethren across the country. Nothing I can do can ever make up for that. But leaving was a start." He brightened. "I've gone into business for myself here in Portland. I expect to do well."

"I see," she said, voice soft in the morning air. "Why have you come?"

Eli gripped his hat so hard his knuckles went white. "Because I've never stopped loving you."

Ellen took a deep breath and let it out slowly. She would test him now. "I am far from a virgin."

Eli shook his head. "I don't care."

"I am a convicted murderess."

"Not in my book."

"I am carrying Bear Paw's child."

He never missed a beat. "It would be as my own."

Ellen could see that no matter what she laid on him, he wasn't going away. "Then come in," she said. "We shall have tea."

They went into the parlor and Ellen poured tea for both of them. They sat facing each other, and talked far into the afternoon as the shadows lengthened in the yard outside. Ellen watched his face, and listened carefully, for any sign Eli was not fully accepting of the path she had taken. She found none. And so it was that when he finally asked the question she knew was coming, she did not hesitate, but reached out her hand to his, fixed her golden-brown eyes upon him, and said, "Yes. Yes I will."

EPILOGUE

MOUNTAIN MEADOWS REST HOME
1930

Strength and honor are her clothing; she looketh well to the ways of her household; her children arise up and call her blessed. . . .
—Proverbs 31: 25-28

"**E**LI WAS A GOOD HUSBAND," Ellen was saying. "He proved to be every bit the gallant gentleman I had always hoped he would be. He loved me so deeply, so unrelentingly, it would have been hard not to love him. He was a wonderful father to Rachel, and to the two sons he gave me. They are all fine children. My sons are successful businessmen in Portland, with families of their own. They don't come to visit much, but I don't worry about them. Eli and I did a good job of raising them to be good citizens and good providers. Rachel you will meet this very day. I've arranged it."

Robbie McIntyre sat back in his chair, exhausted. Sometime before, how long ago he wasn't sure, he had quit writing, so overwhelmed with emotion he was no longer able to move pen on paper. It didn't matter; every word the old woman had said for the last hour was burned into his brain.

"We had forty-five wonderful years of marriage before he passed away twelve years ago," she went on, smiling. "His business prospered, and we traveled the world. He showed me places I had only dreamed of—Europe, the Mediterranean, so much of America—we saw it all, and so did the children. The memories we created helped salve some of my wounds."

"Not that I was welcomed into polite society back home. To the proper ladies in our neighborhood, I was always 'that woman'. *Turncoat.*

Murderer. Indian's whore. They just wouldn't let go of it. It lasted until I finally outlived them all. Eli and I didn't care much. We traveled a lot, to places they could never afford."

Robbie leaned back in his chair, thoroughly comfortable with this woman who had seemed so different, so edgy at first. He felt like he knew her intimately, and could ask her things he would not have dared when they started. "You never got over Bear Paw, did you?"

Ellen smiled at him. "No. He was my savior, my leader, my guide—my friend and master." She turned to look across her small room. "Bring me that rock on top of the dresser, please."

Robbie got up and retrieved the rock he had so thoughtlessly picked up the first day he had been there. He looked at its polished surface in the window light. The pattern he had not been able to make out the first day was now evident to him. The imprint of a bear's paw was etched into the smooth stone. He gently gave it to her and returned to his seat.

Ellen cradled the rock in her hands and turned her face to look out the window. "This rock, and Rachel, are all I have of him now. Except what is up here." She tapped her forehead. "How blessed I was to have the love of two good men! Do not pity me. Some women search all their lives for one." She turned her face back to him. "They never found his body, you know. I like to think he didn't fall to earth, that somewhere between the cliff top and the ocean, he entered the spirit world."

Robbie felt a need to change the subject. "Did you ever go back to Fort Hall?"

Ellen smiled. "Oh yes, Eli and I went back once a year for decades, until I got too old to travel well. It was sad to see all my dear friends from those terrible years grow older, their tribal memories fading and becoming lost. Only Kimama is left now. I haven't seen her for a couple of years, but we write."

Robbie bit his lip, almost afraid to ask the next question. "What happened to the Nez Perce after their surrender?"

Ellen's eyes took on a faraway look. "They were taken from the surrender site and transported with their horses southeast five hundred miles to Fort Keogh. The journey took two weeks over often rough ground. The weather was unrelentingly cold, and the jarring ride was hard on the sick, wounded, and elderly. The once-fine clothes of the Nez Perce had become ragged, their moccasins worn thin, their feet unprotected. The horses suffered too, as they were still plagued with the disease they had picked up weeks earlier that caused cuts and scrapes to fester rather than heal."

"Joseph, for his part, had come to admire Colonel Miles. He had decided to put his trust in this man—and the fate of his people. But this was tempered by his experience that the white man often went back on his word."

"On the other side, Colonel Miles' admiration for the Nez Perce also deepened. He could not help admiring Joseph's calm demeanor, dedication to his people, and superb leadership. Overall, he became convinced that the Nez Perce were a different and far superior breed of Indian than he had encountered before. Over the two weeks or so it took to reach Fort Keogh, Miles became determined to help the Nez Perce in any way he could, and hoped for their eventual return to their homeland. But neither he nor Joseph knew that powerful forces back in Washington had a far different solution in mind."

She paused for a moment and took a sip of water from the glass beside her. "General Sherman—an evil man if ever there was one—had three goals in mind. One, no matter that he too greatly admired his former adversary; he was determined to plant the Nez Perces' faces in the dirt as an example to any other potential rebellious tribes. If even these masterful evaders could be brought low, what chance would anyone else have? Two, he wanted the Nez Perce near lines of supply, where it was cheaper to keep them. And three, he wanted to get them off the Army's expense sheet, and turned over to the Department of the Interior."

"Thus it was that when the party finally reached Fort Keogh, and had settled in in a quite agreeable spot, Miles received orders only a week later that they were to move again. For the Nez Perce, who had believed they would winter here, and return to their homeland in the spring, it was heartbreaking news. But there was no choice but to obey. To further the sadness, this time the Nez Perce's once-magnificent horse herd, the very symbol of their identity, was left behind, given to the soldiers."

"Thoroughly broken in spirit, the tribe was pushed out onto the trail again. It was the depth of winter now, and the going was too difficult to take the entire party overland. It was determined that the party would be split. The women, the sick and elderly, and the children would travel down the Missouri River on fourteen large rough-hewn barges. The men would travel overland by wagon or horseback on what few horses they retained."

"During the journey down the ice-dotted river, one of the boats had overturned, and several of its occupants were killed. It took eight grueling days through the winter freeze for the boats to make it down the river to Fort Buford, ten days for the overland party. But this again was just a temporary stop. They were soon back on the river again, and were informed the trip would take about another ten days."

"This time they reached the frontier metropolis of Bismarck. After an all-too brief stay, the river now being impassible because of ice, they continued on by train. The snorting iron beast terrified the Nez Perce. The journey to Saint Paul was four hundred and fifty miles. Again after a brief stay, the train rolled on, down the tracks more hundreds of miles, finally to Fort Leavenworth, Kansas, arriving in November of 1877. Joseph looked over the landscape, breathed the heavy air, and decided it was not a good place for Nez Perce people. But here they stayed for the rest of the winter."

Ellen paused and looked at Robbie. "Are you absorbing all this, young man?"

Robbie nodded affirmatively. He could see that Ellen's eyes had grown moist at the memories.

"Good. You need to hear it," she said. She looked out the window in silence for a few seconds, then continued. "The next July, the Army—really Sherman—ordered them into motion again. In the midst of a sweltering heat wave, they were herded back into rail cars and sent further south to the Quapaw Agency in Indian Territory—what is now Oklahoma. There were nearly a dozen other tribes there, and one of them—the Modocs—weren't happy about having to share their space with the Nez Perce."

"So The Nez Perce were moved again in the summer of 1879, southwest through Indian Territory to the Ponca-Oakland Agency, where they were settled on arid land with silt-brown rivers, little shade, and biting flies that tormented them. All through the long journey from their surrender point in Idaho Territory, there had been deaths along the trail. The sick and elderly died from the cold, the infants from the heat. Babies were hastily buried in shallow graves, only to be dug up by wild pigs at one spot. Their frantic mothers scrambled to re-bury the remains. By the time they were settled on this new land, there were but 370 left alive out of the 800 who had begun the flight back in the Palouse Country." Ellen paused to wipe her eyes with a handkerchief.

"Are you sure you want to put yourself through this?" Robbie said.

The old woman glared at him. "Yes, I'm sure! Too few people know this story. And I've already forgotten some of it." She took a deep breath and continued. "All through this long journey following their surrender, Joseph missed no opportunity to plead the case for his people to any white official who would listen. Townspeople at various towns they went through put on dinners, with him as the honored guest. He spoke eloquently, and never failed to impress. But I think the whites were more impressed with his celebrity, his civilized manner, and that he could use a knife and fork, than with his message. He even made a trip to Washington D. C., and spoke there. He implored, he pleaded, he begged for relief. The politicians smiled and shook his hand. But nothing was done. His pleas fell on the deaf ears of people who were more interested in entertaining Joseph the legend—for legend he had become—than hearing what he had to say."

"They stayed in this godforsaken land for four years, despondent, ill-housed and ill-fed, devoid of their weapons, horses and saddles, and now of all hope they would ever see their homeland again. But in June of 1883, under great pressure from the Presbyterian lobby in Washington, the government finally relented. The Nez Perce were to go home. Well, a few of them. A small party of thirty-one widows orphans, and two elderly began the journey home to the Lapwai. But it wasn't until May of 1885, eight years after their flight began, that the government, under relentless pressure from a variety of groups that championed their cause, at last allowed the rest to go. When they departed, they left behind over one hundred graves."

"They traveled by train all the way. When they arrived, they were given the choice of returning to the Lapwai and living as Christians, or going to the Colville Reservation in northeastern Washington Territory and living in the traditional way. One-hundred eighteen chose Lapwai, and the remaining 150 chose the Colville Reservation. Two hundred and sixty-eight. That, and the thirty-one who had come in 1882, were all that were left alive from the original 800. It was a great shock to those who came to greet them, looking for relatives and friends that would never come home."

Ellen turned away from the window to face Robbie again. Silent tears tracked their way down her cheeks. "Joseph himself was never given a choice. Stupidly, he was still considered dangerous, a potential unifying force who could once again rouse the Nez Perce to rebellion. Though he pleaded constantly for return to his beloved Wallowa Mountains, he was never allowed to go."

"His daughter, Noise of Running Feet, whom I mentioned was there at the final battle near the Canadian border, had indeed made it to Canada, and she eventually came back to Washington Territory." Ellen lowered her head. "I heard a report that she had been standing near the rail siding at the Lapwai Mission when someone pushed her under a moving train. With her death, all nine of the children Joseph had fathered were dead. There were no survivors to carry on his name, only an indelible and enduring story of bravery, selflessness, and courage that could serve as a lesson to us all, and that too few know to this day."

"What eventually happened to Joseph?" Robbie said.

"He grew old with his wife on the Colville Reservation, having become something of a curiosity, an anachronism, to be trotted out as an invited guest at various functions to liven up the party. He even appeared at a University of Washington football game in 1903. But no matter his age, he never stopped pleading to see his beloved homeland. But the white man never relented in the belief that he was dangerous."

"In September of 1904, in his teepee on the Colville Reservation, he asked his wife to retrieve his headdress from its storage place a short distance away. Feeling that he might die at any time, he told her he wished to die as a chief. She came back with the headdress minutes later, to find that he had pitched forward on his face, having taken his last breath."

Ellen's voice had grown faint and hoarse, and Robbie leaned forward to catch her words.

She looked at him, infinite weariness on her face. "The cause of death was never officially listed. But I think the doctor who came to examine him had it right. He said that Joseph died of a broken heart."

A heavy silence fell on the room. Robbie was drained, and Ellen looked it too. She didn't seem inclined to say anymore. But then she raised her head at the sound of a car out front, and looked out the window. Her expression brightened. "Ah, my daughter is here! She's coming up to the porch." Ellen shifted herself more upright in her chair, eyes focused on the door. There were footsteps in the hall, a soft knock, and the door swung open.

"Young man," Ellen said, "meet my daughter—and Bear Paw's daughter—Rachel."

Robbie had risen from his chair at the sound of the knock. He stood stupidly for a moment, staring at a striking woman who appeared to be in her mid-fifties. She was beautiful, tall and slender with smooth brown skin offset by light-brown hair, grey now at the temples. She had Ellen's arresting golden-brown eyes, and what he could guess was Bear Paw's strong visage. "Hello," she said as she moved with the grace of a cat across the room and extended her hand.

Robbie took it and was greeted with a firm grip he would not have expected from most women. There was nothing ladylike about it. After long seconds, Rachel let go.

"Rachel, meet my visitor these last seven or eight days, Robbie McIntire, a reporter from the *Oregonian*."

Rachel frowned. "What have you been telling him, Mother?"

Ellen smiled up at her daughter. "Everything."

"I was afraid of that."

"Don't mind her," Ellen said to Robbie. "But now, young man, I believe our time has at last come to an end. I want to spend some time with my daughter. It has been my pleasure to entertain your company. Don't forget anything as you go."

Robbie ran his hand through his hair, uncertain of how to end this remarkable string of sessions. But it was clear Ellen wanted him to make an unceremonious exit, so he bent down, scooped up the pile of notebooks he had accumulated during the course of the visit, and headed for the door.

"What will you do now, young man?" Ellen called after him.

Robbie paused at the doorway and turned around. "Well, ma'am, I wish I could say I'll be going back to my job at the *Oregonian* with all this material, but I doubt I have a job anymore. My boss thought I'd be gone only a couple of days. In a way, that would be good, because I know what I want to do."

Ellen looked at him expectantly.

"I want to put all these notes together into a book," he said. "I'll give it your name—Light on a Distant Hill—for the title. And I won't stop talking about it until the world knows this story."

Ellen looked at him for long seconds, as if trying to read his mind. Then she leaned her head against Rachel, who stood next to her, and smiled. "I believe you, young man. May God favor your plan. Be safe as you travel home."

Robbie nodded. "Bless you for what you have taught me, Ellen," he said. Then he turned and went out the door.

Outside, Robbie fired up the old panel truck and drove slowly down the hill to his hotel. In his room, he carefully packed the notebooks, now the most valuable thing he possessed, and prepared for a morning departure. His sleep was troubled that night.

THEN NEXT MORNING, HE WAS up early and finishing his packing when the hotel clerk came to his door and said he had a phone call in the office. When he got there and answered it, Robbie was surprised to hear Rachel's voice on the line.

"She's gone!" Rachel said, her tone frantic. "I came up from town this morning to pick her up for breakfast down at the shore, and she's not here."

"Has Mrs. Maitland seen her this morning?" Robbie said, puzzled.

"No," Rachel sobbed. "She thought Mother was just sleeping in late. She doesn't know either."

"I'll be up there as soon as I can," he said, and plunked the phone back in its cradle. "I'll be staying another day!" he called out to the clerk as he tore out the door.

Robbie stormed up the mountain in the old panel, his head colliding with the roof of the truck over some of the more violent bumps. When the truck wheezed into the yard of the rest home, he jumped out and tore into the residence without preliminaries.

He found Rachel in Ellen's room, seated silently on the bed with Ellen's diary on her lap. The thunder egg was sitting in its customary place on the dresser. He looked around for clues as to what might have happened. "Did she leave a note?" he asked.

Rachel nodded, a grim expression on her face. She opened the diary and withdrew a brief handwritten note.

Robbie read it.

This diary is yours now, daughter. Please guard it with great care, so that one day at a time of your choosing, you may pass it on to your children, and to my sons' children. Tell my sons I love them dearly.

It is easier for me this way.

All my love

Rachel raised a tear-stained face to Robbie. "Where has she gone?"

Robbie looked at the note for a moment, then he turned his head and looked out the window, toward the sea. "Oh My God," he rasped. "I know where she is."

THE RENTED TRUCK WOULD PROBABLY never be the same after its throw-caution-to-the-winds descent of the mountain road. Neither Robbie nor Rachel cared. They careened crazily through the coastal forest and finally came to a halt at the base of the hill that met the surf—the one that could be seen clearly from Ellen's window.

"I was a fool not to make this connection sooner," Robbie said, as he and Rachel began their way up the trail to the top. "Now I know why she chose that rest home."

"She must have bribed the milk delivery man to take her down the mountain," Rachel said. "He comes early."

Rachel had removed her shoes, and now ascended the trail ahead of him at a pace that left him breathless. It was all he could do to keep up. As they climbed, they could see a morning layer of low clouds that formed a cottony blanket over the water, stretching out to the horizon. After twenty minutes, they arrived at the top, Robbie bent over and gasping, and looked around. At first, the top appeared empty. Then they looked out toward the sea.

Ellen was there at the cliff edge. She stood back turned to the sea far below. She was barefoot and clad in a white gown that fluttered around her in the morning breeze. She saw them.

Rachel started to walk toward her, arms out in supplication. Robbie trailed hesitantly behind. They had taken only a few steps when Ellen spread her arms wide, smiling, then leaned back and dropped from view.

Robbie sprinted forward. He reached the edge just in time to see Ellen falling arms spread wide, gown billowing around her, white hair rippling in the wind. She looked like an angel descending. In seconds she disappeared into the low layer of clouds below.

Afte long silent seconds, he turned away, numb, and walked slowly back to Rachel. She had not moved to the edge, but had sunk to her knees, then sat down on her legs. He walked up to her, not knowing what to say.

"We've been expecting something like this for a while," she said dully. "I think she'd been waiting only for someone she could trust to tell her story to. When I heard she was spending a lot of time with you, I thought the time might have come. I was right." She looked up at him. "We never really had all of her, you know. Sometimes when she didn't know I was looking, I saw her face take on a sadness, her eyes a faraway look, as if she was in a different place and time. There was always a part of her she kept to herself, separate from us, certain things she just wouldn't talk about. Maybe she told them to you."

Robbie fought for the right thing to say, and failed. "I'll get word to someone to pick up her body down below when we get into town," he said quietly.

Rachel rose to her feet in one fluid motion and managed a small smile. "I don't think they'll find her there," she said.

Robbie looked at her, puzzled. "If she's not there, where would she be?"

Rachel walked slowly forward to the edge of the cliff. "She's out there," she said, pointing away over the vast blanket of low clouds. "With Bear Paw. She is Taviduaga again, up on her paint mare. Together they ride side by side, streaking across a vast rolling plain, chasing an endless herd of buffalo over the horizon. She's young once more, her long brown hair streaming behind her in the wind. She and Bear Paw hold hands between them as they ride. She is smiling. And she is happy."

AUTHOR'S NOTES

I consider myself an entertainer. This is disparaged in some literary circles, but if it's good enough for John Grisham, Ken Follett, and Clive Cussler, all of whom have said they consider themselves entertainers, then it's okay with me. I also like to educate a little along the way. I hope I have succeeded with both in this book.

While I strive to be correct in what facts I present, minutely-detailed historical accuracy has never been one of my goals. Therefore, it must be noted that I have taken some liberties with Northern Shoshone culture for the purpose of story-telling. Shoshone west of the Rockies, as Bear Paw's tribe was, lived in grass and stick huts rather than tipis. That didn't make for an appealing story, so it was changed. As for the buffalo hunt, buffalo once roamed all through what is now the state of Idaho, but they were gone from that area by 1870. At the time of our story, though, they could still be found on the western border of what is now Montana, and Bear Paw's tribe could have hunted them there. The courtship and marriage customs Ellen encountered were borrowed from the Cheyenne, whose women were noted for their chastity. The attack on Bear Paw's band by the Cavalry was modeled on a massacre of the Shoshone that occurred fifteen years earlier at Bear River. Approximately 250 Shoshone were slain, including 90 women and children. News of the Civil War kept it off the front pages at the time, but it remains one of the largest one-time slaughters of Native Americans in history. Details of the battle were combined with those of the infamous Sand Creek massacre of the Cheyenne in 1864. If I have omitted some of the darker aspects of Shoshone culture (and every culture has them), it was for the purpose of telling an appealing story.

When I started this book, I cautioned myself that I should avoid getting on a soapbox regarding the Indians' plight. In my research, as tragedy piled upon tragedy, it became both harder to avoid and yet increasingly unnecessary. The facts spoke eloquently for themselves. Too few Americans know today the extent of the determined displacement and slaughter Native Americans suffered. It is a myth that the North American continent was sparsely populated prior to Columbus' arrival. There were plenty of Indians in what was to become America. But within a couple of generations, many of them, especially in the east, were wiped out by white diseases they had no immunity to. Entire villages along the east coast disappeared.

The legacy of white settlement in America includes such events as the mass hangings of thirty-eight Sioux at Mankato, Minnesota in 1862 (following a Santee Sioux uprising that killed 800 settlers), and of thirty eight more at the same location in 1864, after another uprising. Were it not for the intercession of President Lincoln, the number hanged in the first event would have been over three hundred. To native peoples, who had no chance for survival from the beginning, it must have seemed as if they had fallen into some kind of inescapable hell. One must bear in mind the stimulus for many Indian attacks on whites. In reality, the white policy of dealing with Native Americans was little different from the Nazis' Final Solution to the Jewish Problem during World War II.

So, what is to be done in our time? Guilt serves no purpose and is a waste of time. Recognition of the extent of the devastation to native peoples—and its enduring legacy— is a start. One insightful idea is offered by Paul Chaat Smith, Assistant Curator of The Museum of the American Indian in Washington, D. C. He suggests in his magnificent book, *Everything You Know about Indians Is Wrong* that the problem is that we like our Indians authentic. One need look no further than the Indian who poses in full regalia for tourist pictures on a ledge of rock overlooking Monument Valley to understand what authentic means. I cannot help but wonder what he thinks as he poses for white tourists, looking out over a land that perhaps once belonged to his ancestors.

Our desire for authenticity in Indians is a barrier to societal integration; it keeps Native Americans apart from us. Smith suggests that Native Americans will be accepted into mainstream white society only when they are routinely accepted as your therapist, the pilot of your airplane, your accountant, your social worker, your attorney—your neighbor.

As Ellen says during her trial, Native Americans were neither noble nor savage. They gambled, drank too much (having little more immunity to alcohol than to the white diseases that killed so many), quarreled and made war among themselves; some engaged in the slave trade, were by turns quick to mirror the white man's often-merciless attacks (admittedly, whites had no monopoly on slaughter), naïve, and just plain foolish. But in that, beneath the strange (to us) dress, beyond the rituals and lifestyle we find so curious, they were very much like us, in our best and worst moments. It would be a step forward to remember that, as a start to someday bringing them back into full participation in the life of this vast land which we have so irrevocably changed.

Ellen would have liked that.

ACKNOWLEDGEMENTS

This book was, as were my previous books, anything but a solo effort. A number of parties contributed vital information that helped bring *Light on a Distant Hill* to life. I tender sincere thanks to Drusilla Gould of the Shoshone Language Project at Idaho State University for the translations found early in the book. I am deeply indebted to Merceline Boyer of the Duck Valley Indian Reservation on the Nevada-Idaho border for providing the translation of Ellen's Shoshone name. My attorney, John Sachs, fixed some glaring procedural errors in my courtroom scene. Thank you! I hope I didn't do too badly with the rest of it. And as always, I am deeply grateful to my wife, Sherry, who as my first-line reviewer found the mistakes I missed.

Cover concept by the author. Cover art by Duncan Long (http://DuncanLong.com/art.html.) Cover lettering by Misty at Arrow Camera, Santa Maria, CA.

SUGGESTED READING

Chief Joseph & the Flight of the Nez Perce, by Kent Nerburn (Harper Collins Publishers, New York). A profoundly moving account of the tragic flight and exile of the Nez Perce, from its precursors, through the flight itself in 1877-1878, and its even more catastrophic aftermath. Reads like a novel. Highly recommended.

Everything You Know about Indians is Wrong, by Paul Chaat Smith (University of Minnesota Press, 2009). A hard-hitting, sharp-edged collection of essays by the Assistant Curator of the Museum of the American Indian in Washington, D. C. Not always easy to confront, but very educational.

Native American Courtship and Marriage Traditions, by Leslie Gourse (Hippocrene Books, Inc., New York). Full of fascinating, quirky and unexpected American Indian courtship and marriage practices.

Rabbit Boss, by Thomas Sanchez (Ballantine Books, New York). If you can still find this novel somewhere, grab it. It tells the story of four generations in the life of a California Indian tribe, from its first encounter with whites in the doomed Donner Party in 1846, on into the 1950s. It remains one of my most treasured possessions.

Bury My Heart at Wounded Knee (illustrated edition), by Dee Brown (Sterling Innovation, New York-London). Still the most complete detailing of the American Indian tragedy I have seen.

Guns, Germs, and Steel: The Fates of Human Societies, by Jared Diamond (W. W. Norton, 1997). The most astonishing and lucid account of why human societies are the way they are that I have ever read. Convincingly shows why agrarian societies will always triumph over hunter-gatherer societies.